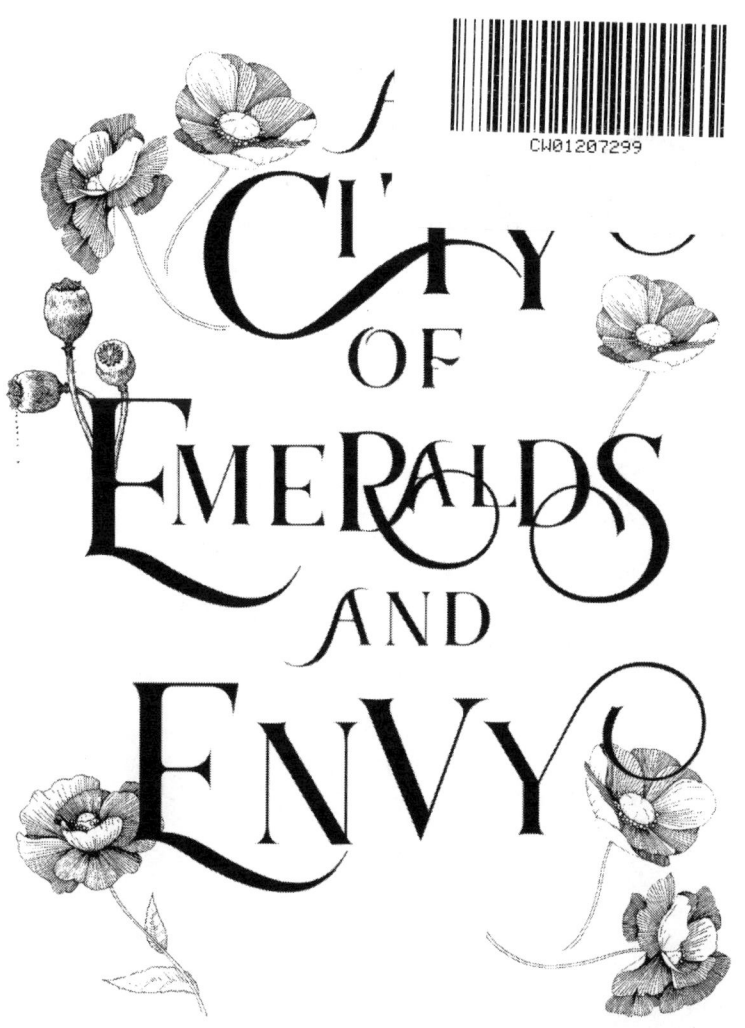

# City of Emeralds and Envy

REBECCA F. KENNEY

This book is a work of fiction. Names, characters, places, and incidents are the product of the author's imagination or are used fictitiously. Any resemblance to actual events, locales, or persons, living or dead, is coincidental.

Copyright © 2023 by Rebecca F. Kenney

All rights reserved. In accordance with the U.S. Copyright Act of 1976, the scanning, uploading, and electronic sharing of any part of this book without the permission of the publisher is unlawful piracy and theft of the author's intellectual property. If you would like to use material from the book (other than for review purposes), prior written permission must be obtained by contacting the publisher at rfkenney@gmail.com. Thank you for your support of the author's rights.

First Edition: September 2023

Kenney, Rebecca F.

A City of Emeralds and Envy / by Rebecca F. Kenney—First edition.

Cover art, RFK Designs

# TRIGGER WARNINGS

couple and group scenes of explicit sex among partners of
various genders,
monster sex, murder, gore, self-harm,
harmful magic, mind control,
abuse, trauma, body horror,
negative self-talk, death threats,
nonconsensual touching

# PLAYLIST

"Ordinary World" Adam Lambert
"I Know What You Did Last Summer" Shawn Mendes, Camila Cabelo
"Devil" Two Feet
"Lost the Breakup" Maisie Peters
"forget me too" Machine Gun Kelly, Halsey
"Natural" Imagine Dragons
"Scarecrow" Alex & Sierra
"Don't Forget About Me" d4vd
"Be Kind" Marshmello, Halsey
"Sleepwalker" Ava Max
"Fearless" Kat Leon
"By the End of the Night" Ellie Goulding
"Say Yes To Heaven" Lana Del Rey
"Francesca" Hozier
"Dancing's Done" Ava Max
"Baby Don't Hurt Me" David Guetta, Anne-Marie, Coi Leray
"Applause" Sofia Carson
"All the Ways" Meghan Trainor
"Over the Rainbow" Judy Garland

# 1

 CAER

Rows of jade pillars rise impossibly high, disappearing into the shadows overhead. If there's a ceiling, I can't see it.

Ahead, translucent emerald steps lead up to a dais, but no throne stands upon the platform. Instead a narrow archway looms above me. Across its mouth ripples a curtain, the smoky gray of the sky before a thunderstorm.

A booming voice rolls from somewhere beyond the curtain, echoing through the great empty hall. "Kneel."

I fall to my knees. There's relief in the act, in the submission, because I've traveled so far to get here, and I'm tired of making my way alone—I want to yield to the will of another.

"What is your request?" asks the Voice.

"You're the one they call the Green Wizard?" I ask. "The one who can do anything—even the most powerful spells?"

"I am."

"I've heard tales of your mercy." My voice shakes, so I pause to swallow, to breathe. "You grant one request to each supplicant who appears before you."

"That is true. And there are many who desire my aid, so make haste. What is your wish?"

I hesitate, glancing around. I haven't seen any other supplicants—in fact, the city was thinly populated, and I spotted only a handful of guards and a few servants on my way to this chamber.

But it was a long journey, with many obstacles. Perhaps many attempt it, but most give up along the way. I'm here out of sheer desperation. I have no other recourse.

"I am Unseelie," I say. "But I am defective. I've been born wrong. I'm not as strong as I should be—I'm too weak, too soft. I need the power to defeat pain and grief, the strength to overcome my desires, and the confidence to face the things that terrify me without running away. I need to be different. I need courage."

"Courage," says the Voice slowly. "What is courage, but the power to defeat any obstacle that stands in your path?"

"Yes, my Lord." I remain at the foot of the steps, kneeling, bracing my palms against the glossy floor. It appears to be cut from one titanic gemstone, and as I stare down, I perceive deeper and deeper into the emerald's green heart, into its slanted inner facets and sparkling layers.

The Wizard must do this for me. He must give me the strength to go back to the Unseelie lands—to face Riordan, if he still lives—to deal with the reality that my mouse, my sweet human, is dead, her heart torn out and eaten, swallowed by that wretched Queen, godsdamn her.

Even now, I can't think of Alice without my whole body turning molten, my muscles contracting and my cock hardening with a compulsive need I can't shake. I was in heat when I left Riordan and Alice behind, and I've been in heat ever since.

A Fae's heat shouldn't last this long—four or five weeks at the most. I've endured months of this torture. I've struggled with a constant burning desire, even as I sailed the seas of Faerie aboard a merchant ship. On island after island, I tried to fuck other Fae to give myself some relief, but my body wouldn't permit it. No matter whom I chose, in the end I couldn't bear their scent or touch. I'm craving one fragrance, one soft mortal body, one set of curious gray eyes. A scent and body belonging to a dead woman.

The need for Alice is driving me closer and closer to the edge of a despairing madness, a ravine so deep I will never be able to claw my way out of it. I've become weaker than a fucking Seelie Fae, as forlorn and weepy as any frail human. I can't even muster the fits of rage that used to give me some relief when I encountered something beyond my control.

I need more than a temporary spell or potion. I need something that will change the very fabric of who I am.

The Voice has been silent, as if in contemplation, and I'm afraid to push for an answer lest he deny me.

The curtain within the archway blows outward, detaching from its frame and rising high, a silvery, undulating veil. The black archway dissolves into dust, and the curtain itself condenses, shaping itself into the shimmering, indistinct form of a person, floating high above the dais. Looking upon that figure, I'm overwhelmed by worshipful awe, by the desire to serve this powerful being. I need someone, something to—

"Your wish is granted," says the Voice. "I will give you the courage and strength you requested,"

"Thank you, Magnificent One," I breathe, bowing lower. "And it will be permanent?"

"Unless I reverse it… yes."

At the last word, a thrum of power passes through my chest. My heart hammers fiercely as it swells, larger, larger. My blood pumps faster as magic rushes along my limbs.

I'm changing, and not only on the inside, as I expected. My body is altering as well.

"What is happening?" I cry, but my voice is swallowed in a heavy, panting, growling sound.

The Voice beyond the curtain chuckles, low and malevolent. "Why so distressed, little Cat? Is this not exactly what you wished for? The courage of a lion?"

# 2

## A FEW MONTHS AFTER FAERIE

Autumn is usually my favorite season. But it's as if *this* particular autumn knows I could use some clear blue skies, crisp breezes, and brilliant leaves—and it's being extremely contrary, determined to deny me all those things.

It's been the wettest autumn on record for a hundred years. Crops rot where they stand in the fields, and my father comes home every night in a worse mood than usual, which is saying something. My mother is unable to thoroughly dry the clothes for her laundering business.

The only good thing about this dreadful autumn is the opening of a new school, which occupies all but the littlest of my seven siblings for most of the day. I told my parents I would return to my post as a maid for Lord Drosselmeyer, if they would let my siblings attend the school at least four days a week—and my parents agreed, since they rely on my wages.

Lord Drosselmeyer provided the location for the school—a refurbished building on his property—and he's funding most of it himself, with some contributions from his loyal patrons, who follow him in whatever new scheme he concocts.

The first half of the day is spent teaching the children the basics—reading, writing, arithmetic, and history—while the afternoon consists of optional sessions on science, biology, and engineering, occasionally taught by Lord Drosselmeyer himself.

Most mornings I walk five of my siblings to the school before continuing on to Lord Drosselmeyer's mansion. As I dust, sweep, shovel ash, polish silver, and change linens, I think about what my younger siblings are learning. What I never had the chance to learn.

I read better now, thanks to some of the tricks Caer taught me—but no, I can't think of him. When I remember his sharp, pretty face, his ridiculously wide smile, and his laugh—when I recall how hard he fought to keep me from sacrificing myself—I *hurt*. I hurt so badly I can hardly stand it.

Did Riordan go after him? Find him? Are they both all right? Do they ever think of me?

Not that I *care* if the White Rabbit thinks of me… but part of me wishes he would. I want him to realize he made a wretched mistake sending me home. I hope he's fucking miserable.

Watching the rain run down the windowpanes of one of the front bedrooms, I snap out a sheet with such violence that my fellow maid, Belle, startles and almost knocks over the bell jar she's dusting. "Gracious, Alice!" She sets the bell jar back over a porcelain rose.

"Sorry." I smooth the sheet over the bed, tuck it in, and create neat, sharp corners. "I'm leaving once we finish this room so I can walk my brothers and sisters home." If I'm lucky, one of them might be willing to tell me some of what they learned today.

"You go on," says Belle. "I can finish up here."

"You're a darling." As I leave the room, I pretend not to notice the curious, pitying look she gives me—the look most people give me now. The story of my supposed kidnapping by highwaymen has spread through the nearby towns, as has the rumor that the highwaymen used me in all sorts of ways. It's a more acceptable version of the actual truth—that I jumped down a hole into Faerie, where I was held captive and nearly mutilated by a rabbit-eared Fae who wanted my virgin body for magical research. Well... I *was* a virgin, until the same Fae fucked me back to life, pouring his own heart's-blood into my chest after his Queen ripped my heart out...

Better to stick with the highwaymen story. The only other person who knows the truth is Lord Drosselmeyer, and even then, I only gave him a partial account of what happened to me in Faerie.

Despite the fact that I stole an ancient spellbook, the Tama Olc, Drosselmeyer offered to keep me on as a maid when I returned. I think he felt a little guilty about the whole thing, and also didn't want to give me a reason to tattle about his magical dealings to the people of the area. If they knew some of the things Drosselmeyer has dabbled in, they would come after him with pitchforks and torches. Foul weather has a tendency to make everyone angry and restless, eager to find a culprit on whom to blame their bad fortune, and Drosselmeyer would serve them well as a scapegoat. Some of the people in town are already eyeing his school with suspicion.

I run down the back stairs of Lord Drosselmeyer's mansion, nearly colliding with one of the footmen on the landing.

The footman's arm shoots out, quick as thought, and his palm slams against the wall beside me, barring my way.

"I enjoyed our time together last week." He grins, lashes lowered over hungry eyes. "Can't seem to think about anything else. I've got a little time now. We could have some more fun, if you like."

I knew it was a mistake to have sex with this one. The other men I've chosen since my return from Faerie were gentler sorts, but this one has a brash, dominant side. I selected him because the rest were fairly disappointing—none of them knew how to use their lips and tongues like the White Rabbit did, and none of their cocks came close to his size and girth, or to the brutal, heartbroken passion with which he fucked me. The human males I've been with have tried to be accommodating, but I could tell they were used to getting their pleasure without much care for the woman.

None of them could give me what I need, what I crave, what I miss so hard that my very bones hurt sometimes. Even when I picture Riordan or Caer, during the act, it's not enough, because it isn't only their bodies or the pleasure I miss—it's *them*.

I chose this footman because he's the most attractive in Drosselmeyer's household, and because I heard him brag about his cock's size. He wasn't lying about the length—but size doesn't matter when a man thinks a woman should orgasm immediately the moment he enters her. He rutted into me jerkily and awkwardly, saying over and over, "That's it. That's what you fucking need, a real man's cock."

Actually, no—what I need is Fae cock. Fae eyes, Fae lips, Fae claws and teeth and tongues. Glittering smiles and wicked, long-lashed glances. Sleek bodies and lethal grace.

I'm not about to repeat my interlude with this man, since there's no hope of him being willing to learn.

"Not today." I move to pass him, but he brings his body closer to mine.

"You're a tease, you know that? It's not fucking fair."

Footsteps on the stairs above make him step back, and I take the opportunity to hurry down to the kitchens. Fearful that he'll follow me, I pause for only a moment in the mud room to switch my house shoes for my boots and take my cape from its hook. The cape has a huge hood, for which I'm grateful as I step out onto the mud-slick pavers of the back courtyard.

Holding my hood in place against the rain, I hurry along the path that skirts the house and cuts through the dripping garden. I cast a glance toward the great rosebush, one I'm almost sure came from Faerie. There are no roses on it now, but it has pushed out more thorns. Its leaves hang limp and damp. It looks as wretched as everything else.

My boot-soles squelch in mud as I pass through the garden gate into the lane beyond. I trudge along the low hedge toward the schoolhouse. Lord Drosselmeyer never did say what the building was used for prior to the school's founding. It's big as a barn, but it doesn't look like one. Maybe he once stored some of his inventions there.

Rain streams off the edge of my hood, and my woolen cape is slowly becoming drenched. I feel as if I might never be dry again, as if the dampness is a perpetual, moldering presence in my life now. The heavy clouds will never part, and the sodden sky will keep leaking, leaking onto the dark and shivering landscape.

I wait under a tree by the schoolhouse until a bell rings and a line of children file out. As we walk home, my brother David tells me a few things he learned today—about a battle that occurred near here, four centuries ago, and about the method by which plants transform sunlight into food for themselves.

When we crest the low rise and see our farm, I frown. There's a strange horse tied by the gate, its head hanging low in the gray rain. No one has bothered to offer it shelter.

"David, see to that horse," I tell him as we pass through the gate. The other children run off toward the barn to visit the animals before going in the house, but David hands me his lunch pail and moves to take the beast's bridle.

The horse doesn't belong to Dorothy, the girl who looks after my littlest siblings. Her family's farm is small—pigs mostly, and they live so close to us that she always walks over, no matter the weather. Sometimes she brings her dog along—a tiny black terrier, a delight to the children. Until the dog's first visit, my siblings had never seen an animal whose purpose wasn't work or food. Dorothy has never told me where the dog came from, or why her parents let her keep it. She's an only child, so maybe they thought she needed companionship.

I trudge into the farmhouse, set down David's lunch pail, and scrape my boots on the mat before pulling them off and wedging them into the pile of shoes by the door. Humid air hangs thick in the hallway, tinged with the savory-stale reek of bacon from this morning's breakfast. The steady drumbeat of rain on the roof makes me nervous. I've already got buckets in the attic bedroom, catching drips. Any more leaks, and I won't have a dry place to sleep.

As I start to take off my cape, I realize my mistake.

I always change out of my maid's uniform when I leave Lord Drosselmeyer's house. The blue skirts don't reach my knee, and the neckline shows a generous amount of cleavage. They're absurdly immodest uniforms by the standards of this region, and draw quite a bit of admiration from Drosselmeyer's male patrons when they come to visit.

This is the first time I've forgotten to change. I was so eager, first for knowledge and then for escape, that I forgot to put on my plain brown dress. And now I'm in trouble.

Maybe I can slip upstairs and change into something else before Mam or Pap notice me—

"Alice?" Mam leans into the hallway from the front room. Her pinched face looks more drawn than usual. "What's taking so long? Come on, girl. Get in here."

She's keeping her tone under control, refraining from the names she typically calls me. Which means we *do* have a guest.

When I don't move at once, she reaches out and grabs my shoulder with an impatient huff, dragging me forward into the shabby sitting room, which also serves as a work area, a gathering space, and my father's bedroom when he falls asleep drunk on the threadbare sofa.

Pap is more or less sober at the moment, sitting in a chair across from a heavyset man with greasy black hair and a greasier smile.

"There she is." The man rises and fiddles with the bristly black scruff under his chin as he surveys me. "Well, take off the cape, girl. Let's have a look at you."

"I'd rather keep it on, thank you," I reply, but Mam snarls under her breath, "Don't be rude!" and pulls the cape off me.

Alarm flashes into Pap's eyes at the sight of my uniform. Little does he know I've worn far more scandalous things, like the scanty blue silks Caer gave me on that wonderful night when he and I fought, played games, and read books together before cuddling in the nest he made us.

*I want him, I miss him...*

The scruffy, greasy man is grinning wider, a lecherous light in his eyes. I've seen that light in Fae eyes before, but it was different, somehow. Did I welcome it only because my Fae captors were beautiful, and this man is rather revolting? Is that the only difference between their lust and his? Am I that vulnerable to beauty?

Pap has recovered his powers of speech. He clears his throat and says, "This is Mr. Gulch, the tavern-keeper in town."

"How do you do," I say, in as flat a tone as I can manage. Pap probably owes this man money. I can think of no other reason why he'd be here.

"Call me Paul." Mr. Gulch scoops up my hand and gives my knuckles several bristly, ale-scented kisses. He doesn't release my hand, but engulfs it in both of his. "My dear wife recently passed on, and I'm looking for a good hardworking girl to share my bed and my business."

Mam chokes a little at the vulgarity. "An offer of marriage, Alice. He's proposing to marry you."

"Is he?" Fat chance of that happening.

"It's time we found you a good place," Pap adds. "A settled place. People are beginning to talk about you working at Lord Drosselmeyer's, and with good reason, it seems, judging by what I see."

"And they'll talk less when I'm a tavern-keeper's wife?" I lift an eyebrow.

"Maybe, maybe not. I won't lie, you'll collect a king's ransom in tips with those fine titties," chuckles Gulch.

My father pales a little, but he only says, "Mr. Gulch and I have already come to an arrangement."

Until he said that, I thought I had a choice—that it was only a matter of toying with this man for a moment before rejecting him. With my father's mention of the word "arrangement," fear twitches in my chest. "But I work for Lord Drosselmeyer. You need the money I make."

Pap won't meet my eyes, and Mam is still standing just behind me, so I can't see her face. When I turn, she looks away, her lips pinned together.

"Truth is, your father's indebted to me," says Gulch. "Run up quite the bill at the tavern, he has. I told him, I says, 'Don't worry about it for a moment. You and I, we'll settle up square, call it even—I'll marry your daughter, and then we'll be all right, seeing as we're family.' I'll forget the debt, and your pappy here will drink free for a year. We'll give your family your tips for the twelve-month, see? I'm always one for helpin' out my neighbors."

"So I'm no better than a cow, to be traded and bartered?"

"It's a good deal, Alice," says Pap sharply. "The debt forgiven, free drinks, and all your tips going to help the family until next harvest."

"You sure he's not planning to whore me out?"

Mam steps forward and slaps me across the mouth. "Watch your tongue."

A few months ago I might have submitted to this. But since I went to Faerie I've gained confidence, knowledge, and a staunch belief in myself. Dying for an entire kingdom will do that to a person.

"No," I say firmly, quietly. "No, I will not marry this man. I will not settle your drinking debt, Father, or enable your future indulgence. Good afternoon."

With my head held high, I walk out of the room and head for the kitchen.

But Mam follows me into the hallway and grabs my wrist. In the slanted light leaking from the kitchen, her face looks more gaunt than ever. "What do you think you're doing, you ungrateful wretch? Do you want to be a burden to us forever? Saddle us with the cost of clothing you and filling your belly?"

"No, but—"

"You must marry, and he's the only one who will take you, now that you've been soiled. You have no choice. Who else do you expect to marry? What do you expect to do with your life—work for His Lordship until your looks fade?"

I stare at her, immobilized by the question.

*What do you expect to do with your life?*

"I don't know," I whisper. "I don't know what I want."

"Then want *this*," she says. "Want this for us, for your family. The crops are rotting. What Drosselmeyer is paying you won't cover your father's debt, and this bargain gets us out of it right now, free and clear." The chatter of voices and the thumping of childish feet come from the kitchen, and Mam tightens her grip on my wrist. "Do it for *them*. If you don't, we'll have to send the three oldest out to work. No more schoolin'. Is that what you want?"

Anger churns in my heart. She knows how much I crave an education, how much I want it for my siblings. She's using that desire against me.

And what right do I have to refuse? What great plans do I have for my life in this dreary place? I had some vague idea of saving up money to move away, but I've been fooling myself—with the ever-growing needs of my family, that was never going to happen.

Tears slip from my eyes. I have as much hope of holding them back as our battered roof does of keeping out the rain.

A figure appears in the kitchen doorway, blocking some of the light. It's Dorothy, the girl from the neighboring farm. "I'm heading home in a moment. The baby's been fed and changed, and dinner's warm on the stove."

A small black dog rushes past her feet, coming to sniff eagerly at mine.

"Hello, Fiero." I stoop to pet him, and take the opportunity to furtively wipe a few tears.

"Keep that thing in the kitchen, Dorothy," snaps my mother.

"Yes, ma'am." Dorothy crouches to collect the dog, and as she does, she looks into my eyes. Hers are different colors—one rich brown, one vivid blue. The brown hue of her skin and the deeper brown of her hair remind me painfully of Riordan's coloring.

She surveys me carefully, as if interpreting my mood. "I'll stay a few minutes longer, until you're ready." Scooping up Fiero, she returns to the kitchen.

"This marriage is happening," Mam says. "It must."

She turns and heads back into the sitting room. I don't wait to hear what she'll say to the men, so I turn and run up the stairs to the garret where I sleep. In the past, one or more children would crawl into bed with me and sleep tucked against me as if I were a warden against bad dreams. But since my return from Faerie, I can't ward off my own nightmares, which are so frequent and loud that my little siblings have decided in favor of staying in their own beds at night. Which suits me fine, because it gives me the privacy to touch myself sometimes, if I want a bit of comfort and pleasure.

Hunching under the rafters, I thread my way between the drips and the buckets to my bed. I plunge my hand under the pillow and draw out the Tama Olc, the ancient Unseelie spellbook I stole from Drosselmeyer. I gave it to Riordan, and he returned it to me just before he sent me home.

Fuck him for sending me away.

It's not as if I haven't thought of going back. Last month I tentatively approached Lord Drosselmeyer about it—just a nudge— "What if someone wanted to visit Faerie?" and he informed me that he was banned from Faerie, and that he has destroyed all the items he possessed that could have enabled travel between realms.

That door is closed to me. I doubt he'd help me go back, even if I begged him. Which is what I feel like doing right now—begging and pleading on my knees, in tears.

If he won't help me, maybe I can help myself.

I've read the Tama Olc cover to cover many times since I returned. Most of the spells include revolting ingredients, or substances that can only be found in Faerie, and a number of them are designed to produce some truly terrifying results. Others include words I don't understand, in some ancient Fae dialect.

Even if I could understand every spell and had access to every ingredient—I don't have magic. Not a lick of it. At least— I don't have *accessible* magic. Riordan says all humans have magic, but it's the dead kind, locked in our mortal forms, unusable, killing us slowly. It's the reason we're mortal. Only sorcerers like Lord Drosselmeyer can access their innate magic for spells, so they live longer than regular humans. For Faeries, the magic in their bodies and souls is active, easily accessible. It fuels and regenerates them in a symbiotic flow that allows them to heal quickly and live for hundreds or thousands of years.

Even without active magic, maybe there's something in the Tama Olc that I've overlooked—something to help me change my parents' minds or improve my future.

Something that will help me *go back*.

If I'm honest with myself, that's what I want. I want to go back there, to *them*. To the two Fae males who held me captive, terrorizing and charming me by turns. We experienced something together—a crisis of kingdoms, an intimate bonding, a visceral sacrifice. One of them ran away because he couldn't bear to see me die, and the other rejected me.

Damn them both. At the very least I need to go back just to smack their savage, beautiful faces—to swear at them and bruise them with merciless kisses.

With the spellbook in hand, I clatter back down the attic steps and hurry through the hallway, past the sitting room door where the voices of Gulch and my parents are still joined in conversation.

In the kitchen, the baby lies in a crib by the window, playing happily with a wooden rattle. The other children are already sitting down to bowls of stew at the table. Little Saylie waves a plump hand and gives me a bright smile, so I pause to kiss the top of her head before heading to the back door. Dorothy joins me there as I slip on my only other shoes—a pair of beaten clogs I use for work in the farmyard.

"I thought I'd go ahead and feed the children, in case you need a moment alone," Dorothy says quietly, under the loud chatter of the little ones.

"I do need a moment. Several moments." Tears prickle at the backs of my eyes again.

My brother Ben approaches us, carrying his bowl.

"Dorothy, my stew is too cold," whines Ben. "Can you warm it up like you did yesterday?"

Ben is very particular about the temperature and texture of his food—an unfortunate quality for a child on an impoverished farm.

"Don't bother Dorothy with that, Ben," I protest.

"But she has a special way of doing it."

Confused, I glance at Dorothy.

Her brown cheeks flush a deep rose color. She glances at the other children, who are oblivious to our conversation. "That was supposed to be a secret, Ben."

"But we don't have secrets from Alice," he counters.

She sighs. "Right. Well… hand over the food."

When he passes it to her, she cups her hands under the bowl, her brows contracting for a few seconds. Steam begins to rise from the stew. Ben smiles, accepting the bowl. "Thank you!"

He hops back to the table and digs in, while I stare at Dorothy. She gives me a tentative glance—wary, as if waiting for a blow.

"I'm not a sorceress," she says.

"Oh, I fucking hope you are," I whisper, seizing her arm. "Come with me."

# 3

# DOROTHY

People think I'm nice.

And I am—mostly. To people worthy of niceness. Like children, for example.

I enjoy children—they're so full of wonder, so easily impressed, so quick to trust. Their minds are wide open, far less suspicious or cautious than those of adults. You can push any imprint into those malleable little brains, and the harder you press, the longer it will stay, becoming part of them forever.

Alice isn't a child, but I like her anyway. Her brain is quick, yet she's childlike in that her mind is eager, curious. Trusting.

When she saw my magic, she didn't scream or gasp. She didn't order Ben to back away from me. She grabbed my wrist, a curse falling from her lips, and she dragged me outside, to the old barn—a ramshackle version of the bigger barn that now houses her family's animals.

I'm not sure how I knew I could trust her with my secret. I suppose I have a sense about such things. My instinct tells me when I can let my mask slip a little, when I can ease out of the confining skin I wear every day—the disguise of the kind, simple, rural virgin. It's rare that I get to reveal even the tiniest sliver of my true self.

Alice and I sit crosslegged in the old barn, facing each other across the damp straw, our faces lit by the lantern she brought along. The barn roof bellies inward, sagging and rotten, but it offers decent shelter from the rain. Fiero snuffles around while Alice tells me the strangest story I've ever heard—all about magic and faeries, and what really happened to her when she disappeared.

Anyone else might have trouble believing her tale. Not me. I've lived with magic ever since I can remember. And I've been waiting for a moment like this—a gateway into bigger things, into knowledge. I can see the door now—it's open a crack, and all I want is to charge through it.

Best not to act too eager, though. I must be careful, and not let my mask fall off entirely.

"This is the book?" I point to the volume she's clutching. "The one you took from Lord Drosselmeyer?"

"The very same. Only its true owner can use it, so if I gift it to you, you should be able to work magic with it, and perform a spell for me."

I keep my voice soft, wondering, and uncertain. "But I've never done anything more than a bit of—well, I call it 'agitation.' I can agitate the small particles that make up non-living things—move them faster."

Alice tilts her head, keenly curious, so I explain further. "I can feel the tiny bits that make up a substance like the stew or a cup of water, and I can agitate those bits, which produces heat or vibration. I can't do it to living things—but if a living creature is already in motion, I can make the whole movement faster—speeding up a horse's gallop, for example. I don't use my power often, because… well, you know how wary everyone is around here. When I do risk it, sometimes I mess up the magic. But people usually attribute my mistakes to clumsiness or bad luck."

"Yes, I know how people are around here." Alice nods sympathetically. "And I won't tell anyone what you can do. All I'm asking is that you accept the book. Maybe we can find a spell that will let me return to Faerie."

An urgent need coils serpentlike around my heart, constricting it so fiercely I can barely breathe. The longing vibrates my nerves, sings in my blood, louder and louder as my fingers creep toward the book she's holding out.

*Wait. Not too eager. Slowly, now, carefully.*

I have to say the things she'll expect me to say.

"To Faerie?" I lift my eyebrows. "But what about your family? I can't imagine leaving mine, no matter how fascinating another realm might be." I feign a shiver. "By your own account, Faerie is a rather terrible place. Why do you want to go back?"

Color stains Alice's pale cheeks. Her eyes glimmer with a mix of desire, fear, excitement, anger, and determination.

"Have you never been curious?" she says. "Have you never wanted to understand something so badly you'd do anything to figure it out? Have you never been seized by the desire to learn, to grow, to *know*?"

I have, and I like her all the more for the confession. But the Dorothy I'm pretending to be has simple thoughts and simple wants, and in her voice I say, "I don't feel like that. Mostly I try to finish my work as quickly as possible so I can sew. I love sewing. Are you saying you want to go back to Faerie just to— learn things?"

"That, and—there are some people I need to see." She blushes deeper.

"The Fae males you mentioned. The ones who held you captive." When she was telling me her story, I could hear the passion in her voice when she spoke of them. She did not tell me everything, but I suspect Alice is no longer a virgin. Another similarity between us.

"They were—indescribable," Alice says quietly. "And I—can't stop thinking about them. They're in my head, always—one of them like a poison I'm addicted to, and the other as a sweet pain, the most precious kind."

"Sweet pain," I echo. That, I understand. The pain of a tender love, a first love. My love can never return, so there is nothing to hold me here.

"I'll look through the book with you, but I can't promise anything," I tell Alice. "And if you do find a way to get back to Faerie, you have to say goodbye to your siblings before you go. Your first disappearance was hard on them."

I don't tell her that when she was gone, Saylie cried for hours in the dark. Sometimes I crept into their house at night, past the drunken father and the exhausted mother, just to check on the child. If she was weeping, I made pretty, soothing visions dance above her trundle bed until her lashes drifted shut. Too young to keep a secret, she talked about them in the morning—but everyone else thought she was speaking of her dreams.

"I won't leave until I say goodbye," Alice promises. "Do your parents know what you can do?"

"They know I have an ability, but we don't discuss it. I use it at home sometimes, but only when they're not looking. They don't like to be reminded that I'm different. We don't talk about awkward things in my family, only cheerful ones."

"Sounds better than the constant arguments in my house." Alice gives me a wry smile.

"It's quieter." I return the smile cautiously, feeling that flicker again, that instinct—*this is someone I can trust.*

Alice and I have never spent much time together—she's always leaving the house as I arrive, or returning home when I'm heading out for the evening. She's nearly a year older than I am, and though I'm as pretty as she is, I'm rather envious of her lovely gray eyes. Mine are mismatched. My real pride is my thick brown hair, which I usually keep bundled into two loose braids to cover my misshapen ears.

"Here." Alice holds out the book. "I give you the Tama Olc, ancient spellbook of Faerie, to be your own possession."

I reach out, and my fingers close on the spine.

My blood ignites.

Power roars through me, currents of shrieking flame that race along my veins and scream inside my brain. My heart thumps, huge and volatile, and in my head echoes a voice, chanting strange words. My lips crack apart, forced open, and the voice from my head issues into the air of the barn—air that is whirling, round and round, tossing my hair and Alice's. Her fingers and mine are still galvanized to the book. I can't let go, and I don't think she can, either.

"What are you doing?" Alice calls over the rising wind. But I can't answer. The voice has taken over my body—it is deep, sonorous, ancient. My will rises up, furious at being overtaken, but I'm no match for the voice, because it's *inside* me, it's my own blood, my bones, my past and my future.

On and on the voice speaks, a chant sucked from the book into my fingers, then vomited from my unwilling throat.

This wasn't my plan. I intended to take my time with this— I don't understand what's happening, and I don't like being controlled, but I can't break free. I can't even struggle. It's as if a deeper call from within me is answering another call somewhere beyond my physical hearing—a beacon in the infinite distance, beyond sight.

The invocation ends, and the voice speaks through me one more time, a bellow over the violent whirlwind circling the barn. "Blood calls to blood," it intones.

The beams of the barn are cracking, the walls shuddering. Fiero leaps into my lap, and Alice screams.

Magic pours out of me, an uncontrollable flood, joining with the purpose of the book and with something else—

something that is *pulling* me, pulling *us*, compelling my soul with the force of its need. A face flashes into my mind—too briefly for me to grasp its features, but I have the strangest feeling I'll know it if I see it again.

With a violent lurch and a snapping of timbers, the floor shifts beneath us, and the whole barn lifts up, borne on the howling, whirling wind.

"Stop it!" Alice screams, but I can't—I'm only a channel. I open my mouth to explain, but something heavy thunks against the side of my skull, and I slump to the floor, my words slipping away as I drop into the dark.

# 4

# ALICE

A chunk of broken wood hits Dorothy on the head, and she slumps over, unconscious. Just my luck. Now she can't undo whatever she has done.

My fingers won't unclamp from the Tama Olc, which terrifies me nearly as much as the fact that the barn is fucking *flying* and I am inside it. The unfastened door is flapping, banging, but I can't see anything outside except a streaming gray blur. The little dog, Fiero, huddles against Dorothy's prone body. She's still gripping the Tama Olc, too.

With my free hand, I reach toward Fiero. "Everything will be all right." My voice cracks, but Fiero seems to appreciate the effort and settles under my palm while I scratch his ears.

The barn jolts horrifically, sending the little knot of us skidding across the floor toward the loose barn door. I brace my heels against the doorframe just in time to keep us all from sliding out.

Another lurch sends us back across the floor the opposite way. The lantern drops from its hook, smashing into a pile of straw, which thankfully is too damp to burn, so the flame gutters and dies.

Then the barn begins to spin, round and round, faster and faster. Oh gods, I'm going to be sick. I clamp my eyes shut.

"I can get through this," I hiss through clenched teeth. "I've had my heart ripped out of my chest by a mad Fae Queen—I will survive this, too. I *will*."

After a few nauseating minutes, the house stops spinning, but it keeps rising. I don't know how high we've gone, prey to the circling currents of the storm—but it's high enough that when the house drops suddenly, I scream.

We're plummeting down, hurtling to unknown depths. My stomach is thrilling horribly, and I feel as though I left half my insides up in the sky somewhere—oh gods, we're going to smash into splinters when we hit the bottom—

A terrifying jerk, and our descent halts for a second before continuing. I scream as the barn races down, down, down—halts again—then *smashes* into solid earth.

My fingers come unglued from the Tama Olc, and the book drops to the floor. I lunge away and vomit into the straw, heaving up the scanty remains of my lunch.

"Shit," I sob. My whole body is shaking, but I'm alive. I'm alive.

"Dorothy?" I crawl toward her. She's still unconscious, blood seeping through her dark-brown hair. A rivulet of gleaming scarlet runs over her temple, down to her cheekbone. But she's breathing.

She has released the Tama Olc as well, so I pick it up and tuck it into the pocket of her blue gingham dress. I'm still wearing my blue maid's outfit and my white apron—both dreadfully smudged now.

The unlatched door of the barn has swung shut. I can't see outside except through a few cracks between the boards, but a glow leaks in—bright yellow sunshine, the kind I haven't seen in days.

By its light I notice something more disconcerting than the flying barn. Dorothy's work-worn leather shoes are melting away. Her stockings vanish next, leaving her legs bare—and then new shoes appear, encasing her feet. The shoes are heeled slippers that glisten silver as starlight, and they're dotted with tiny rubies, as red as drops of Dorothy's blood.

That's magic. And it wasn't performed by Dorothy herself, which means we've landed in a place where magic is as organic and natural as breathing.

"Fiero," I whisper. "I don't think we're in the human realm anymore."

Rising on trembling legs, holding onto the barn wall for support, I hobble to the door and push it open.

Sunlight streams in, so bright I have to close my eyes for a few seconds.

But I'm desperate to know where we are, so I force my lashes apart, just a crack.

My brain revolts, denying what I see. I have to close my eyes again and *breathe*.

When I was in Faerie last time, I didn't see anything beyond the White Rabbit's home and the Dread Court. But Clara told me how startlingly beautiful the landscape of Faerie can be—that its glory can overcome the human mind.

A place this gorgeously overwhelming *has* to be Faerie.

*Breathe, breathe. Then just a glimpse.*

I inhale, then release the air slowly, three times.

Cautiously I open my eyes again.

There are people staring at me—Fae, not humans, lots of them, all robed in blue, but I can't look too carefully at them yet. I need to acclimate to my surroundings first.

Behind the crowd of Fae lies a village. Houses built of blue-gray stone, their domed roofs thatched with blue grass. Balconies draped in glittering blue ivy. Multicolored flowers as glossy as varnished wood.

Gleaming white quartz paves the streets instead of cobblestones. In the distance, beyond the buildings, I glimpse bits of a high wall.

Trees grow here and there between the houses, each ten times the height of the average Fae male. The trunks are smooth and soft green until the top quarter of the tree, where azure foliage bursts out in shining abundance against a pale blue sky.

I've never seen such trees. If only I could study them—but I have a more pressing desire, and that is to find out where I am, so I know how close I might be to Caer and Riordan.

My brain feels clearer now. This place is truly dazzling, but I don't think I'll go mad from it. Maybe my previous visit to Faerie did immunize me a bit, despite my limited exposure to the landscape.

I drop my gaze from the trees to the Fae. Some have wings or horns, and they all have a stark, preternatural beauty. Every one of them wears the same color and style of hooded blue robe, with adjustments for their physical differences. Many have tattoos decorating their faces, throats, or hands. Odd, because I never saw any Fae with tattoos at the Dread Court.

"Is this the Seelie Kingdom?" I ask.

"The Seelie Kingdom?" A woman steps forward, her ochre skin contrasting with the navy blue of her tunic. Bright pink freckles dot her cheeks, and she has a pair of translucent dragonfly wings, pink-tinged, that remind me of the Sugarplum Faerie. How I wish he and Clara were here to help me befriend these Fae! But at least we all speak a common language. The human realm is similar to Faerie in some ways—the other side of the coin, as Riordan once told me.

"She thinks this is the Seelie Kingdom," repeats the freckled Fae woman, glancing over her shoulder at the others. They chuckle quietly. I can't tell if the sound is friendly or not.

"You're on the Isle of Oz, love," says the woman. "I thought you would know that, given where you landed—a spot too well-chosen for coincidence. You knew what you wanted to destroy, didn't you?"

"Have we smashed someone's house?" I gasp, turning around.

Fiero followed me out, and he's nosing at something along the edge of the half-collapsed barn—a pair of bare gray legs sticking out at strange angles. Blood soaks the blue grass where the legs disappear under the barn.

Slowly my hand comes up to cover my mouth. I turn back to the winged Fae woman, dread throbbing in my heart. "We killed someone. I'm so sorry—"

The Fae woman steps forward quickly, right into my space, speaking in a low, urgent tone. "Pretend you meant to do it, human. They'll be far less likely to kill you."

Horror clenches my gut, but on my last visit to Faerie I learned to be adaptable. To hide the depth of my shock over what I saw and heard.

"I'm so sorry—that we didn't smash that person sooner," I amend loudly. "They had it coming."

The Fae woman winks one sparkling pink eye at me. She is some kind of leader in this place, judging from her behavior. "The East Witch did indeed have it coming, as we all know too well," she says to the gathered Fae. "That bitch has terrorized our village long enough. Thanks to this lovely human sorceress, we've been freed from the East Witch's thrall."

My mind races, taking in the information, gauging the expressions of the crowd. I know what a witch or sorcerer is in my realm, but here in Faerie, where everyone has magic, the word "witch" must have another meaning. Explanations will have to wait—first I need to solidify our standing with these Fae.

Shuffling footsteps from inside the barn catch my ear, and as Dorothy emerges, I speak quickly, loudly. "I wish I could take credit for freeing you from the Witch who kept you in thrall, but I am not the sorceress. The power belongs to her." I point to Dorothy, who leans in the barn doorway, looking taller than usual in the silver heels.

"She wears the shoes!" cries the Fae woman beside me. "She is indeed the one responsible for the East Witch's death!"

The leader of the village touches her forehead and bows slightly, and every other Fae in the group repeats the gesture toward Dorothy.

Dorothy glances sidelong at me, then bends to collect Fiero, cradling him in her arms, fondling his ears as she takes in the body pinned beneath the barn, the crowd of Fae, and our surroundings. Unlike me, she doesn't seem overwhelmed by the exotic beauty of the landscape. Her gaze holds wonder, delight, and a sharp satisfaction, but not rapturous awe or dazzled madness. She smiles, quiet and cool, while blood drips down the side of her face.

And in that moment I realize my neighbor Dorothy is far from what she appears to be.

# 5

# DOROTHY

I step out of the wrecked barn, holding my head high. This is Faerie, of course—it must be. There are Fae looking at me, bowing to me. I'm not sure why they're all wearing the same robes. And I'm not sure why I've got these shoes, or how Alice and I ended up here, but I've had practice concealing my reactions to the unexpected. My mask remains in place, tweaked slightly to exude confidence and purpose instead of modesty and innocence.

My gaze meets Alice's briefly. Suspicion crystallizes in those gray eyes of hers, and her lips part, ready to ask questions I don't have the answers to. All I know is that somehow, I'm connected to this bright world—I always have been. There's a joy in my blood, like the flicker of contentment I feel when I'm home with my parents and Fiero in the evening, curled up by the fireplace, sewing or whittling or reading—only this joy is stronger, wilder, more gleefully certain. And there's a tug in my heart, too, as if something or someone important is nearby—the other end of the tether that pulled me here. I need to figure out who or what it is.

Holding Fiero's warm, silky little body to my chest, I take another step forward.

But a shiver passes through the air—a crackle of suspense, like the sting of anticipation right before lightning cracks overhead.

The faeries shrink back from us. Only the pink-freckled one remains near Alice—but her face tightens with fear.

Green smoke uncoils from the ground between Alice and me, explodes into a roiling green cloud. A sharp, crisp scent fills the air—rain-washed leaves, cold wind, and a freshness so enticing I want to lean closer and inhale.

A figure becomes visible as the smoke settles. He's taller than anyone in the crowd—the top of my head would barely reach the middle of his chest if I were standing beside him—and I'm wearing heels. His limbs are as skinny as the wooden staff he grips in one long-fingered hand, and his tight black clothing makes his body look even thinner. He has tousled black hair whose glossy waves curl along his nape—and when he whirls to face me, I gasp, like I've been struck in the face by cold water—like he reached out with sharp nails and ripped the invisible mask from my face. Eyes like glittering spears plunge into mine, piercing down to my very soul.

He's wretchedly beautiful. Smooth, satiny skin, as green as the smoke from which he appeared. A savage jawline, lips made for whispering debauched curses, cheekbones designed to lacerate anyone who might dare touch him. Thick black lashes fringe his dark eyes.

His gaze slants from me, down to something pinned beneath the barn. The bloodied, barefoot corpse.

"You killed my sister." His voice is like wind through a green forest under threat of storms—a shimmering ripple, but with a rolling undercurrent of thunder.

I can't speak. I've never been so thoroughly shaken by anyone. Back in the human realm, I moved quietly through life with the secret confidence that I was the most powerful person in any room or gathering. But the very air around this Fae male trembles with ominous magic, with a power greater than mine.

Alice steps nearer to the newcomer, speaking low so the crowd of Fae won't hear. "Her death was an accident, my lord." I'm not sure why she adds the honorific, but I suppose she's been around volatile, powerful Fae before, and she knows how to handle them.

He turns. Looks her up and down. Whips his attention back to me. "Is this your pet, sorceress?"

I glance down at Fiero. "Yes, this is my dog."

"Not that scrap of fur," he sneers. "The hapless human." He jerks his head toward Alice. "She's yours?"

My eyes widen, locking with Alice's. Her lips tighten, but she nods.

"Um, yes. She's my pet." I lift my chin haughtily.

"Hm." He spins on his heel and rams the end of his staff down on the quartz pavers with a resounding *boom*. When all the Fae jump and whimper, he chuckles, turning back to me. "I wasn't especially fond of my sister. But she was family, so I must avenge her. You understand, of course. A death for a death. How would you like to die?"

Alice turns white as the paving stones. She leans over to the pink-freckled Fae woman and murmurs something to her.

My first instinct is to use my magic—but I'm not sure how it can help me. I can't agitate the inner particles of *living* things—I can only speed up rhythmic motions they're already performing. Maybe I could speed up the particles inside the rocks under the skinny bastard's feet—superheat the stones until they burned him, or maybe explode them—but that would take time, and I've never done anything that dramatic before.

I need to keep this vengeful Fae distracted until Alice and I figure a way out of this, so I say, "What are my death options?"

He advances, looming over me so I have to tilt my head back to look up into his smirking face. He holds out elegant, bejeweled fingers to Fiero, who sniffs them cautiously. "A quick blast of magic to the heart is one option. Or if you prefer, I can slit your throat." He lifts the same hand and traces one sharp nail across my neck. "I can conjure a blade to cut off your head, or slice you open and eviscerate you." The pointed nail leaves my throat and digs into my belly, drawing a vertical line and stopping just below my navel, where he lets all five clawtips rest against my lower stomach.

A quiver of uncertainty passes over his face, and he bends closer, sniffing my hair. My face flames.

"Are you sure you're quite human, little sorceress?" he asks. "Your scent—it's—unusual."

"Of course I'm human." Every bit of my body is alive and humming, danger and desire writhing at my core.

"You can't kill her," comes a voice from behind him. It's the Fae woman with the pink freckles and dragonfly wings. "She wears the shoes."

Alarm flashes into the green-skinned Fae's eyes, as if he just remembered something important. He draws back sharply, glancing at the corpse's bare feet and then at my silver heels. "Fuck."

"You know the rules that govern possession of the shoes," the Fae woman continues. "When the former owner is killed, the shoes and their power pass to the one responsible for that death. For seven days, the new owner of the shoes may not be slain in vengeance."

He whirls and snarls at the Fae woman—actually snarls, a guttural, ferocious ripple from his throat. "But I can kill her pets. I'll destroy the helpless blonde, and the little dog, too."

He reaches for Fiero, and I react without thinking—pure instinct, my hand thrown out. A burst of concussive magic blasts from my palm, sending the green-skinned Fae back a few steps.

I've never been able to do *that* before.

"Try it, fucker," I say, breathlessly. "That's only a taste of what I can do."

Turning my attention to the rocks beneath his feet, I focus on setting their particles in motion. It takes a monumental effort, and my magic feels sluggish, as if some inner reservoir is far lower than usual. Which makes sense, considering all the power I channeled to bring us here, because of that book—

The book, the Tama Olc... where is it?

But the moment I think its name, I can sense it. The spellbook is mine, and it's in my pocket. Not that it's any use to me right now.

The tall Fae glances down at the rocks beneath his feet, which are barely vibrating. He looks back up at me, eyes narrowed with a mix of anger and interest. Then he stalks toward me again, tension in every line of his long limbs. I don't blast him away this time—I think I've spent that power, whatever it was.

He leans down, his brilliant dark eyes, sharp nose, and wicked mouth a whisper from my face. "I'll let you and yours live a little longer. But trust me, sorceress, I'm coming for you. No one leaves this island. You're trapped here with me, in this godsforsaken corner of Faerie. And when your seven days of protection wear off, I'll be waiting. I want to kill you personally. Slowly." His lashes dip, his eyes finding my mouth. "Intimately."

"You can try," I say, with a confidence I don't feel.

When he glances past me, I follow his gaze—and to my shock, I see that the bare gray feet of the dead Witch are forming tiny cracks, like stone struck by a mallet, on the verge of shattering.

"She'll be gone soon," he says tonelessly. "She'll crack into pieces and dissipate into dust."

I search for a pang of sympathy, but there's none inside me. "Who are you, anyway? So I know what name to curse."

"I don't give my true name easily," he says. "For now, you can call me West."

"And I'm Dorothy," I reply. "In case you want to beg me for mercy."

His mouth tilts in a half-smile. "Dorothy," he says softly. "Oh, this is going to be fun. I'll be seeing you soon, little sorceress."

And with a bang and a cloud of green smoke, he disappears.

# 6

# ALICE

I'm back in Faerie. But I've ended up in the wrong part of this realm, and I'm in the company of my docile-looking neighbor who's been hiding magical abilities and who now possesses a pair of magic shoes—and who seems a little too comfortable here, for a human who was just tossed into a new world.

When I question the freckled Fae leader about the shoes, she says, "I believe they augment a person's existing abilities, whatever those may be. The East Witch owned them for two centuries, and I'm not sure what else they can do. The only thing I know for certain is the law of seven-days' protection for the next owner. No one can kill your friend in vengeance until that time is up. Of course, she could die in other ways."

"How encouraging," Dorothy says with a hard, bright smile.

Despite that dire reminder, the Fae woman seems friendly enough—perhaps because, with the East Witch dead, she has full authority over the town. She even tells us her name—Glenna.

The rest of the villagers seem glad of the East Witch's death, but I don't quite like the way they look at us. As if they'd devour us whole if they didn't owe us something. Our welcome here is a fragile one.

The sunlight fades to dusk as Dorothy and I are led through the village. One of the Fae swipes the blood from Dorothy's temple with a long brown finger and licks it clean with a sigh of delight. Dorothy doesn't jerk away, but she shoots me a look of abhorrence and alarm.

The Fae who tasted her blood looks a bit confused at the flavor, but shrugs and takes another lick before ambling off.

As we continue toward the center of town, I explain quietly, "The Fae like the way humans taste and smell."

"No shit," she whispers.

When I told her my story, I limited the tale to the basic facts. Maybe I should have explained more of the interesting bits, so she'd understand Fae behavior. But I never expected us to end up here so soon, and certainly not *together*. Using the Tama Olc for inter-realm travel was supposed to take time. At the very least I expected a few hours to prepare and say my goodbyes.

No such luck.

When we reach the village square, preparations for an outdoor feast are already underway. Benches float into place by magic, and platters of food appear along the tables. A bonfire springs up, its light dancing on the ominous shapes of a gallows, several stocks, and two crosses with bits of rope fluttering from the crossbeams, where bodies must have once hung.

Beyond those structures rises a narrow, triangular building, a single wedge of dull black jutting into the evening sky. Symbols of crows, wheat, corn, and scarecrows decorate its ebony surface.

"What's that building?" I ask Glenna.

"The Temple of the Crows. It has stood here since the Isle was formed, millennia ago." She seats herself at the head of a table and gestures for me and Dorothy to take seats to her right and left. "Bring wine for our guests!"

I stare hard at Dorothy, trying to communicate a warning about eating and drinking what faeries provide, but she's too busy settling Fiero into her lap. At least she's somewhat protected, thanks to her magic. I should probably worry more about myself.

When I first fell into the clutches of the White Rabbit, my curiosity and cleverness saved me. Riordan liked my eager mind and appreciated my genuine interest in his work. I can't count on meeting someone like him this time.

My throat tightens as I picture Riordan's handsome face—the gashes in his cheeks, his scarred hands. Those fingers—so methodical, so gentle. Capable of relentless horror and exquisite pleasure.

For a moment, the pain of missing him is so acute it makes me physically nauseated.

*I hate him, I hate him, I want him...*

Fortunately a distraction arrives as two robed Fae set down brimming goblets and heaping plates before Dorothy and me. The rest of the Fae file into spots along the benches, making room for each other's wings or tails.

Glenna rises, lifting both hands. The center of each palm is tattooed with a bird skull—a crow, I think.

"The Witch is dead," she says, with an exultant grin. "And the Village of Crows is free! No longer will she force us to breed and sacrifice while absorbing the magic of this place herself. No longer will we be drones, operating in thrall to her will. With her gone, all of us will be able to benefit from the Dark Blessing."

A monotone chorus of gratitude rises from the throats of the robed Fae.

"Let us drink to the fertility of our bodies, so we may continue the sacrifices for our own benefit, and no other's!" Glenna cries, and the Fae respond with another groan of agreement. "And let us drink to the health of our cornfields, from which comes our sustenance."

Again her people respond with an answering drone of devotion.

"Eat, my people," says Glenna. "And then we will dance with our guests, the saviors of this village."

Everyone along our table bends over the food, devouring it with a noisy gusto that rivals the tumult my siblings make during dinner. In fact, there are a number of Fae children in the group—far more than I would expect, given what I know about Fae fertility cycles. Their presence, coupled with Glenna's speech, makes me anxious. Something isn't right here, and the wrongness goes deeper than an entire village being under a witch's rule. There's another kind of wickedness at work.

What did Glenna say about the food being created from the crops? And yet there's meat on my plate—a lot of it. I poke at it gingerly with my fork, debating whether or not to sample it.

Besides me, one other person at our table isn't eating—a tall, broad figure, clad entirely in silver armor. He wears a helmet with a grate for a mouthpiece and narrow slits for the eyes. Even his hands are covered with jointed silver plating, ending in sharp metal fingertips. He wears a blue cloak over the armor, the color marking him as a citizen of this village—perhaps a guard. Several of the other Fae wear a chestplate or pauldron over their robes, but that individual is the only one clad head to toe in metal.

"This is delicious," Dorothy says with her mouth full. "I've never tasted anything so good."

I wrench my gaze from the metal-clad man and cringe at the sight of her gobbling the food like the others.

Glenna smiles. "Everything you see on this table, even the meat and fruit, was alchemized from the ancient corn we grow in the field beyond the wall. We serve the crows, and the crows bless the fields."

I'm still suspicious, but I'm also starving. Cautiously I nibble at the fruit and sample the wine. At my request, one of the Fae brings me a cup of water, which I drain. I don't mind going hungry, as long as my thirst is quenched.

Dorothy seems to have no concern about the dinner, even though Fiero turns up his nose whenever she tries to feed him a tidbit. She's acclimating a little too well. I don't think she intended to end up here with me, and yet she seems calm and comfortable in this place. A normal human shouldn't be this unconcerned their first time in Faerie. I need to talk to her alone.

But first, I need to talk to Glenna, and learn everything I can about the Village of Crows and the Isle of Oz.

"Can you tell me more about Oz?"

Glenna sips her wine. "Of course. You are an honored guest, human."

"I'm Alice."

"Alice." She lifts her cup first to me, then to Dorothy. "The Isle of Oz is one of the largest islands in the realm, but it is so far from the Seelie and Unseelie kingdoms that they've left us to our own devices for thousands of years. Over the past several centuries, one family has ruled the Isle, but with the fading of the matriarch, her four children took over, dividing the Isle into quadrants—East, West, North, and South. The royal siblings bickered and squabbled sometimes, but for the most part we lived pleasantly enough. Until the Green Wizard arrived."

"That's the green bastard we just met?" Dorothy asks.

"No, no—that green bastard, as you call him, is the West Witch. He's one of the four royal siblings, and his skin is only green because the Green Wizard made it so."

Dorothy glances at me, confused, but I only shrug.

"No one knows where the Green Wizard came from." Glenna swirls the wine in her cup. "They say he fell from the sky—plummeted into the royal city of Caislin Brea one day. Smashed a good deal of the place, I'm told, though I've never seen the damage. I haven't been allowed outside the Village of Crows since the East Witch appointed me as its overseer…" Her voice fades, and her eyes glaze over.

"More wine?" suggests Dorothy.

Glenna nods, and while Dorothy refills her cup, I venture a question. "Why is he called 'wizard?' What kind of magic does he possess?"

"To us, the word 'wizard' means a wish-granter," Glenna explains. "The Green Wizard grants one wish to each supplicant who seeks him out. He gives you what you ask for, though not always in the way you expect. Do you not have wizards and witches where you come from?"

"We do," I say, "but we use the terms differently. Can you explain what you mean by a 'witch' here in Oz?"

"A witch is someone with the power to control the minds and actions, not just of humans, but of other Fae. The four siblings of this Isle were particularly gifted in that respect. They were immune to each other's powers, but they could maintain control over large numbers of Fae from a distance, for long periods of time. Those of us in this village were thralls laboring under the oppressive will of the East Witch, unable to make any significant choices on our own."

"That's horrible," I breathe.

"It was." Glenna's wings stiffen, as if galvanized by the painful memory. "It's a relief to talk like this, without someone else curbing my speech."

"Happy to have been of service in setting you free," Dorothy says, popping a chunk of fruit into her mouth.

"The history of this Isle is so fascinating," I add encouragingly. "Please tell us more."

"Shortly after his arrival, the Green Wizard became the North Witch's lover," Glenna says. "She was besotted with him—even transferred the allegiance of her thralls to him. About a year ago they had a terrible argument, and she made her one wish to him—a wish no one ever heard, but rumor has it he distorted her request and used it to curse her instead. As part of the curse, she was exiled to the Unseelie Kingdom."

A small group of Fae on the doorstep of the temple begins to play music—a wild, swaying, seductive tune. The melody teases the ear, begs to occupy my whole mind, soul, and body. It's so enticing that I struggle to concentrate on Glenna's next words.

"After that, the Green Wizard began to conquer the entire Isle. The other siblings tried to avenge their banished sister. But the Wizard killed the South Witch and claimed their thralls. Then he fought with the West Witch and stole some of his magic. After that, the East Witch, our ruler, agreed to operate under the Wizard's rule and pay him tribute. She was always the most ruthless of the four."

"Worse than her brother?" Dorothy raises her eyebrows.

"The West Witch allows his vassals some freedom," says Glenna sourly. "The East Witch preferred to keep us firmly under her control, allowing us only the smallest of choices. But such oppressive control was draining for her, so she gave me and some of the guards a little more leash than the others—a bit more authority in the day-to-day workings of the village, just to keep from having to make too many mundane decisions herself. Her power was the weakest of the four siblings. Sometimes, when she traveled too far from here, her control would slip, or she would struggle to maintain her hold on the strongest of us. But those lapses were never enough to give us a chance at freedom. In this village, those with stronger wills are tortured until they weaken, then imprisoned to await their doom."

I suppress a shudder.

"Why didn't the West Witch enthrall us, when he appeared today?" Dorothy asks.

"As I said, the Green Wizard stole that power from him—siphoned it away so he could use it himself. Since then, the West

Witch stays within the borders of his territory, refusing to swear allegiance to the Emerald City. And for some reason the Wizard hasn't killed him yet."

"Will the Green Wizard take control of your minds himself, now that you've been freed?" I ask.

"He hasn't enthralled anyone for months. Some say the power, which is permanent with the royals of Oz, wanes when it is stolen by someone else. So we may be safe from his control, but not from his rule. I would send someone to make a wish for our village's independence, but unluckily for us, no current or former thrall can make a wish to the Wizard."

"Interesting," I comment, momentarily distracted from the delightful music. "I suppose the compulsion magic and the wish magic clash somehow."

Glenna nods. "The Green Wizard tried to have his own thralls make wishes to himself, on his behalf, but it didn't work. Or so the East Witch said." Glenna's face turns smugly triumphant. "She may have stolen my choices, but she did not steal my ears. She would often speak freely before us, thinking of us as drones without thought—but I remember everything she said."

"And he will grant a wish to *anyone*?" My heart pulses with sudden, panicked eagerness. "Could he send someone to the mainland? To the Seelie or Unseelie kingdom?"

"Since the Wizard's arrival, no one has been able to leave the Isle," Glenna replies. "The sole exception was the North Witch herself, and they say her banishment was because of something she wished for."

"What about a ship?" Dorothy suggests.

"Any vessel that tries to leave finds itself headed for shore again. We used to trade a little with some neighboring islands, but since the Green Wizard arrived, sailors quickly learned that those who come here never return. Occasionally Fae miss the warnings and come here anyway, seeking the Wizard's help, only to find out, after their one wish is granted, that they cannot leave. But in your case, if your one wish is to depart, he might allow it."

"And how do I get to him?"

Dorothy sets down her wine goblet rather hard and stares at me, incredulous. "Alice, do you really want to go visit this magic-stealing murder-wizard?"

She has a point, but I'm desperate. "Nearly everyone's a murderer in Faerie. There's not much of a moral code here."

Dorothy's expression shifts, interest overtaking her features.

"You don't have to go with me," I tell her. "But I have to try this, if there's no other way to leave the Isle. I have to find *them*."

I don't speak their names. She already knows who I'm looking for.

"Fine," she relents. "How do we get there?"

"When the Wizard and his lover built the Emerald City, they also created golden paths throughout the Isle of Oz, all leading to the city's gate," Glenna says. "Once you leave the village, you'll see the road immediately. But you'll need to stay inside the village walls until we've put out a scarecrow, or you'll be eaten before you get very far."

Dorothy's jaw drops.

I'm more used to the idea of being eaten—after all, the Unseelie Queen devoured my heart, and Caer used to hint that he wouldn't mind a mouthful of me. Still… "Eaten by what?" I ask, in a forcedly casual tone.

"The crows. They don't disturb us as long as we remain within the walls, or under the shadow of the trees, but swarms of them haunt the fields between the town gates and the forest. Tomorrow at dawn, we'll set out a scarecrow to distract them so you can make it to the woods."

"That's—kind of you," I say hesitantly, though it doesn't make sense that a scarecrow of straw and rags would distract flesh-eating crows.

"It has nothing to do with kindness," Glenna says, with a cold, brilliant smile. "In Faerie, we return the favors paid to us. You destroyed the East Witch, freeing our minds, so I will do this thing for you. It is no trouble—we already have a scarecrow prepared and marked as the next sacrifice."

The word *sacrifice* alarms me still more, and I suppress a shudder, feeling slightly frantic at being alone here with Dorothy, protected only by the favor we did for these Fae. I glance down the table again, wondering when the feast will finally be over—and my gaze latches on the silver-armored guard again. His helmet is angled toward me, like he's watching me, though it's impossible to tell with those eye-slits. There's a tension to his massive shoulders, a suppressed threat emanating from his whole body. Maybe he hates humans and doesn't like the fact that his village is beholden to a pair of them.

The music surges suddenly louder, a compelling song that tugs at every heartstring I possess. It slides into my chest like a golden river, softening my anxiety, blurring my concerns until they seem like silly little worries. The music laughs with me, begs me, lures me to flow along with it.

All the Fae rise from the feast tables, eager to dance by the light of the bonfire, beneath the stars.

I heard Fae music at the Dread Court, but that was a wild clash, a hectic throbbing explosion. This melody is a different style altogether—mystic, irresistible, dripping with salacious secrets. I realize I'm on my feet, though I don't remember rising.

Dorothy orders Fiero to stay under her seat, out of the way, while she and I leave the table and mingle with the whirl of robed figures. Some of the Fae catch my hands, passing me to one another.

Dorothy is laughing, her eyes alight with wild glee. "I've never been able to dance this well before!"

"Do you think it's the shoes?" I call back.

"I have no idea!"

Before tonight, I've barely danced at all. There's never music in our farmhouse, and when I hear music at Lord Drosselmeyer's, it's usually during one of his parties, when I'm serving his guests. And those songs were never this entrancing.

Maybe there's sorcery in the blue shadows of the night, or in the crystalline gleam of the stars, or in the soft sway of the trees over my head—or maybe the music itself lends grace to the hearer—but I find myself carried along with the melody, my body freed to move like it never has in my life. I'm not so much dancing as *floating* along the earth, my feet light as stardust, borne along by magic and music.

I can barely remember why I was concerned—everything seems too wonderful for worries. I'm *here*. In Faerie. Still far from the two Fae I'd most like to see, but I made it back, and that's half the battle won. I'm *glad* to be here, truly. Hope races through my heart—hope and joy because I *will* see Caer and Riordan again—nothing will stop me.

I'm dancing in a blissful frenzy, laughing, eyes full of firelight and stars, when I notice the armored guard in the shadows, leaning against the wall of a building. Again, I have the sense that he's watching *me*. Not Dorothy and me, but *me* specifically.

Something about his stance, his solidity, is like a tether—a lifeline in the sea of endless, reckless melody. My heart craves that stillness, that calm.

I dance toward the guard, letting my body bend and sway and ripple with the music, every movement a challenge. But instead of rising to the bait, he withdraws deeper into the shadows and pauses there, his metal-clad arms still folded, until my continued advance is unmistakable. I'm headed straight for him, and he knows it.

He straightens, and his arms fall to his sides. He stands absolutely still, as if he has rusted in place, but I can feel the tension and anticipation rolling off him.

The way he's standing... something about his posture...

I stop dancing and approach him cautiously.

"Why are you watching me?" I ask, moving closer.

He shifts slightly, a scrape of metal boots on the quartz pavers. It's a small movement, but it betrays his agitation.

"You don't talk? Or maybe you can't." I survey his armor—strangely smooth, no marks of battle. This close, I can tell it's not made of actual silver—probably fabricated from some Fae metal I don't know the name of.

"This is Talon," says Glenna, appearing at my elbow. "He'll be your escort to the woods tomorrow. He doesn't speak much, do you, Talon?" She smirks, then downs another goblet of wine. "He came to us some time ago. The East Witch couldn't enthrall him for some reason, but he vowed to be a good citizen, so she let him stay with us. I've never seen him remove his helmet, or any other part of his armor, for that matter. He doesn't eat, drink, sleep, or piss—not that any of us have seen. Perhaps the armor is actually empty." She reaches out and raps the chestplate with her knuckles. "I'll wager there's something solid in there. Maybe you can convince him to—expose himself." Still chuckling, she wanders back into the dance.

I place my fingertips against the chestplate, right where the guard's heart should be, if he has one. "You never take off the armor? I wonder if you're cursed. Maybe that's why the Witch couldn't enthrall you. Certain types of magic don't mix."

A ragged inhale from inside the helmet. "Always so clever, kitten."

*Kitten.*

*Kitten.*

*Kitten.*

The nickname echoes in my mind as a horrible thrill rolls through my chest. Goosebumps explode over my skin, and every nerve in my body tightens, shrill and taut, a fraction of a second from snapping.

Only one person in all the realms calls me that.

I can't breathe.

The armored man remains motionless as I recoil from him, staring, stunned.

"Say that again." My voice is razor edges and tears tinged with blood.

"Kitten." His voice is muffled, but I'd know it anywhere. "Why have you come to this wretched place? Still no sense of self-preservation, I see."

"*No.*" I back away. "No, no—this isn't how it's supposed to happen. You're not *him.*"

"Keep your voice down."

"I will not. I—"

But he reaches out, pressing metal fingers against my back, and hustles me around the corner of the building. "You must not reveal who I am, do you understand? These Fae are unusually volatile. Make a wrong move, and you'll be the scarecrow they hang tomorrow, to amuse the crows while your friend finds safe passage to the forest. Who is she, this sorceress who brought you here? There's something about her…"

"No!" I nearly shout it this time, shoving both palms against his metal-covered chest. "You will *not* fall for her. I'm the only hapless human girl you get to seduce, understand?"

I don't even know what I'm saying—tears are blurring my view of him—but it's not him, is it? It can't be him locked inside this case of metal. Desperate, I pound on it harder.

"No use, kitten. I've tried. It's unbreakable."

"You're not Riordan," I grit out. "Maybe you're some kind of Fae mind-reader, pretending to be him. Faking his voice."

"To what purpose?" he says quietly. "Besides, would any other Fae know how you taste?"

He's covered in bulky metal and the heavy blue cloak, so how, *how* does he make my skin heat and my clit tingle, simply by tilting his head?

"Tell me what I taste like," I whisper.

His answer is a low murmur from within the helmet. "Like rose petals and sweet surrender. With a faint tang of lemons and a hint of vanilla."

I have no way of knowing if he's right—if *that's* how I tasted to him when he licked me to climax over and over all those months ago.

I want to look into his crimson eyes and be sure it's him. I want to lift off that helmet and punch him straight in the mouth, and then kiss the lips I bruised. But instead I snarl, "How the fuck did you get yourself into this mess?"

"I went after Caer, like you told me to," he retorts. "I found out he'd come here to make a wish to the Green Wizard. By the time I arrived at the Emerald City, he had already doomed himself."

The earth seems to drop out from under me. After the shock of hearing Riordan's voice saying, "kitten"—to have him tell me that Caer *doomed himself*—that he is—is—

It's too much. I can't bear it.

"So he's gone," I whisper. I sink to the ground, my head ringing, stars dancing before my eyes. The world is whirling away into a black and endless void.

"No, love, no," Riordan says hastily, crouching beside me with a creak of metal joints. "He's alive. But his wish changed him."

"Oh, thank the gods." My voice cracks and I bow over, clutching my chest. "Fuck you, Riordan! I thought you meant—I thought he was dead." I take a moment to collect the pieces of my half-shattered heart and reassemble it before I manage to ask, "Changed him how?"

"I think that's too much for you to hear right now."

I draw in a slow breath. Maybe he's right—black spots are still swimming across my tear-filled vision. "You still haven't explained how you got into that armor."

"When I found out what had happened to Caer, I knew I couldn't handle him on my own. My magic is not the aggressive kind, as you know. I'm not like Finias, with his flamboyant attack spells."

There's a twinge of jealousy in his tone, and that, more than anything else, convinces me that it's really him.

He rises from the crouch, a sigh gusting hollowly through his helmet. "I asked the Green Wizard to give me something that would help me face Caer without him killing me. Within seconds of my wish, this suit of armor formed around me. It's impenetrable. Preserves my body in perfect health, even though I can't eat, drink, shit, or fuck. I haven't felt the air on my face in what feels like a lifetime."

I peer up at him. "Your ears must be horribly cramped in there."

"It's torture." The agonized quiet of his tone sends an answering pang through my heart.

What is wrong with me? I refuse to feel bad for him—I'm *angry* with him. I'm fucking furious. He sent me back to the human realm, because he was convinced he knew what was best for me. He thought he understood my emotions better than I did.

He was wrong. So wrong.

"You were a fool to make a wish to the Wizard," I snap at him. "Especially after you found out what Caer's wish did to him. And I'm strong enough to hear the truth, by the way."

"Not tonight," he says. "No more revelations this evening, kitten—you've had more than your share of shocks today. And you may call me a fool, but aren't you and your friend headed to see the same wizard tomorrow?"

I wince. "Yes."

"And what will you wish for?"

"I *was* going to wish to be transported to the Unseelie Kingdom."

"The Wizard would have fulfilled your request—he has no choice, you see. He is forced to grant a wish to each supplicant, not out of mercy, but because of some dire compulsion. So yes, he would grant it—but you'd have landed in a den of Unseelie monsters, most likely. He twists every wish into a curse."

"Well, I still have to visit him. I have to at least *try* to free you two boneheads from your respective curses." I rise, brushing off my dress. "Waste of a perfectly good wish, if you ask me."

A muffled chuckle from the helmet.

I narrow my eyes at him. "Are you *laughing*?"

"No matter how you may feel about me, Alice, I am glad to see you."

His use of my name sends a tremor through me, mostly centered between my legs. He and Caer have featured prominently in my fantasies each time I touched myself. Every memory I had of them has been teased out, relived, and expanded during many lonely nights.

The fact that Riordan is here, just as untouchable and just as supremely infuriating as ever—it's more than I can handle. And I hate to admit that, almost as much as I hate the barrier of metal between me and his mouth.

# 7

# DOROTHY

I could dance like this forever, reeling beneath the stars, surrounded by swirling blue figures.

"Do all the Fae wear blue?" I could swear I asked the question in my mind, but one of the villagers near me replies, "Blue is the color of the sunny sky, the hue of the arch in which the crows fly. We wear it as a sign of respect for them. It is the natural color of reverence and truth. All servants of the crows know this in their bones. You and your pet wear it too. You must be true servants as well."

"True servants—yes, that's me and Alice." I laugh lightly, mockingly, but unease twitches inside me as I glance around, searching the dancers for the pale-haired girl I came with. She's nowhere to be seen.

I don't naturally care about the wellbeing of others, but I've taught myself the patterns followed by people who do care. I can propel myself through the thought chain a normal human would follow, and thus determine what my emotional response should be, what action I should take.

Alice is an acquaintance with whom I've shared a significant experience, which brings her closer to friend status. We're in a strange place, with potential dangers, and my acquaintance-friend is out of my sight, either by her own will or someone else's. She could get hurt, which, as her friend, should disturb me. I should want to prevent that. Which means I should go look for her.

Expressions of concern are a familiar part of my mask, so I assume one and move toward the edge of the crowd. Glenna is flying over the heads of the dancers with a few other winged Fae. She's drinking deeply from a jug.

I call up to her. "Have you seen Alice?"

"She was just there." Glenna points to the corner of a building—a shop of some kind.

When I reach the corner I whistle, sharp and quick, a note so high it's nearly inaudible. The sound cuts through the Fae music, and seconds later Fiero runs up to me, dodging Fae feet as if he's been reveling in other realms his whole life.

"Come on," I tell him. "We need to find Alice."

As I walk into the shadows with Fiero trotting at my side, I sink one hand into my pocket, reassuring myself that the Tama Olc is still there. It's a small book, but thick and heavy. I felt it bouncing against my thigh as I danced.

A quiver of power slithers from the spine of the book into my palm, and I feel the same tug I felt when I touched it back in the old barn on Alice's farm. It's a rhythmic pull, tightening with every step, every heartbeat. I'm nearing the thing that's been drawing me all along.

*Blood calls to blood.*

I round the corner, and in the gloom I see Alice, standing in front of a metal-clad figure, a guard of some kind. He's speaking in a low, male voice, but he stops abruptly when I appear. His head lifts, like a hound scenting the breeze, and then he walks around Alice, straight toward me.

"Who are you?" His tone is belligerent, but there's a thread of curiosity in it.

"You're the one who pulled us here," I say.

"Pulled you here?"

"Yes. When Alice and I both grabbed this—" I take the book from my pocket— "I felt something tugging, just here." I touch my heart with my other hand.

The helmeted guard nods. "I feel it too." He touches his own metal-clad chest.

Alice stares at us, a desperate fury in her gray eyes. "Dorothy, I like you well enough, but if you're fated to be his mate or something, I'm afraid I may have to kill you."

The guard turns. "I thought you were angry with me, kitten."

"I *am*. I'm furious. That doesn't mean someone else gets to have you."

"No one will be having me until I get out of this armor," he says dryly. "And don't think you're going to distract me from the fact that you gave away the Tama Olc to some insignificant human sorceress."

Alice shrugs. "Seemed like the thing to do. Other than Drosselmeyer, she was the only person I knew who had magic."

"A fact you discovered mere hours ago," I add. "There's something I'd like to make very clear—I'm no one's mate. Nor will anyone be killing me, and also I object to being called 'insignificant.' Is there something I'm missing here? Do you two know each other?"

Alice sighs. "Dorothy, it is my great *dis*pleasure to introduce you to Riordan, sometimes called the White Rabbit."

"I dislike that name," says the armored man. "My ears don't make me a rabbit, and I don't wear white all the time—"

"Most of the time. Whenever you're not wearing armor that looks as if it's made from tin. Would you rather I called you 'Tin

Man'? Has a nice ring to it—" she bangs on his armored chest—"and it's shorter than 'White Rabbit.'"

My mind is spinning. Too much wine, dancing, and new information. "Wait... he's one of the two Fae who held you captive? No wonder we were drawn here. You wanted to see him."

"I did not." Alice bristles when the armored man looks down at her. "I wanted to find Caer, not Riordan."

"You didn't want to see me, yet no one else is allowed to have me. A contradiction we can discuss later," says Riordan. "I know where you're both meant to stay. I'll take you there, and then you can tell me exactly what happened when you traveled here."

The cottage we've been given for the night is small and plain, with two cots, a washstand, and a chair. There's a tiny privy closet with a toilet, as well, and Fiero immediately runs in to inspect the smells in that space. Three glowing orbs hover overhead, providing light.

I reach toward one, and it flies into my hand, not quite touching my skin but hovering there until I wave it away.

The armored man seems to be staring at me, his arms crossed. "You're part Fae."

"I don't think so," I reply.

"Only the Fae can manipulate the orbs so easily. Humans cannot affect them, and sorcerers can't either, not without a spell."

Alice seats herself on one of the beds and crosses her legs, letting the short skirts of her maid's outfit ride up nearly to her crotch. She's clearly doing it for Riordan's benefit. "If she's Fae, does that explain the 'tug' you feel between you?"

"Perhaps," he replies. "Tell me everything that happened to both of you today."

He stands motionless while Alice explains. I supplement her tale with a description of how I felt, both when I touched the book and during the whirlwind.

"I would need more data to be sure—tests that I cannot perform while I'm locked inside this shell." Frustration tinges Riordan's voice. "The cursed metal hinders my magic. But I can theorize, if you like."

"Please do," Alice says.

"I will supplement the information you provided with two facts—firstly, that the Tama Olc recognizes a member of its author's bloodline—my ancestor's bloodline. And secondly, in certain Fae families, relatives can sense each other's presence, sometimes over great distances. The closer the familial bond, the stronger the connection. I would guess that when both of you were touching the book at the same time, a link was established between the three of us—two former owners of the book, and one current owner. Alice and I have been bonded in the most intimate of ways—her heart was literally grown from my—"

"We don't need to tell Dorothy all the details of how you saved me." Alice's cheeks are scarlet.

"Very well. Suffice it to say that you and I are forever connected, kitten, and if you had a desire in your heart to come to Faerie, to see me, the book discerned it. At the same time it came under the influence of Dorothy, whom I can say with certainty is part Fae—and I would guess she is of my family. My blood."

"Blood calls to blood," I breathe.

"Precisely."

"But neither of my parents are Fae."

"Could one of them be in disguise? Glamoured? Have you ever noticed anything odd or inexplicable about them?"

I shake my head. "I'm the only odd, inexplicable one."

"Perhaps you were found by your parents, or given to them."

He says it so coolly, so matter-of-factly. As if he couldn't imagine that it would bother me to learn I might have been adopted.

And the strange thing is—it doesn't bother me. Although I know it should. Any normal person finding out such a thing about themselves would be shaken by the news—troubled at the very least—perhaps even agonized.

I feel nothing but a mild surprise. My emotion for the two people I call my parents remains the same—a nebulous, comfortable warmth. I'm not sure I could call it love—that word doesn't seem to fit, exactly. I've only loved once, and that felt different.

Sometimes I think I'm broken. Wrong. That I don't understand what it means to be human.

But according to this strange armored being—I'm not entirely human. I'm part Fae. Part of his family.

"So you two are related." Relief mingles with the interest in Alice's voice. "That's good."

"None of this matters," I say. "It has nothing to do with where we are, and no impact on what we'll do next."

Alice stares at me, and I swear I can feel the helmet staring, too.

"It matters because—because *knowing things* matters," Alice says. "Investigation, discovery, understanding—those pursuits matter."

"Indeed," says the armor emphatically. They look at each other, and damn me if I can't feel the very air between them humming with unsaid things.

"We should sleep." I say. "We've got a long and dangerous journey starting tomorrow."

"But... we should *talk*," Alice says, looking at the armor.

"You can talk tomorrow, while we're traveling," I say. "I assume you'll be coming all the way to the Emerald City with us, Riordan? Not just escorting us to the forest?"

"The people here will expect me to return to them," he says. "But I owe them nothing."

"Why are you here, anyway?" Alice asks.

"Making myself useful. I had nowhere else to go. Without the need to sleep, eat, or drink, I'm the ideal guard."

"What do you guard?" I eye him suspiciously.

"There's a jail here, to hold travelers and any villagers for whom the East Witch's compulsion isn't fully effective. I know of one whom she was never able to compel at all. So yes, guards are needed, because the prisoners try to escape occasionally. Sometimes monsters find their way into the village, or the wards become thin and a few crows slip through. And the East Witch's brother likes to show up and cause trouble. I also serve as an escort when anyone needs to go beyond the wall." He clears his throat. "Sometimes I help place the scarecrows in the fields."

Alice frowns, her lips opening to question him, but he hurries on, "And there's an advantage to being just here, not far from the woods. These are the woods where he... where we..."

Alice leaps up and finishes his sentence. "Where Caer is! Oh god, Riordan—that's why you're really here—because he's nearby. I want to see him."

"He'd rip you apart, kitten. He wouldn't recognize you."

"You can't know that for sure."

They bicker a little more, while I use the privy closet. When I come out, Alice has her back to the silver suit of armor, and he's got his arms crossed again.

How do they *care* so much? It makes me exhausted just watching them.

I fling myself onto one of the beds, and Fiero rears on his hind legs, poking his snuffly black nose over the edge of the mattress and staring at me mournfully until I lift him up and set him beside me.

It's easier for me to care about the little dog, or to care about children like Alice's siblings—maybe because they tend to look up to me, depend on me, and idolize me, which feels right—feels like my natural state. Adults stare appraisingly, judging me, gauging my actions, wondering why I'm not already married at age twenty.

I had someone I wanted, once—Archer, the son of a carpenter in the village. I wanted him fiercely—gave myself to him a few times, when we could manage to be alone. But he was killed while he and his father were constructing the third floor of a shop in the village. An act of the gods, people called it. A fall that shouldn't have been lethal, except for his head striking the ground at an odd angle. One quick snap, and the brightest-burning thing in my life was gone.

Archer is how I know that I can love—or I could. I think maybe his death killed that feeling within me. I'd never felt so passionate about anything before him, and I haven't felt anything that intensely since—until today, in the barn, when I touched the book—and afterward, when I met the Witch of the West.

I can perceive emotions in others, and I feel them powerfully sometimes—but most often my emotions are muted, muffled, like Riordan's voice inside the helmet as he bids Alice goodnight.

When he leaves the cottage, she stands in the center of the room, her hands clenched tight at her sides.

For a handful of seconds she stands there. And then she rushes to the door and flings it open.

He's still there, on the other side. Hasn't moved a step.

"I just wanted you to know," Alice says, breathless. "That I hate you for sending me back, after everything."

"I understand," he replies.

"And I didn't miss you," she goes on in a rush. "Not at all."

He inclines his helmet, a slight nod. "I assumed you'd miss me a good deal less than I missed you."

Again they stare. I'm not sure what Alice is staring at—the slits in his helmet?

"Promise you'll be here when I wake up." Her voice quakes on the edge of tears. "Promise."

"I wouldn't dream of being anywhere else."

When the door closes again, Alice walks stiffly to her bed and lies down.

I lift my fingers, making a squeezing motion at one of the orbs overhead, and it winks out. The gesture was instinctive, natural. Dispelling the orb took no energy at all.

I pinch out the second orb, leaving the third to provide a faint nighttime light for the cottage.

"Did you know?" Alice says into the dark. "Did you suspect that you were Fae?"

"No."

But when she finally turns over and her breathing settles into a slow rhythm, I reach beneath the loose part of my hair above my braids, and I feel the shape of my ear, as I've done over and over throughout my life. I usually keep my ears covered because they're shaped differently—lines of cartilage positioned in odd places, a subtle peak at the top.

Half-Fae.

It all adds up. The way the food tastes here—the vibrancy of the colors, the foliage—the music, the movement—the sense in my blood and bones that I've returned to a place where I belong. My magic. The reaction of the book to my touch. The way I knew Riordan was still on the other side of the door, even before Alice threw it open—because he and I are family, in a visceral way I've never known.

It fits, all of it.

I think I've been wanting to go home my whole life. And now that I'm here in Faerie, unfamiliar as it is, I never want to leave. There's no place like it.

# 8

## ALICE

Against all odds, I slept. A solid, dreamless sleep. I was exhausted—but maybe it also had something to do with the fact that my heart knew Riordan was near, and that Caer is closer than he has been for months.

I don't let myself define how I feel for the two Fae males—why the urge to be near them, *with them* is even stronger than my love for the family I left behind. I'm worried for my siblings, of course—but they are ultimately my parents' responsibility, not mine or Dorothy's. My parents chose to have all those babies. It's about time they actually cared for the children themselves. And if they don't—if they refuse—the older two should be able to help out. David turned ten while I was gone, and Bertha will be ten soon, as well. It's too young, of course—but I was even younger when Mam started handing me the babies to feed, change, and swaddle.

Much as I love my siblings, they aren't mine to raise. Staying would have locked me into a wretched future, including a marriage to a man I loathe. Chained to the tavern and its keeper, I likely wouldn't have seen much of my family anyway.

All that is behind me now. I must focus on myself, and on the people who need me *today*.

In our tiny cottage, Dorothy and I wash up quickly using the supplies in the basket under the washstand. Not all Fae are skilled with cleansing magic, so there are scented soaps, as well as herbal paste for cleaning teeth, for which I'm grateful.

As we prepare to leave the cottage, Dorothy tips her head to one side. "He left for a while, but he's back now."

"You can sense him that clearly?" Despite the fact that they're related, not fated, I'm still a little jealous of their connection.

Dorothy nods. "It's a bit annoying, actually. Like not being able to take off these shoes. I had to wear them all night."

"We need to find out more about those shoes. Unfortunately the one who would know the most about them is that green witch."

"Wonderful. Can't wait to talk to him again," she says dryly.

"I don't know." I study her face. "You two seemed to have something. An attraction."

She stares. "Alice, he's *green*."

"So? Riordan has the ears of a rabbit, and Caer has cat ears and a tail."

"Yes, but—*green*."

Chuckling, I push open the cottage door.

Fiero runs out immediately. Cool morning air flows over my bare arms, and I shiver. Beyond the blue foliage overhead, pink tinges the sky.

A few paces from the door, the suit of armor stands rigid while Fiero snuffles around his silver boots. He isn't wearing the blue cloak today.

My stomach flips at the sight of him. How awful it must be for Riordan, existing inside that cursed shell! And it happened because he went to find Caer, like I asked him to.

I wasn't sympathetic enough last night. I still think he was stupid to make a wish to the Wizard, but as he pointed out, I plan to make one as well. Except mine will be airtight, worded so carefully the Green Wizard can't possibly twist its meaning.

When the armor doesn't move, the eagerness in my heart melts into worry. What if Riordan is somehow gone? What if I imagined him, or what if—

"Dawn is nearly here. We must go." It's his voice, the same voice that once spoke to me so calmly of my own future dissection—the one that murmured encouragement as I climaxed for him, so many times—

Damn it, I'm getting wet again.

"Why is it important to leave now?" I ask.

"The crows sleep for a few hours between midnight and dawn. When they first wake, they're a little sluggish, and they will head for the easy prey—the scarecrow—while we make for the forest."

"Why not travel while they're sleeping?"

"Because if they are startled awake in the night, they are twice as vicious. Not to mention the other things that roam this Isle in the dark."

Dorothy picks up Fiero. "He needs something to eat. I gave him water this morning, but he didn't touch a bit of food last night."

"He's an intelligent scrap of fluff," says Riordan. He nods to a large basket nearby, its contents folded within a blue-checked cloth. "One of the Fae packed some supplies for the two of you, but I'm not sure you should partake. All the food here is magically crafted from the corn the villagers grow, which is fertilized by the remains of the crows' meals and imbued with their strange dark magic. I've not seen this kind of symbiosis between Fae and arcane creatures in all my years. It merits further study, but—"

"But we don't have time," I tell him. "We need to find Caer and get you both un-cursed."

"True." He sighs and speaks to Dorothy. "There will be something in the forest your pet can eat. We should go."

Her lips press into an unhappy line, but she doesn't protest as she picks up the basket. "Whether we eat the food or not, there might be something useful in here."

"True." I hesitate, scanning the quartz-paved paths that wind between the blue houses. There's not a single Fae to be seen. "Should we thank them? Bid them farewell?"

"The only ones awake are the guards who prepared the scarecrow. The rest won't be up for hours. Come."

He stalks along the path. There's a metallic clanking as he moves, and his boots ring against the stone.

Fiero whines and wriggles in Dorothy's arms until she puts him down. The poor dog is probably starving. So am I, but after what Riordan said about the alchemized food, I'd rather wait and eat in the forest. Surely he can tell us which berries and nuts are safe.

We move through the village square where the feast was held. Not a trace of the tables, benches, or bonfire remains—just a clear space with a fountain I didn't notice last night—a huge crow carved of ebony stone, wings outspread, spewing crystal water from its serrated beak. A shudder passes through me as we walk past it.

Riordan leads us around the triangular temple, along another winding street lined with squat blue houses, until we reach the high wall surrounding the village. The frame of the gate towers ridiculously high, almost as tall as the trees, and the double gates are ebony wood, meeting in a sharp point that mirrors the shape of the temple.

Riordan lays silver jointed fingers against the black gates. "The influence of the trees and the village's protective charms will fade once we pass through here. Stay close to me."

The familiar, hated sensation of helplessness rises in my chest like a diseased serpent. "We should have asked these Fae for weapons."

"They have few of those," Riordan says. "The Witch did not permit it, in case they should somehow break free of her control and rise up against her. Even now, freed of her thrall, I believe they prefer to continue along as they always have, with the same traditions and practices. It's easier to succumb than to resist."

His words weren't directed at me, but they sting a little. Last time I was in Faerie, I resisted him for a while—but eventually I submitted. I gave him the book and yielded myself to his will. And it worked—when I finally gave in, Riordan couldn't bring himself to hurt me.

But I submitted in another way, too—I *let* him send me home. When I found out he didn't want me to stay, I bowed to his decision. I should have fought harder.

I've been blaming *him* for it, when I was at fault, too.

Riordan's helmet turns my way. He must think I'm pondering the state of things in the Village of Crows, because he says, "It is a shame. They've been sitting here, consuming polluted magic, using it for nothing except to maintain their current way of life. They could do more with this piece of land—they could even purge the crows from their fields, if they would put forth the effort. But I doubt they will. The crows are a religion to them as well as a threat."

Dorothy snorts derisively. "Religion and threat pair well together, I've found."

"I've heard about human religions from my subjects," Riordan says. "It is a fascinating study."

"Not really." She shrugs. "Weaklings need a crutch so they can hobble through the agony of life. Men who want power devise the crutch, then use it as a cudgel to keep everyone subservient."

I don't like her disdainful tone, but maybe she has a point. I've never found much use for religion—even less since I discovered Faerie was real. What shocks me more, though, is how crisply and clearly she spoke her philosophy. She has obviously learned and thought much deeper than I expected, and I'm a little jealous. How did she educate herself? And how has she hidden her true nature for so long? When I've seen her in passing, she has simply been my neighbor Dorothy—quiet and pretty, with unusual eyes—occasionally clumsy, good with children. The sheer depth of what she was hiding unsettles me.

I have no time to address it with her now, because Riordan is pushing open the gates. A swath of golden-green cornfield widens between the ebony doors, and winding through that cornfield is a yellow brick road.

Dorothy and I step over the threshold of the village onto the road. Riordan closes the gates and then strides ahead to take the lead, while Fiero trots at his heels. The dog seems fascinated by the shiny man of metal, though he startles back if Riordan moves too suddenly.

"We have to hurry," says Riordan. "The crows will be rising soon, and the scarecrow won't keep them busy long. There's not much meat on the boy's bones."

"Wait..." A cold sweat of alarm breaks out on my skin— terror and dread. I walk faster, coming abreast of him. "A boy? What are you talking about?"

"The scarecrow." His helmet angles toward me. "You heard them discussing it, yes? Not a scarecrow in the traditional sense, but a sacrifice to the crows, to distract them."

"I heard that part, but I didn't think it would be a *person*."

"What did you think it was?"

"I don't know—a cow? Some animal?"

"They don't keep livestock. No, they breed much faster than other Fae, because of the crows' magic, so the sacrifice is always one of their own—usually a troublemaker. Someone who doesn't fit into their society. In this case, it's a young Fae whom the East Witch was never able to enthrall—he was immune to her power, despite not being part of the royal bloodline."

Riordan hesitates, and when he speaks again, his voice is quieter, almost regretful. "In the fields where the crows hold sway, there is an ancient well—the Well of Undoing. Its waters remove a Fae's powers temporarily, and wounds created while under the water's influence heal slowly, if at all. The villagers occasionally fetch a little of the water, at great risk, for use in their ritual tattoos, and every sacrifice is dosed with the water, to sap their strength and prevent them from healing while the crows devour them."

"And you've seen the villagers do this before?" I dart in front and plant both hands on his chest to stop him. "You've watched them tie someone up in the field? Right now, you're allowing an innocent person to be eaten alive so we can get safely to the woods?"

"I would do far more despicable things to ensure your safety," he says coolly.

"You—you—" I'm swelling with disbelief, with rage. I can barely speak. I bang on his metal chest with my fist. "You're absolutely *heartless*, you know that?"

"Keep walking, Alice."

"No! You're going to show me where they put up this scarecrow. I assume you know where they usually do it?"

"Yes, but—"

"We're going to find him and free him. Show us where he is, Riordan. Now."

"Must we, though?" says Dorothy in a bored tone. "We don't know him. What does it matter if he dies, as long as we don't have to watch it?"

I grit my teeth, and my fingers curl into fists. "You two are so—*Unseelie*."

"Is that a compliment?" Dorothy smiles, not the gentle, placid smile I've seen from her back home. This smile has wicked edges.

"Riordan, please." I turn my attention back to him. "You know this is wrong."

"He is a sacrifice for the greater good. Not much different than the humans I've offered up to the cause of magical research over the years." He's walking again, his chestplate pressing against my palms. He's moving me backward along the road by sheer brute strength.

"Fuck you," I spit, and I dodge out of his way, off the road and into the cornfield.

"Stop, Alice!" His voice booms inside the helmet, but I'm running along a row, ducking between stalks, then racing down the next row, quickly and quietly as I can. I don't see any crows. If I hurry, I can find the sacrifice before he's torn to pieces.

I'm no stranger to fields like this, to the sharp edges of the crooked leaves, to the papery rasp of the breeze slithering through the stalks, to the sticky silks trailing in bunches from swelling cobs of corn, sheathed in green. My father would give his right arm for a field like this—a field fat with the promise of a rich harvest.

Of course he wouldn't care for the feathered fiends that haunt this place. There's one on the ground, and my heart jumps at the sight, but I think it's dead. It's lying on its back, wings outspread and tail splayed, its claws curled and its beak open.

It doesn't move as I tiptoe cautiously past.

The farther I run into the field, the more thickly the ground is littered with dead crows. Perhaps we've been lucky—maybe they were tethered to the East Witch somehow, and they died when we crushed her under the barn. Maybe some curse of the West Witch or the Green Wizard took them down.

I walk more confidently, but I still avoid stepping on the motionless birds. I can't hear any sounds of pursuit. If Riordan and Dorothy are following me, they're moving just as quietly as I am—which, in Riordan's case, would be difficult.

As my fear ebbs, I begin to realize that I could hunt through this field for days and never find the Scarecrow they put out here. I need to locate some higher ground—any swell of earth that will give me a vantage point.

Pausing to scope out the crow-littered earth between the stalks, I notice a slight upward slant in one direction. So I head that way, and sure enough, the ground continues to slope up until it rises sharply, forming a hill clad only in yellow grass, dotted with a few scarlet flowers.

I part the last of the cornstalks and look up, squinting slightly against the brilliant blue of the sky. The sun has risen, and its new light floods the scene, illuminating the grass—gleaming on the golden hair of a figure tied to a wooden stake at the peak of the hill.

The young Fae male has been stripped to the waist, left with only a pair of ragged blue trousers. His bare feet are tied to the pole by the ankles, and more ropes circle his thighs. His arms are pulled back behind him, securely fastened to the crossbeam of the post. His ribs have been tattooed with stalks of grain, and across his chest is the tattooed shape of a crow spreading its wings—one feathered, one plucked to the bone. The male's left shoulder and upper arm bear another tattoo—a hideous scarecrow made of branches.

The sun shines through a straw hat that was probably on his head but now hangs at his back, held by its leather string, a mocking nod to the role he's supposed to fill—a living scarecrow.

He isn't handsome like Riordan, or wickedly beautiful like Caer—but he's so fucking pretty. Delicate features, soft lips, sorrowful blue eyes. His sharp ears poke through a tumble of curls as golden as ripe grain.

He's looking down at me, and he doesn't look surprised, or hopeful, or even angry. But the sadness in his eyes breaks my heart. He's been abandoned here, his body given up to the appetites of savage creatures, and I know how he feels because I've been there, too.

"Go, before they notice you." His voice is gentle, musical, a lullaby meant to keep wicked things from waking.

He didn't ask me to free him. He doesn't even know me, but his first thought was for my safety.

"Couldn't you break free?" I reply, in a voice as quiet as his.

He shakes his head, sunlight glinting on bright blue earrings. "I have been robbed of my magic and my strength, such as it is."

I lift an eyebrow, surveying his lean, toned figure. "You look strong to me."

"Not strong enough. Please go, before they devour you too." His eyes dart to the left, and my gaze follows.

One of the dead crows lies there. As I watch, its beak clicks shut, and its claws stretch out. The limp wings twitch.

In the distance, against the blue sky and the creamy clouds, black-winged shapes are rising, one after another, wheeling through the morning air.

Fuck, they're not dead. All the bodies I saw on the way here—they're living birds. And I'm out here, weak from hunger, weaponless, alone with this helpless Scarecrow.

Where is Riordan? Did he give up on me so easily?

Struggling up the slope of the hill, I duck behind the Scarecrow and pick frantically at the knots. Why are there so many of them?

"It's not that I'm ungrateful," says the Scarecrow, "but if you do this, you'll die as well."

"I won't let you be eaten to bones just so we can get to the forest." I manage to loosen a loop of the knot holding one of his arms to the crossbeam. "I wish I had a knife, or Fae teeth, or magic—"

An idea springs into my mind—a mad idea, but it's the only one I've got. As Caer once said, everyone's mad in Faerie.

I dart to the crow that's twitching awake and seize its body in both my hands. It flails suddenly, emitting a croaking screech that's cut off by a skillful flex of my fingers and the *snap* of its neck. I'm a farmer's daughter. I know how to kill a bird.

Holding its body with one hand, I pinch its head between the fingers of my other hand, forcing its beak open. The serrated edges are just what I need—and I'm shocked to find there are tiny rows of actual teeth inside the crow's beak, too.

Frantically I saw at the ropes around the Scarecrow's ankles, but my actions have stirred the nearby birds, and they're rising. One after another they hop upright, stretch their wings, and take to the sky. They fly in slow circles at first, but their speed and the intensity of their cries increase with every passing second. The sound of their flapping wings fills the air, a thunderous threat.

The Fae's ankles are free. Now for the ropes around his thighs. His pants have been torn nearly off him, and as I work on his bonds, I notice ravens in flight, tattooed along the inside of his right leg.

"So many tattoos," I mutter, breathless with the effort of sawing as fast as I can.

"I've been marked for sacrifice since I was very young," he replies. "I will beg you one more time, sweet stranger, to leave me and run."

"No."

His thighs are free, but the crows are a thick tempest now, darkening the sky in a storm of midnight wings. None of them have descended toward us, though—they just keep whirling round and round in a cyclical formation. Strange.

As I move behind him and set to work on the ropes binding his arms, two figures emerge from the cornfield onto the grassy knoll—Riordan in his armor and Dorothy, her eyes fixed on the sky. She has managed to sling the basket onto her back, and both her hands are lifted, her fingers crooked with tension. Fiero trots at her heels.

"Hurry," she says. "I have them in a holding pattern, but I'm not sure how long I can maintain it."

I'd forgotten that she has two variants of her ability—moving the inner molecules of a non-living substance, and speeding up movements that living things are already performing.

"That's brilliant!" I exclaim. "Keep it up! Riordan, help me get him down."

"You'll get us all killed," he growls, but he climbs the hill, towering over the young Fae bound to the post. He slices through two of the ropes with one slash of his sharp metal fingers.

The Scarecrow falls forward, crashing onto his hands and knees. As I help him up, his scent rushes over me—warm and sweet and wholesome, like summer grass and freshly baked bread. His skin is soft, hot, and smooth. He manages to stand, one arm draped over my shoulders. With his other hand he tears off the straw hat that was hanging against his back. The crown and the top of the brim have been painted with strange symbols—probably another spell.

He tosses the hat away as Dorothy says, in a strained voice, "We should probably start running for the woods now."

A rumble of frustration issues from Riordan's helmet. "Since you refuse to leave him behind…" He steps in and picks up the Scarecrow in his metal-plated arms, like a knight carrying a damsel in a fairytale. "Go," he says tersely. "You and Dorothy run north, and I'll bring up the rear."

"Don't abandon him, Riordan. Please." I stare into the eyeholes of his helmet, wishing I could see those molten scarlet eyes of his.

"Run," is his only answer, and Dorothy races past me with a panicked, "Run, Alice!"

Her cry is punctuated by a shift in the air, and the sudden enraged screams of a thousand ravenous crows.

# 9

## DOROTHY

When Alice ran off into the field, I was alarmed, of course. But as she disappeared between the cornstalks, the suit of metal she calls Riordan made a sound so broken, so wretched, so full of terror that I felt an echo of his misery in my own heart.

I would have followed her anyway—it's what a friend is supposed to do. But his reaction confirmed my choice. I didn't want to hear Riordan make that noise again.

He and I followed more slowly—he was concerned that his armored bulk might rouse the crows. When they began to wake, he asked, in a voice deep and woeful, if I thought there was any magic I could do to protect Alice.

I sped up the birds' natural formation and kept them stuck in that pattern, moving round and round, faster and faster, adding more and more birds to the cloud as they awoke. But eventually I came to the end of my strength…I had to let it all go, and they exploded from the spiral in a tempest of screaming fury.

And now I'm running through the rows of corn, with Fiero just ahead, his stubby black legs moving in a blur. Alice's panting breaths and light footsteps are right behind me, and farther behind are Riordan's heavier footfalls and the metallic clanking of his armor.

Something thrums inside me—a latent energy. It's not magic, exactly, but it is *potential*. I have the power to run faster if I want to—inhumanly fast, and I'm not sure if it's coming from the silver shoes, or if it's my Fae side awakening, but tapping into that speed would allow me to reach the forest alone, leaving everyone else to their fate.

It makes sense for me to save myself. But I've trained my thoughts to follow the patterns of morality. For years I've guided my mind to function in socially acceptable ways; and I know, objectively, that leaving friends to die is considered *wrong*. If I do such a thing, and Alice survives, she will never forgive me or trust me again, and I need allies to survive this strange isle.

I have to stay with them, even if it means we all perish together. It goes against all my instincts of self-preservation, but I force myself to maintain my pace, and run only a little faster than Alice.

Ahead, above the clumps of cornsilks, the forest looms, a towering wall of shimmering leaves and deep, shadowed green. But it's still too far away, and the crows are darting down, beaks open.

I wave both arms wildly, and a concussive blast pulses outward from me, knocking back a few dozen of the birds. But hundreds more are descending, and that defensive attack seems to be usable only once—I can't summon enough energy to do it again. They're upon me, screeching and clawing and flapping. A crow manages to gouge a chunk from my forearm, and another clamps its talons onto my back and digs its beak into my shoulder. A scream tears from my throat as more wings and beaks descend, ripping my clothes. One of them aims for my eyes, barely misses, and carves a groove across my forehead. Fuck it, I'm going to have to abandon the others and run, run for my life—

Several sharp bangs erupt among the cornstalks, followed by a hissing sound and multiple explosions of green mist. Thin columns of smoke streak up to the sky and expand like mushrooms. The mist spreads rapidly between the stalks and the smoke unfurls into the air, while the crows screech and wheel away from it. They soar back up into the sky, one massive, churning cloud of black feathers and beady eyes. And there they remain, flying in great circles and screaming their rage.

"What is it?" Alice gasps from behind me as the green mist envelops us.

"Try not to breathe it in," admonishes Riordan, but it's too late—I've already gotten a lungful of it. The mist doesn't seem to be hurting me, though. In fact, it smells familiar—like brisk, cold wind and fresh leaves after rain.

A backward glance shows that Alice and the others are bleeding, but still functional. Still running. They show no signs of distress from the green mist. Harmless as it seems to us, the smoke is clearly abhorrent to the crows, who keep swooping down and then streaking skyward again when they encounter it.

The green cloud extends all the way to the eaves of the forest. I can see the trees far ahead, at the end of the row along which I'm running—and in the far distance, at the edge of the woods, I glimpse a skinny figure standing amid tall blue grass.

The figure is turning, moving away into the forest. If it's the person I think it is, I'm not about to let him leave—not without an explanation.

Since the crows have retreated, I drop the basket I'm carrying and let myself go, unleashing my latent power to run faster than ever before in my life—faster than any human. I leave behind Riordan, the Scarecrow, Alice, and Fiero, and I dash under the boughs of the forest, into its blue-green depths.

The bushes and undergrowth grow thick and thorny, but there are patches of lush grass, blue as sapphire, here and there under the canopy. This must be where the villagers get the thatch for their roofs. Tiny star-bright flowers bloom amid the grass, but I barely glance at them because the slim, long-legged figure I'm chasing is almost out of sight among the trees.

I race after him, shouting, "Stop!" But he's fast—little more than a skinny wraith darting here and there in the emerald gloom. It's all I can do to keep him in sight, what with the quivering leaf-shadow and the blood dripping into my eyes.

Finally the figure swerves and disappears into a thicket.

I run to the spot and plunge in, thrashing through branches and ducking under vines until I stumble into an open space, a clearing in the center of several trees, surrounded on all sides by leafy green walls. I wade through the tall sapphire grass, scanning the shadows.

Hesitantly, silently, I move forward, listening.

A tempestuous force whirls against me, lifting me off my feet and pinning my back to the trunk of a tree. The West Witch holds me there, at a height that brings us face to face. The crush of his chest against mine makes it hard to breathe.

"Kin-Slayer," he seethes.

Again I feel the rush of fear, the awareness of his power flooding my bones. My body recognizes a superior force, an apex predator—and the resulting terror is also a strange delight.

The Witch's nostrils flicker. He tips his face up, tongue slipping out, and licks the blood from the gouge on my forehead.

A shudder passes over him, vibrating through me. "Deliciously human, yes, but Fae as well. Unseelie by blood, on your mother's side, I think."

"You—" I struggle to find words, to find breath. "You saved us."

He licks my blood from his white teeth. "Only because I want to kill you myself."

He runs both hands up my arms, through the shredded fabric of my sleeves, until he's cupping my shoulders. His body grinds more firmly against mine as he leans in, his rough breath against my ear. "Understand that I can and will do anything I want to you—any form of torture I desire, short of killing you," he murmurs. "I will peel transparent slices of skin from this lovely body and snap these clever little fingers, bone by bone. I will fuck you hard and leave you bruised, bare, and sated for your friends to find. I will incinerate them without warning, if it suits me. They exist for my pleasure, and so do you."

He leans back a little, creating a sliver of space between our upper bodies. When he looks down at the ragged bodice of my gingham dress, I follow his gaze.

His fingers leave my right shoulder and skate along my collarbone before moving lower, teasing the fabric that barely covers my chest. I watch, hardly breathing, as he drags it down with a single claw, until one brown breast is exposed, its dark nipple tight and peaked in the valley of air between us.

My body thrills, my pulse thumping fast and hot.

The Witch dips his dark head to my breast and takes the pointed nipple between his teeth. Tiny pricks of pain burst from the spot as he bites me, lightly, and a corresponding throb of arousal pulses through my pussy.

With a low, rough sound of urgency, he rakes my dress down off both shoulders, until my other nipple pops free, and he bites that one too. He takes more of that breast into his mouth, while I hang there, helpless to the molten delight pooling between my legs.

After a moment he lets me slide down the tree where he pinned me, until my feet touch ground again. Roughly he cups my chin, jerking my face up. "Your eyes are different colors. Even among the Fae, that is rare."

"Is it?"

"Yes." He bends low, until his breath skims across my lips. "I'm going to fuck you, Kin-Slayer."

"No," I whisper, writhing.

"Oh yes," he croons, nuzzling along my cheek. "And I'm going to come inside you." He licks the wound on my forehead again. "I've always found sex with a human to be more satisfying, and you're only part Fae, which is close enough." He ducks down to pull one of my nipples into his mouth again. "These are so biteable."

I almost moan, because the tugging, pinching suction of his mouth is sending tiny spears of pleasure right through my clit—but a distant shout catches my ear. Alice is calling my name.

Immediately the Witch spins me around and holds me with my back against his chest, clamping a hand over my mouth. "My fun will have to wait," he murmurs in my ear. "Keep that pussy wet for me. I'll be back to claim it. And be careful in the forest. There's a monster in these parts who is too dangerous even for me. He is sensitive to sound and movement, so if you encounter him, be very still and silent until he goes away."

With that, he vanishes, leaving me panting and half-naked, with only a wisp of green smoke to prove he was ever there at all.

# 10

## ALICE

Dorothy emerges from a thicket, tugging at her torn dress. A blush darkens her brown cheeks, and her eyes are liquid and bright. Maybe she's ashamed that she got scared and ran so far ahead.

"Are you all right?" I ask.

She nods. She's bleeding in a few places. So am I, and so is the golden-haired Scarecrow.

When she dropped the basket of food the villagers packed for us, I picked it up. It hangs on my arm now, tugging at one of my wounds. If we're lucky, maybe the villagers put some healing supplies in there, too.

"Let's sit," I suggest. The azure grass is thick and pliant, almost pillowy as I sink down into it. Fiero turns around a few times, making himself a little nest before settling in.

Dorothy sits carefully down next to her dog, keeping her thighs pressed together. She looks stunned.

"You saved us," I tell her. "Thank you."

"I wasn't the only one," she says.

"The green witch," Riordan says, still holding the Scarecrow. "Why would he help us?"

"Because he wants to kill me himself when the seven days are over." Dorothy swallows, looks away, and begins plucking the heads off small white flowers.

"By then we'll have reached the Wizard and wished ourselves off this isle," I assure her. "He won't be able to touch you."

She shoots me a look I can't interpret, the flush on her cheeks deepening.

Riordan bends stiffly and lets the Scarecrow roll out of his arms. The blond Fae tumbles into the deep grass, where he lies motionless, looking for all the world like a pretty, broken angel I might see in a painting at the village chapel back home. Not that we ever visited there much. And those angels wouldn't have sported such fascinatingly dreadful tattoos.

"Would you care to tell us your name?" I ask him.

He laughs a little, faintly. "You saved me. Of course I'll tell you my name, gladly. It's Jasper." He gazes up at Riordan's armored form with admiration, then turns worshipful eyes to me. "What can I do to repay you?"

There's a flicker of carnal suggestion in his eyes—and it surprises me, though it shouldn't. Innocent as he appears, the Scarecrow is Fae, after all. During my last visit, Riordan taught me about the Fae's need for sex—how it's connected to their magic, their healing abilities, their longevity. I suppose even this angelic-looking male has had dozens of sexual partners in his lifetime.

"You can repay me by resting and recovering your strength," I reply.

Jasper smiles. "As you wish."

I pull the basket closer and lay back the covering. The cloth is bigger than I thought—more like a sheet, folded in half and used to line the basket. Under parcels of food I discover an herbal-smelling paste and some neat white cloths, perhaps intended as napkins or handkerchiefs.

"These will work just fine as bandages." I unfold one, spreading it out on my knee.

"I wish I could heal you," Riordan says tersely. "But I can't, not with this armor on—and *he's* too full of cursed water to be of any help." He jerks his helmeted head toward the Scarecrow, then glances at Dorothy. "And *she* can't even heal herself. She's half-Fae, but she's been raised in the human realm, so her innate Fae powers were unable to fully develop."

"Sorry I'm so useless," Dorothy snaps. "At least I kept the crows off our backs."

"I never said you were useless," Riordan answers in an exasperated tone. He falls to one knee at my side, takes one of the cloths, and slices off a strip. Then he lifts my arm and ties the bandage around the worst of my wounds, careful not to lacerate me with the sharp edges of his metal fingers.

"You're very good at that," says the Scarecrow admiringly, his blue eyes following Riordan's every move. "I never imagined I'd be rescued by such wonderful beings—so strong, beautiful, and kind. And you're all so full of confidence and plans! It's marvelous, how you freed everyone in the village. I was in my cell when it happened—I was watching one of the guards and I saw the East Witch's control over him dissipate, like fog in the sun. I hoped I would be released, but they gave me to the crows, and I thought that was the end. Now that I'm going to live, the world seems so full of choices and pleasures…it's dazzling! But it's frightening too, the idea of being alone, of not having a place to be, or someone to—"

"Hush, would you?" snaps Dorothy. "I'm trying to think."

Jasper falls silent instantly, his head bending, golden hair tumbling around his face as if he's used to being hushed, as if he expects a blow.

"You can talk if you want," I say defiantly on his behalf. "Dorothy can plug her ears if she needs to think."

Dorothy shoots me a glare, but she doesn't protest. Cautiously Jasper lifts his head, and I meet his gaze while Riordan meticulously binds more of my wounds.

In the Scarecrow's blue eyes I see that pain again, the look he had out in the field. The ache of repeated rejection—years and years of it. I'm not sure how old he is—younger than Riordan, I think. It's difficult to tell with Fae.

"You can come with us," I tell the Scarecrow gently, and his face lights up with pure, passionate, grateful joy, so intense that I can't help smiling, almost laughing.

Riordan scoffs inside his helmet. "He doesn't want to go where we're going. Look at him. He's a delicate, forlorn creature, not much better than that scrap of fur Dorothy calls a pet. He'll be devoured before we reach the Emerald City."

"Don't judge him so harshly. You didn't think much of me when we first met."

"Yes I did," Riordan mutters. "*You* were clever. He's…well…"

"Hush!" I jab my elbow against his metal arm. "We'll be all right. We've made it this far."

"Small comfort," Dorothy says darkly. "Your friend is out here. The monster you spoke of. He haunts these woods."

Riordan's helmet dips, a nod of assent.

"He's sensitive to sound and movement, isn't he?" Dorothy continues. "If we see him, we should be still and quiet until he moves on."

"But I need to talk to him," I protest.

She sighs. "You'll get us all killed."

Riordan tears off another bandage. "How do you know those things about the beast, Dorothy?"

She grimaces, then says, "After the green smoke came, I thought I saw the Wicked Witch of the West in the forest. I chased him, and I spoke to him. That's how I knew for sure it was him who helped us, and why. It's true that without him, we would have died out there, in the cornfield. But that doesn't mean any of us are safe from his magic. He's capricious. Vile. Another beast we have to worry about." She plucks at the grass, refusing to meet my eyes.

"Did he hurt you?" I ask.

"No." She gets up suddenly, almost angrily. "We should keep moving."

"Can you go on?" Riordan asks me, low.

"I just have scratches and surface wounds. I'll be all right." I give him a wry smile. "There was a time you would have cut me to pieces yourself."

"But I would have done it elegantly, neatly. For research."

"That's such a comfort." I use his shoulder as a prop while I climb to my feet. Despite my insistence that I'm all right, my legs wobble. Maybe the shock of being chased by flesh-eating crows and nearly eaten alive affected me more than I thought.

The Scarecrow hasn't spoken for a while, so I glance over at him. He has relaxed into the grass, and his golden lashes have fallen shut. His chest rises with slow, steady breaths.

The sight of him makes my heart ache. He's covered in chafe marks from the ropes, scratches from Riordan's armor, and gashes from the beaks and claws of the crows. The only time I've seen a Fae in worse shape is when I helped Caer recover from an attack of the Heartless.

"He's sleeping off the cursed water they dosed him with." Riordan nudges the Scarecrow's arm with his foot. "He won't wake for a while. Best not to move him while his body repairs itself—if it can. He may have scars, or worse, depending on how much they gave him."

I sigh, sinking back into the grass. "When he wakes, we need to find that yellow brick road again."

"I'll go look for it," Dorothy says. "I'll bring Fiero with me, so he can hunt for a squirrel or something to eat. The road can't be far. And since we're connected, I can always find my way back to *him*." She points at Riordan.

"Be careful," I warn her.

She flips a thick brown braid over her shoulder. "You too. Come on, Fiero."

She practically saunters off into the forest, as if she belongs here, as if she has roamed this area all her life.

"Wish I had her confidence," I mutter.

Riordan adjusts his position in the grass, stretching out his stiff armored legs.

How terrible it must be for him, trapped in that shell, unable to eat, sleep, drink, fuck, or do magic. Worse than the lack of physical comfort is the emotional and mental toll—which must be horrific. Riordan comes across as cool, ruthless, cerebral, even emotionless, but he holds a depth of passion I've never experienced from anyone else. Messes, dysfunction, waste, and ignorance disturb him deeply, almost painfully. He's surprisingly sensitive, and for a soul like his, this curse must be excruciating.

My sympathy almost obliterates the memory of him rejecting me and sending me away.

"You're suffering, aren't you?" I scoot nearer to him and place one hand on his armored thigh. "I wish I could help. I promise we'll get you out of this."

His voice grates from within the helmet, a caustic rumble. "Are you sure you want me out of it?"

Weariness washes over me at the words and the prospect of a long, emotionally difficult conversation. "We're not doing this now. I barely know how to talk to you when you're in that thing."

"We might not have the opportunity again. You're likely to die tonight, shredded by the claws of someone we used to know, while I'm forced to watch."

"That won't happen. Dorothy can help us—"

"No." He barks the word so sharply that Jasper frowns in his sleep and lets out a soft whimper. I move between him and Riordan, stroking the silky golden waves of the Scarecrow's hair. He settles under my touch, his brow smooth again.

"Dorothy's magic isn't strong enough to defeat Caer," Riordan says. "The Green Wizard made him too powerful. I'm not sure what the idiot wished for—strength, power—"

"You shouldn't call him an idiot. He didn't hear what Fin told us, about the Green Wizard being the one who cursed the Unseelie Queen. You knew all about that, and you wished anyway."

"I was desperate. I had tried everything to get close to Caer without being ripped to pieces. And I went into the Emerald City intending to *confront* the Wizard, not make a wish. Once I got into his throne room, I couldn't seem to remember anything I knew about him except that he could help me, if I would only ask."

"You think he charmed you somehow?"

"I think he wields an influence beyond that of any normal Fae, witch, wizard or otherwise. He's either a god-star, or the priest of one. Which makes our task all the more difficult."

"We'll find a way." I let one of Jasper's curls slide through my fingers. It stretches smooth, like a gold satin ribbon, before it bounces back into place. Then I stroke the edge of his ear, admiring the delicate tip and the soft lobe pierced with a single sky-blue earring. Idly, hardly knowing why, I trace his smooth chin and the sharp corner of his jaw.

Something in me reaches out to him, wants to draw him close, protect him, kiss him and whisper to him and soothe his heart. I want to reassure him that he won't be rejected or sacrificed again. I think, if I did those things, he would follow me around forever, loyal and devoted. He would do anything I wanted… anything at all…

"You obviously wish to fuck him," Riordan says tightly. "So do it."

Startled, I glance up. "I don't want to fuck him."

"Don't lie to me, kitten. I can smell you, even through this damned helmet. Go on. Wake him, and see if he'll oblige you. Sex might restore him faster."

"I think you want to watch," I throw at him.

"Maybe I do."

His candid admission catches me off guard. How I wish I could see his face right now... "Then you—you think he's pretty."

"Any being with eyes can see that he's beautiful." In a lower, more grudging tone, he adds, "During my stay here, I occasionally served as guard over the prison where he and other sacrifices were kept. He reminds me a bit of Finias, only Jasper is far more Seelie. In fact, he's the most Seelie Fae I've ever encountered. Just now he kept thanking me for carrying him, praising my strength—yet if not for you, I would have left him behind to die. He's too soft and gentle. Unfit for existence. No wonder they wanted to sacrifice him."

"I don't have much experience with Seelie Fae, but I agree he's one of the sweetest people I've ever met. Far nicer than most humans."

"And that doesn't bother you?"

"Why should it?"

"Extravagant goodness is irritating."

"Perhaps because it reminds people of a moral standard they've failed to meet, an expectation they have not fulfilled," I say coolly.

"Or perhaps it is annoying because truly good people rarely know how to have fun."

I snort. "Like you're the king of fun." I do my best imitation of his voice—serious and darkly dramatic. "'No, kitten, I cannot allow myself to *snuggle* with you and Caer, or indulge in your frivolous games. I must study and dissect and experiment during every spare minute.'"

"I know how to have fun," Riordan counters. "You met me when I was deeply engrossed in the small matter of saving the entire Unseelie Kingdom from the ravages of a cursed Queen. And still I found time to gamble with Caer and lick you to climax—"

"That doesn't count!" I interrupt, blood rushing to my cheeks. "You did that so I would fall asleep, so you could take my dreams."

His voice is lower, softer. "Surely you don't believe that was the only reason?"

"I... I suppose..."

"Your scent was maddening, Alice. It still is. The way I crave—" He breaks off the sentence.

We sit there, he and I—his silent bulk, expressionless except for the tension of his posture—and my squirming, blushing, heated self.

"You're aroused. And I'd like to watch you come," he says at last. "I enjoyed it then, and I want to witness it again. And if I can't pleasure you myself, I can watch him do it."

I swallow hard. "I remember you losing your mind over Caer nesting with me. You told him I belonged to *you*."

"Caer is different. That selfish little bastard will take anything good all for himself. Never learned to share. But I suspect this youth has too noble a heart to crave sole possession of you. Besides, once I'm free of this cursed armor, I will..."

He stops himself.

I stare at the helmet, listening to his labored breathing. "You'll what, Riordan?" I ask softly. "What will you do to me?"

Low and rough, an answering whisper. "I'll fuck you."

"Tell me how." I press in closer, aching for him. "Tell me all the ways you'll fuck me."

A long silence, so lengthy that I start to pull away, and then he says, "After I saved you, I held myself back from taking you again, because I knew if I did, I would not be able to let you go. But you found your way back to this realm, reckless girl, and all I can think of is stripping you bare, laying you flat on your back, and burying my face between your legs. I want to drink you like wine, savor your liquid like the sweetest syrup. When you walk through Faerie, I want to know that your thighs are slick with need for me, and your words are flavored with my cum. I will splay you on my silver table, pin your beautiful pussy wide open, and study every tiny bit of your flesh until I find the most delicate ways of teasing out your desire. You will climax again and again, until you can scarcely bear to be touched, and still I will force you to come for me. I will watch every spasm, and then bathe your sore little clit with my tongue."

My fingers have crept between my thighs, and I'm burning, flaming, barely breathing. When he lets himself confess his feelings, Riordan can give the most shockingly erotic speeches.

"I wish you could touch me," I breathe.

"At least you can touch yourself," he says hoarsely. "I've been like this for months, and now that you're here, I am so hard I can barely think, kitten. I may go mad."

"Don't," I whisper, pressing my palm to his breastplate. "We need you. *I* need you, Riordan."

"Fuck..." The word cracks from him. "I almost came when you said that. I think—I think I could come without a touch, if presented with the right view. It would be an immense relief."

"The right view—of course." When I glance down at the Scarecrow, I notice that even though his eyes are still closed, his face is flushed, and there's a distinct bulge under the ragged pants.

I smirk as I survey him. Our voices roused him, and he's been listening.

I lean closer to him and murmur, "Are you awake?"

His blue eyes blink open. "Yes."

"Good." I run my hand over his warm chest. He has such silky skin. "Would you be... um... interested in..."

"Yes," he says quickly.

I can't hold my smile back this time. He looks so eager, so adorable.

"I know you're still weak, so I'll do the work," I assure him. "And we'll make it quick. Dorothy will be back at any moment."

Strangely, the thought of her catching us is only mildly mortifying. Once you've been naked before the entire Dread Court of the Unseelie, a simple fuck in the forest doesn't seem as embarrassing.

The skin along the edges of my cuts twinges and pulls a little as I remove my clothes. But the injuries are small, and the discomfort blurs, softening and fading into the heat of my body, into the swirl of need low in my belly.

As I stand bare before him, Riordan climbs slowly to his feet, metal scraping on metal. He remains a few steps away, watching as I unbuckle the Scarecrow's belt and ease his pants down, over his hips.

Jasper's cock bounces out, slim and erect. It's smaller than Caer's or Riordan's, but it's neat and well-shaped. I like it immediately. There's a trickle of arousal glistening at the tip.

I look at Riordan, waiting. Not that I need his permission, because he and I were never committed in any real way—he was fucking the Unseelie Queen during most of the time I was his captive. Sexual connections are not as restrictive in Faerie as they are in the human world. They are broader, more fluid, more open to the changing needs of those involved.

I deserve to take what I need from the blue-eyed Fae I rescued. But I do not want to injure Riordan's heart. So I look at him, and I wait.

He wraps both metal-clad hands around a tree branch. Then he inclines the helmet, a wordless agreement.

With his consent warm in my soul, I lick up the underside of the Scarecrow's pretty cock. He jerks, whimpering, his whole body taut with need. I let my fingers wander over the hard planes of his stomach, over the tattoos on his ribs and chest.

"Kiss him," Riordan orders.

I crawl up Jasper's body, careful of his wounds, and I softly press my bare torso against his skin. His cock is pinned between us, a hot ridge against my clit.

Rocking my hips a little, I touch my lips to Jasper's mouth. He makes a small sound of yearning, as if all he has ever wanted is to be kissed like this. It's sweet, and hot.

I kiss him again, languidly, savoring the warmth of his mouth. His teeth aren't sharp like those of some Fae, so I don't have to be careful.

"Tell me how he tastes." Riordan's voice is cool, the tone of a physician or a researcher—but I can hear the thickness of arousal under that feigned coolness.

"He tastes exquisite," I say. "Like vanilla cake, or golden honey." I move back down Jasper's body, pausing to lick his nipple while I tease the underside of his cock with one finger.

"You've gained experience in this area," Riordan says, his voice suddenly colder.

And there we have it. I knew he would figure it out.

"When you rejected me and sent me home, I was angry." I kneel astride Jasper, reaching between us, stroking his cock head along the wetness of my pussy. "I had sex with the stable-boy and one of the gardeners at Lord Drosselmeyer's mansion. And also a footman. And—"

A low hiss of anger emerges from the helmet.

"Don't," I say tightly. "I'm sure you fucked others after I left."

Riordan doesn't indulge my curiosity. After a long moment he says, "Far be it from me to resent you for deepening your understanding of a new field of study. Fuck him, then, Alice. Show me what you've learned."

Jasper groans at the words. "I should tell you—"

"Sshh." I rub my thumb over his soft lips. "This will help all of us. Just relax, and look at him." I gesture to Riordan.

Tucking the Scarecrow's tip between my folds, I sink down, taking him in.

The dalliances I mentioned to Riordan were unsatisfying, and I felt wrong and wicked the whole time. I feel wicked in this moment, too, but in an entirely different way. The heart I carry inside me now isn't the one I was born with—it was grown from Riordan's body, from the essences he poured into me while I was turning into one of the Heartless. Fucking someone else in his presence, with his permission, is a hectic delight. I want to make him come helplessly, without a single touch. I want him to paint the inside of that metal shell with his release, forced out of him by the sight of me fucking another male. Riordan is the prisoner now, not me. He is subject to my will, my actions, and though I care about him, I can't help admiring the justice of it.

I'm about to begin moving on Jasper's cock when a startling thrill buzzes through my sex.

"The fuck?" I breathe.

It happens again—a light vibration through my pussy lips, through my entire channel. It feels mind-bendingly amazing.

"Oh gods," I gasp.

Jasper half-smiles, blinking gold lashes at me. "I was going to tell you."

"Tell her what?" Riordan grits out.

"His cock vibrates," I whimper. "Oh... oh..."

I'm coming already. I can't help it. Thrills chase each other through my belly as my pussy flexes against Jasper's cock. He chuckles breathlessly, reaching out to wrap his fingers around mine. "Sensitive little human," he murmurs. "Why didn't you let me warn you?"

I'm gasping, gripping his hand, my hair spilling over my shoulder and my breasts trembling as I lean over Jasper's chest. As the pleasure ebbs, I manage to lift my hips and move myself on him, up and down, slowly. His head tips back, his eyes closing.

"I'm going to fuck your pretty cock until you come for me," I tell him, more for Riordan's benefit than anything else. "Do you feel how my pussy is squeezing you? You made me come so hard. Fill me up, beautiful one…I want your cum inside me…"

"Oh fuck," Jasper whimpers, and his hips yearn upward.

Riordan gives a great, heavy groan, wrenching at the tree branch he's holding so hard it cracks clean off. I can hear him gasping inside the helmet—panting with relief.

Jasper comes in a warm trembling rush, followed by another long vibration of his cock. With that stimulation I come a second time, a squeal of surprise bursting from my lips. My eyes roll back and I shudder as bliss washes through my limbs. I have never felt anything as exquisite as the delicious buzzing hardness of him.

A distant bark makes my heart jump, and I lift myself off Jasper quickly, hurrying to pull my clothes back on. Still lying in the grass, he lifts his hips so he can tug his pants into place. Once they are fastened, he throws his arms above his head, a huge sigh gusting from him.

"I feel better," he declares.

"And you?" I ask Riordan. "Did you…?"

"Gods, yes. It wasn't entirely satisfying, but it was a relief."

My pussy feels warm, swollen, and sated, an afterglow that I try not to show on my face as Dorothy picks her way through the undergrowth toward us. Fiero is with her, still mouthing bits of whatever he found to eat. Some of the hairs of his muzzle are stained red.

Dorothy looks unhappy—or disappointed—but as she enters the clearing, her expression changes, smooths itself into one of pleasant companionship. "The road is that way." She points.

"Do you think you can manage?" I ask the Scarecrow.

He gives me a bright, adoring smile. "Anything for my rescuer."

Riordan snorts a laugh and stalks away, in the direction Dorothy indicated. He's likely to be a bit uncomfortable, walking around in armor he just splattered with his own cum. But maybe the relief he experienced was worth it.

After helping Jasper to his feet and making sure he can walk on his own, I follow Riordan. I want him to understand that no matter what I just did with the Scarecrow, Jasper isn't the one I've been missing all these months. He's not the one I crossed realms for. No matter how angry I've been, Riordan is mine. And I need him to know it.

But when we step onto the road, and I walk side by side with the silent suit of armor, I can't make myself say any of those words. So I do the next best thing.

"Ever since I left, I've been thinking about the *comhartha dia*, and the god-stars," I say. "You mentioned the Green Wizard is either a god-star or the priest of one."

"Since he performed a god-curse on the Eater of Hearts, those are the only two options," Riordan says.

"And the curses laid on you and Caer—are those *comhartha dia?*"

"It's possible. Wishes twisted into curses. In which case the only way to break them is a retraction from him, or water from the Unending Pool. And since we can't leave the Isle of Oz to fetch water from the Pool—"

"The Wizard's mercy is our only hope," I finish. "Tell me more about the god-stars and their priests. I want to know everything."

"I have conducted extensive research into the topic," Riordan begins, and the quiet eagerness in his tone makes me smile.

We continue on together, while Riordan explains the lore of the god-stars, creators of the Fae and of all living things. He walks straighter and faster as he talks, and I draw closer to him, lured by my own curiosity, seduced by the inexhaustible fountain of his knowledge.

This is something no curse can change—this passion we share for investigation, for understanding. No wizard, god-star, or priest can ever sever that link between us—a connection beyond anything physical. A true marriage of minds.

# 11

# DOROTHY

The West Witch didn't appear to me when I was alone, searching for the yellow brick road. I'd half hoped he would make good on his promise to come back and claim me. But I suppose someone like him has other business to deal with. He can't always be lurking in the woods, trailing after me like a ravenous hound.

Why am I so much more interested in him than in my own blood-relative? Maybe once we get the cursed suit of armor off Riordan, I'll be more inclined to speak to him and connect with him. To be fair, he doesn't seem too interested in me, either. We've been traveling the yellow road for hours, judging by the angle of the sunlight through the trees—and he's been absorbed in conversation with Alice the whole time.

The golden-haired, pretty-boy Scarecrow tried walking next to me for a while, but I glared at him until he understood the message and fell back to walk behind me. He and Fiero seem quite taken with each other. There's a puppyish quality to the Scarecrow, a "please-let-me-follow-you-and-be-your-friend" look in his eyes whenever one of us glances at him. Obviously he can't go back to the village that sacrificed him, and Alice invited him to come along, so we're stuck with him for a while. Maybe he'll be useful to distract the monster in this forest—provide it with a tender snack while the rest of us get away. Though I doubt Alice would agree to making use of her precious rescued puppy like that.

I suppose my emotions on the matter are rather Unseelie, but physically, I don't feel Fae in the least. I feel human, and my feet hurt, and my magic still hasn't quite replenished itself. Alice is still carrying the basket with the food, but I doubt she'll let me eat any of it, since it's contaminated by foul magic. So I'm starving as well.

"How far is it to the Emerald City?" I ask.

"That's the trick of it," says Riordan. "It takes as long to get there as the Green Wizard pleases. The length of the journey is different for everyone who follows his yellow roads."

I dislike the sound of that. "And what if we walk *beside* the road? What then?"

"Only by following the road can you find the Emerald City," he replies. "Otherwise the Wizard's location will remain hidden from you."

"That sounds like some very powerful magic."

"It is."

"Can we stop for a bit and rest?"

The Scarecrow, Jasper, speaks from behind me, his voice threaded with apprehension. "It's nearly sunset. The beast will be roaming soon."

"He prefers the night, yes. But now and then he roams in the daylight," Riordan says. "His patterns are unpredictable. I should know—I spent weeks attempting to chart them. His form changes, too, depending on how great a threat he judges you to be. The best we can hope for is to make it through these woods without attracting his attention. If I had supplies, and if this armor didn't block magic, I could craft something to disguise

Alice's fragrance—but as it is, I'm afraid he will scent her from miles away."

"I could try a little magic," Jasper offers. When I glance back, he's holding Fiero in his arms, scratching behind his ears so gently that the little dog is melting, eyelids drooping and drowsy. "My illusions are weak, but I could disguise her scent a bit."

"Do it then." Riordan stops on the road so abruptly I nearly crash into him.

"No," Alice protests. "I *want* Caer to find me. I told you, I want to try to speak with him."

"Speak with him?" Riordan scoffs. "You'll be lucky if you get in a scream before he takes a mouthful of you."

Alice glares at him, so potently that if she were Fae, the sheer power of her eyes might melt through his armor.

"Look at it this way," Riordan says. "Shielding your scent, at least partly, might give you a chance—however unlikely—a very *slim* chance of speaking with him before he kills us all."

Alice shakes her head at him. "You've gotten so much worse. You used to have a little hope, and now—nothing."

His voice from inside the helmet is cold and sharp. "It's not as if I've had much to hope for, lately."

"I suppose not." She puckers her lips. "All right, I'll do it. Jasper can disguise my scent, just for tonight."

"Come here, then, lovely." Jasper sets down Fiero and extends a hand to Alice, his smile warm as sunshine.

She goes to him with an answering smile. He cups her face between his hands and closes his eyes in concentration. There's a warmth, an intimacy between them that wasn't there before I left to look for the road. What were they doing while I was gone?

I scoop up Fiero and hold him to my chest while Riordan stands stiffly beside me.

"How do you think we're related?" I ask.

"Judging by the strength of the link between us, I would say you're my half-sister. But there's no way to be sure until I get free of this curse and I can do a few tests."

After a moment, I force out more words. "I should be happier about it. If Alice found out she had a Fae half-brother, she'd be overjoyed. Curious. Fascinated. But I am—"

"Indifferent," he finishes. "I didn't know my mother, but she was probably Unseelie like my father—which means you are also Unseelie. Your Fae blood doesn't reveal itself strongly in your appearance, but it colors your mentality and emotions. You lack the inbred morality and social sensitivities of humans. Instead, you have the natural apathy, self-interest, and tendency toward cruelty that our people possess."

"So the Unseelie do not love their families," I murmur, remembering what West said as he gazed down at his sister's body, crushed beneath the barn—that he didn't much care for her.

"That is a common misconception," Riordan replies. "In some Unseelie families, circumstances prevent the formation of loving connections among siblings and parents. In others, those links are so thickly forged that the death of one nearly destroys all. When the Unseelie do feel, they feel with a depth beyond what most Seelie Fae experience. But it is no use forcing an emotional bond. Our relationships develop suddenly, within days or even hours—or they build gradually, over centuries. There is rarely an in-between."

"So you don't mind that I'm not leaping for joy over this."

"Not at all."

"Do you—do we—have other siblings?"

"I had a brother," he replies. "He saved me from our father, who was despicable even by Unseelie standards. My brother and I bonded immediately, and when he was killed, it cleaved my heart to the core. You and I may develop a bond within the next few days, but if we do not, I am perfectly content to part ways as casual acquaintances. However—if we should find ourselves inclined to a deeper affection, I will be loyal to you until death."

A strange warmth curls around my heart at those words. No one has ever said such a thing to me. My parents love me, but it's with a cautious, tentative love, one that carries the awareness of my strangeness, my secret abilities. I can only imagine what it would be like to have a staunchly devoted brother, a companion, a friend gifted with magic, and an ally for life against all that might threaten me.

It sounds too good to be true.

Jasper takes a step back from Alice, his fingertips lingering against her cheek a moment before his hand drops. "I've done what I can."

"Which isn't much," growls Riordan. "I can still smell her. She's like a fucking beacon." He marches on, up the yellow brick road. "We may as well look for some kind of shelter."

As we continue walking, the forest shifts into a grove of knobby, crooked trees, similar to apple trees, whose leaves are dark purple with sage-green undersides. Their boughs stretch over the yellow-brick road, so heavy with fruit they nearly brush the top of Riordan's helmet. My mouth waters over the ripe, round offerings, frosted purple and sugary pink.

"You there—Haystack," I say to Jasper. "What are those fruits?"

"A type of sugarplum tree," he says.

"Edible? Not poisoned or corrupted by magic?"

"No, but you probably shouldn't take—aaaand you're already picking one." He sighs as I polish the fruit on my arm. "Don't blame me for what happens next."

I pluck another fruit. "Alice, catch."

She turns just in time to capture the flying sugarplum. "Oh, it smells divine."

We both bite at the same time. As my teeth punch through the sugared skin and the juices explode over my tongue, I can't help laughing out of sheer joy. "How is this so good?" I gasp, while the sticky syrup of the fruit runs over my fingers.

Riordan stopped walking when Alice and I did, and at my exclamation, his helmet turns toward me. "The food of Faerie is your true sustenance. As you consume it, and as you breathe the air here, your healing power will develop. You'll never heal as swiftly as a pure-blooded Fae, but it's an ability worth having."

While I gnaw deeper into the fruit, I seize another and toss it onto the road, in case Fiero wants a taste. He sniffs cautiously before nibbling at it.

A shivering rustle runs through the tree above me, followed by a shudder from the next tree, and the next, until all the trees bordering the road are quaking, branches groaning and thrashing, leaves showering the yellow bricks. A breathy wail rises from the trees, a keening sound of loss and rage.

"I *told* you!" Jasper shrinks from the tree nearest him. "We should run."

"Why?" As the word leaves my mouth, a branch snaps out, smacking me hard on the temple. Stars dance through my vision, and my eyes water with pain.

Fiero erupts into frenzied barks, his ire aimed at the trees. He's barking so forcefully his entire furry body practically bounces off the ground. More branches swing across the road, knocking against Alice and Riordan.

"They don't like us stealing their fruit," Jasper explains. "Run!"

All of us pelt along the road between the rows of wailing, tossing trees. A sapling lashes at me like a whip, but Fiero springs between us and bites it, right near the roots. Still barking, he runs farther into the forest.

"Fiero, come back!" I almost dart after him, but Riordan charges forward. "Let me! They can't hurt me."

He plunges in among the trees, while they hammer his armor as heavily as they can. They keep attacking me, too, but I manage to dodge most of the blows. Jasper holds Alice against his chest and curves his body around her, trying to shield her as best he can.

Between the swaying, groaning branches, I can make out the lines of Riordan's shape. He bends—with surprising swiftness for his bulk—and catches Fiero around the middle. I'm worried that his sharp fingers will shred my pet, but when he works his way back to us and delivers Fiero into my arms, there's no sign of blood.

My terror subsides a little as I hold my dog carefully against my heart. He wandered onto our farm one day, years ago, and from the moment I saw him, I loved him, more earnestly than I love my parents. Gratefully I look up at Riordan, remembering what he said about the Unseelie and how they form relationships. *Immediately, or not at all.*

"Thank you," I manage.

He grunts, as if unused to expressions of gratitude, but he gives me a stiff nod. "Come on."

We keep running, until the knotty sugarplum trees disappear and the forest resumes its usual appearance—tall trunks, leafy undergrowth, a thick canopy overhead. Shadows are thickening beneath the boughs, and velvety darkness shortens my sightline in every direction.

"You grew up around here," says Riordan to Jasper. "Is there somewhere we could take shelter?"

"There might be a place. It's been a long time since I was allowed to roam free." Jasper gives Riordan a sweet, pained smile. "I'll see if I can find the spot."

After a short walk, he shows us a clearing a few dozen paces from the road, at the base of a rocky hill. There's an enormous tree, half-grown over a boulder, and between the tree and the boulder there's a gap, large enough for all of us to sit together. The hillside, the great rock, and the tree's massive roots form walls, of a sort. Riordan tucks us all inside the hollow and settles himself in front of the widest opening, like a wall of metal.

The tree's roots are twice as thick as my body, and the branches looming overhead look even thicker, giant beams spreading outward from a colossal central trunk. The breeze murmurs above us, a soothing hum through the leaves.

"Try to rest," Riordan advises. "You, boy—you'll help me protect them if anything disturbs us."

"I'm not a boy," says Jasper. "I'm thirty years old."

Riordan snorts. In terms of Fae lifespans, thirty must be considered quite young.

"And I'm not helpless," I put in. "I should be able to do magic again after a little sleep."

"And I'm—well—I'm fucking useless," Alice says glumly.

"It's all right." Jasper seats himself beside her and puts an arm around her shoulders. "I will gladly give my life for yours. You are my savior, and I love you."

"For the gods' sake!" Riordan snarls, rising abruptly with a clank of metal. "Alice may have partly untied you, but Dorothy held off the crows, and I carried you from the cornfield. Do you love us as well?" His tone is utterly sarcastic, but Jasper doesn't seem to notice.

"I think I could," he says, genuine conviction in his blue eyes. "You, at least. *She* doesn't like me." He shoots a glance my way.

"I think you're sweet, but rather simple," I say candidly. "Perhaps you could ask the Green Wizard for greater intelligence when you meet him."

"Dorothy!" Alice snaps.

"No, no, she's quite right." Jasper strokes Alice's pale hair soothingly as she bristles in his defense. "I don't have much by way of brains, nor is my magic very powerful. That's one reason they wanted to sacrifice me—that, and my immunity to the East

Witch's thrall. They only kept me alive so long because Glenna liked using my cock."

Even in the gloom, I can see Alice's cheeks flush red. "You don't have to be useful, or brilliant, or attractive, or pleasant, to be worth something," she says decidedly. She's weaving her fingers with Jasper's, but she's looking at Riordan. "You have value for no other reason than *being yourself.* That's enough. You don't have to justify your existence to anyone."

"That's beautiful." Jasper lifts her hand to his mouth and kisses her knuckles. Alice looks at him, smiling a little, and he leans in closer, slowly, until he softly seals his lips over hers.

She allows the kiss for a second, then pushes him gently away, with a cautious look at Riordan.

Riordan turns his back to them and settles down in the opening again, a silent guardian staring down the rustling dark.

# 12

# ALICE

I think Dorothy is asleep, and I know Jasper is—he's curled against my side, his golden head on my breast. Riordan didn't protest when he fell asleep there.

I've tried to rest, but I can't stop worrying about Riordan, in his metal prison, and Caer, roaming the wilderness, alone and wretched. My eyes keep popping open.

The night breeze must have picked up, because although it can't shift the massive limb above me, it's stirring the leaves more strongly now. In fact—it almost looks as if the branch over my head *is* moving, but that's not possible. It would take a huge weight to move such a giant limb—it's the size of a tree trunk all by itself—

No, it's *definitely* moving—bobbing and bending as if something heavy is pacing along its top side.

Carefully I shift Jasper's head off my chest and sit up. The breeze swirls around my face, lifting the ends of my hair.

A low growl ripples through the night. It's coming from the branch directly above me.

Riordan notices—I hear the faintest scrape of metal as he moves, just barely.

The monster is here. Caer is here. Silent as death, he must have crept onto that branch without us noticing, and now he is waiting to pounce.

Dorothy said we must stay quiet and still, to avoid an attack. I should do that, I suppose. It's very good advice. But when have I ever listened to my own advice, or anyone else's for that matter? Jumping into the hole with the White Rabbit was the stupidest thing I've ever done, and also the best. Perhaps this choice is akin to that one.

"Don't." A single, breathed word, barely a rasp from Riordan's helmet.

How well he knows me. He can sense what I'm about to do.

Slowly I rise from the ground and stand beneath the great limb, my eyes trained on it. From this new vantage point I can see two glowing purple eyes with vertical slits for pupils. Cat-eyes.

Caer's eyes.

I can't make out much in the dark, but whatever else he might have become, he's still the grinning Cat who taught me how to gamble.

I'm taking a risk now. I'm betting on him.

"Caer," I say softly.

The night explodes with a roar—thunderous, earthshaking, deafening. I'm engulfed instantly—caught up in a tempest of fur, claws, hide, and muscle. Tossed in the air like Pap might toss a forkful of hay—then seized between a pair of serrated jaws. The teeth begin to puncture my back and stomach in two huge semicircles, and I scream, "Caer! Caer, please!"

The fangs halt, barely penetrating my flesh. The monster's lips close on me firmly, but he doesn't bite any deeper. I feel the tensing of his gigantic form as he crouches, then bounds away into the night with me in his mouth.

What hurts more than Caer's teeth is Riordan's bellow of fury and anguish. But it fades with terrifying speed as the monster leaps from tree to tree, then bounds up a hill and down another. I can't watch where we're going—I have to shield my face and eyes from the whipping branches and sharp thorns. I have to try to keep breathing, even though the racing speed of the monster makes it difficult to suck in a breath.

The thump of the beast's paws changes to a softer, more padded sound, and when I risk a peek between my eyelids, we're galloping through a grassy meadow, silvered with starlight.

How far have we gone? Will the others be able to follow?

The beast opens his jaws, and I spill from his mouth into the grass.

Rolling onto my back, I get my first good look at him as he bounds away and then circles back, crouching low, his purple eyes narrowed.

He's like a living nightmare, a thunderstorm brought to life and given razor claws and fangs. His shape resembles a creature I saw in a book once—a panther, coated in silken ebony fur, with an elegant sloped face. But this beast's mouth can open impossibly, terrifyingly wide, and he has far too many teeth for anything less than demonic. He has a thick mane like a lion, but black and glossy.

And he's huge. Far bigger than a normal lion or panther has any right to be. Big enough to carry me in his jaws as if I'm a kitten—or a mouse.

"Caer," I whimper, pressing my hand to the shallow, bleeding cuts on my stomach. "You hurt me. You promised you wouldn't."

He snarls, swiping at his own muzzle with a clawed paw, opening gashes on his snout. As if he's punishing himself.

"It's all right." I push myself up to a sitting position. "I'm not angry. I'm so glad to see you."

He pads nearer, nostrils flexing. A low moan issues from his throat.

I sit perfectly still and breathe as evenly as I can while he sniffs me. His great nose prods along my shoulder, my throat, the side of my face. He could easily bite my head off. But he hasn't yet.

There's a faint miasma of animal, of fur, but mostly he smells like himself—like violets and the dark cool of night, but with an afternote of bitterness.

"Caer, darling, I missed you," I say soothingly. "I've been so worried about you."

His jaws open again, and this time there are words—a deep groan from his chest. "You... not... real."

"I *am* real. I survived, Caer. Riordan saved me after the Queen took my heart. He didn't tell you his plan ahead of time, because he wasn't sure it would work, but it *did*. Afterward he sent me to the human world, but I came back for you—for both of you. You've seen Riordan, haven't you? Did he tell you I was alive? Maybe he didn't think he should, since I'd gone back to my world. Or maybe you didn't give him the chance."

At Riordan's name Caer recoils, snarling, his claws digging into the turf on either side of my legs. He throws back his head and screams to the moon, while I cover my ears in a desperate attempt to preserve my hearing.

When he's done shrieking his rage, he looks different, more human in shape. He's standing on two legs now, and he's a little less bulky. He still has the thick mane and the preternaturally huge, fang-filled mouth. But there's more of Caer in his leonine features now, and I can see the outline of his pectorals and abs clearly through the short, silky black fur covering his body.

Riordan said his form changes with his mood. Maybe when he's less angry or afraid, he becomes more human.

"There's nothing to fear," I tell him softly. "Come to me."

His fanged muzzle opens. "Mouse?"

"Yes!" Tears spring to my eyes. "Yes, it's really me."

He takes a step forward, and his long tail snakes out and curls around my throat, a silken noose. He doesn't tighten it, but as he advances, I notice the erect length between his legs—thick, rock-hard, curved slightly upward.

He showed his cock to me once—although it was paler then—and he told me how during his heat, tiny barbs would extrude from it, locking him inside the female he was fucking.

As if he senses my gaze, his cock bobs convulsively.

"I need..." he rasps. "I've needed... so long..."

A shock thrills through my belly. He was in heat while I was in Faerie—he couldn't still be in heat, could he? It's been months.

"Are you—are you still in heat?" I breathe.

The agony of his answering groan tells me everything I need to know.

"Oh shit," I whisper.

His tail slithers away from my throat. He's prowling over me, pushing me back down to the ground with black furred fingers, tipped with lethal claws. Those claws drag at my clothing, shredding what's left of it, baring my stomach and breasts. He sniffs the wounds on my belly and growls.

"You did that," I say shakily. "But you won't hurt me again. I'm not afraid of you."

The rest of my dress shreds easily under his claws, and he scrapes it away before inhaling deeply between my legs. As the fur of his muzzle tickles along the hollow of my hip, I try to repress a shiver—but then I realize it's not a shiver of disgust. I'm lying amid the rags of my clothing, torn and bleeding under the night sky of Faerie, while a monster nuzzles my pussy, and I'm not repulsed at all. Not even when a broad, wet tongue laps along the seam of my sex.

"You have another scent on you," he snarls.

No sense lying when he can smell the truth. "Yes, I fucked someone else."

Again he recoils, hissing, his fur and mane bristling into an enraged mass.

"Don't run." I reach for him. "Please, I want you, Caer. Right now, in this moment, you're the only one I crave. Please, please, come here. Taste me—see how much I want *you*, just you." I hold his gaze, and I blink once, slowly.

He stares back—and then his eyes blink slowly in return. As his fur settles, he dips his head between my legs and licks again, deeper this time. He moans with delight when he reaches the taste of my arousal.

"Oh my gods." My hips buck into the contact, into the luscious friction of his tongue. "Fuck, Caer..."

He keeps licking, slathering my pussy with his tongue until I'm mewling, helpless, melted underneath his massive body. A shaken groan rolls from him, and with a shove from his paw, he turns me over, onto my stomach.

His claws clasp my thighs, moving them apart, drawing my opening toward him. I feel his huge cock head nudge at my entrance.

I don't know if I can take him, or trust him.

But if he's been in heat all this time, he's probably half-mad with need. Maybe letting him fuck me will soothe him, and then I can explain what we're doing—that somehow we're going to convince the Green Wizard to undo the curses.

As the bulging head of his monstrous cock pushes between my soaked pussy lips, I let all those rational thoughts escape my mind, because the raw truth of it is this—I want him. It's as simple and wicked as that. I want to be fucked wildly, messily, brutally by Caer in this beastly form.

He's pushing deeper, and suddenly I'm more grateful than ever for the times I experimented back in my world. If I hadn't fucked those men, I wouldn't be able to handle Caer without ripping apart. He's enormous, and it burns—gods—

I bite my wrist, eyes squeezed shut as he works his way in. He's not thrusting madly, not yet. But I can feel the trembling force of his lust, of his primal need. He's shaking, panting heavily.

And I make a choice. One I might regret—but I've been torn apart before, and I survived. I can handle this.

I stop biting my wrist and lift my head, staring into the thin, shimmering leaves of the blue grass. It smells impossibly, delicately sweet.

"Fuck me the way you need to, Caer," I say. "I can take it."

His velvet-furred fingers wrap around my throat instantly, and using that hold for leverage, he pulls my ass tight against his abdomen with a low roar of furious need. I cry out as he slams in to the hilt—and then he's gripping me whole, clasping me by throat and waist, using my body like a toy, like the sheath for his cock. He pumps that huge length through my insides, over and over, and it hurts at first but after a few thrusts it doesn't hurt anymore—I've given myself up to being used and it's a relief, it's bliss not to have to think about anything but the monster cock filling me up tight, dragging out, and shoving in again.

Every time he drives in, a rich throb of pleasure rolls through my clit, stronger with each thrust.

"Yes, yes, Caer—" My words are a half-squeal, and he roars aloud and jerks into a new rhythm. He's purely a beast now, rutting me in a frenzy. His hips pound against my ass, and I think I'm going mad from raw, carnal sensation, from the heady smell of sex, of his thick fur and his hot skin—and because it's him—it's Caer, and he isn't quite *my* Caer yet but he will be. I will make it so.

His tail writhes along my belly, then moves right over my clit, a silken glide.

And I come undone.

Because this man, even though he's imprisoned by a curse and tormented half out of his mind, is thinking of my pleasure even as he's taking his own.

Caer fucks the orgasm out of me—his hands, his cock, his tail—and as I'm thrilling with violent bliss, he comes.

Tiny pinpricks of pain erupt along my channel, and Caer holds me in a vise grip—holds me perfectly still, growling a warning.

The barbs along his cock—they're gripping my insides, locking us together, and he doesn't want me to struggle, doesn't want me to be torn.

I don't fight him. The glow of my orgasm blurs the pain as his cock throbs and throbs, flexing in a surging rhythm, pumping a flood of his cum into my womb. I've never felt anyone come so much.

Back home, whenever I had sex, I took a tonic to prevent pregnancy, purchased with a few coins from my wages. Here in Faerie, I'm not sure what will result from mating with a Fae in heat, much less a Fae in a cursed monster form. But this moment is so intimate, violent, and primal—I can't bring myself to worry or care.

We stay that way for several minutes, locked together, while he holds my throat and his tail coils softly around my waist, twitching reassuringly against my skin.

At last, the twinges of pain have completely ebbed, and Caer's cock has softened. He draws it out of me slowly, and I feel the immediate rush of cum dripping from my hole, down my legs.

He makes a faint sound of displeasure and crouches behind me, licking the cum and pushing it back inside me with his tongue. When he's satisfied, he drapes his monstrous, lionlike bulk in the grass and pulls me close, with my back to his chest. He curls around me, possessively, protectively, like he did when he made me the nest of pillows back at the Dread Court.

He feels different, but his sigh of satisfaction is the same, and it makes me smile. I nestle against him, my skin warmed by his body heat and my insides warm from his cum. Talking must be hard for him in this form, or I'm sure he'd be chattering to me.

"I like you this way, and all ways," I whisper. "There is no form of yours in which I would not care for you. But we are going to free you from this curse, you understand?"

He sighs again, and there's a thread of hope in the sound.

After a few more minutes, I venture, "You know Riordan is probably going mad right now, worrying about me."

Caer's chest rumbles. I can't tell if it's a growl or a purr.

"You need to take me back to him. He's been through enough pain."

A louder rumble. Definitely a growl.

"You're still angry with him. I understand. But his plan to sacrifice me to the Queen *did* work. I didn't die. And then he came after you, Caer. He wanted to find you. You're important to him, to both of us."

It's hard to tell how much my sweet, savage Cat understands in his cursed form, so maybe a demonstration of my intent is in order.

"I'm going back to Riordan." I start to rise from the ground, but with a throat-ripping snarl he tightens his grip, pinning me in place.

Though the grass is pliant and pillowy, and the stars are lovely as sugared snow on dark-blue velvet, a trickle of fear seeps into my soul. I'm naked and vulnerable in a meadow, clasped in the arms of a monster. The small cuts where his claws poked me earlier are stinging more now.

What if Caer won't let me leave? What if he keeps me here, prevents me from seeking out the Green Wizard and bargaining for the dissolution of his curse?

"Caer," I say quietly, tears in my voice. "Please."

He's breathing faster, a hectic rhythm. After a moment, words grate from between his jaws. "Not yet."

"All right. But soon."

"Soon."

# 13

## DOROTHY

For the first few minutes after Alice is taken, I'm sure Riordan will lose his mind. He runs after them a little way, but he's slow in the armor. Once he realizes they're already far out of his reach, he begins dashing his metal-clad body against trees, roaring curses.

Jasper sits with his knees pulled up and Fiero cuddled to his heart. Jealousy twinges through me, but I don't demand that he put my dog down. He looks as if he needs the comfort more than I do.

"I can't—fucking—do—anything!" bellows Riordan. "Fuck, fuck, *fuck*!"

"If you're done," I say dryly, "Maybe I can use the Tama Olc to track her or something, with your help."

Riordan whirls and stalks back toward me so threateningly that I recoil, putting both hands up defensively like I did to the West Witch and the crows. A pulse of power bursts from my fingers, sending him crashing backward onto the ground.

"What the fuck?" he snarls.

"Don't *prowl* toward me like that."

He climbs to his feet. "If you can find her, do it."

I pull the small spellbook out of my pocket. "It will take a while for me to figure out which spell might help us."

"By then he might have eaten her." Riordan slams a metal fist against the tree.

Jasper's blue eyes dart from one of us to the other, and he says meekly, "If it's a matter of finding her, I can help."

"Can you indeed?" Riordan's voice drips with disbelief.

"I can. One of my few gifts is tracking, and the ability is stronger if I've been intimate with the person."

"Intimate?" I frown at him, then look at Riordan, who turns away. "Wait… did the Scarecrow fuck Alice while I was looking for the road?"

Riordan's silence is answer enough.

"And he did it in front of you? Shit. Things really are different in Faerie." I tuck the Tama Olc back into my pocket. "Very well, Scarecrow—find her."

"I'm going with you," Riordan says.

Jasper eyes him doubtfully. "Can you be quick and quiet?"

A low sigh from within the helmet. "You know I can't."

"Then I should go alone."

"You'll die." Perhaps it's callous of me to say it, but it's true. "That thing is beyond reason."

"Reason, maybe. But he did recognize her, at least on a primal level," Riordan answers. "He took only her, and left the rest of us untouched. He knows who she is. That doesn't mean he will not devour her, or damage her irreparably." His anger spent, he sinks to the ground, with his back to the trunk of the great tree.

A new voice sounds from a few paces away—a cool, mocking voice. "Poor little human. Mortals are so soft and toothsome… they never last too long in these parts."

My stomach flutters and my blood heats immediately.

The slim, long-legged figure of the West Witch emerges from the darkness. He ignites a handful of tiny glowing orbs and sends them sailing into the air over our heads, providing a dim golden light.

Riordan doesn't rise, only tilts his helmet back against the tree and sighs again. "What do you want, Witch? Come to put us under your spell?"

"You know very well that I can't, thanks to the stars-damned Wizard. I'm here for one simple reason—I'm fucking bored." His gaze has been fixed on Riordan, but it slants to me suddenly and my heart jumps at the dreadful intensity of those dark eyes. He smiles, his sharp eye-teeth glinting. "Kin-Slayer. I told you I'd be back for what's mine. Come here."

I know he can't compel me to do anything, and yet I feel his voice, his will, tugging at my very bones. Maybe there's an echo of his former compulsion ability still left in him. Or maybe I'm being lured by a hunger so deep I've scarcely dared to acknowledge it.

One step. I take one step toward him.

And then Jasper sets down Fiero and leaps up, planting his body between me and the West Witch. "Leave her alone," he says firmly.

"How precious," croons the Witch. "You have *two* guard dogs now. And how will you defend your lady, Scarecrow?" He moves nearer to Jasper, running his fingers over the crow tattoo on his chest. "You're barely Fae at all. A little tracking magic, a few weak illusions—that's all you're good for, isn't it? If you had intelligence to make up for the lack of strength and magic, that would be something, but there's not much going on in your pretty blond head." He flicks Jasper's cheek with his sharp nails, and Jasper flinches, turning his face away from the Witch's piercing gaze.

"What are you most afraid of, I wonder?" continues the Witch. "Oh, I've just had the most wonderful idea for a game.

Let's play, all of us, shall we? I'll guess your deepest fears, and if I'm right, you'll be plagued by those fears until you guess mine."

"We can't play games with you." Riordan gets to his feet heavily, as if mustering the energy for a thread of hope is a monumental task. "We need to get Alice back."

The Witch takes a dark glass marble from his pocket and tosses it once. "I'll show you where she is, and then you'll play my game."

"No," Riordan says.

"Are you quite sure? With this, we can see exactly what's happening to her. Might set your heart at ease, if you've still got one in there." The Witch bends, pretending to listen at Riordan's breastplate. "Never had one myself. Hearts are such dreadful nuisances, don't you think, Kin-Slayer? All that anxious 'is this right' or 'is this wrong,' worrying about kindness and loyalty and love—ugh." He shudders. "A wretched business."

Part of me understands what he's saying. Echoes it, and affirms it. Throughout my life, fitting in, learning the moral and social rules, and pretending to function normally has been so damn exhausting. Letting it all go and not worrying about right and wrong, or the problems and pleasures of others, sounds utterly liberating.

"I am Unseelie, as you are," says Riordan. "I am not kind. My loyalty and love belong to a rare few, and two of them are somewhere in this forest."

"All the more reason to take a look." The Witch spins the marble in his hand, and it grows to a ball the size of a melon, made of dark glass and swirling with formless shadows.

"That's a scrying stone," Riordan says.

"Indeed. A tool of witches like myself and my siblings, to help us keep an eye on our thralls. But it can be useful to spy on others as well. I can observe anyone, provided I remember their face and know their name."

The West Witch holds the glass ball toward Riordan, grinning. The bastard has been watching us this whole time. Whenever he likes, he can spy on our group—on *me*.

"Don't indulge him," I say sharply, but Riordan is already leaning in, the eye-slits of his helmet angled toward the glossy surface. The shadows within the ball condense into a spiral, then fade, leaving behind an image of Alice and the monstrous beast who stole her away.

She's naked, on all fours in a meadow, while the hulking monster ruts into her from behind. He's less beastly than I expected—I can see the form of his Fae self beneath the fur, the fangs, and the panther-like aspect.

"See there, she's perfectly fine," says the West Witch. "Being thoroughly bred by a giant cat. Nothing to worry about."

"Where is this?" Riordan grits out. "I have to get to them before he kills her."

"Trying to go back on our deal? Naughty, naughty." The Witch waggles a long green finger at Riordan. "You took a peek, and now you play the game. Though it isn't as much fun when your worst fear is so easy to guess. Take another look."

He lifts the glass ball closer to Riordan. The beast is still fucking Alice, but now she's slowly coming apart, as if the seams of her flesh are ripping, revealing bloody swaths of red muscle and bulges of glistening organs. She's screaming, too—a faint, hideous, garbled sound. And the beast is weeping as it fucks her—weeping, and crying out for help in the voice of a young male.

Riordan releases a cry of agony, transfixed to the vision.

The West Witch steps back, bringing the glass ball with him—but a translucent copy of the scene remains in midair before the motionless Riordan, as he watches it play over and over again. The air around Riordan is watery, wavy, as if we're looking at him through the ripples on the surface of a pond.

He's trapped within the illusion of his own worst fear, watching the torture of the two souls he loves most. I'm concerned and shocked, of course, but I'm mostly worried about myself. What will the West Witch show me?

"Stop it," cries Jasper. "Stop tormenting him!" He turns to me, his blue eyes wet with tears. "Dorothy, do something."

"You're Fae. You fix it," I say. "I'm tired of everyone relying on me for magic. Riordan should know that isn't real—he heard the terms of the bargain. All he has to do is guess this green bastard's real fear, and he's free."

"Correction—if *one* of you guesses it, you all go free," interjects the Witch. "So very generous of me, isn't it? Of course my motives are quite selfish—if I leave you all trapped in illusions, I'll be bored again. So it's in my best interest for you to find your way out—eventually."

"You fiend." Jasper's fists tighten. "I won't let you do this to the people who helped me." And he leaps for the Witch, teeth bared.

But he freezes mid-spring, caught in a watery illusion like the one Riordan is suffering. He's surrounded by figures, both Fae and human, and they're all facing him at first but then, one by one, they turn their backs on him. He calls out to them, pleads, persuades, but no one responds. Even when his body alights and begins to burn, none of them look at him. Ashes flake from his charred flesh—he's shrieking, crumbling, and still no one in the vision notices or cares.

"Too easy." The Witch yawns. "You, Kin-Slayer, are a little more difficult to read. Let's try a few things, shall we?"

He snaps his fingers, and the cries of Jasper and Riordan vanish, muted by magic. When he turns to me, Fiero leaps forward, barking, sensing my peril—but the Witch swirls him into an illusion of hunting tender rabbits through a green forest. Harmless enough. The Witch could have done far worse to my pet.

I reach for my own power and find that it's there again—but the brush of my mind against that inner energy is half-hearted. I'm uncertain what to do with the power I do have, not sure how to use it to turn the tables on him. Besides, what he's doing right now is physically harmless, and I hesitate to use my magic when I'm not in serious danger. I might need it later.

And perhaps I'm a little too curious about this game of his. Perhaps part of me wants to be known—split open to my core and touched at the quivering, vulnerable center of myself.

The Witch stands opposite me, a smirk tweaking the corner of his mouth, one eyebrow hitched more sharply than the other, as if he's waiting for me to notice something. His gaze lowers, just for a second.

When I look down, my clothes are gone. It has to be an illusion, because the Tama Olc is still in my pocket—I can sense it there. But it feels so real, right down to the whisper of night air against my skin.

Someone walks out of the forest—no, several people—a mixed group of Fae and humans. At the sight of me they pause, then form a half-circle around me and stare openly at my body. Some of them look disgusted, others merely bored. Their whispered comments swirl around me—comments about the squareness of my shoulders, my narrow hips, and my strange-looking ears, neither Fae nor human. They criticize the unevenness of my skin tone in places, the moles on my thigh and my right side, the contrast of my blue eye and my brown eye. They comment that my ass is too flat, my legs too scrawny, my elbows too pointy, and my knees too knobby.

Anger churns inside me, but I'm not afraid of them. I grit my teeth and plot how I might kill them all—until they vanish, and I remember that it's an illusion. I can't see the Witch, or Jasper, or Riordan—I'm alone in the forest, naked, or so it seems.

Movement on the ground catches my eye. Out of the undergrowth slither two pale snakes, their scales as white and glossy as milk. I step back as they slither toward me, but they're too quick—they're already coiling around my ankles, sliding up my bare thighs. One glides around to my backside, and the ripple of its smooth, tiny scales over my ass cheek sends a flood of arousal through my body. The snake continues up my spine to my throat, where it coils, tightening slowly.

Meanwhile the other serpent is nudging between my legs, parting the lips of my sex with its head, worming its way inside me, coils of its body disappearing into my entrance—I part my legs and look down between them, gasping as I see the tip of the white tail vanish into my pussy. I can feel the snake moving in my lower belly, but strangely, I'm not frightened.

A flicker of alarm runs through me as the snake around my neck pushes its head between my lips, into my mouth, and begins pouring itself into me, filling up my throat. Still, I'm not terrified—I'm titillated, fascinated by how marvelously full my body feels.

A second later, the slithering sensation in my throat and my belly disappear, and I remember, once again, that it was all an illusion. Every time another waking dream begins, I seem to forget what's happening.

"Most women would have screamed." The West Witch appears a few steps away, tapping one finger against his lips thoughtfully. "I know many an Unseelie who would have cringed at that, and you didn't flinch. You're a little pervert, Kin-Slayer."

"And you're being too gentle," I retort. "People ridiculing my body, telling me I don't belong? Snakes entering my holes? Surely you can do better than that."

He peers at me. "That's a challenge. Ah, Dorothy, how foolish of you. Very well then—prepare for the most terrifying night of your life."

# 14

## DOROTHY

I shouldn't have challenged him.

I don't know how long he bombards me with swarms of spiders, delusions of drowning, visions of monsters, and images of my parents and friends being skinned alive. Apparently nothing provokes the reaction he's looking for, because he gets progressively more frustrated every time he appears to me, between illusions.

After one particularly harrowing vision of Alice's little siblings being boiled and eaten, he lets all the veils drop. I'm no longer naked, and I can see our camp again, with Riordan and Jasper still trapped in their fears. If either of them have managed to comprehend what's happening, they still haven't guessed his fear correctly.

The West Witch charges me, collars my throat with his hand. He towers above me, his eyes snapping with vicious intent. "What is wrong with you? Is there nothing that terrifies you? I've sensed disgust, fascination, arousal, concern, anger, vengefulness, and moderate fear, but not true terror. Nothing that constricts your heart and makes you crumble into ash. What more can I do to make you afraid?"

I stare up at him, caught in the storm of his rage, riveted by the sense of sheer, unstoppable power flowing from his fingers into my body. He's so much stronger than I am—the things he could do to me—the things I want him to do—

"Wait..." He frowns, peering into my eyes. "Wait... I wonder..."

And in a blink, everything drops away. His touch, the forest, everything. It all disappears.

I'm alone. Just me, in a dull black void. Nothing above, nothing below—a vast nothing stretching endlessly in every direction. I have no magic, no strength, nothing except the dread certainty that I have been cast out by both Fae and humans because I am *wrong*. I am too different. I don't belong to either race—I am something Other, some rejected thing floating like a bit of rancid shit in the bowels of the universe. And worse than the encroaching panic is the horror, the certainty, that this place has no escape, and no end. It is interminable, unbearable monotony. There's nothing I can try, no magic I can do or words I can say. I am voiceless, powerless, and isolated, doomed to be conscious amid all this nothing, forever. Nothing to invigorate my mind or entertain my senses. No power of imagination I can summon for relief—my brain is entirely flooded with wretched, debilitating terror.

I can't scream. I can't die.

I am doomed to exist alone in timeless, merciless Nothing.

But one thought quivers in my stricken brain. It comes to me in pieces, and I struggle to assemble it, to make it coherent until it finally takes shape and struggles to the forefront of my consciousness.

He couldn't scare me with anything else, so he used the thing that scares *him* the most.

"This is your worst fear, Witch," I gasp out. "Yours and mine."

Abruptly I'm back in the forest, in the liquid gloom of green leaves and golden magic, while the West Witch stares at me with shattered black eyes.

Jasper and Riordan are still motionless, but their illusions have shifted to harmless dreams, like Fiero's. I barely note the change before I meet the Witch's gaze again.

The air between us thickens, a heated throb of blood, of lust, of tension tightening, coiling and coiling until—

I snap and lunge for him. He wraps one hand around my skull and crushes my mouth to his, and it isn't pleasant, it's brutal, wretched, savage. There's blood in my mouth—I'm not sure which of us bit the other.

His scent crashes into my mind—-cold wind and the vivid freshness of green grass. I suck in great breaths of him, desperate for that fragrance. His teeth scrape along my jaw; he sucks on the sensitive skin of my neck, leaving a bright bloom of pain behind when he releases it.

My fingers tear into his clothing, wriggling into the gaps, anywhere I can touch his hot flesh. I want to slice him open and drink him down.

With my hair doubled around his hand, he yanks my head backward and grips my jaw, brutalizing my mouth, lips and teeth and flaming liquid tongue. I make a sound—not a whimper, more like a frustrated half-scream, and I wrench at the row of tiny hooks keeping his black pants closed tight. They yield to me—he pushes them down and tugs out his cock, smooth and green.

A quick blast of magic, and I'm knocked to the ground, the breath gone from my lungs. He leaps on top of me—he's shoving up my skirts, tearing aside everything in his way. I am volcanic, molten, a river of heat, and I *demand* to be filled. If he does not get inside me now I will *scream*.

His nails rake my thighs, drawing blood as he spreads me wide open, lines up his cock head, and shoves inside me in one brutal rush. His lean body hunches over mine, his chest and throat right above my face. Every explosive thrust is a shock to my senses. I can't breathe. I reach up, grab fistfuls of his hair, and pull until he snarls and shoves both my wrists down, pinning them to the ground while he fucks me viciously.

I've always had to be quiet during sex. But this time—gods, the sound of it, the thick, wet, sloppy noises—and I still can't breathe, not until he slaps the side of my face lightly and barks, "*Breathe*, Kin-Slayer," and something breaks free inside me and I can finally inhale.

A white-hot explosion is building behind my eyes, surging in my body—my legs are curled up tight on either side of his hips and I'm choking out screams. He releases one of my wrists, wraps that arm around my head, and press his jaw against the top of my head while his hips buck, pushing his cock into me faster, faster—

*Shit*—

A bolt of keenest ecstasy sears through my body, splitting me in two. Shrieks erupt from my throat—I can't help it—never felt anything like this—never, never—oh gods—waves of bliss keep bathing me, over and over. I've never had an orgasm that lasted this long.

The Witch is still fucking me, slick and full and deep—and then he comes, harsh male cries of pleasure breaking from him while his body goes rigid with bliss. I can feel the spasms of his cock inside me as he spills everything.

He shoves in one more time, hard and tight—another groan—and then he relaxes, panting. Pulls out and moves back—then tumbles aside onto the ground and lies there, blinking and gasping and muttering, "Fuck."

With shaking fingers I push my skirts back into place, and as I do so, he pulls himself to his feet with a jerky movement that's almost angry.

"A bargain was made," he says acidly. "You guessed my fear, so all of you will be free to go. But I'm not done with you yet, Kin-Slayer. Next time you'll take me in your mouth, and swallow my cum." He leans down, catches my chin in a rough grip. "The day you killed my sister was Day One. Yesterday was the second day, and tomorrow is the third. When the sun sets on the seventh day, I will end you, do you understand? Sex is not softness to the Fae. Fucking you does not mean I'll spare you—far from it. I will kill you in the most horrific manner I can devise."

Eyes narrowed, I let some of my magic leak into the ground, causing a rumble beneath his feet. "Not if I kill you first."

A flash of interest and humor in his eyes—gone so quickly I might have imagined it. "Keep dreaming. And keep that pussy wet for me." He shoves his slim booted foot beneath my dress, pressing the hard leather against my soaked center. I gasp a little, and he grins, shifting his foot a bit, grinding the toe of the boot over my clit. "I think you'd come on my foot if I let you."

I want to beg him for it. But I have a nagging twitch in my mind—not guilt, exactly—I don't usually feel guilt—but an awareness that I should probably care more about the welfare of my traveling companions than about my own sexual cravings. So I scoot backward, away from the contact. He merely shrugs, waggling his dark eyebrows at me before he vanishes in a puff of green smoke.

# 15

## ALICE

My consciousness crawls out of sleep, becoming gradually aware that I'm moving. I'm swaying with the movement of someone's steps, carried in a pair of silken arms. The face over me is strange—a panther with mane like a lion, but there's intelligence in his purple eyes. His feral beauty is a blow to my gut because it's Caer, and I'd know him in any shape.

His chest and torso are distinguishable as human, like last night. Beneath his short black fur, I can feel the contours of the muscle beneath. He's walking on two legs, gracefully and steadily enough, but by the twitch of his ears and the thunder of his heart I know he's not at peace.

He glances down at me. Manages two words. "Nearly there."

Is he taking me back to Riordan?

He lifts his head, sniffs the air. A tremble runs through his limbs, and he seems to instantly grow bulkier, his shoulders gaining a hulking mass they didn't have before. A strangled sound issues from his throat—a pained growl.

"You're all right," I tell him, pressing my hand over his heart. "Calm down. It's only Riordan."

He huffs, shakes his mane. His body is changing more, taking on greater size and threat. He drops me naked into the underbrush and crashes to all fours while his limbs and claws lengthen.

He's terrified of facing Riordan. And if I can't calm him, I might lose him.

"Caer, stay with me." Cautiously I move nearer, placing my hand on his great shoulder. My pale fingers look so fragile and small, splayed against that hulk of black furred muscle.

"We've been through difficult things before, you and I," I say soothingly. "Remember when you came to me, all torn apart by the Heartless, and I made you the potion you needed? Remember when we fought each other, and then you taught me Jacks-and-Antlers and helped me practice my reading? And then you built me a nest, and we snuggled there together. We're friends, you and I." I hesitate, swallowing the emotion that's trying to clog my throat. "More than friends. I missed you, Caer. I'm here now, and I won't leave you again, not even if you tear me apart. My life is yours, my heart is yours. You don't have to be afraid. And if it's Riordan you're scared to face—trust me, he cares for you deeply. He came out here searching for you—he made a terrible wish that became a curse, all because he wanted to help you. He—he loves you."

The monster shudders, growls, but the growl ends in a low whine.

"Come on," I tell him. "Let's find him together."

We continue on, and I keep my hand on his shoulder the whole time, as if the touch is a tether, a line from my heart to his, a tangible way I can keep him grounded, prevent him from losing himself inside the monster's form.

Together we pace out of the forest into the clearing where we camped—me, naked as a sheared lamb, marked with dirt and blood, and Caer in the guise of a gigantic black panther with a lion's mane and the wide, wide, fanged mouth of a monster.

The Scarecrow is sitting on the ground, leaning against Riordan's armored shoulder, cradling Fiero in his lap. Judging by Jasper's pallor and the defeated forward bend of Riordan's helmet, something happened to them while I was gone. Dorothy is pacing the clearing restlessly, her hands in her pockets.

When Caer and I appear, she stops short. Riordan's helmet lifts, but he doesn't move otherwise. He stays silent, rigid.

But Jasper gasps softly at the sight of the beast beside me. He rises from the ground with slow, cautious grace and a wondering light in his blue eyes. Fiero, tumbled from his resting spot, gives a sleepy sort of half-bark and scurries over to Dorothy, who scoops him up.

Jasper keeps moving forward with one hand outstretched toward Caer. "This is him? The friend you were looking for? He's beautiful."

Caer gives a sharp snarl that fades into a displeased, ongoing rumble in his chest.

Jasper smiles, brilliant as sunshine on golden grain, and steps nearer.

Sinks his fingers into Caer's mane.

With his other hand, he strokes the beast's glossy black muzzle. "A pleasure to meet you," he murmurs. "Aren't you lovely?"

I keep my hand on Caer's shoulder, terrified that he might bite off the fingers of the golden-haired Fae male who's petting him—but although he bristles, he doesn't attack.

For a moment longer I wait, until Caer's unsettled rumbling shifts into something closer to a purr. And then I leave him with Jasper and approach Riordan, who's still frozen, sitting by the tree. He doesn't say a word.

"Did something happen to him while I was gone?" I ask Dorothy.

"The West Witch came by and tormented us with visions of our worst fears," she explains. "I won his game, and he left. But they were trapped in terrible illusions for quite some time. And I think Riordan felt it more deeply than the Scarecrow did."

"Are *you* all right?" I ask her.

She frowns, looking surprised, as if she didn't expect me to care. "You're the one who's naked and bleeding."

"True." I kneel beside Riordan, placing my hand on his breastplate. "Caer was afraid to come here. As you told me, the brutality of his form is tied to how much fear he feels, how strong he thinks he must be to protect himself. I think he needs to hear it from you, that you're not angry with him. That you care about him."

A rasp from inside the helmet. "It goes without saying."

"It doesn't, though. Unseelie or not, you have to be able to say it. Riordan, please. I can't bear for the two of you to fight. Look what happened to you two when you were apart!"

"When *all three of us* were apart." He speaks so low I barely hear the words.

My breath catches. It's the first time he has put the three of us together like that—as if we're a trio, linked on a level deeper than friendship.

"Perhaps we shouldn't be apart," I whisper. "Any of us. Ever again."

"A fine triad we'll make," he replies. "The lion, the tin man, and the tender little human. We'll tear you apart, Alice. Sooner or later we'll be the death of you. Look at yourself, kitten."

"Scratches," I say dismissively. "No worse than a run-in with a restive colt or a troublesome rooster."

A hoarse laugh from the helmet. "I will speak to him. But only for a moment, and then we must make for the Emerald City as fast as we can. Is he coherent enough to travel the yellow road, without killing you and the others?"

"I think so." I bite my lip, hesitating before I forge ahead. Riordan may as well know everything. "Caer has been in heat since I first met him, and it has only gotten worse. I think that may have spurred part of his madness and violence. But he—I let him—that is, we—"

"He bred you, and now he feels better," Riordan says tightly.

"Well... yes."

"It's odd, him being in heat that long. Unusual, particularly for an Unseelie Fae. I shall have to ask him some questions about it."

"But not now. He can barely speak."

"Later, then. Once the curse is broken."

Dorothy speaks up, startling me—I didn't realize she'd come closer. "And we're certain the Green Wizard will let Alice use her one wish to free you and this beast?"

"He must," I say simply. "And then, Dorothy, you can wish us back to the mainland of Faerie—preferably to the Court of Delight. We have Seelie friends there."

Riordan snorts. "'Friends' is a strong word."

"Very well." I push his shoulder playfully. "*I* have friends there. Friends who can help us. We'll be safe."

Dorothy puckers her lips and glances around at the forest, which is slowly lightening as day dawns. "Safe in the Court of Delight. Sounds exciting."

"Better than this place, where curses abound and nothing makes sense." I rise, clasping Riordan's arm and tugging vainly. He's too heavy for me to move on my own, but he concedes and climbs to his feet.

Jasper is still ruffling Caer's mane, scratching his ears, and talking quietly to him. Shock and pleasure mingle in the Cat's purple eyes as he allows the attention. His stiff-legged stance eases the longer he's petted. But his posture hardens again and his mane ruffles up as Riordan approaches him.

I take the Scarecrow's hand and pull him gently away, allowing Riordan and Caer to face each other—the huge beast, teeth bared and hackles raised, glaring at the silver suit of armor.

As I watch them, Jasper pulls me against his side, a comforting grip. He looks down at my nude form with appreciation, despite the bruises and blood. "You look beautiful," he whispers in my ear.

"Shut up." But I can't help smirking, even as I refocus my attention on the two cursed males.

They're staring at each other. Wordless.

Dorothy sighs, leans against a tree as if she's settling in for a long wait.

"You unutterable fool," Riordan says at last. "You fucking moron."

"Oh shit," whispers Dorothy, clearly expecting those words to start a fight—but I hold up a finger for her to wait.

I've seen these two interact. I heard the last words they said to each other, during a violent fight over my fate. I saw Riordan kneeling astride Caer—heard his broken whisper. That he couldn't watch Caer die. That he would sacrifice *me* before he would let that happen.

These two loved each other long before I loved them. They've just refused to admit it.

Maybe now—maybe here—

"Follow us on the yellow road, or don't," Riordan says caustically. "Alice wants to wish us both free. You can help me protect her on the way there, or you can run back to your den."

Caer hisses savagely and snaps, his terrifying teeth nearly raking against Riordan's helmet. When Riordan doesn't budge, Caer growls thickly, "I will follow."

"Fine. The road is that way." And Riordan stalks off through the trees.

Caer slinks after him, head lowered and shoulders tight, as if he's stalking the suit of armor, ready to pounce.

I stifle a groan. These men—why are they so pig-headed?

"I need something to wear." I glance around the clearing, my eyes latching on the basket of supplies sitting beside the boulder.

"Why must you wear something?" Jasper blinks innocent blue eyes at me. "I like your naked form. It is enchanting."

"But I would like to be covered as I travel."

"I see." He watches me as I tug the blue-checked cloth out of the basket, leaving the food and napkins behind. The cloth is large enough for me to wrap it around my body and knot it on one shoulder, leaving my other shoulder bare. It's an odd sort of garment, very drafty—but it's better than nothing.

# 16

## DOROTHY

Traveling in Faerie is strange enough, but traveling in the company of a monstrous cat, a man encased in metal, a faerie covered in sacrificial tattoos, and the girl from the neighboring farm... it's beyond preposterous.

Riordan stalks ahead, every tense line of his armor proclaiming that he does not want to be touched or spoken to. The hulking, maned panther prowls behind him, rumbling occasionally, and sometimes baring a horrifying number of dagger-like teeth.

Jasper walks confidently between the monster and Fiero. The Scarecrow seems to like animals, from my tiny dog, trotting as fast as he can on stubby legs, to the great leonine beast pacing nearby.

Alice falls back to walk beside me, exhaustion and discomfort evident in each of her stiff movements. Her wounds are shallow, but she seems to gain more and more of them, the longer we're in Faerie.

"Your last visit wasn't like this," I say bluntly.

"No." She winces. "I spent most of my time in a cell, until my heart was gifted to the Queen."

I try to imagine how it must have felt. "You trusted your survival to *him*. To Riordan."

"I did. I knew he'd do everything possible to save me."

"How did you know that?" Frustration edges my voice. "Sometimes I can read people—what they're feeling, what they want—and other times, I'm lost. At least back home the emotions were simpler. Here, everything is so complex, and the relationships are—" I lift both hands, interlocking my fingers.

"Tangled. Yes, that's a good way to describe it. And I don't see any of it untangling until we get to the Wizard."

I hesitate, aware that what I'm about to say might be considered rude back in the human realm. But I can't see how playing into her delusion is helpful. "You think the Wizard can solve everything. You seem to be willfully ignoring that he twists every wish people make—distorts it into something terrible."

"I'm aware. But I've planned the precise words I'm going to use. I can't think of any way they can be twisted." She glances sidelong at me. "What about you? Don't you want to see Riordan's true face, and find out for sure how you two are related?"

"I suppose. But it won't change my life much, one way or the other."

"Because the West Witch wants you dead. Maybe you thought I'd forgotten about that, but I haven't. Once we get Riordan and Caer back, we can focus on protecting you. That's why I suggested the Seelie kingdom as our destination. You'll be safe from the Witch there, since he can't leave the Isle of Oz."

"Oh…yes." I try to muster some enthusiasm about the concept of safety, but all I can feel is a hollow dread at the thought of never seeing a certain dark-eyed, green-skinned Witch again. "I suppose that is the best option."

"Of course you could always ask the Wizard to send you back home." Alice peers at me, her gray eyes keen as a blade. "The rest of us can figure out our own way to the mainland of Faerie. But I don't think that's what you really want, is it?"

"Home?" I say sourly. "Where I had to conceal my magic and work incessantly to seem like a normal, pleasant country girl? Where I often caught my parents whispering anxiously, only to stop the conversation as soon as I entered the room?"

"But you love your parents," Alice says. "And they'll miss you—"

"As your siblings will miss you. Yet I don't hear you talking about going back. You're planning to stay here, aren't you? With *them*?" I gesture to the group of males ahead.

"If they'll have me," she says quietly. "Last time, Riordan didn't want me to stay."

"The fuck he didn't."

She giggles at my outburst, and my answering smile is genuine.

"I never knew you were like this," Alice says once her merriment subsides. "I think, if I'd known you better, we could have been great friends. In case you haven't noticed, I rather like Unseelie types."

"I wish I had spoken to you more openly as well," I reply. "If nothing else, you could have told me about Lord Drosselmeyer being a sorcerer. I could have sought him out for information about what I am, and what I can do."

"Yes, well… he's never been friendly to the Fae." Alice winces. "Perhaps it's best that neither of you knew about each other's abilities."

I'm about to answer when I notice the light growing brighter ahead. Sunshine floods between the pillared trees, turning the yellow bricks to radiant gold.

We're coming to the edge of the forest.

Riordan turns around. "This happened last time I headed for the Emerald City. I came out of the woods and I could see it up ahead, across grassy meadows."

Alice sucks in a quick, eager breath. "We're nearly there."

"He's dangerous," Riordan warns. "I don't remember everything about the city, or the palace, or how he looked, or what he said to me before I made my wish. The encounter is blurred, which is no doubt what he intended. As I said—if he isn't a god-star himself, he's the devoted servant of one. And we will be entirely at his mercy. Once you are in his presence, you may not even remember the exact wording of the request you wished to make."

I throw out my hands, an exasperated gesture. "That's what I've been saying. Why visit this terrible person?"

"Because he's their only hope," Alice replies, her gaze on the man of metal and the hulking beast.

With a quick intake of breath, she forges ahead, moving past all of us, out of the gloom of the woods into the brilliant sunshine. Fiero scurries after her, and so do Jasper and the monster. Obedient dogs, the lot of them, trotting after their mistress.

Sighing, I move to follow them, but Riordan puts out his hand to stop me. "Don't feel beholden to us, or obliged to wish for something," he says. "We can find our own way. I'd rather not risk you making a wish that can be used to harm you. In fact it might be best for you to wait outside the palace with your little pet."

His concern pierces the blankness of my emotional wall—stabs right through it, into the flesh of my heart—reminds me that I have one.

Riordan wakes me in a different way than the Witch does—stirs in me feelings of blood-loyalty, of family commitment, of security that I never felt with my parents.

I can't be sure he has formed a familial attachment to me. But the tone of his voice seems to hint as much. And strangely, it makes me eager to return that bond, that loyalty, that concern.

"I should have acted more quickly last night," I burst out. "I should have saved you from those awful visions faster."

"The fact that you saved me at all is enough. I will repay it."

He doesn't thank me as a human would. He promises a fair exchange, and somehow I like that better.

"I'll go with you into the Emerald City," I tell him. "Whatever your fate may be, I want to witness it, and to help if I can."

He makes a brief hum in his throat, a sound of assent and approval. "So be it."

We walk together into the sun, and it feels right that I'm here, on this golden road, stepping into the flood of dazzling light with him, with my own blood, with someone who knows what I am, what I can do, and doesn't fear me, because we are the same.

I blink against the brightness, and then I stop short.

The brick road twines between meadows, just as Riordan said—but they aren't grassy—they're blanketed with red flowers—poppies, I think, or the closest Fae equivalent. The sun glances through the petals, turning each one a vivid, translucent scarlet, like a pane of ruby glass. So thickly do the flowers grow that they nearly cover our path. Their stems arch over the yellow bricks, narrowing the way, lining it with banks of nodding crimson blooms.

Far in the distance, beyond the fields of poppies, rises the Emerald City—columnar towers of rich green against the blue sky.

My heart leaps at the brilliance of it all, at the sheer glorious color, so much brighter than anything in the human realm. This is the kind of beauty I've been craving all my life, though I didn't realize it until the tornado of magic dropped me here.

A laugh bubbles up inside me, and I feel as incandescently joyful as when I first heard faerie music back in the Village of Crows. The buttery yellow of the road, the blood-red of the flowers, the bright green of the palace, and the impossible blue of the sky—I'm so happy I could scream.

Laughing breathlessly, I dance forward and drop to my knees amid the blossoms, inhaling their heavy, spicy fragrance. It's so rich and sweet—I could breathe it in forever.

"It wasn't like this before," says Riordan, and I swear I can *hear* the frown in his voice, though I've never seen his face.

"They're flowers." I pluck one of them, admiring the delicacy of the petals. "What harm could they do?"

"This is Faerie. The loveliest things are usually the most dangerous."

"You worry too much." I glance ahead to where Alice, the monster, and the Scarecrow have paused to wait for us. As I watch, Jasper bends and lifts Fiero, who looks strangely limp.

Fear clutches my heart, stealing the joy as swiftly as it came. Jumping to my feet, I hurry forward and take my dog from Jasper's arms. "What happened?"

"I'm not sure. He simply... fell over." Jasper looks up at me, my own concern mirrored in his lovely blue gaze.

For some reason his anxiety infuriates me.

"He's not yours to worry about," I snap. "He's mine."

Jasper withdraws a step, hurt pooling in his eyes—but then sympathy replaces it, and he smiles at me with soft understanding. "You're right. I've been taking him from you too often. He's adorable, and I let myself become enamored, I'm afraid. It's a bad habit of mine."

His gentle comprehension makes me angrier still. The rage is a poisoned lash inside me, rising too fast for me to plan a reaction or summon my usual mask. Words spill from my lips in a venomous tide. "I don't need your understanding or your empathy. I just need you to leave my dog the fuck alone. Why do you have to be so *good* and *gentle* all the time? Why are you even with us? You serve no purpose and you want nothing from the Wizard. Go on your way! No one's keeping you here."

Pain flickers in his gaze. "You're right," he says quietly. "I have no place with your company. I thought perhaps I had friends at last. But as always, I am useless and unpleasant. I will go."

He brushes past me as if to head back into the forest. And then two things happen at once.

First, I realize how strange it is that Alice didn't rebuke me for my outburst.

And secondly, the panther-beast leaps past me in one fluid bound. Snarling, he plants himself on the road, blocking Jasper's way into the woods. As if he doesn't want the Scarecrow to leave.

I'm about to yell at the beast when a quiet thump draws my attention.

It's Alice. She has toppled right over among the flowers.

Riordan hurries forward with a grating clank of armor and kneels stiffly at her side. "She's unconscious, but breathing." Relief floods his voice.

The panther-beast prowls over to her, moaning a little in his throat. His shoulders and hindquarters swell larger, his form increasing in bulk, synchronized to his distress. His tail lashes, a thin black whip snaking through the air. A guttural roar bursts from him, while his claws lengthen and sink into the soil. One great front paw tears up a clump of the flowers, and the other lands dangerously close to Alice's prone form.

Riordan pulls Alice away from the beast's claws, but the sharp fingers of his armor cut her arm a little in the process.

Jasper leaps forward, hands outspread, crooning to the beast. "Softly now, my friend, softly. You're in no danger, and she'll be all right."

But the beast screams in his face—a hideous nightmare shriek—and slaps him with a mighty paw.

Jasper's head whips aside with a snap of spine, and his body flies some distance away, dropping amid the flowers.

He's Fae; he'll heal. I'm more concerned for the rest of us.

Riordan is shouting, "Caer, calm yourself! Dorothy, stop him!" But I don't know what to do, how to fix this. I dare not lay Fiero down for fear the monster will step on him, yet I need my hands for magic—I can't do it only with my mind. The Tama Olc burns in my pocket like a mental flame, a jolt to my consciousness, but there's no time to hunt for a spell.

I'm backing away from the raging beast, my mind racing—I won't run, but I can't stay—

"Dorothy!" Riordan calls again.

His voice—it's blood calling to blood, it's the tether that drew me here, that brought me home. I can't abandon him. The monster might not be able to kill Riordan, but it can kill Alice, and that will destroy my half-brother as surely as any physical death.

I run a few steps, lay Fiero down, and turn, hands lifted. "Beast!" I scream. "Turn and face me!"

When the monster whirls toward the sound of my voice, I push my magic into the movement. I keep that whirling momentum going so that he can't stop—he's spinning round and round, just like the crows kept flying in circles under my command. There's a drain on my energy since he's so big, but I can keep it up for a while.

"Take Alice and run," I call to Riordan.

He staggers to his feet, burdened by Alice's weight—or by something else. His movements are heavy, slow, as if he's slogging through some thick, viscous substance.

"Go!" I scream, but Riordan falls, his armored limbs crashing into the flowers while Alice's limp form tumbles away, half-disappeared beneath the blooms.

It's the damn poppies. They're putting everyone to sleep.

The drain on my energy is growing, suctioning more of my power to maintain the beast's spinning motion—because he, too, is lagging, slumping. Thanks to his sheer size he's the last to fall—except for me.

I break the tether of magic between us, halting the beast's spinning movement. He groans, shuffling a few steps before collapsing in a great black mountain.

Helplessly I stare at the fallen bodies of my companions. Is this a natural essence from the poppies, or is it a spell? And why am I not affected? Is it some test the Wizard has laid in our path, or—

"Kin-Slayer," purrs a voice behind me.

Of course.

I whirl to face him, and my breath catches because every time he's away I forget how fucking tall and gorgeous he is. He's smirking, lashes lowered over dark eyes that glitter with mockery.

"What did you do?" I snap.

"I bought us some time together." He reaches out, caresses my jawline with his fingertips.

I knock his hand away. "I don't want time with you."

He cocks his head. "Your heartbeat says otherwise."

"Anger tends to make a heartbeat quicken."

"True. So does lust."

"That was—I don't want *that* again. And you're sick, wanting to fuck someone you plan to kill."

"But that's what makes it so exciting." He moves into my space, his chest against mine, and his hand thrusts between my legs, cupping me roughly. "I know this tight little pussy won't exist much longer, so I want to enjoy it while I can."

I can barely breathe. My entire existence centers on the curl of his fingers through the fabric of my skirt, the possessive grip between my legs.

Why do I feel most alive at the touch of the enemy who wants to kill me?

He ducks his head, his lips at my ear, his low tone hoarse with desire. "Give me your cunt, Dorothy."

My mouth is dry, scanty breaths skipping over my tongue, and my entire skin vibrates with awareness, with sheer quivering delight at the visceral need in his voice.

"No," I hiss, more to see what he'll do than out of actual reluctance.

With a growl he wraps his other arm around me, yanking me tight to his body. "Give me your mouth then." His lips ghost over mine, hot and hungry.

"Why are you fascinated with me?"

"I told you. Your transience, your impending death at my hands—it makes the game more interesting."

"But that isn't the only reason, is it?" I tip back my head so I can meet his eyes. "We are similar, you and I. We both carry that vision of an endless Nothing, one that grows until it swallows us whole, cuts us off from everything and everyone else. We both dread being locked away from adventure, from experiences—abandoned with nothing to entertain our minds. Doomed to endless boredom and uselessness…and loneliness."

"I'm not lonely." His lip curls in a sneer.

Into the space between his bared teeth and my trembling breath I confess something I've never spoken aloud. "I *am*. I've been lonely since I lost the one person who understood who I am, inside. He understood how apathetic and wicked I can be, how dark my thoughts sometimes are, but it didn't matter to him."

West frowns, dark eyes sparking savagely. "It didn't *matter?* That's bullshit. Who you are *should matter* to the person you love. They should love you because of it, not in spite of it. They should celebrate it, revel in it, devour it—" His lips graze mine, soft and wild and scorching.

"Maybe," I murmur. "I don't think anyone could love the wickedness and carelessness of me. I hurt people, or I watch people hurting—and I don't really *care*. I try to care. I pretend to care. But so often I don't, not really. Not deep inside where it matters."

"You're Unseelie."

"But that's no excuse, is it? Because I'm also human. I should have more compassion, but I'm broken, wrong. I'm missing something that everyone else has."

"Not everyone." His mouth closes over mine, a velvety-smooth press. Just a moment of that glimmering contact, and then a breath of space and he speaks again. "Unseelie are supposed to be capable of a few deep attachments. I've never formed one of those. Not once. Not with any of my siblings, or our parents. I've been watching them—" he jerks his head toward my slumbering companions— "seeing how they interact, the power of the bonds they've forged. I hate it, and I want it. Part of me wants to unravel them and watch them bleed pain, because I can't *feel* like they can. I want to triumph over them and laugh and know that I am better because I don't feel such things. But at the same time I envy them so badly that I want to seize the world and crumble it into dust between my fingers, out of sheer rage."

"Yes!" A frenzied understanding seizes me and I grip his arms. "Sometimes I have this cool, blank apathy, and at other times I have so much rage, discontent, and envy. How does that make sense? And then sometimes I feel so wildly joyful I think I could soar straight up out of my body—but that feeling is usually linked to an experience or sensation, not a person. Except when—"

I bite my tongue—literally bite it—to stop the confession I nearly allowed to escape.

*Except when I'm with you.*

West studies me for a moment, then tips my face up and kisses me again. His tongue sweeps between my teeth, sliding over the bloody spot where I bit my own tongue. He hums with delight, savoring the wound.

"Except *when*," he mutters into the hot darkness of my mouth.

My arms snake around his neck and my fingers twist into his hair, pulling until I know it hurts him—he bites my sore spot in return, and my soft yelp disappears into the wet slide of his tongue.

He angles his head, opens his mouth wide to fit all the edges of mine, as if our souls are screaming to crawl up our throats and slither down into the other's chest cavity. As if I could swallow his heart and it would settle warm between my lungs, pumping slow and heavy, feeding me something better than blood.

West travels my skin with his lips, wet heated circles along my jaw and throat.

I tug at his clothing, ripping it aside to reveal the smooth green skin of his chest, a tight dark-green nipple. In a blink he makes the rest of the clothes leave his body, pants and vest and undergarments strewn across the scarlet flowers.

"What are they?" I ask as I shuck off my dress. "The flowers? Are they poppies?"

"Yes. You have them in the human realm, too, but their potency is felt in a different way there. I enhanced these so they would work on your friends quickly, yet leave you unaffected."

"You could have let me succumb and then taken me while I slept."

"What would be the fun in that?" He wraps one of my braids around his hand. "Your sharpness, your intensity, your savagery—that's what I find so enticing. I like you vivid and alive under my hands... for now." One palm runs up my bare back, while the other skims over my breast.

Then he drags both hands down my body, sinking slowly to his knees before cupping my thighs. His thumbs probe between the lips of my sex, pulling them apart so he can see my clit. With a low chuckle of satisfaction he puts out his tongue and licks the little bud of flesh.

I whine faintly and grab his head, sinking my fingers into his hair again, widening my stance to give him better access.

"A pity I won't be able to taste this pussy again after I kill you," he murmurs against my clit, and my hips jerk forward, aching for pressure. Laughing, he nuzzles deep, his nose pushing in just the right spot while his tongue bathes the area around my entrance.

Shaken sounds of pleasure quiver on my tongue, leaving my lips in a tremulous cry as he works me closer and closer to the edge. His tongue thrashes over my pussy and I come hard, curling my body over his kneeling form, grinding my mound into his face.

When the shock of pleasure is over, I melt into the flowers, letting my legs fall open for him. He wipes my wetness from his face with one hand and kneels between my thighs, his thick green cock pointing toward me.

He hitches my thighs and bottom up higher. Spreads me wider. Grips himself and guides his cock head between my slick lips.

He doesn't sink in right away. He teases me with my own wetness, swirling through the slick before pushing fully inside.

The slow fullness of his entry warms my body, a surge of glowing delight that makes me realize I'm not done—I can come again. I *need* to come again, with his hardness filling me up.

West teases my nipple with a claw, sweeps sharp nails under my chin, and draws lines across my throat like he's planning where he'll cut it. "You're godsdamn beautiful."

"Stop teasing and fuck me," I whisper.

He laughs and leans over me, beautiful as a glittering blade. "How do you want to die?"

I don't plan to let him kill me once the time is up. But I'll play along. "I want you to slit my throat while I'm coming on your cock."

His length twitches inside me. "Perfection."

He starts fucking me in earnest then, and I can only gape in delirious wonder. What would the humans back home think if they could see me being taken by this sharp-eared, green-skinned, wickedly pretty creature? They'd probably burn me alive afterward.

I am never going back home. Never. Never…

Energy spikes through my body, and my magic takes over, speeding up West's movements, driving him into me faster, faster. His eyes widen as I fuck myself with his cock, as I lock my legs around his waist, my silver shoes pressed to the small of his back. He gives a choked cry as he comes hard and helplessly, prey to the frantic friction.

I keep using him, careless of everything but my own climax. He gasps, whimpers at the overstimulation. That sound—the sense of my power over him—it finishes me, and my body convulses with a hard, brilliant burst of ecstasy. I scream faintly, clutching his shoulders… and then I let the magic go, releasing his body from my hold.

He moans, the rocking of his hips slowing, stilling. He's gasping brokenly, almost sobbing.

When he straightens his arms and pushes back, looking into my face, our eyes lock.

"You, Kin-Slayer, are a magnificent fuck," he says hoarsely.

"You're not bad yourself."

He cracks an incredulous laugh and shoves himself off me. In his movements I can feel how shaky he is, and it thrills my heart.

"Not bad, eh?" he says wryly. "That's just what every powerful Fae male wants to hear from the women he beds."

"I don't give effusive praise."

"Effusive." He stares. "Where did a farm girl learn that word?"

"From stolen books. The lover I told you about—he used to help me steal them." I rise, pulling on my dress again. "He would explain the motives of the historical figures or fictional characters in each volume, and he'd help me understand human thought processes and emotions, so I could emulate them. He helped me design the mask."

"The mask?" He's lying in the meadow, a naked emerald god among rubies, one arm tucked behind his head.

I stand up straight, shoulders back. With my arms relaxed at my sides, I assume a neutral expression, then a pleasant smile, taking care to soften my eyes, to give them warmth. I know how each tiny muscle of the mask feels, how it should move as I speak, how it reacts to different feigned emotions.

"Good afternoon," I say warmly, pleasantly. "How is your father feeling? My mother sent me over with some warm broth for him. Is there anything I can help you with while I'm here? Oh, it's no trouble at all! What are neighbors for?"

West stares at me, shocked. "Oh fuck. Now I really want to rip your throat out."

I shrug. "Humans like the mask. It makes them feel comfortable. Without it, they can sense something is wrong with me. They watch me, and give me strange looks. So I learned to wear it all the time. Even at home."

"How exhausting."

"It was." I seat myself among the poppies, pluck a blossom from its stem, and tug the petals free, one by one. "Sometimes I would go to the barn during a thunderstorm and scream until I lost my voice. My parents hated that. I frighten them, you see."

"Do you know which of them slept with a Fae?"

"Maybe my father? I look more like him than my mother."

West nods. "Your father could have bred a Fae woman while she was in heat. It's rare that children result from such a union, but it can happen. As an Unseelie, she wouldn't have wanted the trouble of a half-human baby. She would have either eaten you, sold you, or given you to your human father. In this case we know which she chose."

"I should be grateful, I suppose."

"You should." He rises and summons his clothes back onto his body with a twitch of his fingers.

I watch enviously. "Can I learn to do that?"

"Fae powers vary depending on the individual. Some are inborn, determined by the season, the setting, and the position of stars at the time of birth. Others are learned as the child grows up in Faerie."

"You mean, since I didn't grow up here, I missed out on learning certain things. If I stay, could I learn them, over time?"

He studies me, his dark eyes calculating. "But your life is going to be so short, Kin-Slayer. You won't have time for any of that."

The sincerity in his voice stings. He still plans to kill me, after what we just did. After the confidences we shared.

"You're an insidious bastard," I hiss.

He shrugs. "When an Unseelie Fae's sibling is murdered, vengeance is expected. I have to avenge my bitch of a sister, whether I liked her or not. I don't have a choice. We must all wear the masks we are given."

"Then I will have to kill you first. Pity." I give him a slow smile. "You have a tolerably serviceable cock."

"Tolerably serviceable..." He shakes his head, a frustrated laugh skating between his teeth. For some reason, my jabs at his sexual prowess actually unsettle him. Something to remember for later.

He walks over to Riordan and kicks the armor lightly. "I'll wake your friends in a few moments, so you can run to the sparkly city and beg the Wizard's favor. Just remember, no wish of yours can protect you from me. I have ways of killing you no matter where you go—even if you flee to the mainland of Faerie."

I already knew he could spy on us anytime with his scrying stone, but I'd forgotten it until just now. He overheard my conversation with Alice about our wishes. Fuck.

West smirks, pleased at my shock. "That's right, Kin-Slayer. No matter what you wish for, you're mine."

He vanishes in a swirl of green smoke before I can respond, before I can determine why those last two words prompted a thrill through my belly that wasn't fear, but something else entirely.

# 17

## ALICE

When I wake, my eyelids feel sodden and heavy, and my skull aches. I'm cold—deeply cold, all the way down to my bones. My stomach churns as I try to get up, and I give a dry retch.

Dorothy pushes me back down. "Lie still until you recover."

Something crunches under me, and I turn my head to the side.

A carpet of flowers stretches in all directions—but instead of a glowing, living red, they are crisply frosted, encased in ice. The sunlight has changed—it's grayer, colder, and it sparkles on the dead flowers, turning the meadow into an expanse of frozen blood-red diamonds.

It's so beautiful I want to sob, and also to throw up.

Riordan lies beside me, his armor coated in a thin layer of delicate frost.

"What happened?" I ask Dorothy.

She has Fiero nestled in her lap. He's awake, but he's droopy and unhappy. The poor little creature needs decent food and a warm bed.

"The scent of the poppies put you all to sleep," Dorothy says. "But their effect has been muted until we can pass through."

"Is that so?" I rise cautiously on one elbow. "And who's responsible for this mercy?"

She meets my gaze. "I think you already know who it was."

"He likes you, doesn't he?" I narrow my eyes at her. "The West Witch."

Dorothy scoffs. "He hates me. He plans to kill me as soon as he can."

A laugh rises in my chest, but it cracks in the middle on the way to my lips. "That's how Riordan and Caer and I began. Death threats. I thought I would be raped, eaten, dismembered, flayed, skinned—any number of terrible things. It's not that they aren't capable of such atrocities—but they became attached to me, and they couldn't bring themselves to do any of it."

"Why?" Dorothy scoots closer, confusion and curiosity in her eyes. "How does that connection happen between enemies?"

"I'm not sure. I think it's a kind of magic no one will ever understand. You seem so wildly different at first, and then you discover that deep, deep inside, where it matters, you're more the same than you ever suspected. And it's those moments of mirrored thought, those little shocks of realization—they fuse souls together until you can't break free. And then you realize you don't really want to be free, after all. Or maybe there's a new kind of freedom, the kind you craved all along, though you didn't know it."

Dorothy's stare makes me self-conscious. I can't discern her reaction to my words. But I'm freezing, and I can't lie still any longer, nausea or no—so I struggle to my feet.

Some distance away, Jasper is stirring amid the frozen blossoms. He sits up jerkily, his neck snapping into place with a terrifying crack. His golden tan looks a shade paler, more sickly, but he immediately turns toward me and chokes out, "Are you all right?"

Warmth rushes through my chest. He's truly the sweetest person I've ever met. "I'm fine."

He starts struggling toward me through the fragile frozen blooms, crushing them, leaving scarlet carnage in his wake. He's shirtless, shivering. Fae don't normally feel temperature extremes too strongly, but this freeze is magical, and must be affecting him more deeply. Either that, or he's just weaker than most Fae. Maybe there's human blood somewhere in his background.

He crawls to me, lifting dark golden lashes decorated with snowflakes. The intense longing and concern in his bright blue eyes startles and thrills me. I reach for him, pull his cold body close, and tuck my face into the curve of his neck and shoulder.

He's precious to me, and it's frightening how quickly that happened. From the moment I saw him, I knew he was mine. Couldn't be anyone else's. He'd been waiting for me, needing me, and when our eyes met we both knew it.

I turn my face up to his at the exact moment he looks down, and he gives me a soft smile right before he kisses me.

But then, with a creak of metal, Riordan begins to move, and my heart practically leaps from my chest toward him. I twist in Jasper's hold, stretching to lay my hand on Riordan's thigh.

"You're awake," I breathe.

He shifts nearer and reaches for me, metal-clad fingers shaking. He doesn't touch me, but his hands hover over my body, as if he's desperately checking for more injuries. "Kitten."

"Darling," I whisper back.

A rasp of caught breath from inside the armor.

Jasper reaches behind me to clasp Riordan's shoulder. "I'm glad you're all right, my silver guardian. While you recover, I'll go check on the beautiful beast."

He gets up and walks over to the bulky, unconscious shape of Caer. Dorothy follows, stroking Fiero's furry little head and surveying Caer with cool disinterest.

Riordan grunts into his helmet. "The Scarecrow gives his affections far too readily."

"He means well. I think it's rather adorable."

"He's an idiot. And not an idiot like Caer, who is clever but foolishly impulsive. In the Scarecrow's case, I'm afraid there isn't much inside that golden head."

"Does there have to be?" I glance at Jasper, who is stroking Caer's mane and talking quietly to him. "Not everyone needs to be as intelligent as you."

Riordan scoffs. "That's fortunate, because so few beings are."

"So humble," I say dryly. "I may be centuries behind in my education, but I intend to catch up to you one day, you know. Humans don't age here in Faerie, right?"

"They do, but far more slowly than in your world. Here, with some luck and the right healing potions, they can live for hundreds of years." A few moments pass, and then he says, "So you intend to stay."

"You don't have your precious pocketwatch with you. You can't send me back this time."

"I have nothing." His voice is taut, pained. "Nothing to offer you."

My face heats, but I force the words out. "Nothing except your love. That's all I need, Riordan. To know that you regret sending me away. That you love me, with the passion I tasted when you saved my life. You remember, don't you?"

"Remember?" he says hoarsely. "I will never forget how it felt, when my heart's-blood gushed into your body. When I kissed your mouthful of fangs and felt your claws slicing my flesh. When I drove myself inside you, invaded you with all the strength of my will. It hurt me to do that. But it was also the greatest ecstasy I have ever felt—so great I thought my heart would crack from the force of it."

"You tore yourself open for me. Risked your own life to save mine. Why are you holding back now?" I curl my fingers into fists, crushing two handfuls of poppies. "I've given you every opportunity to tell me outright that you care, that anger isn't all that's left inside you. That you love me, and Caer, too."

"Love." There's a dark twist to the word, a dreadful pathos in his tone. "I loved my father, and he tortured me. I loved my brother, and Drosselmeyer killed him. I loved you, and I had to sacrifice you and send you away. I can't love you again, and I can't love *him*, because to lose either of you would finish me. I can't do it, kitten. Please don't ask me."

"The terror of losing someone doesn't kill your love for them," I reply. "The love remains, no matter how you deny it. The fear only holds you back, keeps you from enjoying a life with them while you can. It steals the future *and* the present from you and the one you crave. Fear is a stupid reason not to love." I jump up, brushing flowers and frost from my makeshift garment. "I thought you were smarter than that."

I stalk away before he can reply, and I help Jasper get Caer on his feet. Once he sees me, Caer's monstrous shape recedes until he looks more like himself and less like the beast.

"Your neck." He speaks to Jasper through his wide jaws, his voice slightly clearer than before. "I struck you. I heard your spine snap..."

"I'm all right." Jasper grins and rubs the back of his neck. "I survived." He cups Caer's muzzle and plants a kiss on the beast's nose. "You're forgiven."

It's a marvel to me how Jasper has so much love, poured out so freely, while Riordan keeps his affections barricaded inside his chest. And Caer is an altogether different matter—he seems shaken from the experience, and slinks along next to me as we find the yellow brick road and continue our journey. He walks on two legs this time, and I loop my arm through his bulky furred one, since it seems to steady him.

When we left the forest, the fields seemed to stretch on forever, and the Emerald City was a green jewel in the distance. But now it seems much closer, as if the golden road has folded on itself, bringing our current location and our goal much closer together. By mid-morning we're standing at the edge of a broad moat, eyeing the translucent emerald bridge leading to the gates.

The Emerald City is like nothing I've ever seen, not even in the paintings and books of Lord Drosselmeyer's mansion. Towers pile upon towers, all of them glittering green, and where the sun shines on the jeweled walls it's painfully bright. There's something uncanny in the height of the towers, their clustered forms—something soaring and dreadful, terrifying and ethereal. It affects me like the overwhelming brilliance of Faerie, but instead of delirious madness I feel a horrible, sickening weight in my stomach, a hollow void opening in my mind.

"It feels wrong," I murmur. "So wrong."

The others don't reply. We move ahead, crossing the bridge to the entrance. Riordan clasps the knocker in metal fingers and bangs it three times—each impact a hollow, booming thud that seems to echo through the sky and across the landscape.

No porters or guards appear, but the gates split and fold back to reveal houses and shops of pale-green stone—rows and rows of them, bordering narrow streets paved with yellow bricks. Even the sky overhead has a green tint.

Tall green-clad Fae move silently here and there. They seem to be occupied with daily tasks, but sometimes one will pause and stare into the distance, as if they've forgotten what they meant to do. The silence is uncanny—unlike any town or village I've ever seen.

No one stops or questions us as we wend our way through the city, toward the central cluster of towers. When we reach the palace, motionless guards, armored and helmeted in jade-green metal, flank a broad flight of emerald steps. They don't try to prevent us from mounting the steps or entering the great doors.

My jaw drops as we step into the grand hall. I've never seen such a place, not in paintings or storybooks or my most fantastical dreams. It's as if the entire palace was grown from a gemstone, rooms and staircases cut from its faceted heart, crystals allowed to bloom along its walls and ceilings. The entire place is a glittering haven set with ornate furniture in pristine jade and rich gold. There are green marble tables, crystalline settees covered in tasseled pillows, and jade fountains trickling with green-tinted water.

Jasper's eyes are wide and wondering, and Riordan is moving forward mechanically, wordlessly. Caer is panting, his form rippling and shifting under the influence of clashing emotions. Dorothy stares around, an odd smile on her face, but Fiero squirms in her arms, barking and snarling our surroundings.

Something about Dorothy's expression frightens me. She looks dazed and compliant—the complete opposite of her nature. Riordan mentioned feeling a magical effect when he was last here—a kind of blurred trance. But Dorothy is half-human—she should be able to shake off the enchantment.

I step in front of her and grab her shoulders. "Wake up," I tell her, low and urgent. "Something about this place is very wrong."

She blinks, and the glaze of her eyes clears a little.

"The Emerald Palace affects the Fae," I say tightly. "You have to fight it. Your human side is a strength now, not a weakness. You and I have to keep our heads. We have to remember why we're here."

"Our wishes," she says, blinking. "Yes. We need to be careful."

We follow a pillared hallway that ends in ornately paneled doors, before which stand two guards and an exquisitely gorgeous Fae male with a sheet of shining green hair all the way to his feet. He holds a long roll of parchment that curls in endless loops along the tiled floor.

"Names." He poises his quill over the roll.

"Caer, Riordan, Jasper, Dorothy, and Alice. And Fiero," I add hastily.

The Fae scribe frowns a little. "Two of you have already had an audience with the Wizard. Those two must wait outside. The rest of you may enter."

Obediently, Riordan and Caer move aside. Their silence and compliance makes me so anxious I can hardly bear it. Ever since I've known those two, they've been fighting for control of their own fates and future. I hate that this Green Wizard—this godstar or whatever he is—has taken that from them so easily.

Jasper seems less meekly obedient—just overwhelmed by the beauty of the place. When I glance at him, he actually meets my gaze. He was resistant to the compulsion of the East Witch; maybe he's immune to the effect of the Wizard as well.

"Stay outside with Caer and Riordan," I tell him. "Watch them. See that they don't move from this spot."

"And hold Fiero." Dorothy pushes the dog into Jasper's arms. "If he barks or growls, listen to the warning." She catches me watching her and gives a tight shrug. "I may not like it, but Fiero is safer with him than in *there*." She nods toward the doors the guards are opening for us. "If I lose myself during this audience with the Wizard, I give you permission to slap me."

"Agreed. One more thing—don't make any wish until I say so. Let's see what happens with my wish first."

A shadow of uncertainty crosses her face, but she nods.

"First things first," says the scribe. "You can't appear before the Wizard in that." He grimaces, eyeing the blue-checked cloth I'm wearing, then Dorothy's ragged dress. At a wave from him, a Fae woman steps forward and places a shining emerald cloak around my shoulders, fastening it in front with a gold pin.

She sweeps a second cloak around Dorothy and fastens that as well.

Satisfied, the scribe steps back and gestures us forward with a flourish. Impulsively I take Dorothy's hand, and together we enter the throne room of the Wizard.

# 18

# DOROTHY

My silver shoes ring against the glassy green floor as Alice and I pace forward between soaring columns, toward the dais at the end of the long room.

An archway of twisted green metal stands on the platform, and from its peak hangs a swinging perch—and on that perch is the loveliest bird I've ever seen. It has feathers of green and yellow, an enameled beak of jade and gleaming gold, and sparkling emerald eyes. Its tail sweeps in a long, graceful curve, brushing the floor.

"I wish we had Clara here," whispers Alice. "If he really is a god-star, she'd be able to see his true form. I'm fairly sure *that's* not it."

"How clever." The bird speaks in a cool ripple of unearthly sound, and its body shifts, condensing, then lengthening into the lithe form of a cat. Parts of its body are still enameled—blue, green, and gold—while others are cloaked in rich green fur, like the softest grass.

"What do you think my true form is, human?" says the cat, leaping smoothly to the floor as the perch vanishes.

A strange sensation flows over my body—a compulsion, a desire to kneel, to prostrate myself, and to speak the one true wish of my heart before this great Being, this One who deserves all my worship—

My fingers slacken in Alice's hand, but she renews her grip, squeezing hard until a flash of pain clarifies my thoughts again.

"I have no way of knowing your real form, my lord," Alice says.

"It is just as well. You could not bear its glory."

"Once my master, Lord Drosselmeyer, called all his servants out to the lawn to observe an eclipse," Alice counters. "He gave us special glasses so our eyes wouldn't be damaged by the power of the sun. Are you saying you can't manage a similar feat?"

The cat's lips twitch back, baring its teeth. "Of course I can." A gilded box appears before us. "Open it."

I bend and unlatch the lid. Inside is a tangle of spectacles, all different shapes and sizes, most of them opulent in style, with colored lenses.

"Choose," says the cat, "and I will reveal myself to you. If you choose correctly, I will grant you two wishes instead of one. Choose wrong, and you will be struck blind, and will have to use your one wish to reverse the condition."

Alice's terror is palpable in the strength of her grip. I twist my hand free and lean farther over the chest, peering at the glasses. "What color is the opposite of green?" I ask her. "Red?"

"I think so." Alice stirs the tangle of spectacles, then pulls out a small plain monocle with a clear lens, not a shadow of tint to the glass.

I take out a pair of gilded goggles with deep ruby lenses. "Together?"

Alice nods, placing the monocle over her right eye and closing her left. It's a smart choice—if she's struck blind in the right eye, she'll still have sight in the other. I should close one of my eyes as well.

I settle the red goggles over my face and try to close one eye—but I can't. Both my eyes are pinned open somehow—by magic, I suppose.

Terror stabs through my gut as a bone-chilling laugh unfurls from the cat, echoing through the infinite hollows of the hall as his form changes. His catlike limbs vanish, sucked into a single dancing orb, a blazing star a thousand times brighter than the sun. It sears my eyeballs and stabs blades of white light deep into my eyes, into my brain. I scream, agonized. I scream and scream, while my world blackens, until the only thing I can see is that malevolent white star burning and burning in my mind.

"Enough!" Alice's voice explodes through my screams.

The star winks out, leaving me in darkness.

I try to recall images, colors. A scarlet poppy. West's wicked green face. The pages of the Tama Olc.

But there is nothing. I can remember the names of things, but I can't form mental images to match them. The god-star didn't just steal my sight—he stole my memories of sight as well.

"You chose wrong," whispers a velvet voice at my ear. "Use your wish. Ask me to return what I took from you."

Tears race hot down my cheeks, pouring from my sightless eyes. I don't want to use the wish for this. But I have no choice.

I open my mouth to speak the words—*Return what you took from me*—but Alice cries out, "Think first! Choose your words carefully."

Heart racing, I form the wish, and then I speak it aloud. "I beg you to return my sight and my memories, just as they were before I saw your glory."

"Clever woman." The voice sounds disappointed. "Very well."

My sight flashes back, revealing the throne room with all its colors, contours, and edges.

The Green Wizard stands directly before me, tall and sharp-faced and green from head to toe, dressed in a suit with a long tailcoat. He tosses and catches a small, thick book—the Tama Olc.

He took it from my pocket while I was blind. If I'd wished for him to return what he took from me, he'd have given the book back instead of my sight.

I glance at Alice. She's pale as death, and her right eye is pink with strain, laced with broken blood vessels, but she seems to have her sight in both eyes. With her timely warning, she saved my sight as well.

I owe her for that.

"The Tama Olc cannot belong to you," I tell the Wizard, "unless—" I can't quite remember the conditions, so I turn to Alice.

"Unless you steal it and keep it for a night and a day without the owner's knowledge, or unless it is freely given, or unless the owner dies, in which last case you must wait a year before using it," Alice says.

"A human who knows every condition of use for this arcane spellbook." The Wizard examines her with interest. "A human who chose correctly from the chest, and witnessed my true form without blindness. Most intriguing." He tosses the Tama Olc carelessly back to me, and I tuck it into my pocket again as he nods to Alice. "You have two wishes, human. Make them quickly, before I change my mind."

"I wish for my friends, Caer and Riordan, to be returned to their former selves, alive and whole as they were on the day before they came to you and made their wishes—with all their memories from before that day and since then."

The Wizard tuts. "That's a very complex wish. And since it involves two individuals, it counts as two wishes."

"That's not fair," I interject—but the Wizard whirls, his gaze swerving to me, and it's a force more ancient and terrifying than I can bear. A compulsion to worship him overcomes me, and I nearly crumple; but Alice catches my hand again and moves closer, supporting me.

"Very well," she says. "My wish stands, and I agree that it shall count as two wishes since two Fae are involved."

"I will restore your friends to their previous forms." The Wizard traces his lips with a gleaming emerald nail. "But since you did not specify how long you wanted them to remain as their former selves, the restoration shall be temporary, lasting for only four days."

"You wretched motherfucker" is what I intend to say, but the sense of awe in my mind reverses the words, and they leave my lips as, "Most glorious and generous lord."

"Why thank you." The Green Wizard turns away from us, and his body begins to dissolve, to disappear. "I believe our business is concluded."

Alice is weakening—I can feel her body trembling. But she pulls herself upright. "There must be something I can do for you," she says calmly. "Something you want, as payment for making their restoration permanent."

"Something I want?" The Wizard turns back around, solidifying again. "As a matter of fact, there is. Something I can't retrieve myself, due to—unfortunate circumstances. But you could get it for me. Yes… yes, I think we have a bargain. Complete two tasks for me within the next four days, and your wish shall be permanent."

"What are the tasks?"

"Kill the Wicked Witch of the West, and bring me his scrying stone."

"What?" I gasp. "No, we—I—he's—"

"Too powerful," interjects Alice. "He's too strong for us."

"Not if your Fae friends have their natural forms and their magic back. And you—" The Wizard turns flashing green eyes on me. "You have the Tama Olc, and your pretty silver footwear. I know where the shoes come from—my ally, the Witch of the East. You have killed her, and now you possess the enviable power of the shoes."

Enviable power? All I've noticed so far is a mild increase in my energy levels and speed. That, and my seven days of protection from vengeance.

My doubt must show on my face, because the Green Wizard cocks his head. "Can it be that you haven't yet discovered all the properties of your new footwear? Oh, this is delightful."

"Will you tell me what they do?"

"Ah-ah!" He waggles a finger at me. "That would be too easy. The East Witch told me about those shoes, but I'd rather you work for the knowledge. A visit to Caislean Brea might prove enlightening. It's the ancestral home of the royal clan of this isle. And fortunately for you, it's on the way to the West Witch's domain. Well—nearly on the way. When you come to the three red hills, a short detour south, off the main road, should bring you there. It was once a magnificent city, ruled by a gifted family. There's only one of that dynasty left now, since you smashed the East Witch. How tragic."

"Killing the East Witch was an accident," Alice puts in.

"Oh, of course it was. I've heard all about it. I have eyes everywhere—well, nearly everywhere." His lip curls. "I used to not need spies at all, you know. I could see everything myself— turn my focus anywhere I liked, until my wretched family dumped me here."

"You mean the other god-stars?" Alice says cautiously. "They put you here?"

His form judders, fading out and then back in, except he's taller now—growing taller and more terrifying by the second. His voice is a thin, distant, ethereal wail. "Fallen, fallen. They felled me, banished me, and for what? A small infraction—perhaps several small infractions—petty interferences in the flow of the cosmos—and for that they bound me to this isle, forbade me from interfering in any part of the realm beyond it. I almost outwitted them—I branded my old lover with a curse that would have enabled her to ruin this realm and others. But she was foiled, destroyed."

His head is nearly out of sight now, high above us in the shadows that hide the ceiling. His body is a slim, swaying column, smoothing itself into a pillar of green—and then the color drains away, leaving shining white scales. The serpent's head snakes down, its body undulating, coiling around the columns of the hall. It's immense, long enough to weave itself into a white web between a dozen pillars.

"Witches are wondrous things," the serpent hisses. "Fae with the power to compel other Fae. I drained that power from the South Witch when I killed them, and the North Witch when I banished her, and the West Witch when I cursed him. I used their powers to enchant most of the inhabitants of the Isle. The enchantment lasts, but the power doesn't—not for me. I can spend it, but once it's gone, I have no innate ability to compel anyone. I let the East Witch keep her power so she could help me control the Isle, but I always planned to take it from her eventually. Now she's dead, so I can't get more of that delicious ability. That's why I'm just a little *enraged* at you two. You don't belong here, and you've caused a great deal of upheaval. It's time for you to make it right."

"By killing the West Witch," I manage. "Why don't you do it yourself?"

But Alice speaks up, her gaze fixed on the great ivory serpent. "You can't, can you? You're limited somehow. Limited to illusion magic, wish-granting, and shape-shifting. You have the influence of a god-star, some aura that makes Fae muddled and worshipful when they approach you. But other than that, the only magic you're capable of is through wishes."

I stare at her, impressed. No wonder Riordan admires her mind.

The serpent slithers out from among the pillars, building itself into a column, coil upon coil, while its white scales shift to a lurid, poisonous green. "Clever little human. Yes, my fellow god-stars thought I should be taught a lesson. They wanted me to spend some time serving others, granting their requests. I am forced to grant one wish to each supplicant."

"But instead you corrupt every request," Alice says. "You twist wishes into curses. That's what you did to your lover, the North Witch. She made a wish—something to do with hearts, didn't she? Perhaps she wished to have every heart she desired, after you broke hers—and you created the curse that deformed her. You made her crave actual *living* hearts, and transformed her into a monster capable of producing the Heartless."

"My best work. I'm rather proud of it." The snake shrinks, transforming back into the tall Fae in the tailcoat. "Her brother the West Witch also made a wish, in a moment of weakness, and—well, you've seen him. I turned his skin my favorite color and snatched his power for myself. Unfortunately I also had to grant his request, and I can't reverse a wish unless the supplicant *asks* for a reversal…most irritating. His domain is forbidden to me and my thralls, so I can't deal with him personally. But he's the last of those pesky royal siblings, and with him gone, this Isle of Oz will be entirely mine."

"And the scrying stone?" I cut in. "Why do you want it?"

The god-star narrows his eyes at me. "You know, I think I've answered quite enough questions for one day. Your group may remain here tonight—I'll give orders for you to be housed in the finest rooms of the palace. You'll have privacy, comfort, new clothes, and the most delicious of dinners. Tomorrow will be the first day of your four allotted days. I'd get an early start if I were you."

"And my friends?" Alice tries to keep the plaintive note from her voice, but it doesn't escape me. "Have they been returned to their original forms?"

The Wizard's body vanishes, and his head expands, growing fearsomely large until it shadows the entire dais. His giant eyes blink, and his great mouth opens, releasing a deafening voice. "Leave my presence, and see for yourself."

# 19

# ALICE

I practically run from the Green Wizard's audience chamber.

My heart is booming inside my chest, so violently I'm afraid it might give out. My mind holds no distinct thoughts, only an agonized swirl of *wanting*.

I explode out through the doors into the reception area where Dorothy and I left the others—and there—

And there—

A tall, slim figure stands with his back to me, poised with lazy, lethal grace, his long tail swishing above perfectly rounded ass cheeks. I follow the groove of his spine up to his neck, where silky black hair lies in glossy curls. His black, furred cat-ears twitch.

Caer turns from Jasper, who is gaping at him—and his violet eyes meet mine. His wide, wide mouth stretches in a hideous, glorious grin.

I scream and leap for him.

He catches me in his arms, wraps me up tight against his lean body. His chest is heaving hard, as if he's struggling with sobs.

"Mouse," he whispers into my hair. "Don't leave me again, I beg you."

"Never," I hiss back, clinging to him, digging my nails into his shoulders. "I'm staying with both of you—" And then I remember Riordan, and I jerk back from Caer, my stomach thrilling with anticipation.

The suit of armor has vanished, leaving Riordan's body bare. His smooth brown skin flows over swelling muscles; he's more powerfully-built than Caer, taller than Caer, his features more elegant, more naturally mournful. Each of his cheeks bears an open gash that shows the roots and edges of his sharp teeth. Those wounds, and the scars on his hands, were left upon him by the father who used him as a subject for demented magical experiments.

The illumination from the floating light-orbs behind him glows through his long, sensitive ears, turning their insides pink. His brown hair tumbles in unruly waves around his face, brushing his high cheekbones and sharp jaw. Thick lashes fringe his scarlet eyes—eyes that don't glisten with tears—no, they *burn*, they sear, they enflame me—they immolate me whole, and he hasn't even touched me, or so much as twitched a muscle to move in my direction.

His lips part—I remember the velvety heat of them, their broad smoothness caressing my mouth.

He doesn't speak. But his eyes, oh how they *burn*.

Slowly I disengage myself from Caer and walk toward him, stretching out my hands.

Riordan meets me, scarred fingers sliding through mine. "Kitten," he says quietly.

He pulls me in, pressing our linked hands to the back of my waist, and he kisses me.

Despite being in that armor for so long, he doesn't smell rancid like a human would—he smells like oranges and rich earth, with notes of copper. And he tastes, as he always has, like blood and bittersweet passion, like salt and citrus.

Smooth arms flow around me from behind, and Caer's warm, naked body presses along my back as he encompasses both me and Riordan in the hug. Riordan twitches as if he's going to pull away, but he doesn't.

I could die like this, perfectly happy, surrounded by the two of them.

But I'm not dead, and they're both very, very naked. I defy any mortal woman not to be wildly aroused by two gorgeous Fae males pinning her between their nude bodies. And it doesn't escape my notice that Jasper and Dorothy are watching us.

I break the kiss with Riordan and try to wriggle free, but the two men hold me tight.

"You should find some clothes," I manage breathlessly. "We're staying here tonight—dinner and rooms—"

"And baths, I hope," Dorothy adds.

"And baths, yes." I glance from Riordan to her. She's staring at him with a wondering light in her eyes—and I can't help a double-take, because with Riordan's face revealed, the similarity between them is startling. Dorothy's skin is the same brown shade as his, and her hair, like his, is a deeper brown. Her features are feminine, with an intensity and a darkness that she never showed back in the human realm—and while it's a different expression from Riordan's somber one, there's something alike in both their gazes. They are brother and sister. I don't need any of Riordan's magical tests to confirm it.

Riordan gives her a nod and a half-smile, which she returns with a delighted grin.

It's a heart-warming moment and I hate to ruin it, but I have to tell Caer and Riordan the truth. "Your forms aren't permanent.

Not until we kill the West Witch and deliver his scrying stone to the Wizard."

"I thought it was too much to hope that he'd actually released us," Riordan says morosely. "Did you discover anything about what he is?"

Briefly I tell him about the Wizard's true form, and his story.

Riordan frowns. "Then he's not merely channeling the power of a god—he's a fallen god-star himself. I could learn so much from him—I have so many questions. Or perhaps it would be enough simply to worship him—"

I pull one arm free and snap my fingers in front of his face. "Shit, I thought he'd released you from all that. His presence seems to enchant Fae—it makes them want to submit and worship him. It can't be the compulsion powers he stole from the Witch siblings, because he has used all that up. This must be a natural aura of his. Maybe it's stronger the closer you are to him—or stronger if you're under one of his spells or curses. We should see if—"

"If dinner's ready," Dorothy cuts in. "I'm starved. How do we find our rooms, and the food?"

The Fae woman who gave us the cloaks earlier steps forward. "It would be my pleasure to show you to your rooms. The Wizard has given orders that you shall have everything you desire for your comfort."

"How did he give those orders?" I ask curiously. "He hasn't come out of his audience chamber, and no one has gone in since we emerged."

"I hear him. In here." She touches her temple and gives me a stiff, dazed smile. "You will come with me."

"I will require food for my pet as well. This one," Dorothy clarifies, patting Fiero's head before lifting him carefully out of Jasper's arms.

The Scarecrow hasn't taken his eyes off Caer and Riordan. He seems to have been struck speechless by the sight of their true forms. There's a fascinated kind of adoration in his wide blue eyes, and I recall that none of the Fae in his village had animal ears or tails—nor did they bear marks like Riordan's slashed cheeks and scarred hands. Perhaps it's those oddities that have captured his attention, though I suspect it's more than that. Among the Fae I've seen, Riordan and Caer are certainly notable for their beauty. And Jasper seems adorably susceptible to the charms of anyone who shows him a scrap of kindness.

More of the Wizard's servants approach, folding long emerald cloaks around Caer and Riordan, guiding us through hallways and up staircases until we reach a long, carpeted passage lined with mirrors. The female Fae guiding us opens door after door to beautifully-appointed suites, one for each of us, with bathing chambers adjoining the bedrooms. I've never seen anything so luxurious, not even in Riordan and Caer's home at the Dread Court.

We're ushered into separate suites before I can figure out how to protest the arrangement. I don't want to be alone, not when Caer and Riordan have just regained their true forms—but it seems I don't have a choice.

A table laden with steaming platters and frosted glass bowls is rolled into my room, and more servants follow with an array of green clothing and a basket of cosmetics, soaps, and towels. One servant explains that a healing serum has been added to my bathwater.

After depositing their burdens woodenly, the servants file out of the room and close the door, leaving me alone in the opulent, cavernous bedroom. The door shuts with a loud click, and when I try to open it, it won't budge.

Fuck.

They've separated us and locked us in. I probably shouldn't eat or drink anything, shouldn't trust this place—but the Green

Wizard needs us to accomplish the task he has set, so killing us would make no sense. Despite the annoyance of the locked door, this room is probably the safest place I've been since I returned to Faerie.

My stomach gurgles at the delicious aroma of the food, so I take a few bites before wandering into the bathing chamber. Steam curls from the enormous jade-green tub, and the water smells inviting—like rain-washed grass with a touch of fresh mint. I strip off my makeshift garment and yield my aching bones and scratched skin to the heat of the bath. Awestruck, I watch Caer's claw-marks and all my other injuries heal almost instantly, thanks to the infused magic of the water.

At last, clean and flawlessly healed, I climb out of the bath, towel off, braid my wet hair, and wrap myself in a silken robe. I take more bites of the food—creamy ice-green pudding, frosty green grapes, slices of white fish flecked with green herbs, and green leafy vegetables, lightly sauteed and salted. As I'm munching a slice of green cake, the door to my room swings open.

And then it shuts, having admitted no one.

Or so it would seem.

I hide a delighted smile and continue eating, while my skin prickles with the anticipation of the touch I know is coming.

Along with his natural form, Caer got back his powers of temporary invisibility.

Claws dance along my skin ever so lightly, teasing the robe off my shoulders. The silk slides low, parting in front and nearly baring my breasts.

Warm breath travels the back of my neck, right beside the braid.

"Caer," I whisper.

Faint words, sweet with desire and heavy with hurt. "They took you away from me."

I turn, but he's still invisible. Lips I can't see touch my forehead, a swift kiss, playful and tender. Then the glide of a furred tail along my leg.

His bared teeth and his eyes reappear first—a pair of purple, slit-pupiled orbs and two rows of glittering white fangs. "I was alone for so long."

"Caer." Tears crystallize my vision as I reach for him.

He sinks down before me, between my knees, and leans his head against my stomach, his black hair like raven's feathers against the green of my robe. The rest of him comes back into view strip by strip—his lean, bare torso, long legs clad in loose silky pants of forest-green. I delve my fingers into his hair, massaging at the roots of his cat-ears, while he strokes my calf with elegant claw-tipped fingers.

"Will you tell me what happened?" I venture.

"You already know."

"I think you need to say it."

His head lolls back as he stares up at me. "Very well, mousie." The faintest flash of his old grin, a hint of purple tongue between his sharp teeth. "I was afraid, so I wished for courage. And the Green Wizard gave me the monstrous form you saw, in which I was more fearsome than any living thing. Yet still I was afraid. And the greater my terror, the more monstrous I became."

"And you were in heat…"

"And I was in heat," he confirms, "which made the madness of my terror worse. During my wanderings, before I reached this gods-cursed isle, I tried to slake my lust, but I could not manage it. I craved only one scent, only one body." He slinks lower, between my knees, and turns his face inward, inhaling deeply at the juncture of my thighs. "Fuck… that's it. That's the scent."

"Are you still… in heat?"

"Yes, though the urgency has eased since I took you in the field. It will continue until my body is satisfied that you've been thoroughly bred. That doesn't mean you have to carry a child of mine—there are herbs you can take afterward, spells—"

"So I'm not already pregnant?"

"I would smell it if you were."

His reassurance is a relief. I've spent years caring for children—I'm not ready to have any of my own, not for a long time. Certainly not the half-Fae babies of the mischievous cat-eared Unseelie who slipped into my room. "By the way, how did you get in here?"

He tilts his head, sharp and questioning. "Through the door, darling."

"But it was locked."

"No, it wasn't."

"Strange. I could have sworn it was when I tried it. Maybe someone unlocked it while I was bathing."

"Mmm, you… bathing… I'd like to see that…" His voice fades—he's running both hands up my legs, still mesmerized by the place that's emitting the scent he craves—the tender, trembling part of me that's barely covered by a fold of my silken robe.

His tongue writhes out and traces his lips, leaving them wet.

My body is flush with health, newly healed and still vibrant with the joy of seeing him and Riordan in their true forms again. It responds with a rush of wetness at the mere sight of Caer's wickedly pretty face so close to my sex.

But a faint frown puckers his brow. "Did I hurt you?" He looks up at me, violet eyes flooded with remorse, longing, self-loathing. "In the meadow, did I—"

"No, precious." I take his face between my hands. "It was exactly what I needed."

"Me as well," he breathes, a manic desire lighting his gaze. "May I eat you, sweet mouse? May I devour you until you're too hoarse to vent another scream of pleasure?"

I'm about to beg him to lick me, bite me, fuck me into oblivion—but the door to my room opens again. This time the entrance is filled by a tall, well-toned Fae whose long ears brush the top of the doorframe.

Riordan is shirtless too, every gleaming muscle of his torso on display. His scarlet gaze leaps from me to Caer like a living flame.

"I should have known." His words leak through clenched teeth. Through the slashes in his cheeks I can see how hard he's grinding his jaws. "I'll go."

"No!" I push Caer gently aside and leap up, tightening the belt of my robe before snatching Riordan's hand. He found gloves somewhere—mint-green ones that contrast beautifully with his rich brown skin. But I hate the gloves because they mean he's hiding his scars again.

Riordan lets me pull him into the room, and the door falls shut behind him. I drag the glove off his hand, exposing the scars that crawl over his flesh.

"You don't hide from us," I tell him firmly. Then I half-turn, reaching out to Caer. "And *you*—you don't run from us."

A breath's hesitation, and then Caer rises—a fluid, graceful, catlike movement—and places his hand in mine.

And we are linked, the three of us.

A tenuous, fierce heat quivers in the air. I can feel it building between Caer and Riordan—a violent, frenzied swell of unspoken passion.

"Say it," I whisper. "Whatever you need to say to each other—say it."

Caer bites his lip, pointed teeth denting the soft flesh. His hand flinches in mine, ready to withdraw, to turn coward and flee from this. But I squeeze his fingers, a reassurance, and he swallows... and he stays. Waiting.

"You left me to do it alone." Riordan's voice is hoarse, wretched. "You pushed me to care about her and then you *left* me to sacrifice her heart to the Queen, alone."

Caer's eyes spark. "When have you ever wanted my help? For anything? When have you ever called me any name besides idiot, moron, wretch, fool? When have you ever wanted me around for something beyond errands and games of chance? When did the splendid, oh-so-intelligent Riordan ever require my presence for any of his plans?"

Riordan's hand drops from mine, curling into a fist to match the hand that's still gloved.

Caer takes a step forward, sneering. The two of them are in front of me now, chest to chest, except Riordan is taller, more threatening, looming over the Cat.

But Caer doesn't back down. "Tell me," he hisses. "When have you ever truly needed me?"

"Always." The word cracks from Riordan's throat. Scintillates in the air, a bright match to the kindling that has piled up between us, the unspoken thing made of our heartbeats and blood and teeth.

Caer is struck silent, his violet eyes fractured with bright emotion.

My stomach tightens, and my skin flames. My heart, my nerves, my very bones ache with the depth of what I feel for these two stubborn, beautiful men.

I step closer to them both, tightening the space. "Riordan… you said I shouldn't ask you this… but I am asking." I look into his scarlet eyes—blood and embers, the windows to a desolate heart that feels so much more deeply than he'll admit. "I'm asking everything of you, for my sake and Caer's. I never want to be apart from you again, and I know he feels the same way."

Closer I move, while Riordan's chest lifts and falls, the only sign of the battle within. Slowly I take up his fist, uncurl the fingers, and tug the second glove from his hand. "You're mine, beloved," I whisper. "And you're his, too. You're ours. And we belong to you. Not a burden you have to carry. Not two dependents you must protect. Equals. Among the three of us there is enough cleverness, courage, and heart to sustain us through anything."

Riordan exhales, half groan, half chuckle. "When did my little human farm-girl learn such beautiful words?"

"You should know by now that I'm full of surprises." I rise on my toes while he bends and meets my mouth hungrily. Then I turn and touch Caer's parted lips with mine, giving him a taste of Riordan on my tongue.

Caer lifts his eyes, looking past me to Riordan. In that look there's a promise so beautiful, so courageous, it makes me want to shriek for pure joy.

Riordan makes a strangled sound in his throat—lunges forward, grips the Cat's jaw with a scarred hand, and crushes his mouth against Caer's.

Through Riordan's wounded cheeks, I can see their tongues thrashing—teeth and fury and need. Riordan's unrelenting grip travels to the back of Caer's neck and clamps there, possessive.

An unbound thrill races through me, watching them. Their lips separate, but their foreheads are pressed together, a hard kiss of bone on bone, savage gazes locked. Caer is panting, light and quick, and Riordan growls, "You beautiful fucking idiot."

Caer laughs, breathless—and then both of them turn their faces to me, a fluid, synchronized, predatory movement.

Chills skate over my skin as they both stare at me, their heads tilted against each other. Caer grins, all playful desire, and Riordan's full lips twist, his eyes narrowing with a manic, aching lust.

Their entwined scent rushes over me, violets and midnight, citrus and salt.

My fingers find the knot of my belt and tug it loose.

# 20

# ALICE

When my robe slips to the floor, Caer and Riordan exhale hungrily, eagerly. They could have anyone, these two. Anyone beautiful and powerful, Fae or human. But they want me. They have chosen me, and they belong to me. That assurance leaves no room for self-consciousness.

They shed their clothing—Caer in a frantic rush, Riordan with slow purpose. We don't speak of how tonight might be our only chance to join like this. We simply slide together, fitting as if we are all three pieces of a puzzle designed by the gods themselves. My breasts glide hot and full against Caer's lean chest while his claws trace up my sides. His length pushes against my thigh.

Riordan approaches behind me, undoing my braided hair with the same studied gentleness he used to examine me when I was his captive. The hot tip of his cock pokes at the groove of my ass, and I remember the thickness of that cock, the girth of it shoving into me when I lay Heartless and suffering.

This is as it should be. Not choosing between them—I could never. This is the knot we were meant to tie, all of us. I close my eyes and surrender to sensation.

Hot skin, silky smooth over firm flesh, encompasses me from all sides. The strength rolling from both of them, the swell of muscle and hardness of sinew—it steals my breath, fires my blood to the shimmering heat of a summer's day in the fields. One of my hands travels the slope of Caer's waist and side, while I reach back and grab Riordan's hip with my other hand.

Caer plays with my curved human ears, traces them with his claws, nips at them with his teeth, while Riordan's hips surge against my backside and his hand slips over my sex, between my legs. I whimper at the brush of his fingers across my clit.

"Yes, kitten," he says, low, and then kisses Caer again, right by my ear, while his central finger slips into my wet entrance. He has vanished the claws, but the scars are ever-present, their texture strangely titillating as he adds a second finger.

Caer shifts from kissing Riordan and takes my mouth, his long purple tongue flickering over mine, exploring, filling me with the taste of violets from him and citrus from Riordan. He's careful with his teeth, as I'm cautious with my tongue.

Riordan's fingers pull slowly out of my pussy, and then Caer gasps, a sweet helpless sound passing from his lips into my mouth. The White Rabbit has wrapped his hand around Caer's dick and he's pumping—I can feel the motion against my thigh.

"I get your pussy," Riordan breathes hot against my ear. "Caer takes your mouth."

"Yes," I gasp.

Somehow we move toward the bed, limbs interlaced, hips urgently bucking, spines arching, sharp exhales issuing from each of us in turn as questing fingers find new hollows, new points of heat and pleasure. I'm kissing Riordan now, utterly abandoned to the raw, glorious agony that is his wicked, ravaged mouth. He tastes like sweet, dark death and mortal fire. It hurts, and I cut my tongue and lips a little on his teeth, but I keep kissing him through the salty blood because I've wanted him so much, for so long.

"I fucking love you," I whisper savagely to him, and his grip on my back tightens.

Caer is behind Riordan, running his fingers wonderingly over his friend's body as if he can't quite believe he's being allowed to touch Riordan this way. Once, when his claws pass over Riordan's nipple, Riordan nearly snarls at him—but his cock bobs at the stimulation, and Caer notices. The Cat grins wickedly and reaches both arms around Riordan from behind, cupping Riordan's pectorals and then playing with both nipples at once.

Riordan only allows it for a few seconds before he whirls and tackles Caer bodily, wrestling him down onto the bed. I watch, fingers tucked between my legs, helplessly wet for both of them. I've seen them fight before, less playfully, and it's even more arousing this time. Their taut bodies curve around each other, sinewy arms straining and long legs thrashing. Caer slashes Riordan across the chest, and Riordan throttles him down, red eyes gleaming, settling astride Caer's hips. In this new position, their cocks are pressed together, and Caer chokes out a groan of bliss at the friction.

Riordan bends down and kisses him ferociously, leaving blood on the Cat's lips. "On your knees on the bed," he orders. His hips buck once, firmly, grinding their dicks together before he climbs off the Cat.

Flushed and disheveled, Caer rises upright, both knees planted on the mattress. As his eyes meet mine, his cock twitches. I take a second to admire it—pale pink, fading to delicate lavender at the tip.

"Come here, mouse." He gives me a slow, sultry blink of his cat-eyes and circles the base of his shaft with his fingers.

"Don't worry—since I'm coming in your mouth, there won't be any barbs this time."

I crawl onto the mattress and bathe the tip of his dick with my tongue. The sweetness of his precum is tantalizing. He lets out a faint cry, one hand clasping my head, fingers sunk into my hair.

In this pose, my rear must be too inviting to resist, because Riordan's hand closes on one cheek of my ass immediately, and the huge, hot end of his cock prods at my entrance. I freeze, desperate for that fullness. My pussy lips feel swollen, heavy, almost sore—aching for him.

"Together," he says to Caer, and they move into me as one. Caer's dick slides between my lips, over my tongue, and Riordan's enormous cock surges into my pussy.

I forget to breathe.

Caer tastes like he smells—faintly floral, with a midnight sweetness. And Riordan feels like I remember—so big, so smooth, so warm and huge and *filling* that I sob a little around Caer's dick, tears pooling in my eyes.

"Mousie, don't cry." Caer strokes my hair from my temples and shifts back, slipping his cock out of my mouth.

"Maybe you taste terrible," Riordan grunts, seating himself deeper inside me.

"Want to judge for yourself?" Caer gives him a lascivious smirk.

"You taste delicious," I manage. "It's just—I've wanted this—with both of you—for so long—" I'm not going to cry. I will *not* ruin this moment.

"Oh mousie." Caer crouches low on the bed, cupping my face, bending to kiss my cheeks and lick my tears. "Sweet one." His tongue glides across my mouth, and his soft lips follow, a reassuring pressure. Meanwhile Riordan has reached under my stomach and is manipulating my clit with such studious skill he has me gasping into Caer's mouth before I can form another coherent thought.

"Oh gods," I pant. "Oh gods, oh fuck—"

"Come for us, pet," coaxes Caer.

"She always comes for me," Riordan says quietly, while the pad of one finger jiggles my clit with merciless expertise. "She can't help it, can you, kitten? Not when I know every bit of you so well."

The motion over my clit increases until I'm frantic, I'm venting tiny screams of helpless need, while Caer laughs and kisses me over and over, sweet wet fire and wicked tongue.

Riordan's voice deepens. "Come on my cock, Alice. I want to feel you tremble around me. Come, beloved."

And at that word, I come, my pussy tightening around Riordan's thick shaft. Caer swallows each whimper I release into his mouth.

I'm shaking, tears of bliss slipping from my eyes. Caer laps away more of my tears, then rises on his knees again and feeds me his cock. I suck it eagerly, rocking forward on him and backward on Riordan's length, the three of us finding a swaying rhythm.

"Come with me," Caer says between gasps, reaching out, but he's not speaking to me. Out of the corner of my eye I see Riordan grasp Caer's offered hand—and then I feel them both tensing at the same moment—Riordan filling my pussy with warm jets of cum, Caer spilling his hot, sweet release over my tongue. I am full, so full—I'm whole at last, bound to them now—I can sense the intangible link connecting us, a golden chain of pleasure and devotion. Their joined male groans are the most beautiful, erotic thing I have ever heard.

But in a half-second of silence between those groans, I hear another moan—from somewhere else in the room. The two Fae hear it too, but Caer waits until I swallow every bit of his cum and suck the head of his dick clean, and Riordan takes his time easing his cock out of my pussy.

Then the White Rabbit swings off the bed and stalks over to a pair of gilded green doors—a closet.

He throws the doors open, and there stands the pretty blond Scarecrow, cock in hand, his cheeks scarlet. His pants are around his ankles.

# 21

# ALICE

Riordan grabs Jasper by the back of the neck and drags him out. "Spying, were you?"

"I didn't mean to!" Jasper chokes. "My room was too big, and I missed Alice, so I came to see her. But then I heard her leaving the bath and I... well, I knew she doesn't like to be observed while she's naked, so I went into the closet. I thought I'd come out again once she was dressed, but then she seemed so happy to be alone, enjoying her feast—and then *he* came in—" He points to Caer. "And... I never seemed to find the right moment to come out of the closet."

Caer leaps off the bed and prowls behind the Scarecrow, his grin wider than ever and his purple eyes alight with mischief. "How naughty of you," he purrs. "I didn't think you had it in you to do anything remotely sneaky. Such a good boy, you are." He snaps his sharp teeth together, right by Jasper's ear, and Jasper startles.

Riordan moves his hand to grip Jasper's throat. "Did you like what you heard, Scarecrow?"

"Clearly he did." Caer lower himself to a crouch, his mouth on a level with Jasper's erect cock. Jasper whimpers a little, his cock buzzing softly.

Caer's eyes widen. "Shit. Riordan, did you see that?"

"It vibrates." Riordan tries to say it casually, but his voice is thicker than usual, and his own cock is stiffening again. "What of it?"

"I'm only saying—it looks rather tempting." The Cat tilts his head, eyeing the precum beaded at Jasper's tip. "I don't usually take a cock in the ass, but this one—I could make an exception."

Riordan stares down at him. "You're joking."

"I'm not joking. I think it would feel marvelous." Caer licks his teeth and leans in. "But I don't think this soft little Fae could muster the backbone to do the job properly. He's a tender little dumpling, aren't you?" He pinches Jasper's ass. "You couldn't fuck me thoroughly, not if your life depended on it."

I've had enough. I rise from the bed, conscious of the slickness coating my inner thighs, and the fresh flood of wetness brought on by Caer's games.

"Stop teasing the poor thing," I order. "Riordan, let go of him. He's mine."

Riordan releases Jasper's throat, and Caer retreats, snarling softly in his throat.

Jasper stares at me as I approach, adoration in his eyes as he surveys my bare body.

I reach up, slide my fingers into his golden curls, and tug his face down for a kiss.

Caer snarls again, and I'm reminded of what Riordan said—that the Cat never learned to share. But he did well enough sharing me with Riordan just now, and he's clearly attracted to Jasper. I think he can be persuaded.

Softly I break the kiss, letting my body skim against Jasper's. His dick vibrates against my thigh, and I smile up at him. "Would you like to play with us?" I murmur.

He swallows hard and nods, his blue eyes bright with hope.

I turn to Riordan, relieved to find his gaze fiery with interest.

"He can join," says Riordan, low. "But he must agree to obey our commands. Our last pet proved to be rather stubborn, didn't she, Caer? Rather too strong and independent to be truly submissive. I think we have space for a new one, as long as he knows his place."

"Oh, I like that." Caer stalks nearer again, his tail swishing against Jasper's rear. "Can you do that, precious? Can you be our soft little pet?"

Jasper's face lights up still more. "I would love nothing more than to serve all of you, in anything you ask."

"But we won't ask anything dreadful," I assure him. "Or anything you'd rather not do." I throw a warning glare at the Cat and the Rabbit. Caer gives me a joyously devilish grin, and Riordan smirks.

Caer darts in, one hand at the small of my back, the other curled around Jasper's chin. "My first command to you, pet, is to show how quickly that vibrating dick of yours can bring our delicious Alice to orgasm."

And so begins the longest, most decadent night of my life.

I come with Caer's long purple tongue writhing inside me and Jasper's vibrating cock touched to my clit, while Riordan murmurs, "Open for me, kitten," and coats the surface of my obedient tongue with his cum.

When Caer lies on his back on the bed, legs up, and takes Jasper's dick in his ass, I come again, with Riordan's fingers on my sex and my hand around his cock.

I climax again with Jasper's face buried in my pussy, while Riordan bends Caer over and fucks him until he screams and comes hard, all over the floor.

I lose track of how many combinations we've tried—how many hours have passed. I only know that eventually there's a lull, a gradual emergence from the frenzied haze of sex. We're no longer clawing and humping and exchanging frantic, hungry kisses... we've settled into a soothing, mellow contentment. Naked skin against skin, with the scent of cum and arousal heavy in the air.

I'm lying limp and blissful in the center of the bed, with Jasper softly kissing one of my breasts and Caer playing with my hair, winding it around his slim fingers and combing it with his black claws. I'm sated, or so I believe—but Riordan thinks otherwise. He's between my spread thighs, lapping my swollen clit, determined to coax one more orgasm from my body. He kisses my pussy, over and over, so tenderly I want to cry. When I fumble for his hand, he gives it to me. Gripping it for leverage, I feed the tiny spark of arousal I feel, nurturing it while Riordan bathes my pussy lips, the inside of my entrance, and my clit, over and over.

Jasper closes his mouth over my nipple, his lips soft and wet, sucking gently. Caer licks my collarbone, nuzzles against the pulse point of my neck, and whispers, "Make that pretty little pussy flutter for us one more time, mousie. Such darling, tender, suckable flesh you have, so very biteable—" and he nips my shoulder, while his claws travel in a slow circle over my other breast.

I'm panting, rising to the peak again, and Riordan senses it in the force of my grip on his hand. "Jasper," he says through another lick. "I need your cock again. For her."

Jasper shifts his hips, bringing his rigid cock near enough for Riordan to take it and set its tip delicately against my clit.

With a low hum of pleasure at Riordan's touch, Jasper lets himself vibrate, and I squeal softly at the friction.

"Yes, darling, yes," Caer moans against my neck, and with a tiny shriek I come for them, sharp little mewls of pleasure leaving my lips as the bliss bathes me again.

"Good girl," says Riordan, warm approval in his tone. He's stroking Jasper's cock, and within seconds the Scarecrow bucks against my side, clinging to me while he comes, while his release sprinkles my skin.

"Such a good girl," echoes Caer. "And such a good pet, too." His body is aligned with mine on the opposite side from Jasper, the two of them pinning me in a sandwich of naked chests and sleek Fae limbs.

Riordan lets go of my hand and gets up from the mattress, licking my arousal from his broad lips. He stands at the end of the bed, surveying the three of us, and for a moment I fear that he thinks there is no room for him.

"Stay," I beg him.

"We all need rest. And I don't sleep well with others."

"Try it. We'll give you a bit of space, just beyond Caer, see? The bed is big enough."

Caer stops nibbling at my earlobe and says, "Can it be? Is the studious researcher going to *cuddle* with me at last?"

"Keep dreaming," snarls Riordan. He drapes his long body at the very edge of the mattress beyond Caer, maintaining space between them. The lighted orbs in the room dim their glow, and my mind begins to blur with sleep. Before I completely succumb, I wonder if Dorothy is all right, alone in her room. She did not belong in this medley with us, but I hope she is comfortable. Though I can't imagine anyone being nearly as comfortable as I am right now.

I wake in a knot of interlaced limbs, with Jasper's face pressed to the back of my shoulder and Riordan's breath warm on my lips. Caer is curled up at the end of the bed, the semicircle of his body encompassing all our feet. While we were asleep, he must have been busy—he has piled every pillow, sofa cushion, blanket, sheet, towel, and bit of spare clothing all around us, making the bed into a large nest. His tail is curled around my ankle.

Though he seems to be asleep, Riordan is erect, his hardness prodding my belly. I crave him again, with a hollow need beyond the fiercest hunger I've ever felt. Slowly I adjust my position, curling my body and shifting my hips, hooking my leg over his hip until the head of his cock touches my center, a warm, blunt pressure. I want so desperately to push forward, to draw him inside me, but first I whisper, "May I fuck you?"

He stirs, and without opening his eyes says, "Always."

With a soft moan I rock my hips forward and impale myself fully on his cock. For a moment I simply rest there, enjoying the connection.

His dark lashes part, and his scarlet eyes gleam into mine. "Kitten."

My pussy flutters. "Say it again."

"Kitten," he says, deeper, richer.

"Oh gods." I move my body on him, slow deep thrusts. The motion stirs Jasper behind me, and his warm hand slides over my breast.

"Mind if I join you?" he asks Riordan in a soft, sleepy voice.

"Mm," says Riordan, and I murmur, "Yes," though I'm not sure what he has in mind.

Jasper lifts my leg, the one I arched over Riordan's hip, opening me wider.

A trembling warmth stimulates the lips of my sex, and I recognize the feeling of magic. The Scarecrow is doing something to me, to ease the way for whatever he's planning. He swirls his fingers around the place where Riordan and I are joined, collecting my arousal. Then he paints my asshole with the wetness before working one finger inside that tight opening.

"Shit," I breathe, freezing.

"Trust me." Jasper kisses my shoulder, working a second finger into my hole.

Riordan helps him hold my leg up as the Scarecrow eases his slim cock into my rear channel. He takes his time, while I gasp, eyes watering at the faint burn and the overwhelming sense of fullness. Another warming rush of magic, and the burn disappears, leaving only the satisfying bliss of *two* Fae cocks in my body.

Both males begin to move at once. Riordan's huge cock rolls through me slickly, easily, while Jasper's tugs a little with every thrust.

"I can feel you inside her," Riordan grits out. "Gods, that's good."

And then Jasper *vibrates* inside me, and Riordan barks out a harsh sound of shocked pleasure—a sound I've never heard from him before. I moan at the same time, utterly and blissfully stimulated. I don't even have to try for this climax—it's coming to me, surging nearer with every powerful thrust of Riordan's hips, every buzzing thrust of Jasper's incredible dick.

Caer is awake now, blinking at us with sleepy violet eyes. He crawls around our bodies, up to the head of the bed, and slides his cock across Riordan's cheek, right over the gash that exposes Riordan's teeth. Riordan turns his head, opening his lips slightly, and Caer rubs his cock across them, right through the groove of Riordan's parted mouth, over and over. Mesmerized, I watch the two men I love joined in this lewd act, while my body is stuffed with cock and my mind overwhelmed with the scent of their skin, their heat, their arousal.

A stronger vibration from Jasper jolts through Riordan and me, and I clutch his arm, half-screaming, "Fuck, fuck," as the orgasm explodes star-bright through my clit. Riordan roars aloud with the force of his climax, his body shuddering against mine, and Caer comes with a spurt that dapples my face with his cum. Jasper is coming too, pumping a hard release into my ass, moaning sweetly against the back of my neck.

We drift into sleep again, and this time Riordan doesn't protest being woven into the knot of everyone's limbs. I wake on my back, with Caer parting my legs and petting my pussy, and when I nod he slides in, fucking me while I lie between Riordan and Jasper. The little barbs along his dick lock us together again, and when he's done, he exhales a great sigh of relief before pulling out and falling asleep between my legs, with his face pillowed on my lower belly.

Somewhere deep in the dreams that follow, I become aware of a thumping. No, a pounding, knocking—louder and louder—until suddenly there's an explosion I can't ignore—a thunderous, concussive blast that startles me upright.

And there, in the doorway of my bedroom, with her hands outstretched and her eyes blazing, is Dorothy. Fiero stands staunchly at her side, yapping an alarm. What used to be the bedroom door is now a pile of dust.

"By the stars," growls Riordan, dragging a pillow over his crotch. "What the fuck are you doing?"

"Saving your asses," says Dorothly sharply. "You've been in here for two days."

My stomach drops, plummeting into a bottomless well of horror. "What?"

Dorothy nods. "A spell, a charm—something is keeping you in this room, making you lose track of time. I nearly succumbed to it as well, but—never mind that now. Get dressed. We're leaving this wretched place."

# 22

# DOROTHY

Riordan, Alice, Caer, and Jasper are silent as we leave the gates of the Emerald City and cross the bridge. I may not always be good at identifying emotions, but in this case, I can guess that they are stunned, embarrassed, wretched to think they've been fucking each other's brains out, wasting half the time we've been given to accomplish the Wizard's task.

The Wizard's people don't try to stop us from leaving. One even offers us a map, which I'm not sure we can trust—but Alice accepts it anyway.

We travel west, along a plain dirt road instead of a yellow one. Only when we're a good distance away from the Emerald City does Alice speak.

"I'm sorry, Dorothy," she says. "Thank you for pulling us out of there. You could have left us behind."

"You're my friend, and he's probably my brother," I say shortly, with a glance at Riordan. "Besides, I can't defeat the West Witch alone. He might not be able to kill me yet, but that doesn't mean he'll yield easily."

"It seems the enchantment on our rooms hampered our ability to discern the passage of time," Riordan says. "How did you break free?"

"After a bath and a meal, I felt unbearably tired, so I went right to sleep. I only woke up because Fiero began barking. There was someone in my room, sliding their hand under my pillow where I put the Tama Olc. When I woke up, they hurried out of the room. If it hadn't been for Fiero, they would have taken it, and I wouldn't have roused enough to realize that there was no clock in my room, and no window—no way to tell the time. My door had locked behind the intruder, but I broke it down and questioned one of the servants until they gave me a straight answer about how long we'd been in our rooms. I could sense Riordan, so I made my way to your room, Alice. Again, the door was locked—"

"It seems the locks on those doors operate by the will of the Wizard," Riordan says grimly.

"Perhaps. Anyway, no one in your chamber would answer my knocks or my shouts, so I had to demolish that door as well."

Through the gashes in Riordan's cheeks I can see the tight set of his teeth. "I should have realized what was happening. I should not have let my guard down. It won't happen again," he vows darkly.

Alice glances up at him apprehensively, then glares at the mint-green gloves covering his hands. I have no idea why she doesn't like the gloves. We're all dressed in green—Riordan in a crisp shirt and sleek pants, with a brocade vest; Jasper in embroidered green silk, highly unsuitable for traveling; and the former Beast, Caer, in loose green pants and an open, blousy shirt that cinches into a ruffle around each wrist.

Caer stalks ahead of Riordan, Alice, and me, swinging up into a tree now and then and prowling through the branches before leaping back down. He doesn't speak.

Jasper walks in front of us all, tossing sticks for Fiero, who races ahead to fetch the twigs and then carries them back.

Halfway through the morning we pass through a strange village entirely populated by life-size statues. They seem to be made of bone-white porcelain, with painted clothes and faces. Some of them are intact, while others are missing limbs or larger chunks of their fragile bodies. The road is littered with shards of porcelain that crunch and crack beneath the heels of my silver shoes.

As we pass through, I think I see one or two of the figures move slightly. But every time I whirl and look, they are so still I'm convinced I imagined it.

"A wish gone wrong, no doubt," says Riordan. No one answers him, but I spend the next hour wondering what kind of wish could have wrought such a nightmare.

Around noon, the dirt road we're traveling cuts through another town—a more normal-looking one this time—where Caer barters a jeweled ring he stole from the Wizard's palace, in exchange for a basket of provisions. He inquires about horses, or some kind of mount, but he's told there are none for hire.

Alice asks one of the shop owners if we're on the right path to the West Witch's domain, but he won't give us a straight answer, only mutters, "If you know where you're going, you'll get there when you're supposed to."

"We need to stop by Caislean Brea first," I remind Alice as we leave the town behind. "That's where I can find out more about my shoes and their powers."

"Unless that was another trick of the Wizard's," Alice counters. "A detour so we would waste more time."

"It didn't seem to be." But I hate that she could be right.

After another hour, I experiment with using my magic to help Alice's legs move faster, while the rest of us race along the road at Fae speed. But as Riordan explains, every Fae has different abilities, and although Caer and I feel as if we could keep running indefinitely, Riordan can only do short bursts of speed, and Jasper has even less stamina. Besides which, I don't care to use up all my magic to propel Alice along. She doesn't seem to like it, and nearly falls on her face several times. So we continue at the usual pace, which for me feels maddeningly slow.

"What if I run ahead to find Caislean Brea, and learn what I can about my shoes?" I suggest. "Then I could meet you on the road, or at the border of the West Witch's domain. I'll be able to sense Riordan—it's not as if I'll lose you entirely."

"Will she really be able to sense you from that far away?" Alice asks Riordan.

He surveys me with a kind of curious pride. "Once the book connected us, she could sense me across realms."

Automatically my hand travels to the back pocket of my leather pants, where I wedged the Tama Olc. "I'll find you again, I swear."

"Then go," he says. "Do what you have to do."

"But is that wise?" Alice protests. "She doesn't know Faerie very well. What if she runs into some terrible danger?"

"Without you all slowing me down, I can run away from anything I encounter." I pause, surveying my ruby-studded silver shoes. "These seem to give me a speed greater than that of most Fae."

"If you think it's safe…" Alice says doubtfully.

"Nothing in Faerie is safe," Caer puts in. "She's in as much danger alone as she is with us. Makes no difference. Go on, off with you." His violet stare is a challenge.

"First…" I look at Jasper. "I think Fiero should stay with you, in case I run into danger where I'm going. I think he'll be safe in your care."

"I'll protect him with my life." Jasper beams, clearly overjoyed by my approval. I suppose I can see the appeal of his sunshiny, all-too-happy-to-please personality. But my affinities lie with cruel smiles and clever tongues.

I turn away from Jasper so he won't think my blush is about him. After picking up Fiero for a kiss, I surrender him into Jasper's arms so he doesn't try to follow me. "See you soon," I call over my shoulder, and I race ahead, down the road.

Caer runs alongside me for a long while, but eventually I outstrip him. It's true, then—the shoes lend me extra speed, just as they gave me additional grace for dancing. I suppose those benefits outweigh the annoyance of not being able to remove them. Luckily my toes have never been erogenous zones for me, or I'd be more bothered by it.

The warm afternoon air rushes past me, the fields and forest along the road reduced to a bright blur. I run full-out, delighted by the fact that with the shoes, I don't even get breathless, nor do my legs tire.

By late afternoon, the sky has begun to cloud over, looking more ominous by the second. The dirt road has cobbles now, half-buried from disuse, but still visible. When I reach three large hills of red rock, I turn south onto another road, following it between those hills and up to a ridge overlooking a great valley.

On that ridge I pause to survey the dramatic landscape below me.

Under a heavy underbelly of black clouds that flicker with green lightning lies a ruined city. It looks as if some great celestial body crashed to earth directly on top of it, turning half the buildings into a black crater. Blackened streaks extend outward from that primary impact point, giving the appearance of a midnight sun painted across the city. At the north side, several streets remain mostly intact, though roofs have partly collapsed and walls are crumbling. From that sector of the city rises a castle, bristling with black, needle-like towers.

This must be Caislean Brea, the once-great seat of the rulers of this Isle, crushed by the advent of the god-star. Somewhere in those ruins lies information about the shoes I've inherited—

information I'll need if I'm to help my friends defeat the West Witch.

Again, a twinge of regret, of reluctance thrums through my heart. I don't *want* to kill him. But I don't have a choice, because despite the understanding and lust we share, he's going to kill me. It's expected of him. It's the Unseelie way. And my only chance of surviving his vengeance is to slay him first. Not to mention the fact that killing him is the only way my half-brother gets to retain his natural form. Otherwise he'll live out his life in misery, sealed into a suit of cursed armor.

I owe Riordan the loyalty of a blood-bond, just as West owes the same loyalty to his dead sister. And with Riordan and me, the loyalty is joined by a growing affection, one I believe is mutual. I can't abandon that new, fragile bond for the sake of a green-skinned bastard, no matter how good a fuck he might be.

I run through the city, mulling over how much things have changed for me. All those years learning how to fake humanity, how to conceal my callous nature and mimic the emotions and morality of humans—all of it feels wasted, because everything is different here. Though I suppose the effort wasn't truly useless, since it enabled me to survive in the human realm.

I wonder how long I would have been able to keep wearing that mask. Would I have gone mad from repressing my true Unseelie self? Would I have eventually said, "Fuck it," and killed someone carelessly, just to see how it felt? Or would I have slowly become more human, and lost both my Fae nature and the magic that goes with it?

A crack of stone and a rattle of pebbles from a nearby building startles me. I halt, peering around, trying to pierce the shadows cloaking the ruins.

Something is still alive in this city. I can't imagine it's anything good.

Another scrabbling sound, and my stomach does a dreadful flip. I leap ahead immediately, running for the castle.

As I run, I begin to see shapes resolving from the shadows, crawling along half-collapsed walls, leaping from slanted rooftops to broken chimneys. More and more shapes emerge, flanking the moss-coated cobblestone street, swinging from sheets of ivy. Sometimes I could swear I catch the flutter of gray wings beneath the lowering sky. A malevolent chittering noise comes from the darkest corners, carried through the gloomy air on a breeze redolent with the scent of dead things.

"Fuck the Wizard," I hiss to myself as I try to increase my speed, to draw more power from the shoes and outstrip the creatures. There's no doubt in my mind now—he directed our group to this place out of sheer malevolence. He seems like a fickle sort; maybe he can't decide which he wants more—the death of the West Witch, or the defeat and despair of our group. He'd probably love to see Caer and Riordan trapped in their cursed forms forever, with Alice mourning them eternally.

But he didn't expect me to come to the ruined city alone. I'm going to survive this, if only to spite him.

The chittering and clicking noises are all around me now, louder and closer. As I run across an open square, toward the open drawbridge of the castle, I catch my first glimpse of the creatures hunting me.

They have long, stick-thin limbs, coated in blue-gray fur, each leg as lithe and flexible as a monkey's tail—and there are six of those limbs to each bulbous body. Some of them have small wings that can propel them a little way through the air. They have no necks; their faces protrude right out of their furred, lumpy torsos, between their two foremost limbs. The faces remind me of the catfish my father likes to catch and fry—flat and bland, with glum mouths and horribly wide-set eyes.

"Shit," I hiss, and I bound ahead, onto the drawbridge.

Several of the creatures scurry onto the chains of the drawbridge, following me along. They climb up those chains until they're high above me on both sides—and then they leap.

I dodge the first one. Another cartwheels on its flexible legs, right in front of me, then raises itself high and opens its jaws, revealing a cavernous maw lined with rows of teeth marching all the way down its gullet. It looks as if the creature's entire body is going to turn itself inside out and become a rolling ball covered in razor teeth.

And that gives me an idea.

As the creature screeches, opening its mouth wider, I feed my magic into the motion, continuing that stretch past the point of comfort, until the beast's skin and flesh rip and it really does turn itself inside out. With a choking rasp, it goes limp in a puddle of its own blood.

More creatures hail down around me, and I lash out with magic. I boost their momentum, speeding up their descent so they smash against the bridge with a *splat* instead of landing as they intended. When they perform their leggy cartwheels, I feed that momentum and roll them into the slick black water of the stagnant moat.

But there are too many of them. I can't hold them off forever.

Once I've created a clear path, I run for the castle gates, which are stuck partway open. I slip through, pelting across the rubble-filled courtyard to the inner keep. That door is also half open—but when I start to dive through, I skid to a halt, my heart lodged in my throat.

Long limbs, like tails or tentacles, are sliding out of the crack between the doorpost and the great wooden door of the keep. Each limb is as thick as my waist and bristles with coarse, blue-gray fur. The door creaks wider, and a slab-like body squeezes through, bearing a far, far bigger version of the flat, dead-eyed, catfish faces the smaller creatures wore. Once through the doorway, the monster swells, inflating to terrifying proportions.

My scream dies in my throat. I'm mute with terror, backing away from the monster—but peril lies behind me, too.

There's only one person who might be watching this. One person with the power to save me.

"West," I croak through my dry lips. "West...remember what you said... that you want to kill me yourself..."

With a crack and a puff of green smoke, he appears right on top of the beast's body, just above its eyes. It chitters and moves as if to roll and throw him off. But he's holding his staff this time—the one he had when I first met him—and he rams it down, almost carelessly, punching through the furred flesh of the monster into what must be its brain.

He looks rather glorious perched there, wearing a huge flowing coat of dark leather, its shoulders decorated abundantly with raven feathers.

"Hello, Kin-Slayer." He smiles, riding the beast down as it collapses, then hopping lightly off its slumped corpse. "Miss me?"

"No," I gasp.

"Pity." He steps past me, extending his staff. Forks of green lightning shoot from its tip, turning several of the smaller beasts into balls of green flame. The others skitter off the drawbridge and back into the darkness of the ruins.

A crack of thunder explodes from the menacing clouds overhead, and torrents of rain crash down, pummeling the cobblestones, soaking me to the skin in an instant. I clap my hand over the Tama Olc in my back pocket, trying to shield it as I run past the great dead beast into the keep.

West follows me, producing a few small orbs for light, then pausing in the crack of the door to look out at the rain. I pull the spellbook out of my pocket and inspect it anxiously—but it's perfectly dry. Not a spot of moisture anywhere on it, not even from my wet fingers.

"That's a tempting little volume." West peers over my shoulder, rain dripping from his black hair onto the book. Each drop disappears the instant it contacts the page.

"It's mine," I retort.

"Of course it is. And this castle, ruin though it may be, is mine. So I must ask, Kin-Slayer—what are you planning to steal from me?"

His scent, brisk as the icy rain, fresh as clipped grass, suffuses each breath I inhale, thrilling in my lungs, bringing every nerve in my body to life.

I step away from him. "I plan to take nothing but knowledge."

"Ah, but knowledge is the most precious treasure in this place! The only treasure remaining, I do believe. The castle has been thoroughly stripped of anything else which might have the slightest value."

"If you'll tell me where the library is, I'll find the information I need and leave this place," I tell him haughtily, as another roar of thunder shakes the stone walls.

The Witch laughs, dark eyes glittering. In the yellow light of the orbs he conjured, his green skin looks almost golden—a strange effect. "You'll just find the information and leave? You make it sound so easy. Very well, Kin-Slayer, come along."

We traverse echoing, cavernous halls, long corridors, and broad staircases, until he flings open a pair of dusty doors and motions for the lighted orbs to sail through ahead of us. They float upward and multiply, spreading out to reveal a room as big as a dragon's den, inhabited by rows upon rows of bookshelves, scores of them—no, hundreds of them.

"In the Golden Age of this Isle, my ancestors were fascinated with collecting and inscribing knowledge," says the Witch. "They encouraged the composition of many volumes of science, history, and philosophy. And they celebrated storytelling as well… tales of romance and wonder, delight and horror. I grew up reading them all, both true and imagined. I know every book in this vast library, Kin-Slayer."

He slants a triumphant look my way, as my heart sinks with the understanding of how long it would take me to search through these volumes and locate the information I seek. I spent my youth devouring the contents of a few precious stolen books. Whenever I did dream of libraries, I thought of Lord Drosselmeyer's mansion. As the wealthiest man in the area, I knew he must have a large room stocked with interesting volumes. But I never dreamed a library like this could exist. It extends so far into the bowels of the castle that I can't see the far wall—and it's two stories high, with narrow walkways and railings running around the second tier of bookshelves.

"I assume you're looking for information about the properties of my dead sister's shoes." West's voice is low, faintly bitter, tinged with challenge. "I could direct you to the right book, for a price."

My heartbeat kicks into a faster rhythm. "What price?"

"Tell me about your meeting with the Wizard."

"Shouldn't you already know about it?" I hedge. "Since you have the scrying stone and all."

A muscle tics along Wests's jaw. "I can't see into the Emerald City. His influence blocks me. I know you spent two days in there, but beyond that—"

"Beyond that you're ignorant."

He bristles. "Let's put it this way—I have something you want. You have something I want. An exchange of information, plain and simple."

"A bargain."

"Yes."

In the musty, dense atmosphere of the library, our voices sound thick and quiet, and the roar of the thunderstorm is a distant murmur. When I inhale, my nose tickles from the dust our entrance stirred, and I sneeze sharply instead of answering him. West laughs, his green cheeks creasing, dark eyes sparkling. And I almost smile back, before I remember that he plans to kill me.

I can't tell him that my friends and I plan to destroy him, or he might decide to leave me here and go kill them. I'm not sure of the full extent of his power, but I can't imagine they'd survive once he made up his mind to end them. Though Riordan is strong, he doesn't have a significant amount of aggressive magic that could be used in a battle. From what I've heard, his talents tend more toward potion-making and spellcraft. Quick and clever as Caer may be, he's not a match for West either. And the Scarecrow is practically useless.

So I opt for a partial truth that's less threatening. "The Green Wizard wants your scrying stone. I'm supposed to bring it to him."

All humor vanishes from West's face. "Is that so?" He sets his staff against the wall by the door and takes off his wet leather coat, shaking off the rain and fluffing out the feathers clustered on the shoulders. Underneath, his clothes are black, well-worn, even a little ragged, like the outfit he wore when I first met him. Without the coat, he looks less intimidating. I wonder if he wore it for my benefit, so he could make a grander entrance.

"Is that everything the Wizard requested?" he asks, laying the coat over a nearby chair.

"Yes."

He whirls, eyes snapping. "You lie." The words fly from him, sharp as daggers.

"I swear I'm not lying. I'm supposed to take the stone from you and bring it to the Wizard—"

West collars my throat with his hand and rushes me back against the library wall by the door. I grip his wrist, trying to break the hold.

"The only way you can steal it from me is if I'm dead," he hisses in my face. "You've been commanded to kill me."

Oh. Fuck. I didn't realize the two things went hand in hand.

"I don't know why you're so angry—nothing has changed. I was going to end you anyway," I grit out. "Remember? I said I'd have to kill you first, before you kill me."

"As if you could," he snarls. "As if there was anything you could do to me that I could not resist."

A naughty idea slithers through my mind. "Is that a challenge?"

My hand loosens from his wrist and drops to his waist, while my other hand slides between his legs.

His gaze intensifies, but his hold on my neck relaxes. His tongue traces his lips as something hard flexes under his pants.

Oh, he wants me. A gratified glee swells in my chest, but it's mixed with a vindictive anger, because despite his lust for me, despite our connection, he's still a slave to his plan for revenge.

With a swift twist, I break free and duck, lunging for an old ornamental pike in a bracket by the nearest bookshelf. I try to yank it loose, but it's stuck fast. "Shit!"

West is on me, seizing my upper arms, whirling me away from the weapon. I throw magic into the motion, twirling us both faster than he expected—his grip isn't tight enough and I spin free, my shoulder crashing against a bookshelf.

There's an antique letter opener lying on a dusty stack of parchment. I snatch it up, whipping around just as he barrels in. The dull blade rakes along his forearm, slitting his sleeve and opening a shallow cut.

West grapples with me and wrenches the letter opener out of my hand. "Stop it, or I'll—"

"You'll what?" I say, breathless. "You can't kill me... not yet."

"I could put you to sleep. Send a mist into your lungs that would torment your mind and make you cough uncontrollably." He shoves me against the bookcase, clasping both my wrists in one hand and pinning them above my head. "I could incapacitate you in any number of ways, Kin-Slayer."

"Do it then. But you'd be breaking your bargain. You said you'd show me the book I need."

"I said I'd do it *if* you told me about your time with the Wizard. You lied, so the bargain is void."

Fuck. He's not wrong there.

My knee pops up, hitting him squarely in the crotch. Even Fae males are vulnerable to such pain, and as he bends over and groans, I jerk sharply against the wrist-hold and break it.

I stagger back from him, panting. "I gave you a partial truth. That warrants at least a hint about where the book is."

He straightens, still wincing from the pain in his balls. "It warrants nothing."

Enraged, I shove his chest with all my strength—no magic, just me. He barely budges a step. Stands there, smirking insufferably.

"I fucking hate you," I seethe, aiming a punch at his face.

He blocks the blow, his hand closing around my fist. "I hate you back. You've been a fucking nuisance since you got here. I can't get anything done. I watch you all the time—ugh!" He lets out a grunt as I kick him right between the legs again. "That's it, Kin-Slayer. Enough." As I'm lunging for a set of ceremonial daggers on a shelf, he seizes one of my braids and hauls me back to him. I shriek at the pain and fling up a hand, blasting him with my one-shot of defensive magic.

He flies backward into a heavy bookshelf, which shakes at the impact despite its solid structure.

I should have saved that blast for later. Now I'll have to wait until that particular reservoir of my energy recharges.

West is on his feet again, striding toward me, so I retreat, backing away between two long rows of bookshelves. The look of predatory rage in his eyes chills my soul, but there's lust in those eyes too, and that heats my blood, quickens my pounding heart.

I'm not sure what he'll do when he reaches me.

Lifting both hands, I shake the bookcases on either side of me, faster and faster until they topple inward, spilling their contents onto the floor in a cascade of leather, parchment, and dust.

West bounds high into the air—an inhuman leap—and lands lightly atop the slanted bookcases. He crouches, one forearm braced on his knee, head cocked and eyes narrowed. "What's your plan, Kin-Slayer? Destroy my family's library in a vain attempt to murder me? If you're trying to kill me, you're not doing a very good job. One might suspect your heart isn't in it."

My inner rage mounts, and I release it in a screech of frustration. He laughs, leaping down from the bookcases and pacing toward me.

I infuse his gait with magic, speeding his walk to a run, and then I dodge so that he zips on past me down the aisle of books and smashes into a study table at the far end.

A giggle escapes me as he struggles to his feet, swearing.

"Laugh it up, bitch," he sneers. "You'll run out of energy sooner than I do." He springs out of sight, behind the bookcases.

I don't like not having eyes on him. It's like knowing a spider is in the room, but not being sure where it's lurking.

Cautiously I creep down the aisle. The bookcases are sturdily built, with solid backs, so they're an impenetrable wall—I can't peer through them. When I reach the end of the aisle, I peek around the corner.

More rows of books, extending into the gloomy reaches of the library.

Tilting my head, I listen. There's the distant hammering of rain. The occasional quiet slap of my wet clothing against my skin as I walk. My shoes are silent on the thick carpet, and the orbs floating above make no sound. I breathe carefully through my parted lips, trying to catch the tiniest sound that might tell me where West has gone.

A small scuff, barely a whisper. Not down this row, or the next—*above me.*

My head snaps up, and there he is, slightly behind me, standing atop the bookcases. Before I can react, he leaps.

He knocks me down and tries to pin me, but I writhe free. His claws are out now, and they slice through the wet silk of the green blouse I'm wearing, shredding it easily. I jump up and run into the next row, tossing aside the silken rags, clad only in my black lace-up bustier and leather pants.

"I'll make you a deal," calls the Witch. "A book for a book. Give me the Tama Olc."

"Why do you want it?"

"To work spells of greater power," he says slowly, as if he's speaking to a very foolish child. "As I've watched you and listened to your conversations with your friends, I've come to realize how rare a book it is. Give it to me, and you shall have the secrets of your new shoes."

"No. I think I'll use the Tama Olc to kill you instead." After replying, I run a little farther and duck into the shadows behind a case of stuffed hunting trophies—most of them creatures I don't recognize.

"But you haven't had time to learn how to use the Tama Olc." I can hear the grin in his voice. "The spells in books like that usually take time, careful study, and rare ingredients. Things you don't have. Two days, Kin-Slayer. That's how long you have left until you're mine. And then I'll take the book anyway."

He's right on all counts. But at least I can deprive him of one thing he wants. I may not be able to learn to use the Tama Olc in two days' time, but I can prevent him from owning it after I'm dead.

I slide the little volume out of my back pocket and tuck it into the darkness beneath the trophy cabinet. No one has stolen it from me, so no one can lay claim to it. It will remain mine, hidden there until I return to fetch it, or until someone finds it after my death.

Nudging the book further into its hiding place with my toe, I tap into my enhanced speed and race along an aisle to the library wall. Quickly I climb one of the spiral wrought-iron stairways to the second-floor balcony—little more than a narrow walkway with an ornate railing.

From here I can see West prowling between the rows of shelves. And then he stops, chuckles, and takes a dark marble from his pocket.

Shit, he's cheating. He's going to use the scrying stone to figure out where I am.

"You can't have the Tama Olc," I call down to him. "Is there anything else you'll accept in exchange for the knowledge I seek?"

Without answering, he holds out his hand, and his staff comes flying across the room, smacking solidly into his palm. He rises on a cloud of green smoke, soaring up to the balcony where I stand. I try to use my agitation magic on him again, but it bounces off. He has shielded himself somehow.

"Don't run from me," he warns, landing on the walkway.

"Or what?" I retort.

"Or this." He lifts the staff, and an invisible force hurls me backward, pins me to the shelves with my arms outstretched and my legs spread. I can move a little, but my feet can't touch the ground, and I can't pull myself free. When I reach for my magic, it doesn't respond.

He's been toying with me. Letting me think I was holding my own, when in reality he could have overpowered me at any moment.

West stalks forward, props his staff beside my immobilized body, and inspects the sharp black nails on one hand. He disappears the claws for a moment, then flicks them back into existence. "You've lost your shirt." His gaze drops to my breasts, which are lifting and falling with my angry breaths, nearly surging out of the bustier's cups with each inhale.

West runs his claws down my sternum. With a series of deft movements he loosens the string holding the front of my bustier together, draws it out, and flings it aside. The bustier falls open and drops to the floor, baring my upper body to him.

If I begged him to leave me alone, he might. But I don't protest, not a word. Hanging here before my enemy, naked to the waist, is an intoxicating kind of torture.

West vanishes his claws again and moves in close, right beside me, his breath warm against my forehead. He runs long green fingers down my trembling stomach, playing along my hipbone, right at the edge of my leather pants.

His hand glides up again, cupping one of my breasts, fondling its softness. My nipple peaks, and he leans over to suck it briefly.

A soft moan slips from my mouth. Heat roars in my face immediately afterward, because I didn't want to let him know how deeply he affects me—how much I crave his touch.

He pulls back at the sound. Looks into my eyes. "I propose an exchange," he says softly. "You will submit to anything I request for the next hour. And then I will yield the knowledge you seek."

The bargain is a sexual one. I know it, and my belly thrills at the thought. Does he know that I would submit to him anyway, even without the promise of knowledge at the end? I'm guessing he suspects as much. He's letting me off easy, allowing me to give him something we both crave as the payment for the book I need.

It's almost… a kindness.

"I agree to the bargain," I whisper.

"Perfect," he breathes, his lips brushing over mine. "My first order—remove the rest of your clothes. I know you can't remove the slippers, but I'll glamour them invisible. I don't wish to see my sister's shoes while you're sucking my cock."

My clit throbs in response, and I lick my lips reflexively.

"Good girl," he murmurs. "Preparing to taste me already. I'm going to fill your pretty throat with my cum, Kin-Slayer." He strokes my neck, and I swallow against his fingers.

"Fucking perfection." He kisses me, a firm, possessive pressure. His tongue glides into my mouth, and I fight the urge to bite it for a moment before I yield and melt into the heat of his soft lips. He tastes like a rainstorm in the spring, when golden rays glance through the clouds and light up the sparkling drops, when the world smells pristinely fresh and richly green.

A moment later he withdraws, backing away several paces, and I'm released from the immobilization magic. I step away from the bookshelves and work my pants down, over my hips and legs. I have to sit to pull them off, and when I start to rise, West says, "You may as well stay down there. Now the panties."

The bit of black lace is soon discarded, and I sit naked on the walkway before him. I can still feel the shoes, but when I look down, I see my bare feet.

West's lips curve in a smirk. "Crawl to me, Dorothy. Slowly."

On hands and knees, my breasts swaying and my ass in the air, I crawl to him. He takes his cock out while I approach, and he's not smirking now—he looks ravenous. There's a maniacal gleam in his eyes that makes me wonder if I'll make it to him before he decides to pounce. But somehow he holds himself back, waiting until I crawl right up to his feet and rise on my knees.

"Take me in your mouth, Kin-Slayer," he says thickly. "And don't bite, or I promise you'll regret it."

I curl my fingers around the base of his shaft, holding his cock still while I take him in. I suck him quickly, my head bobbing with the rhythm, until he hisses a sharp breath and pulls back.

"Tip your face up and open your mouth," he orders. "Tongue out, and look at me."

I lift my face and put out my tongue. His gaze locks with mine while he lays the head of his cock on the flat of my tongue and strokes himself.

He starts to come—little spurts flinging across my tongue—and then he grips the back of my skull and plunges his cock deeper into my mouth, his hips jerking convulsively as he comes fully in my throat, jet after jet of thick cum. When I gag a little, he withdraws, with a terse order: "Fucking swallow it."

Eyes watering, I obey.

"Show me." He grabs my chin, pushes my jaw down so he can be sure his release found its new home.

"Fae can climax many times in a row," he says, pushing a tendril of hair back from my face and wiping the tears from the corner of my eye with his thumb. "I want you covered in my scent by the end of this hour. But I don't want you docile, Kin-Slayer—I want you wild and writhing, cursing me even as you beg for release. I want you to fight for every climax you achieve, and I want you to make me fight for mine, too. Do you understand?"

I nod quickly, already desperate, already leaking arousal as I kneel before him.

West banishes his clothes, sending them from his body to drape over the railing. Then he catches me by the throat and yanks me to my feet, and when I slap him for it, he grins, as if he's delighted that I understand the game.

And in that moment I abolish my mask.

I destroy every shred of it, and I leap into the frenzied freedom of my Unseelie side. I attack West, flinging my whole body at him, and he topples, crashing to the balcony floor. I seize his cock and lower myself onto it, but I only get the tip between my folds when he twists, rolling his hips aside. With a surge of his lithe body he flips us both over, pinning me to the floor this time.

I manage to get my legs on either side of his and I buck against his thigh, grinding my pussy on the hard-packed muscle, leaving a wet smear on his skin. He doesn't let me hump him for longer than a few seconds before he changes position, settling astride my chest, squishing my breasts together and shoving his cock between them. I buck, trying to throw him off. When he won't let me, I take his nipple between my fingers and pinch until he growls and grabs my hand, slamming my wrist to the floor.

Hunting for my magic, I discover that he has allowed me access to it again. I seek out the concussive blast I use for defense and find a bit of energy there—not strong yet, but it's all I need.

I plant my other hand on West's bare chest and send a quick pulse of magic against him. It's enough to knock him back a bit, and in that scant second I lunge, adding momentum magic and bowling him over. I'm on top now, my pussy settled over the ridge of his cock. When I roll my hips forward, the friction of his length along my sex makes my eyes roll back.

He lets me get close to climax this time. But when I let out a sharp little cry of anticipation—almost there—he leaps to his feet with a gust of green magic, lifts me bodily, and flings me over the balcony railing.

I shriek, terrified—but I haven't fallen. His magic caught me, and I'm dangling upside down above the rows of bookshelves, held aloft by an invisible force. My legs are spread apart—I'm practically doing a split—and my pussy is on a level with the top of the railing.

As I hang there upside down, naked and spread wide for him, West saunters casually to the railing and leans over, taking a long lick between my folds.

For other women, such a perilous position might be more distracting than arousing, but the Unseelie half of me is thrilled at this new experience—so when West's tongue traces through my labia, the sensation is tripled, and I scream breathlessly. "Shit! Oh gods, please—please do it again—*fuck*!" I shriek as he licks me once more, casually, like a man tasting his favorite dessert.

The blood is rushing to my head—I'm dizzy, delirious, whimpering as he slides his tongue to my clit and nibbles there.

"Don't stop, please, please…"

But he does stop. A cloud of green magic lifts me, deposits me back on the balcony floor. I'm shaking, my thighs convulsively pinned together, trying for that last bit of friction.

West shoves me against the bookshelves again—pins me there with his slim naked form, and tucks his fingers between my legs. His fingers emerge dripping wet, and he paints my own arousal along my throat, around my nipples, across my belly. He squeezes a bit of precum from his own cock and reaches up to dab on my cheeks and lips, while I stand quivering, aching, finding each move he makes more arousing than the last.

"Put your fingers into your pussy," he whispers, right by my ear. "And mark me with your cum."

I tuck my fingers inside myself, shuddering in a delirium of need. I've forgotten why we're here. Forgotten my purpose. Nothing matters except his body, and mine, and the relief he's going to give me.

With wet, trembling fingertips I trace lines across his abdomen, then paint another line along his cock. He shivers and exhales as I do it, crowding against me, as if he yearns to be closer.

I have a little of my arousal left on my fingers, so I smear his cheeks with it. He looks at me, his cheekbones gleaming, a strange kind of dread and glory in his eyes, as if he has just done something that scares and thrills him.

Then he gathers me up, lifting me, and as my legs part for him he enters me. No more struggle, no more fighting—we gasp in mutual agreement as he slides inside, and I reach up to clutch one of the shelves above me. I can feel another shelf digging into my back, and I wince, momentarily drawn out of the moment.

West notices and carries me down onto the carpet with him, his cock still sheathed in my heat.

I grip his upper arms, feeling the tightened biceps as he braces his palms on either side of me. When I look into his eyes, there's a challenge in my voice. "See how long you can last without coming."

He makes a frustrated sound. "Same to you, Kin-Slayer. No talking, no other touches, just this." He nods to the place where we're joined, and I return the nod.

I'm determined to outlast him. I'm a woman—for many of us, it takes longer to reach pleasure, and that should be an advantage here, but oh—oh gods—he's thrusting harder, deeper, and there's a place inside me that's lighting up, sending swirls of gilded pleasure through my belly. Fuck, fuck—I'm going to come—I pin my legs around him, heels locked against his ass, and squeeze my pussy around him as tightly as I can. A sharp gasp of surprise breaks from him, and his cock throbs, but he doesn't come yet.

I won't break our bargain. No other touches, no talking… but I can look at him.

I'm nearly there, nearly over the edge, but I take a deep breath and I fix my eyes on his. At first he's looking away, teeth gritted—but it's as if he can sense my stare—his gaze swerves to mine, as he keeps fucking me fiercely, determined to win.

Words fill my mind as I look at him, words I couldn't say, not even if it was permitted in this moment.

*I never thought I would want another man, not after Archer. I haven't felt truly alive for a long time, and it wasn't just Faerie that brought me to life—it was you. When you're here, everything is sharper, clearer, more vivid, more exciting.*

West's eyes are violent and tender and pained, his thrusts slower, deeper, his lips parted as if words hover on the tip of his tongue.

I keep pouring unspoken things from my mind, through my eyes, into his.

*You're lonely, vindictive, cruel, delicious, intelligent. You're the most fascinating person I've ever met, and the one who is most like me. I don't want you dead, and I wish you could let me live. We could do this forever, the two of us—we'd never have to fear being alone again. We'd be so wicked and wild—we could do anything we pleased, and no one could tell us not to. I wish... I wish... I wish... I could love you until I die. I want you to be mine.*

"*Ahh...*" A groan cracks from his lips, and his shoulders tighten, his head bowing in defeat as he comes inside me. "Gods-fuck..."

The slow pulse of his orgasm in my sensitive channel is too much—my hips surge, meeting his final thrust, and I come on him, a hard burst of bliss shattering my senses, surging through my body in rich waves. He's still coming—he rocks deeper and groans again, more warmth rushing from his cock, bathing my insides. Another wave of pleasure catches me, too—a second crest, and I gasp, whimpers slipping from my throat. My legs lock tighter around him, pinning him inside me so I can enjoy every second of the blessed fullness.

After a few seconds he moves to pull out of me, but another rush of ecstasy floods through my body and I arch into it, wordless, soundless, stunned.

"Fuck," he rasps, his body hardening with another orgasm. "Oh fuck."

"It wasn't like this the other time," I manage, breathless. "What's happening?"

He looks shocked, wide-eyed, almost boyish in his surprise. But there's realization in his eyes, too, and a flicker of guilt. He turns his head away.

"What is it?" I reach up and grab his jaw, forcing him to look at me. "What did you do?"

"It was a primal instinct, an impulse," he says, low. "It requires commitment on both sides, so I never thought it would work."

"What does that mean?"

He withdraws from me, and this time there's no extra burst of pleasure, just the slick, pleasant glide of his flesh leaving mine.

"Three so close in a row like that—it's unusual, isn't it? Even for Fae?" I persist.

"Yes, we typically need at least a few minutes to recover." He summons his clothes back onto his body and his staff into his hand, then leaps over the balcony railing, landing catlike on the library floor far below. He disappears among the bookshelves.

"Wait a fucking second!" By the time I struggle into my underthings, my pants, and my bustier, he's already returning, with his coat on and two books in his hand. I clatter down the steps to meet him, feeling clumsy, disheveled, and a little rejected.

"These are what you need." He slams a slim leather-covered volume into my hand. "This journal will tell you more about the Wizard you're working for—how he arrived here, and what he has done."

"We aren't working *for* him," I protest, but he slams the second book on top of the first.

"This is a history of my family's powers and inherited artifacts. Read it, learn to use the shoes, and then come fucking kill me if you can. I'll be waiting."

There's no trace of humor on his face, no teasing glint in his eyes. With a crack and a cloud of green smoke, he disappears, leaving me alone in the great library of Caislean Brea.

# 23

## ALICE

Caer is much more fun to travel with when he's in his natural form. He's in high spirits, running ahead and bounding back to us, climbing trees, and springing from branch to branch. Once he dashes up behind Riordan and leaps onto his back like a child begging for a ride. That earns him a lethal glare from the White Rabbit, who is still gloomy about the time we wasted in the Emerald City, fucking like... well... like rabbits.

Jasper watches Caer frolic with an expression of bewildered delight. "Where does he get all that energy?" he asks me in an undertone.

"I have no idea. He's like a kitten on catnip."

Caer is a few dozen paces ahead, but I notice his ears twitch. Then he disappears into the bushes beside the road.

"He heard us," I whisper to Jasper.

As we draw closer to the spot where Caer disappeared, I fall back, letting Jasper, Fiero, and Riordan move ahead. My skin prickles with a subtle awareness, the instinctive knowledge that I'm being stalked.

I'm nearly to the place where Caer vanished. If he leaps out at me, it'll be from there, and I'll be ready—

An arm wraps around my breasts and a hand clamps across my mouth. I'm yanked against a firm chest, and he whispers in my ear, "Too easy, mouse."

He must have darted into the bushes, turned invisible, and then crossed the road and backtracked to surprise me.

When he takes his hand from my mouth, I gasp, "Well done. You nearly scared the piss out of me."

He chuckles against my neck, flashing visible again even as he keeps me pinned to his chest. He inhales deeply against my pulse point. "Your scent has been tormenting me all day. Do you think Riordan would kill me if I fucked you quickly behind that tree?"

"If it's because you're in heat, he might make allowances."

"And you?" Caer nuzzles up to my ear and nips at the lobe. "Will you make allowances for me?"

"Gods, yes," I breathe.

Picking me up, Caer darts to the great tree he mentioned and whisks us behind it. I wore a green dress today, with nothing beneath—slutty of me, maybe, but I couldn't help myself. I'm ravenous for these Fae men in ways I didn't know I could be—half-mad with the excitement of this new dynamic among us all.

Caer bends me over and groans with delight when he finds nothing in his way. He takes out his cock and slips into me easily, holding my hips while I brace my palms against the tree. His tail coils around my leg, a sinuous, silky caress that I find wildly titillating.

"Every time I fuck you, it's like coming home." Caer speaks the words tentatively, quietly. "It's like an embrace, or a nest made just for me. I love Riordan, I do—but you—fuck, I'm devoted to you, Alice."

He pulls out, flips me around, and drags me close for a passionate kiss, his wet cock pressed against my skirts. His mouth is wide, wicked, and full of teeth. Kissing him is a sweet insanity, a delirious danger. I whimper into the dark space between those serrated jaws, and he chuckles, sending his long tongue into my mouth, a tempting, teasing flicker of heat. Frantically I bunch my skirts around my waist and he lifts me up with one hand, using the other to tuck his cock into my entrance while I hitch my legs around his waist. He sets my back to the tree and fucks me with firm, hard jerks of his hips, while I gasp at the grind of his body against my clit. When he comes, the tiny barbs along his cock extrude again, sealing us together as his cum pools inside me.

He kisses me while we wait, palming my breasts and whispering sinful things in my ear.

When his cock is smooth once more, we separate, and he slides to his knees. He lashes his slick tongue over my clit, then buries it deep inside me, alternating those sensations until I finally come, with one hand in his black hair and the other clamped around my mouth to muffle my own screams.

When we stumble back onto the road, giggling, we find Riordan standing there, arms folded and feet braced apart. Jasper sits crosslegged behind him, playing with Fiero's ears.

"Finished?" asks Riordan coolly.

"I'm in heat," says Caer, with a cocky lift of his chin, as if he's daring Riordan to protest.

"In heat? As if that matters! You'll be in beast form forever if we don't get this done," snaps Riordan. "No more sex until this is finished, one way or the other."

Caer winks at me as if to contradict the order, but there's a shadow of genuine anxiety in his gaze. He walks on without another word, and throughout the rest of the afternoon, his antics are more restrained.

As evening falls, we notice a storm gathering to the south. The edges of it spatter us with light rain, but we forge on, pursuing the western road until Jasper points out something in the far distance—a wall of greenish cloud, barely distinguishable from the overcast sky.

"I see it," Riordan says. "The West Witch's domain, shrouded or protected somehow. I'd be interested to know what spell he used—"

"Never mind that now," Caer interrupts. "The important question is, can we get through it?"

"Run ahead, Cat, and see," Riordan suggests caustically. Caer races away, pursued by Fiero, and Jasper runs after both of them.

Riordan mutters, "I'm going to have to fuck Caer's ass again to remind him who's in charge."

"Equals, remember?" I slide my hand up to his shoulder. "Relax. We've made it this far. Once we get past the border into the West Witch's lands, maybe we can get directions and hire mounts. Although—shit—the Witch can see us, can't he? I keep forgetting. So he knows we're coming."

"He's bound to put obstacles in our path," Riordan says grimly. "And we lost so much time—we have none to spare. We shouldn't have stayed the night in the palace. We should have left at once, after you'd been healed and fed."

I stiffen, frowning. "I'm not a pet you need to care for, you know."

He glances down at me. "I know." His voice is soft, sorrowful. "I don't blame you. I blame the Wizard, and I blame myself for yielding to your charms, for giving in to—all of it. I should have known better."

"Well, I don't regret the time we spent together. Maybe I wish we'd shortened it, but—if this doesn't end the way we want, at least we have those memories."

"Memories I can torture myself with when I'm sealed into that accursed armor again."

"Riordan, stop." I step in front of him, halting his progress, and I seize his gloved hands. "You're giving up, and we're not even close to being beaten yet. Think of how long you struggled secretly against the Queen—"

"I'm tired of struggling." The words break from him, harsh and fierce, as if he's been holding them in for a long time. "First my father, then the Rat King, and then the Eater of Hearts, and now the Wizard, and when—when will it be over, Alice? When will I finally have time to spend with my work and the people I love? My life has been one struggle after another, one conquest after another—sacrifice upon sacrifice—" He wrenches his hands from mine, strips off his gloves, and throws them into the mud with a wet smack. "I'm *tired*, kitten. I'm tired of fighting the will of the god-stars, which is to crush me into bone-dust under their feet. I want peace. I want relief. I am *tired*."

I reach up to him, my palms sliding over the gashes in his face, my thumbs stroking his cheekbones. "Life is a struggle, in any realm," I tell him. "It's exhausting, and sometimes horrible. But that's the very reason I don't regret the time the four of us spent together. When you have a chance for a beautiful moment, or a bit of pleasure with people you love, you have to take it. You have to throw yourself into it and enjoy every second, because you know it will end, and the next struggle will begin. That's what makes love and pleasure more beautiful. They're fragile, like the husks around grains of wheat. The wind comes and carries them away, and what's left is hard, but it's necessary."

Riordan's scarlet eyes burn into mine with a soft, tender fire. He takes my wrists and collects my hands in his scarred ones. "Precious mortal," he whispers. "I think I have loved you since you shut me in my own dungeon. No… perhaps it began when you leaped into the hole so readily. You looked around at the garden, at your realm, and you decided to risk it all for knowledge."

"Foolish of me." I pick up his hand and press it to my cheek. It's warm, and wounded, and mine. "Foolish, and the best choice I ever made. I love you, Riordan. I love you. And believe me when I say I will do anything to save you, even if we don't manage to kill the West Witch. I will stay with you, whether you're in this form or another. If you're in that suit of armor, I'll be your hands—I'll hold books for you, mix potions for you—anything you need. I'll be there for you and Caer. We'll be together, either way. And Jasper will stay, too. I know he's new, but there's something about him, Riordan—he's special. He belongs with us. I know it."

"I feel it, too," Riordan says reluctantly. He sighs, pinching the bridge of his nose. "Fuck me...a human, a wildcat, and a soft-hearted Seelie for my mates, and a half-human for a sister."

"Mates?" I raise my eyebrows.

His mouth twitches, the ghost of a smile. "You don't approve of the term? Partners, then? Lovers?"

"Partners or lovers will do," I say primly, walking on. "I suppose I could get used to 'mates.' And you may keep calling me 'kitten.'"

He keeps pace with me. "How about fuck-doll?" he says, in a low voice that makes my whole body thrill. "May I call you that sometimes?"

"If I'm in the right mood," I say, breathless, suddenly conscious of his height, his strength. *Fuck-doll...* I wouldn't mind being used like that occasionally. An image forms in my mind—all three of them crowded around me, pumping into my holes, shouting and laughing while they take me to fresh heights of pleasure... *our little fuck-doll...*

"Alice." Riordan is looking down at me, grinning. It's glorious to see him smile. "Where did you go?"

"Somewhere naughty," I confess.

"I thought so. Save that fantasy for later, kitten—the others are coming back."

Caer, Jasper, and Fiero are indeed heading toward us.

"Caer doesn't look too glum, so I'm guessing he made it through the barrier," I say.

"That would be my guess as well."

Caer reports that the barrier is nothing more than a bank of cloud, easily traversed. "The question is, do we head through or wait for Dorothy on this side?"

"We wait," Riordan and I say firmly, at exactly the same moment.

And then Jasper says, "If she dies, can I keep her dog?"

"Gods, Jasper," I exclaim. "Don't say things like that."

"I don't mean that I *want* her to die," he amends quickly, turning pale. "Just that I want Fiero to have a home."

"It's a valid question, though," Caer puts in. "Do we allow our pet to have a pet, or not?" He leans in, licking up the side of Jasper's face. The Scarecrow flushes to the roots of his golden hair and throws Caer an adoring look.

"The question is pointless," says Riordan. "Dorothy will return. If she had died, I would sense it."

The link to his sibling makes me faintly homesick. I left my entire family behind without a word, without a goodbye. I can't bear to think how sad my little brothers and sisters must be. And the older ones will worry.

We walk on together, heading for the barrier, planning to wait at its edge for Dorothy. Jasper picks up Fiero, and after a few paces, holds him out to me. "Would you like to carry him? You look as if you need it."

"I'm fine."

"You aren't," he says softly. "Is there anything I can do to ease your suffering?"

"You're sweet." I give him a small smile. "It's not quite so bad as *suffering*. I just miss my brothers and sisters. I don't want them to be mistreated while I'm gone, or to miss me too badly."

"You can't always protect others from being mistreated. I've tried." Sadness suffuses his blue eyes, as if my own emotions are reflected there.

"You tried to help the other sacrifices, the misfits in your village, didn't you?"

He nods. "I wasn't able to save any of them. But I made a difference, even if no one else could see it. Even if nothing changes, you make a difference by *trying*. By being *better*. By choosing to do the right thing, even if the result isn't what you want. You made your family better by being in it, Alice. Maybe it's someone else's turn to be *better* now."

He smiles at me as we walk, and I look into those azure eyes, so full of sincerity and love…

Love. That's what makes him special. Love without measure, without end, so deep that the Village of Crows couldn't dry it up, so vast their cruelty never reached the end of it, so true that the East Witch was never able to hold him in thrall, because that love always conquered. There is strength in his softness, beauty in his gentleness. And that kind of generous, boundless love is exactly what our little family needs to balance Caer's selfishness and cowardice, Riordan's obsessiveness and occasional cruelty, and my own recklessness.

And Jasper needs us, too. He has suffered deeply, endured imprisonment and abuse for years. This journey is too brief for us to untangle everything he has been through, but inwardly I vow to hold his hand and his heart in the future, as he frees himself from that pain and discovers who he was meant to be.

"I love you," I tell him impulsively.

He smiles, and I could swear the gray sky brightens. "I love you, too."

# 24

# ALICE

We wait for Dorothy under shimmering purple trees, by a pool where fiery insects skate through the dappled shadows of its surface, stirring up tiny puffs of steam. I could watch them forever, and Riordan is fascinated too—but his fascination involves plucking one of them off the pond, detaching its wings, and delicately prying its body open, so he can figure out how it burns without incinerating itself.

Caer leans against the rock I'm sitting on, so I play with his silky black hair. He tilts his head into the touch, humming softly in his throat as I massage the base of his cat ears.

Eventually Riordan abandons his study of the insects and stalks over to the wall of green cloud, inspecting it. He stands there for a long time. The only movement is the swivel of his long ears to catch the sounds of Jasper playing with Fiero.

Darkness falls, the fiery insects burn brighter, and Riordan begins to pace, chafing as more of our precious time passes. Caer and I end up curled together on the grass with Jasper, petting each other quietly, not daring to fuck outright lest Riordan rebuke us. But Caer grows bolder, and leans over me, tugging

Jasper's head back by his golden hair and bending to kiss his throat. Then the Cat kisses my mouth and nuzzles against my cheek, while his fingers slide over my breast.

I'm fairly sure things are about to get interesting… but then Riordan's ears stiffen and he turns around. "She's coming."

Dorothy arrives at a run, bursting out of the darkness. She has lost her green silk shirt somewhere, and she's clad only in her leather pants and bustier. Under one arm are two books, and under the other is something in a cloth bag.

"I'm sorry I took so long." She flings herself down into the grass and accepts a storm of enthusiastic welcome from Fiero. "This book tells about the shoes, and the history of Oz's royal family. And this one—this is a diary kept by the North Witch, when the Green Wizard first arrived. Which do you want to hear about first?"

"The god-star, and make it quick," Riordan says, seating himself on the grass. He's nearest to Jasper, and after a moment, the Scarecrow crawls closer to him, laying his golden head on Riordan's thigh. Caer and I exchange apprehensive glances, but after a second, Riordan's scarred hand settles on the golden curls.

Dorothy sets aside the thicker of the two volumes and opens the slender one. "I read some of it in the library of Caislin Brea. The author of this journal is the North Witch, as I said. She's the one who became the god-star's lover and then was cursed as the Eater of Hearts. She ruled the north quarter of the Isle, but she had come to Caislin Brea for an annual meeting of the four siblings. During her stay, the god-star crashed onto the city, causing a giant crater. His form was unstable for weeks, until he managed to take Fae shape. He began to seduce her. She mentions knowing that he was a god-star. She thought it was fate that he should be her lover, because the royals of this Isle all have a unique gift from the god-stars—the compulsion ability that makes them witches. And this part is interesting." She looks up, her blue and brown eyes shining. "The scrying stones the witches use to keep visual track of their thralls? Those are rumored to be the fossilized tears of the god-stars, from when they walked this realm in their titanic forms, back when the worlds were first made. Later on in the journal, she mentions that the Green Wizard smashed every scrying stone he could find, including hers."

"Smashed them?" I exclaim. "Then why does he want the West Witch's scrying stone? Unless—" I meet Riordan's crimson eyes, knowing we have the same thought— "unless the scrying stones can do more than just observe people. There's some other use for them, one that frightens the Green Wizard."

Riordan's eyes gleam with approval. With the gashes in his cheeks and the fiery light from the pond playing over his face, his smile is absolutely terrifying. But I smile back anyway, because I love him—every dark, twisted, brutalized, aching piece of his soul.

"The stone could be a weapon," Riordan says.

"And your shoes?" Caer is lying on his belly, his chin propped in his hands. "What can they do?"

Dorothy smirks. "They enhance gracefulness and speed, like I suspected. And they help me read faster as well as run faster. I suppose that's a handy ability for a Witch to have—the power to skim through magical texts as quickly as possible to find the right spell. It takes a while for them to fully synchronize with a new owner. But that's not the best part. These shoes can transport me to any place I've seen, in just three steps. And I can take someone along with me if I'm touching them."

"Fuck." Caer sits up, envy glinting in his violet eyes. "You've tried it?"

"Not the 'taking someone along' part, but yes." Dorothy nods. "I transported myself from the library to the crossroads by the three red hills. I had to run the rest of the way to meet up with you, but it shortened the journey."

Riordan leaps up, pushing Jasper's head off his thigh. "I must study those shoes."

"Later," Dorothy says. "Once we get through this. I found other things in the palace vault, but I can't speak of them yet." She lowers her voice. "Not while he's listening, and watching. Not until—well, here."

She slides a nondescript wooden box out of the bag she's carrying and opens it. Inside lie several milky-looking marbles.

"Take one, and swallow it," she orders.

Riordan's eyes widen. "These were in the vault?"

Dorothy nods. "In a section for magical supplies. The place had been sacked, mostly, but these must have escaped notice. I only figured out what they were because the North Witch spoke of them in her journal."

Riordan plucks a marble from the boxes and gulps it down. I follow his example, then Jasper, then Caer.

After we've each swallowed one, Dorothy explains, "These orbs are a counter-scrying measure. Each royal sibling took these and gave some to their closest servants and guards as well, to prevent them from being spied upon. These orbs will keep West—I mean, the West Witch—from being able to see us."

"So our attack on him will be a surprise," says Jasper.

"Well..." Dorothy bites her lip. "Not exactly. You see, I would never have found the books without help. The palace and its library are much too enormous. And to get the help, I had to trade information."

Riordan's fists tighten. He glares down at his sister with an expression of scorn and betrayal. "You told the Witch our plans."

"He already knew we were headed his way—he just didn't know *why*," she protests. "I told him we were after the scrying stone—but apparently you can't use a witch's scrying stone without killing the witch first... so he figured out the rest. He knows we're coming to kill him."

"So he's expecting this." My heart sinks. "Which means we have no chance."

"We *do* have a chance," Dorothy says, "if you'll let me explain—"

But I'm furious. Angrier than I've been in a long time. "Did you fuck him?"

Dorothy stares at me. "Alice, I—"

"Did. You. Fuck. Him?"

"That has nothing to do with—"

"It has *everything* to do with this. You told him about our bargain with the Wizard—"

"He'd have found out anyway through his scrying stone," she cuts in. "You're lucky I found those orbs to block his view of us, or—"

"So I should be grateful to you? I should praise you for sleeping with the enemy and telling him our plans? Grateful that you've risked Caer and Riordan's future? You betrayed us!"

"I had to trade something!" Dorothy shouts back. The ground begins to tremble, and the water of the pond shivers, startling the fiery insects into a flaming cloud of frantic wings. "What else did I have except secrets—and myself?" At my frown, she shakes her head impatiently. "No, it wasn't like that. He didn't force me into anything. I did it of my own free will."

Even though I suspected it, the revelation strikes me hard. I teased her about the Witch a little, sympathized with her attraction to him—but I thought she couldn't be too serious about it, given that he has sworn to murder her.

But now her attraction to the Witch stands between me and my happiness.

"You know we have to kill him," I say tersely. "It will happen, even if I have to slit his throat myself."

"Alice, I know." She's breathing hard, looking more emotional than I've ever seen her. "That's why I brought something else along. I found the vault after he left, and I don't believe he saw me take it... he was distressed, and distracted. Too distracted to spy on me again for a while, I think. And he can't see us now, so..." She reaches into the bag again and pulls out a cloth-wrapped object. "After I found the orbs, I saw this among the bits and bobs left in the vault."

When she unwraps it, the light of the pond insects flashes on faceted glass.

"Most of the bottles in the case were broken," Dorothy says. "I almost missed seeing this one. But once I read what it could do, I thought it might prove useful." She passes the glass bottle to Riordan, who inspects the label pasted to the back.

"It's water from the Well of Undoing," he says quietly. "Douse someone with it, and you remove all their powers. There's enough here to weaken a Fae for a single hour."

"The Well of Undoing is near my village," says Jasper. "They use its waters to mix the ink for our tattoos and spells. It allows Fae to be marked with tattoos that never heal. With it, they can weaken each sacrifice they make to the crows. They made me drink it before they tied me to the stake."

"Fuck," breathes Caer.

"I'm well-acquainted with this water, too." Riordan's tone darkens, and he touches one of the gashes in his face. "My father had a small supply of it. He said it was rare as sun's-blood, that the original source was long-lost. Until my stay in the Village of Crows, I had no idea the Well was located on this Isle."

"It's in the cornfields," Jasper adds. "It requires a sacrifice for every bucketful or two they manage to retrieve, so yes—it's rare."

"Can we dump a whole bucket of it on the Green Wizard?" Caer puts in. He's still lying in the grass, his tail curling lazily, his arms crossed behind his head.

"The water wouldn't work on a god-star," Riordan says.

"Doesn't seem fair." Caer plucks a piece of grass and chews it thoughtfully. "I've been wondering why the god-star was able to absorb the witches' compulsion abilities, and yet didn't try to steal any of our powers."

"Maybe he can't," I reply. "The witches' power is a direct gift from the god-stars—isn't that what the journal says? So it's more compatible with what he is. But the powers and magic of the Fae—those are different. Fae are born with their own unique blend of abilities, and maybe a god-star can't take them and use them himself. Even the compulsion power fades for him, though it's permanent for a witch."

Riordan's gaze is still fixed on me, and it has transformed from approval and agreement to admiration and a dark, fierce craving. If we were alone, I believe he'd throw me down in the grass and fuck me soundly, just because he loves my mind. When I smile at him, he licks his broad lips slowly, lecherously, and his fingers twitch at his sides. A fluttering, panicked delight fills my chest. If we can manage this task, living with him for decades in Faerie is going to be the most delicious kind of adventure.

I can't give up the hope of that future. Not for anyone, not even Dorothy. She can't possibly love the West Witch—she barely knows him. We'll kill him, and she'll find someone else.

Guilt crawls through my heart, because every one of those thoughts is hypocritical and selfish. I fell for Caer and Riordan in a handful of days, and *they* were planning to kill *me*. Who am I to judge the connection Dorothy has with "West," as she calls him?

Riordan's eyes are still on me, and I know he noticed my change in mood. Holding my gaze, he says, "We are in agreement, then. We are now concealed from the West Witch, so although he knows our plan, he does not know how or when we'll enact it. That should give us some advantage. We simply have to reach his stronghold, get inside, and make our way close enough to douse him with this water."

"I can get close enough." Dorothy's tone is blank, dull, emotionless. "I'll throw the water on him, and then you can kill him."

"Are you sure?" Riordan swerves his gaze to her.

Dorothy squares her shoulders and lifts her chin. "If I don't, he will kill me. And what kind of sister would I be if I let this opportunity pass and doomed you to spend your days in a metal shell?"

Riordan is still holding the bottle, but he stretches out his free hand to her. It's a stiff, awkward gesture, and she takes his hand just as stiffly. But there's real affection in their eyes—an undeniable bond.

Jasper sniffs, and when I glance at him, the wet path of a tear glistens on his cheek.

"So precious. So sweet," purrs Caer tauntingly from the grass. "The love of family. Is there anything more beautiful than—agh!" He yelps as Riordan shoves the bottle back into Dorothy's hands and leaps on him. They tumble over together, wrestling, clawing, and biting until Riordan manages to get Caer in a headlock.

The Cat's grin widens as Riordan secures his grip. "Tighter," he says. "I'm almost there…"

"Little shit," Riordan hisses in Caer's ear. "Just wait until this is over. I'll…" But his words are too quiet for me to hear, spoken only for the Cat, who looks both aroused and terrified.

"You wouldn't," breathes Caer.

"Try me." Riordan's voice is low, rich, and menacing enough to send a tingle of need between my legs.

"Fuck…" Caer whispers. "I'll be good, I promise. For now." He winks at me over the constricting band of Riordan's arm. "And then maybe, after everything is done, you and Jasper and Alice and I can gamble who gets to do—that thing you said—and who gets to watch."

"I'm in," I say quickly.

Jasper looks at me, perplexed. "You don't even know what it is."

"And she doesn't need to know," Caer says, his eyes shining at me. "Our mousie is always ready for games."

Riordan grunts his agreement and lets the Cat go. "Enough of this. Time is running short, and we still have a long walk ahead."

# 25

# DOROTHY

When I was in the great library, I saw a map of the Isle of Oz on the wall. Once I found what I needed in the books, I took a closer look, and from what I can remember, it seems the map the Wizard's servants gave Alice is accurate.

I could have left the books behind, but I guessed that Riordan might want to peruse them, to confirm the information I relayed—and of course I was right. Once we've passed through the cloudy green barrier surrounding the West Witch's domain, he opens the history book and begins to read. Sometimes he is so engrossed that he wanders off the road, but Alice or Jasper always steer him back.

Night cloaks the forest through which we're traveling, its inky darkness disturbed only by the light of the two small orbs that follow Riordan along, enabling him to read and giving the rest of us some visibility. Caer can see in the dark somewhat, but his night vision isn't perfect.

I suggested that I run ahead to scout the route, then transport back to the group and carry them ahead with me to a farther point along the road—but Riordan advises waiting until it's light before we attempt that. "You aren't used to this ability," he says. "And since it's based on sight, it's best to wait until visibility improves."

It frustrates me that although I can produce enough of a spark to light a candle or a lantern, as I often did back home, I can't produce the glowing orbs that most other Fae conjure when they need light. Jasper walks beside me for a while, coaching me while I attempt it. But finally I give up and walk at an annoyingly slow human pace, carrying Fiero in the basket that held today's lunch.

Strange sounds echo through the forest as we walk—screeches and howls, moans and wails. Instead of wandering as usual, Caer slinks close to Alice, muttering, "Sometimes I rather miss my beastly form."

She doesn't answer, only squeezes his hand.

I envy Alice. I envy the way she communicates with all of them so effortlessly. The way she forms the center of their fucking little quartet. The way she can so easily demand that I give up the one person who made me feel truly alive again, all so she can secure her happy ending with the three Fae males who seem so besotted with her.

Not that I want any of them. Riordan is my brother, for fuck's sake, and Caer is too jittery and wild for my taste, and Jasper—well, I think if I were around Jasper too much, I might kill him one day, simply for being too sweetly, dreadfully *nice*.

But why should pasty little Alice with her silvery-blond hair have all of *them*, and yet want to take away the *one* person who desires me?

My heart knows the answer, of course. West's deadline for me coincides precisely with the Wizard's deadline for this task, and when that deadline passes, West is going to torture me to death. He'll enjoy every minute of it, and when it's over, he'll keep living his life. He might miss my cunt on occasion, but he won't miss *me*. The similarity in our souls isn't enough to dissuade him from his revenge.

"Your shoes and the scrying stones are not the only family heirlooms belonging to this dynasty," Riordan says, jolting me out of my thoughts. Fiero startles awake in his basket.

"Oh?" I say idly, petting Fiero's silky fur until he settles back down. "I saw something about that, yes. But it didn't pertain to me, so I didn't read it."

"There's a golden cap as well, and a belt, and a pair of bracelets," Riordan continues. "The belt gives the wearer great strength, far beyond that of a normal Fae, and the bracelets enable their owner to build anything they can imagine. It says here the South Witch inherited the belt, and North Witch inherited the bracelets."

"Great strength didn't help the South Witch," Caer comments.

"Maybe the Green Wizard didn't build the roads and the Emerald City after all," Alice says. "Maybe the Queen of Hearts did, before she was cursed and banished."

"That means West has the cap. What does it do?" Alice asks.

Riordan's voice is hollow with awe. "It calls the Wild Hunt."

Alice gasps, and I'm struck speechless. Even in the human realm, there are stories about the Wild Hunt—dreadful spirits who gallop across the sky on mystical horses, usually during times of unrest or on holidays like Midwinter Glee or the Bone Festival. They are drawn to the extremes of human emotion—greed, anger, love, grief, and joy. Sightings are rare, and when they do occur, people go missing and are found later, either dead or wandering mad through the forests and fields.

The idea of anyone calling the Wild Hunt on purpose is shocking—impossible.

Alice clutches Riordan's arm, peering at the page. "Have you ever heard of such a thing?"

"I have not. But it says here that the owner of the cap may call upon the Wild Hunt once in their lifetime, to purge injustice from the land. And there is a warning to the one who calls: 'Let them be guiltless, or their life will be the first one taken.'"

Caer scoffs. "Which is no doubt why the West Witch hasn't called upon them to rid his kingdom of the Green Wizard. He's afraid they'll take him, too."

There's a bit more lore about the Wild Hunt in the book, which Riordan reads aloud to us. Alice is noticeably lagging, and after a while Riordan hands the book to Jasper and picks her up, cradling her body against his broad chest. We continue like that, with her dozing in his arms and the rest of us trudging along, until dawn tints the sky.

With the pink light comes the awareness that we've been passing through farmlands dotted with houses and barns. Some of the cattle in the pastures are strange to me—tall, lanky creatures with long necks and scaly wings. Others are squat and roly-poly, like cows, but less able to stay on their feet, more prone to lolling in the deep lavender grass. We pass fields strewn with rotting logs, from which sprout colorful crops of mushrooms, and bushes heavy with small golden berries, like drops of honey. There's corn, too, similar to the cursed fields outside the Village of Crows, and that crop, at least, is familiar.

The houses are low and small, as if hunched down against an incoming blow, or shrinking to escape notice. The few people we see in the fields and farmyards are dressed in varying shades of green. They work doggedly, without paying us much notice, but they don't seem as dazed and enthralled as the servants of the Emerald City.

Riordan insists we leave the main road, since that's the one West will expect us to take, so for the first half of the day we travel by other paths, with me running ahead to survey the route and then transporting back to grab the others and bring them along. Alice screams the first time we transport together, and when we land, Fiero throws up on Caer's blousy shirt. He doesn't seem to mind, though—he strips it off, declaring he prefers going shirtless anyway—a state Alice and Jasper also seem to prefer for him. Riordan mutters, "Nothing I haven't seen a thousand times," but he keeps stealing glances at the Cat's toned body as well.

Around noon, we pause at a roadside market for a little food. No one is particularly hungry, but Alice insists we all need our strength.

I stand on a jutting rock by the road, staring ahead. We're approaching the foot of a mountain range, and West's stronghold is clearly visible now—a castle that looks as if it grew directly out of the dark-gray rock, half-camouflaged by the charcoal cliffs behind it.

So far there's been nothing to stop us. No poisonous green mist, no fields of poppies, no green flames leaping up to bar the path... nothing.

Even if he can't see us through the scrying stone, he knows we're coming. Why hasn't he stopped us?

Caer walks out from behind a nearby rock, grimacing. "I think I just shit out the orb I swallowed. Who wants to go and check?"

"Not possible," Riordan says. "They're magical, idiot. They will stay put until you purge them, or until they dissolve in a few months' time."

"Oh. Good." Caer swings up into a tree and perches on the branch above my head. "What's the plan, then?"

Jasper looks up from where he's feeding Fiero strips of meat. "You turn invisible and climb the walls, then let us all in through a side door. If anyone runs to attack us, Dorothy will speed-run them into a wall or a tree and knock them out."

We all turn and stare at him. He gazes back with innocent blue eyes. "What?"

"It's a really good plan, Jasper," Alice says.

"A bit simple," I add.

"Simplicity might be best here." Riordan gives Jasper a cool nod of approval. "Well done."

It's simple, yes, and it sounds too easy. West may have noticed Caer playing around with his invisibility when we were traveling. He might suspect exactly that tactic.

Whatever his plan is, he's not going to sit quietly in his chambers and let us stride into his castle.

# 26

# WEST

I'm going to sit here and let Dorothy and her little band of assassins walk right into my castle.

The fools think I can't see them. They don't realize the orbs Dorothy found expired years ago—they should last for months, but they only blocked my perception for a couple of hours before the effect wore off. I have the whole group in my sights again.

I hook both legs over the armrest of my leather chair, my eyes fixed on the dark glass ball in which the shapes of the would-be assassins are moving ever nearer.

I tug another berry off the stem with my teeth, then toss aside the empty twigs. The juice swirls over my tongue, sweet as the taste of Dorothy's arousal.

I messed up with her. I did something I didn't plan for, something she doesn't suspect—something that changed the dynamic between us forever. She might be furious when she finds out. Or maybe she'll be relieved, because it means I can't kill her like I planned to. Not without destroying myself at the same time.

I'll wait until she's close enough to kiss, and then I'll tell her everything.

She's taking so fucking long to get here.

With a sigh, I leap off the chair, nearly knocking over the tall wooden stand that holds my scrying stone. I pause to steady it, then stride to the window of the tower room where I spend most of my time. My people continue with their lives, exactly as they did before the advent of the Green Wizard. They're under my thrall, just enough to keep them happy, hard-working, and worry-free, while I take on all the anxieties of keeping this place safe. With my compulsion power gone, I can't enthrall anyone new, or alter the conditions of their obedience. It's just as well—otherwise I might be tempted to summon them together into a great army and compel them to go to war against the Wizard for me. So many of them would die—it would be dreadfully unfortunate. And I am a wise, noble lord. I do not waste my resources.

This little band of wayfarers, though—they could be the tools I need to remove the Green Wizard—destroy him once and for all. He thought to use them against me, but what if I turned the tables on him?

I've tried to defeat him, without success. Every day I wake up regretting the wish I made—thinking of how I could have worded it differently. I wished for the ability to evade the Wizard and his forces, both for myself and my people—and in return I received the protective barrier around my kingdom and the ability to transport myself from place to place, just like the power of my sister's shoes. Unfortunately, neither those shoes nor my new power could get either of us off the Isle.

If I could have left Oz alone, would I have done so? Would I have abandoned my people to the Wizard's mercy? It's something I ponder from time to time, never with a satisfactory answer. My existence here is one long, droning series of dutiful days spent managing the petty affairs of my people. I spend my nights pacing my chambers, gnawing over the same problems again and again.

My wish was carefully worded, but I still came away with an unintended side effect—my new skin tone. The Wizard said he added it to help me camouflage myself in his presence—part of my wish to "evade" him, he said. Of course it was a purely vindictive move, brought about by his rage at being forced to grant the wish. In those first few days, I tried every kind of illusion, glamour, and charm I could think of to regain the true color of my skin. But I barely mind the green now. Beauty is beauty, in any shade, and I'm as gorgeous as ever.

I scan the ground far below my tower window, squinting at bushes and trees to see if I can spot the travelers. They're nowhere in sight. They must be climbing the mountain, planning to approach the castle from the back. They think they're clever.

I'm not afraid for my life. None of them are as powerful as I am, not even Dorothy—not yet. I have conversation in mind, not conflict. A truce, for our mutual benefit.

When they arrive, we'll bargain.

If they would only hurry up.

Walking back to the scrying stone, I run my fingers over its glossy surface. I may be the only being alive who knows precisely why the Green Wizard is so desperate to obtain this, the last scrying stone on the Isle. Once I'm dead, and he has destroyed it, nothing will stop him from conquering this region. The barrier protecting my domain will fall, and my people will be prey to his enthralled armies—my siblings' subjects, gathered from the East, North, and South. He will storm this castle and lay claim to all the magical artifacts I managed to rescue from the ruins of Caislean Brea.

I suspected him from the moment he crashed into the former royal seat, long abandoned by my parents after they faded into the next life, but still an important location for the Isle, particularly when the four rulers wanted to meet at a neutral location.

My siblings were fascinated by the god-star, or the "Green Wizard," as he immediately told us to call him. He promised them power, and they were all too greedy for it.

But I broke into the vault the day after his arrival and took with me all the most precious treasures of our land. I wanted to protect them from him.

My siblings would not believe I was simply being cautious. They considered me a thief, and the Green Wizard fed their delusion until he managed to isolate me. By the time my siblings realized his true nature, it was too late.

Here I have stayed, watching the god-star destroy my family, sitting on a trove of magical items I cannot use. None are powerful enough to take him down, or to break through the spell that prevents anyone from leaving Oz. I suspect that spell wasn't laid by him at all, but by whoever sent him here. This Isle is his prison, and by extension, our tomb.

When Dorothy and her friends arrive, I will tell them all these things. They'll listen, because they have to—because she and I are bound now, forged by a chain we both willed into existence. A poisoned chain, maybe—a twining of toxic serpents—but it's the way of my family, the practice by which we have ensured spousal loyalty. It's the reason why neither my siblings nor I bound ourselves to anyone, until the god-star arrived and ensnared my sister.

I warned her not to bed him. His was an unnatural form, untrue. The bond that was supposed to ensure their eternal love was corrupted from the start because of what he *is*. And when the connection between them was brutally severed, it fractured her spirit so deeply that he was able to send her away from the Isle. By the time he was done with her, the barrier spell did not even recognize her as a living thing, but as something undead, sustained only by the terrible wish she spoke and the curse he laid upon her.

I have no doubt she is truly dead now. I pity those she must have destroyed before she met her demise.

Peering into the scrying stone, I can't hold back a rueful smile. My would-be killers are at the southwest tower, taking weapons from my unconscious guards, preparing to enter the narrow gate.

I turn my back on the orb and walk to the window once more, unlatching it and pushing one side open. The diamond-shaped panes of glass flash in the light of the setting sun.

Soon now. So soon.

My stomach whirls and my pulse quickens at the thought of seeing Dorothy again. She is intoxicating, invigorating. Delectably human, but with such Unseelie darkness in her soul. Her mind is a maze I yearn to explore, even as I ache to taste every curve and hollow of her body. She will agree to this bargain, I know it.

For a moment—just for a moment—I allow myself to imagine a different ending. If she and her friends should manage to defeat me somehow—if one of them has a weapon or magic I haven't seen—if they manage to kill me—

If that happens, Dorothy will die as well.

I imagine it—myself, lying limp and beautiful on the floor of this tower, my sightless eyes reflecting the scrying stone nearby, while Dorothy's lovely body slumps over mine, forever stilled in death. So picturesque.

Her friends and her half-brother would weep over her fate—but only for a little while. They would realize, soon enough, that my death fulfilled their task. Robbed of Dorothy's ability to travel swiftly, they would steal mounts from my stables and race for the Emerald City, carrying my body and the scrying stone to the Wizard. Maybe they would reach him in time, before I decomposed into ash, before their deadline expired. But even if they made it, he would never allow the four of them a joyous future. He is the enemy of happiness, and he would find a way to ruin their love.

A sorrowful ending, romantic in its very sadness.

But that ending will not be mine.

I settle back into my chair, taking a cup of wine from the little table on my right and propping my legs over the armrest again.

No, that is not the ending I will accept. Everyone else can die, for all I care—but Dorothy and I must remain alive.

I have so much more I want to do to her.

# 27

## DOROTHY

Something about this feels wrong. Not morally wrong, but—illogical. Suspicious.

We're inside the castle now. There's been no magic to stop us, and the guards we've met were fairly easy to overcome. I've been using my energy sparingly, since I might need all of it when we face West. So far, my reluctance to use magic hasn't been a problem—Riordan and Caer seem all too ready for a fight, and even Jasper has gotten in a few punches. Riordan grabbed an ax off one of the guards, but at Alice's insistence he's mostly using its back side to thunk people over the head and knock them out. Alice has been carrying Fiero, lingering behind the rest of us, since she has neither magic nor combat training.

Considering how ill-prepared we all are, it's been far too easy.

"I don't like it," I repeat, for the third time, as we flatten ourselves to the wall in a dank hallway. The passage tees off ahead, and I'm not sure what awaits us around the corner.

"So you've said," Riordan answers dryly.

"He's letting us walk in. That can't be good."

"What other choice do we have?" Alice whispers. "We can't stop now. We're running out of time."

"We need to spread out," I say. "Look for a throne room, a great hall, or the royal chambers. Interrogate any servants you find. Jasper and I will go together, and Riordan can go with Alice. Caer should be fine alone."

Caer looks anxious at the thought of prowling the castle by himself. "Me, alone?" he says faintly.

Alice steps forward, as if to encourage him, but I move in quickly and clasp his shoulder. Meanwhile my other hand closes around something in my pocket—the small bottle of water from the Well of Undoing.

"You made your wish because you were afraid," I say, low. "But fear isn't something to abolish. Fear makes you wiser. Sometimes it gives you the strength to do what must be done—to be the person you need to be. You are the best choice for this. I trust you to succeed."

As I speak to him, I'm pushing the bottle into his hand. His fingers close around it, and he nods, understanding.

With a final squeeze of his shoulder, I mouth the words, *Follow me.*

Hopefully Caer will understand and pursue Jasper and me, using his invisibility. I still believe we're cloaked from West's view. But I won't take any chances.

"Come on." I jerk my head, indicating for Jasper to follow. He's armed with a short sword gleaned from a fallen guard, and I've got a dagger.

West's castle is gloomy and appears mostly uninhabited—an empty, echoing maze of stone hallways and square dark rooms draped in tapestries. He certainly hasn't been growing rich off the labors of his people. As for the lack of guards and servants, I suppose he doesn't have much need for them. This land is somehow protected from the Green Wizard, so it wouldn't need a significant military. Or maybe, with his powers of compulsion sucked away, West can't repurpose his thralls and re-task them as a fighting force. Maybe he has simply been sitting here, waiting for an opportunity to overthrow the Wizard—a chance to fight back. Or maybe he's content to spend the rest of his days as the solitary leader of a puppet kingdom under siege. How long can this region endure, walled off from the rest of the Isle, without the possibility of trade by ship or shore?

"Where are we going?" whispers Jasper from behind me, and I realize I've been wandering without much thought... wending my way up a circular staircase without any idea what might be at the top.

"I'm not sure," I whisper back. "But I have a feeling..."

It's not like the tug I feel toward my half-brother, the awareness of his location. This is a whisper in my mind, a nebulous lure teasing me onward, up the stairs, until we reach a broad landing, richly carpeted, with a mosaic table standing by a glossy paneled door.

Other than the throne-room doors in the Emerald City, this is the finest door I've ever seen—beautifully carved from some rich, red-brown wood.

My fingers curl around the gilded handle, and when I press down, the door opens with a quiet *click*.

Slowly I push it open, my heart thundering so fast it's almost to the point of pain.

And there he is. Standing by a half-open window, looking taller than ever. The breeze tosses his dark hair, and a thin black cloak swirls around him. The fading sunlight softens the green of his skin, turning the side of his face nearly golden.

For a moment neither of us move. It's as if we're suspended in time, our gazes woven together across the space between us. I'm barely conscious of Jasper behind me, of the spacious circular chamber, of the scrying stone resting in a stand at the room's center.

Then West moves, quick as lightning. He reaches for his staff, leaning against the wall nearby, but I dive into it with my magic, agitating the tiniest cells of the wood, making it vibrate and heat so that he can't hold it. He drops it, cursing, and raises his other hand, palm out.

Instantly, spirals of green mist rise from the floor and entwine my body and Jasper's. The flow of my magic cuts off abruptly, and when I try to step forward, I can't.

"I need you to listen," says West. "I've been thinking since we parted, and I believe I have a plan that can get both of us what we want."

"And what do you think I want?" I say acidly.

"You want to live." His mouth curves in a slanted smile. "And you want your brother and his partner to retain their natural forms. And *I* want the Green Wizard gone."

"But he's a god-star. He's impossible to kill."

"It's true, he can't be killed. But he can be permanently trapped. Contained. And with your help, I—"

Something dashes into his face—a flash of sparkling liquid from an invisible source. West startles and wipes his cheek with the back of his hand. "What the fuck?"

A serrated white grin dances in mid-air, slowly joined by the Cat as he reappears, strip by strip, until his whole body is visible. He waggles the empty vial in West's face. "Got you."

West grabs for his staff again, but when he points it at Caer, nothing happens. At the same moment, the green mist he conjured drains away, leaving Jasper and me free to move.

"What the fuck have you done to me?" West stares—not at Caer, but at me. Anger and betrayal churn in his dark eyes.

"Water from the Well of Undoing," I tell him. "Didn't you see me take it from the vault?"

"I didn't watch every second of your time in Caislean Brea," he snaps. "I had my own research to do. And I thought I destroyed all those vials. Where did you find that? You didn't bring it from the Village of Crows—they guard their supply too fiercely."

"I found it in a box, buried under the shards of broken vials."

"Shit."

Caer whips out his claws, inspecting them casually. "Want me to slice his throat, Dorothy? That should do the trick. But Jasper can cut off his head, too, for good measure." He darts toward West, who leaps away from him, putting a big armchair between himself and the Cat.

"You don't want to kill me," West says, darting a keen glance at me. "I know a way to trap the Green Wizard for good."

"That's a lie," Caer says coolly. "A rather pathetic one, too, if you ask me. Desperation doesn't suit you, Witch. But I suppose all the tormentors turn out to be cowards in the end. I heard what you did to my friends, torturing them with wretched dreams. Playing with their worst fears." Teeth bared, he stalks toward West again, a hiss slipping between his parted jaws. "Say goodbye, swine."

He bounds onto the chair, and West scrambles out of his reach.

"You don't understand," yells West. "If you kill me, then Dor—"

But his voice vanishes—jerked to a halt in his throat. Eyes wide, he struggles—tries to speak—but he can't even form words.

"A bit of magic I perfected recently," Riordan says, striding into the room. He casts a sidelong look at Alice, who's by his side. "I had to interrogate quite a few Fae in my journey to find Caer. And as I told you, I don't like screaming. This keeps them quiet until they're ready to speak the truth, you see."

Alice gives him a look of mingled admiration and horror.

"Caer, Jasper, hold him," says Riordan. "It should be easy—he lacks his Fae strength. He's weak as a human right now. No healing abilities, either. The marks we make on him now will remain." There's a twitch along his jaw, right near one of his cheek-mouths.

"You were going to kill Dorothy," Alice says quietly to West. "So she should be the one to end you. Unless you'd rather one of us did it, Dorothy... since you... well..."

"You think because I fucked him, I can't kill him?" My voice sounds higher than usual, but it's strong. "I'm Unseelie. I have no qualms about doing this."

Taking the dagger from my belt, I walk forward, while Caer and Jasper shove West back against the wall and pin him there, his arms outstretched. His green skin and dark lips still gleam with drops of the well-water Caer threw on him. His eyes meet mine, deep-brown and sorrowful—almost desperate. Again he tries to speak—and again he can't manage a word through his magic-stiffened lips.

Agony and despair wash over his features, but he nods, mute and resigned. Closing his eyes, he tips up his chin, baring his throat to my knife.

"Do it quickly," Riordan says, tension in his deep voice. "You must transport us back to the Emerald City before midnight, or the bargain with the Wizard becomes void."

"I know," I hiss over my shoulder. Behind me, Alice whispers, "Leave her be, Riordan. This is hard for her." In a louder voice, strained with sympathy, she says, "Dorothy, let someone else do it. Please. You shouldn't have to—"

"Shouldn't have to what?" I whirl, the dagger clenched in my fingers. "Shouldn't have to kill someone I fucked? Someone who understands me better than any of you do—even *you*." I point the knife at Riordan. "Or you, Alice—we were raised in the same realm, in the same region, and yet you understand *nothing* about me. Nothing. *He* does." I whirl back to West, setting the tip of the dagger against the pulse point of his throat. My voice cracks, hoarse and hollow. "He sees inside me like no one else ever has. And yet I have to kill him because all of *you* want him dead. Because you *need* him dead, to ensure your own happiness. What has he ever done to any of you?"

"He's wicked, Dorothy," Alice says gently. "He keeps all these people under his control. His family—"

"The people under his thrall seem perfectly happy and healthy," I counter. "Certainly they're better off than the rest of the inhabitants of this Isle. Sometimes people—Fae or human—need to be controlled, for their own good, by someone who knows what's best for them."

"As the temporary ruler of the Dread Court, for all of one month—I agree with you," Riordan says. "But he has a blood-feud against you. He has sworn vengeance on your head for the death of his sister."

"No." I'm staring into West's face, into his eyes, now open, fixed on me. Hope ignites in his gaze, and a fiercely tender look—the same one I saw on his face the last time he fucked me. I understand the message in those eyes, as clearly as if he has spoken it aloud. "No, he wouldn't. He *can't* kill me, any more than I can kill him."

The knife drops to my feet, and I lift both hands, shoving Caer and Jasper away from West with a blast of magic. Caer lands on his feet, crouched low, snarling, while Jasper smashes into a dresser and picks himself out of the wooden shards, looking deeply offended.

I turn my back to West, my body shielding his. "None of you will touch him," I declare, in a voice more powerful than any I've used in my life.

Riordan advances—so much taller and broader than me. His scarred fingers tighten into fists. "Don't do this. I will not suffer hundreds of years in a suit of armor so that you can play queen to the last paltry king of this godsforsaken isle. I will not sacrifice my own happiness again—not even for you. Not even for my own blood. This I swear."

"You're not a fighter," I say through gritted teeth, while my magic seeps into the stones of the tower, causing the floor to quake. "You can't stop me."

"Oh, but I can, little sister. And I will." Red eyes blazing, he reaches for my throat. To my surprise, I have some of my concussive magic left—maybe my shoes are synced to me at last. I throw that force against my brother's chest, and he flies backward, crashing into a bookshelf.

Caer springs at me next, but I push extra force into his jump and he soars over me, smashing into the open window and nearly tumbling out. Alice screams, drops Fiero, and runs to him, helping him scramble back inside. Freed from Alice's protective arms, Fiero runs back and forth, barking frantically at all of us.

Jasper approaches me, his sword awkwardly angled toward my breast, a tortured look in his blue eyes. "I can't lose them. Not after I just found them—please, Dorothy—"

I agitate the particles of his weapon, heating the metal until he drops it with a yelp.

Riordan is struggling to his feet, but apparently his hold on West's tongue broke, because from behind me, the Witch shouts, "Stop, all of you! I have a way out of this, if you will only listen!"

"They won't listen," I grit out. "No one does. No one ever *cares* enough to listen."

"That's not fair, Dorothy," Alice seethes. She's truly angry now—flushed and flaming.

"Not just them, Kin-Slayer," West says soothingly. "I need you to listen, too. Let's all sit down, and I will tell you why killing me would end your life as well. I'll explain my plan to fulfill your bargain with the Wizard *and* trap him forever."

Alice stares at him, startled. She flings out her hand, and Caer, who was just about to pounce on West again, settles for shredding the leather of the armchair with his ten claws.

Killing West would end my life as well? And he has a plan to trap the Wizard forever? What the fuck is the Witch talking about?

Riordan clears his throat, brushing off his green vest. "Well then. That sounds promising. Why didn't you say so before?"

# 28

## DOROTHY

"Killing you will end my life?" I exclaim. "What do you mean?"

"It's a ritual adapted from the way our ancestors used to claim their mates, millennia ago," he says. "Some Fae still believe in the practice of marking a mate, but usually it is done purely for erotic and emotional purposes, with little magical power behind it. However, for my family, marking a mate with your arousal and theirs, and being marked in return, carries a greater significance. When accompanied by a mutual love and desire to be each other's eternal partner, that act creates a mate bond. I believe the Seelie have something like it in their royal family, but I'm not sure if it is still practiced. Here in Oz, a royal mate bond ensures ultimate loyalty, because the death of one partner causes the death of the other."

The longer he speaks, the more frantically my heart beats.

He marked me. I marked him. And I spoke those words in my head—words of passion and longing.

*We could do this forever, the two of us—we'd never have to fear being alone again. We'd be so wicked and wild—we could do anything we pleased, and no one could tell us not to. I wish I could love you until I die. I want you to be mine.*

"And you two—performed this rite?" Riordan says stiffly.

"The marking was impulsive on my part," West admits. "I didn't explain the significance, because I never expected her to reciprocate what I was thinking and feeling."

"Who says I do?" I snap.

"The proof of the bond occurred immediately afterward." West gives me a significant look, and I remember the three dazzling orgasms we experienced in unison.

My cheeks heat. "Oh. Fuck."

"We still only have your word that killing you would kill Dorothy," Alice points out. "You might just be trying to save your own skin, to buy time until the effect of the well-water dissipates. What proof can you offer?"

"Do you still have the books I gave Dorothy?" West asks.

"They're in a basket outside the castle, concealed under a bush," she replies.

"I'll get them." I rise quickly, and with a click of my heels and three quick steps, I'm in the darkening forest outside the castle. Since I've seen West's chambers, it will only take me a second to transport myself back there—but I pause after retrieving the books. I clutch them to my chest, my head bowed over them, and I drag in a few long, shuddering breaths.

Those words in my head—were they truly a commitment? A confession of love? Apparently they were enough to lock me into this "mate bond" with him. I hate that my thoughts and my acts with West are being dragged out into the open for everyone to inspect and evaluate.

Maybe I won't go back in there. They can sort this out themselves, can't they?

But then West will be alone with the others.... helpless, powerless. What if they decide to kill him anyway, while I'm gone? What if he's already dead?

I click my heels and take three steps, breathless with terror.

When I snap back into West's chambers, he's still alive, lounging on the biggest armchair in the room, pointing to the scrying stone. "—a god-star's actual tear," he's saying. "God-stars can observe humans whenever and wherever they like. The scrying stone grants a limited form of that ability to certain humans with god-star gifts—like compulsion. The god-star who fell to this Isle has been stripped of most of his powers, as you know—including his abilities of coercion and omniscience."

"So he could use the stone to spy on people?" Alice asks. "But if that's his goal, why would he destroy the stones that belonged to your siblings?"

"Because the stones have another power. They pose a terrible threat to a god-star like him—one who has been weakened and cast down. I found some information on the matter a long while ago, but I gave up hope of being able to use it, since the spell I would need was inaccessible to me." He leans forward, his dark eyes glinting. "You see, a scrying stone can be used to trap a fallen god-star in their true form. But such a feat requires a spell from one of the most ancient of spellbooks—"

"The Tama Olc," says Riordan.

"Exactly." West's eyes are bright with triumph. "I knew you carried a book with you, Dorothy, but until our time in the library I wasn't sure if it was truly the Tama Olc. Nor could I recall for certain whether the Tama Olc was the book I needed. When I left you in Caislean Brea, I came here and searched my personal library until I found the reference to scrying stones being used to trap god-stars. And my suspicion was confirmed—the spell I need is within the Tama Olc."

"So I'll have to hunt for the spell," I say, my heart sinking at the thought of all the pages of close-set script and complex lists of ingredients. Even with my ability to read quickly, it will take a while to locate the right pages. "I have to find it as quickly as possible so we can gather all the ingredients and return to the

Emerald City by midnight—and then what? Trick the Wizard into believing we killed you? Deliver him the scrying stone?"

"It will require precise timing," says Riordan thoughtfully. "A sequence of events that will ensure the outcome we desire."

"Perfect." Caer groans and flings himself onto the settee where Jasper is sitting. When Fiero leaps out of the Scarecrow's lap with a disgruntled yip, Caer settles his head on Jasper's thighs instead. "Just what I love—sequences of events that must be performed in precise order."

Jasper soothes him by stroking his hair and playing with the gold piercings along his black furred ears.

"No need to worry your feline head about it," says West, his tone gilded with condescension. "You and the Scarecrow are simply set pieces in the little play we'll perform for the Wizard."

"Who threw the well water on you and took all your powers away?" Caer asks loftily. "Why, that was me, wasn't it? Maybe you'd like a few permanent decorations while we're waiting for your powers to return." He flexes his ebony claws.

Setting the books on a table beside West's chair, I stalk over to a sideboard and pick up the ornate hourglass standing on its surface. I turn it upside down so the emerald sand begins pouring through. "If anyone harms the Witch in the space of the next hour, they will answer to me."

I can practically see a scathing retort forming on the Cat's lips. Jasper quickly bends down and kisses him, effectively sealing off the words. Caer mumbles a protest, but after a moment, his body relaxes and his hand drifts up to caress Jasper's cheek.

"Show us the information about your family's mate bonds," Alice requests, nodding to the books on the table. I pass the historical volume to West, and he flips through several pages before passing the tome to Alice.

"I should go fetch the Tama Olc," I say hesitantly.

Riordan's eyebrows rise. "*Fetch* it? You mean to say you don't have it? Where the fuck is it?"

"Keep your trousers on. It's safe, in the library of Caislean Brea. I can have it back here in an instant, provided all of you promise not to hurt West while I'm gone."

"Your concern for me is quite moving, sweetheart." West splays a hand over his chest. "I could almost believe you care for me."

He's mocking me, but there's a faint edge to his voice—a question he's too proud to ask.

He wants to know if I love him. Wants to know what I was thinking while we were fucking.

The realization springs into my mind, so sharp and obvious that I'm shocked it didn't occur to me before.

The mate bond has to be a mutual agreement. If my will and my thoughts expressed words of love and commitment that sealed the bond—he must have expressed something similar.

A wild excitement sparkles through my veins, and for a moment I think I might perish on the spot unless I know exactly what he thought in that climactic moment.

But I don't want to hear those words in front of the others, nor do I plan on voicing my own thoughts until West and I are alone. And then I'm going to wreck him for daring to perform even *part* of a mating ritual without my consent. After which I will fuck him until he yells my name.

I'm smiling at him. Shit, I didn't realize it. And he's smiling back, a wicked grin that's both surprised and avaricious.

"Shut up," I snap at him, and he grins wider as I tap my heels together and disappear.

# 29

## ALICE

Dorothy takes a few minutes to fetch the Tama Olc, so Riordan and I sit together on a couch and skim the pages West pointed out to us, until we're satisfied that his story about mate bonds is true. There's a list of death records that show royal couples dying within minutes of each other—not just the King and Queen of the Isle, but other relatives in the family tree as well.

"It's a strange way to ensure loyalty and love." I look up at Riordan. He's engrossed in reading, but his long ears twitch toward the sound of my voice, and I can't help a little smile.

"Some might consider it romantic," he says, low.

"It's certainly possessive."

His dark lashes lift, his scarlet eyes meeting mine, and my breath catches at the torturous beauty of him. Even if magic could seal the gashes in his face, I rather prefer them. They are *him*—proof of a past he survived. They are the explanation for his occasional ruthlessness, and the witness to his indomitable nature.

"Never assume that because I share you with Caer and Jasper, that I am any less possessive of you." His words are quiet, meant only for me, but there's a depth and power to them that makes my whole body tingle. "I plan to have you all to myself, kitten, many times. You and I will explore all the ways your pretty human body can come apart for me."

Breathless, I stare into his eyes, caught up in the magnetic force of his personality, the brilliance that first drew me to him. I can't speak, so I nod, and his eyes warm, a smile that never touches his mouth.

With difficulty I break the bond of his gaze, glancing over at Caer and Jasper. They're still kissing, with an increasing ardor that seems to amuse the West Witch.

Dorothy appears again, snapping into existence out of thin air. She's holding the Tama Olc. "Now for the long job of perusing every page, trying to find the right spell," she says dolefully.

"I think I can help with that." I rise from the couch and walk over to her. "When I owned that book, I spent hours looking through it. I couldn't do anything with what I found, but I practically memorized the titles of all the spells. I don't remember a reference to 'god-star,' but maybe there's another word used in the book—a term for god-star that I don't know."

"*Dia Réalta*," says West, looking at me with renewed interest. "Or *Rí Gréine*."

"*Rialóir Mór*?" suggests Riordan, and West nods.

"*Dia Réalta*," I muse, while my brain skims through my memories of the book. "The Tama Olc doesn't belong to me anymore, so I can't find the spot for you, but—Dorothy, try about two-thirds of the way through, somewhere near the spells for corpse reanimation and moon-phase conversion. If you hit the spell for living limb replacement, you've gone too far."

Dorothy opens the book, and with my help, she navigates to the spell within minutes. "*Príosún Dia Réalta?*" she reads aloud.

"Fuck me—that's the one!" exclaims West.

"What does it require?" Riordan asks.

Dorothy reads off the ingredients—an encouragingly short list. "We must create this potion and bathe the scrying stone with it to prepare it for containing the god-star. Then someone must speak the incantation."

"I'll make the potion," Riordan says, leaping up with such eagerness I almost laugh. He's so fierce and brooding, yet so fucking adorable.

"Fine." West waves his hand airily. "Never was much of a hand at potions. There's a supply room, fully stocked, though some of the ingredients may not be what you'd call *fresh*."

"I'll make do. Shouldn't take long. I'll need a little of your blood, Witch—and yours, too, Dorothy. I must also create a potion that will simulate a state of death for the Witch, and the blood of his lover is a key ingredient for that spell. Best not to trust an illusion or glamour when we're dealing with a god-star. We must convince the Green Wizard that his enemy is dead and fading."

Once the samples are collected, West rings for a servant, who leads Riordan off to the supply room. The rest of us move from West's chambers to a parlor on the first floor of the castle, where he insists we partake in some food and wine, presented by a pair of affable servants. I can't convince myself to nibble any of the food, though I'm sure it's delicious. This entire situation reminds me far too much of the time when Riordan and I forged our alliance with Finias and Clara to take down the Eater of Hearts. The experience was hours of unbearable suspense followed by horrific pain. It worked out for us in the end, but I'm not sure we'll be so lucky tonight.

Last time, Caer turned tail before the final confrontation.

My gaze travels to him as I take a tiny sip of wine. He's restlessly prowling the edge of the parlor, stealing glances at Jasper, who sits beside Dorothy, feeding Fiero bits of roasted fowl. West is leaning over Dorothy's shoulder while she reads lines of the incantation aloud.

When I look at Caer again, he's watching me. He curls a beckoning claw and darts out of the room into the hallway.

I follow him, my skin warming at the anticipation of his touch. But when I step into the corridor, he's leaning against the wall, his slim tail writhing gently and his ears pricked forward.

"You keep looking at me with this apprehensive stare," he says quietly. "Like you think I'm going to run."

I pinch my lips together and turn my gaze to the floorboards.

"Darling Alice." He tucks a knuckle under my chin and tips my face up. "I made that mistake once. I won't do it again. I've never been so terrified as when I had to exist without you and Riordan. Love you or lose you, I'm here to stay. You're stuck with me."

I force a smile, but I know it doesn't reach my eyes.

"You don't believe me yet," Caer whispers, his gaze tender. "But I'll show you, mousie, I promise. I will never be so selfish again. Even if I have to watch you suffer, sicken, scream, and die in front of me, I will stay. I will try to save you, and if I can't, I'll comfort you at the end."

It's a strange thing for a lover to say, and stranger still that it's exactly what I need to hear. I find his hand and slide my fingers between his. "I vow the same to you. Whatever form you take, I will be there, playing with you, talking to you, cuddling with you—and yes, fucking you, monster or not."

He releases a low, breathless laugh, tilting his forehead against mine. "I love you."

"I love you, too. I love you so much I can't breathe sometimes."

His other hand wraps around the back of my head and he kisses me, a warm, fierce promise. "Mine," he whispers. "I may share you with the others, but you belong to me."

I laugh against his mouth. "That's what Riordan said, too."

"Riordan." He smirks, shaking his head. "Lovable asshole, isn't he? Speaking of assholes—do you think he'd ever let me..."

"Maybe," I say doubtfully. "I think he likes to be the one taking, not being taken."

"I'll wager Jasper and I can convince him sometime."

"I'd pay money to see that," I breathe. "Does that make me a wicked little slut?"

"Oh, it does," he purrs. "*Our* wicked little slut. And also our cherished queen. Both."

After a few more kisses, we return to the parlor hand in hand. Despite the reassurance from Caer, I'm still wretchedly anxious about our timetable—we're only two hours from midnight now. The green hourglass emptied a while ago, and though West didn't boast about the return of his powers, there's a renewed confidence and cockiness about him, a wisp of green smoke hovering over his fingers as he perches on the armrest of the couch near Dorothy.

The two of them haven't spoken alone since we arrived, and neither one seems eager to make that happen. Maybe they don't want to face the reality of their bond until after the situation with the Wizard is resolved, one way or the other.

At last Riordan strides into the parlor, holding a vial in each hand. He looks taller and more handsome than ever—beautifully triumphant, fortified by the return to his true calling—the science of magic, and the creation of spells and potions.

"One to prepare the scrying stone," he says, lifting the purple vial. "And the other to mimic a Fae state of death." He raises the second bottle, which gleams green.

West grimaces, but he nods. He produces the scrying stone from his pocket and expands it from its marble-sized form to its larger size. When Riordan pours the contents of the purple vial over the stone, the liquid soaks into the glossy surface, as if the stone drank it all. Its color alters slightly, threads of white smoke lacing through the customary dark swirls of cloud inside it.

"I suppose that means it's time to go." Dorothy rises from the couch, a little stiffly. Reluctantly.

"Wait!" The word jerks out of me, more loudly and sharply than I intended. "I mean—please, I'd like a moment with Dorothy first."

"Of course, love," says Caer. "Whatever you need." Jasper nods enthusiastically, and Riordan bows his head to me.

West doesn't protest. As Dorothy and I move into the hallway, Fiero trots after us and begins nosing along the baseboard.

"I'm sorry." I force the words out, my hands twisting together. "I know Fae don't like apologies, but you're part human so... either way, I owe you an apology for behaving as I did. I was incredibly selfish... so blinded by the nearness of the future I wanted that I was willing to do anything to get it. I sacrificed myself once, you know—sacrificed *everything*. I believed I was going to die. And then, when I didn't—well, I supposed I got greedy for the things I never thought I could have. It made me a little mad, I suppose. As Caer would say, everyone's a little mad in Faerie." I release a faint laugh. "But that doesn't excuse how I behaved toward you—what I asked you to do to the person you—" My voice cracks. "Dorothy, I'm so sorry."

She regards me coolly, as if she's gauging my emotions, my sincerity. Calculating what her response should be.

"You don't have to forgive me," I add hastily. "You have every right to be angry as long as you need to. I just had to say it, before we—you know."

"In case we die."

"Yes. That."

"I understand why you wanted me to kill West. You love Caer and Riordan. You can't bear to think of them existing in torment." She nods. "You acted as I would have if our circumstances were reversed, and I can't fault you for that."

"Then... we're all right, you and I? Friends?"

"Friends." She seems to be testing the word, seeing how it feels in her mouth. "Yes."

She heads for the parlor again.

"I hope this works," I blurt out. "Not just for me, but for you. I think you are more yourself here than you ever were back home."

Dorothy glances over her shoulder, with a mysterious half-smile. "But this *is* home. And I think I've always been trying to get here."

When we return to the others, West is holding the potion, preparing to drink it, but he says, "There's one final piece of this puzzle. We need the Wizard to take his god-star form, otherwise he can't be trapped inside the stone."

"He showed that form to Alice and me," Dorothy says. "He might do it again. But if we ask, he might get suspicious."

West shakes his head. "We can't just ask. We have to force him into that form. Someone has to make a wish."

"But each person gets only one wish, and we've all made ours," says Caer. "Can you have one of your servants do it?"

West shakes his head. "People who have been under thrall cannot make wishes to the god-star, even if they've been released from the thrall by their master's death. There's a conflict of magic there.... Or perhaps it's a fail-safe the god-stars instituted, to prevent the Wizard from becoming too powerful during his exile."

Everyone falls silent, but my eyes snap to Jasper, who's standing by a sculpture, his fingers tracing the contours and details with wondering admiration.

"Jasper hasn't made a wish," I say. "And he's never been under thrall. The East Witch's power didn't work on him. He might be the only one on the entire Isle who can do this. Certainly the only person we can get on such short notice."

Every head in the room turns toward Jasper. He stares back, blue eyes widening as he grasps what I've said.

"Fuck," growls Riordan. "I suppose it's a good thing we rescued him."

"Of course it is," says Caer. "With a cock like that, killing him would have been a terrible waste."

"Oh gods, Caer." I shove his shoulder, and he grins.

"Right, then." West plucks the stopper from his vial. "I suppose it's bottoms-up for me, and then Dorothy, you'll take us to the Emerald City."

She holds his gaze. "If we both survive this, we need to talk."

"Of course." He winks at her. "I'd be happy to—*talk*—with you."

Her mouth twitches slightly—the barest hint of a smile. "Drink up, motherfucker."

# 30

# THE WIZARD

I am sick, sick, sick of being here. Sick of being trapped on this fucking Isle, barred from the rest of Faerie, from the other realms. Prevented from expanding through the universe as I'm used to doing. Confining me here is like taking a magnificent dragon from the skies and jamming it into a thimble. It's barbaric. It's fucking infuriating.

I've tried various schemes to free myself, to reach out and *hurt* the ones who put me here. My devices and schemes have all failed. And the more they fail, the greater my disquiet grows. I'm weakening—I can tell. Each wish I'm forced to grant drains me a little more. It gives me some joy to distort the wishes, to cause pain and terror whenever I can, but even that joy wears thinner every day.

Except for a few children in the Village of Crows, there are none left on the Isle who can wish for anything. Newcomers arrive every so often, hunting me down, demanding their due. I like hurting them for their insolence, but I hate the sense of power leaking from my form each time.

My so-called transgressions did not warrant this wretchedness. I did not *deserve* this punishment. As a god-star, I need not cling to any moral code, nor follow any canon of justice. There is no such thing as guilt or law for one such as I. A pity the other god-stars did not agree. They disliked my favorite amusements—torturing entire races in various realms. I even created two fully populated realms of my own, just so I could torment and dismantle them. But when I decided to destroy one of the twelve primary realms—well, that spurred my fellow god-stars to action.

I thought them too indolent and self-absorbed to care about what I did for amusement. I was wrong.

Someday I will devise a way out of this prison. And then they'll wish they had never dared to punish me. I will rain such devastation upon every realm they love, upon every race we've ever created, that they will burst apart from the pain of it. And I alone will be left, ascendant, triumphant. Utterly liberated.

But before I can aspire to such goals, I need to rid this Isle of the final risk to my existence—the West Witch and his scrying stone. I don't believe he knows the threat it poses to me—how could he, puny Fae fool that he is? He is a quivering idiot, incapable of facing me on his own, cowering in his protected region, behind the barrier I was forced to erect for him.

If he knew what that stone could do to me, he'd have used it by now. Besides, the spell he needs to trap me in the stone is securely in the hands of the assassins I sent to kill him. That cold Fae girl with the brown and blue eyes won't let the Tama Olc out of her possession, so I need not fear it falling into the Witch's hands.

It irks me that my people failed to steal the Tama Olc from her, and that I was forced to let her walk out of my castle with it. But she's a weakling half-Fae. There is no possibility of her learning to use such powerful magic. Not now, not when the deadline is almost up.

I pace faster, aching for an end to all this. I want to see the West Witch's corpse, cold and gray and granite, lying before me. And then I will take his scrying stone and grind it into powdered glass.

If the human, the half-Fae, and the two curse victims fail to kill him, I will have the lesser pleasure of learning about their deaths, and hearing the survivors plead for my mercy. There is love among the little band of fools, and there is nothing I like better than twisting love into despair, rotting it with cruelty, shattering hope into horror.

Either scenario will be a savory treat.

I stalk my throne room in my Fae form—the shape I took so I could seduce and fuck Evanelda. She was amusing for a while. And then I grew bored, so I broke her. It was the best fun I've had since I fell—digging into her black heart that pulsed with love for me, driving my thumbs into the vessels, popping them so the dark blood gushed out, ripping the muscle with my nails. I ate her heart myself, and gave her the craving for the hearts of others.

She was the nearest thing I found to a kindred being in this place. But in the end, she was like all the others—boring, insipid, feeble. Her weakness practically begged to be abused and tortured.

A thread of awareness enters my mind. The steward at the throne room door is mentally announcing the presence of several supplicants. It's the group I've been waiting for, and a vicious glee soars through my consciousness.

Swiftly I change my form to that of a great beast—the heads of three lions, the body of a bear, the claws and wings of an eagle, the antlers of a stag, and a hundred bulbous eyes. I relish the shock on their faces as they approach me down the length of the great hall. The rabbit-Fae and the one with cat ears are carrying a body slung between them—the stony, gray corpse of the West Witch.

He's dead. The fools actually managed it.

I'm ten times larger than any of them, and when I bend my central head closer to inspect the body, they all cringe. I love it. Their fear is better than any psychedelic potion the Fae have invented. It carries me to screaming heights of delight.

The West Witch is dressed in black, his skin a solid, cold gray from head to feet. Tiny cracks are already beginning to branch through his body. Soon he will disintegrate, and his dust will blow away until he is entirely faded. I'll have his body left here in my throne room so I can watch it happen.

"Well done," I boom, and my roar makes the supplicants tremble. But the human girl who wished for the two Fae to be freed steps forward, her pale hair billowing with each huff of breath from my great nostrils. I'd like to cleave her in two with a giant cock, then eat the pieces of her torn flesh. But I am bound to honor her wish. I've twisted it as far as I can, and now it must be granted.

"And the stone?" I demand.

The girl motions to the other one with the braids—the one with the mismatched eyes. She steps forward and sweeps a cloth off the object she's carrying.

It's the scrying stone. The only way anyone on this Isle could possibly end me.

I shift into my Fae form and hold out both hands. "Give it to me."

But the blonde girl shakes her head. "Not until you proclaim that these two Fae are forever free of their wishes and their cursed forms, as we agreed."

"It is done," I confirm, my expression twitching slightly as a bit of power leaks from me. "They will forever retain their natural forms."

"One more thing," says the girl with the braids. "Our friend Jasper has not yet made a wish. Before we leave, he has a request."

I'm about to insist they give me the stone first, but the golden-haired Fae, Jasper, advances, already speaking. His voice is smooth, golden, calming. Almost worshipful. "I wish that I may perceive your glorious true form for five minutes, without losing my sight or memories, and with no harm to my friends."

I almost laugh. It's a stupid wish, a simple one, easily performed, and I'll lose no power by granting it. The boy must be an idiot to waste his wish on such a thing. I should expect no more—humans and Fae are generally foolish, incapable of higher thought. The number of idiotic, foolishly-worded wishes I've granted is enough to boggle even such a great mind as my own.

The terms of my punishment are acting upon me already, compelling me to grant the wish, forcing me to shift into my true form—a searing ball of energy, white-hot and glorious, far beyond the comprehension of mere mortals or Fae.

But as I change, a suspicion jolts through me.

The scrying stone, the gods-tear, gleams in the brown hands of the girl with the one blue eye…

And I have been forced into my true form by the boy's wish…

Fuck.

They are doing this on purpose.

No. No, no, no…

The West Witch sits up.

Not dead.

Not dead, not dead, no, this *cannot* be happening, no… I struggle to change forms, but I cannot fight the wish. I am trapped like this for five minutes.

The girl with the braids takes a book from her pocket and hands it to the West Witch. "I give you the Tama Olc, of my free will, to be yours…"

*No*, I want to scream aloud, but I have no lungs or mouth in this form. I cannot make a sound.

I can only burn.

The West Witch accepts the book and rises from the hammock in which he was carried. He stalks toward me, his eyes wide open, green magic flickering around his body as it reverts from stony gray to cursed green. He's intoning a spell... *the* spell. The one I fear above all else.

The others are watching, circling, closing in, their faces avid and hungry. They are scrawny, crook-necked, grotesque vultures, ravenous for my demise.

The old words on the West Witch's lips are sapping what little strength I have left. Each phrase lashes around me, sentence after sentence forging invisible chains of arcane power. The other god-stars were fucking *fools* to let the Fae have magic at all. They thought it would be a wise balance to our cosmic power, but it was moronic, tragic.

In my fury I claw at the binding force of the wish, seeking a loophole. I have little time and even less power, but...

Jasper wished to retain his sight and memories... to have no harm done to his friends...

Ah, there's the crack in their scheme, the hole in the wording.

No harm to *his friends*.

But I can do harm to *him*. Not to his sight or his memories, but I can hurt him. I can *ruin* him.

A bolt of energy snakes out from me, striking its target just in time, just before I cave inward. I hear screams of shattered love and mortal anguish echoing through my throne room. They are the sweetest music...

But I have barely a second to enjoy those cries.

I am crushed, shrinking...

Growing smaller...

Fighting... I can fight this...

Smaller

Until I am
So very small

And the last line of the spell sucks me into the orb
Where I float, muddled and dazed
The dragon squished into the head of a pin, and there is no more room for plans or thoughts

There is barely enough room to be

And I am not even sure

What
I am

# 31

## ALICE

The bolt of white lightning strikes Jasper full in the chest and he falls backward, slamming onto the emerald floor. My scream rends the air of the throne room.

His lovely face is tipped up, blue eyes sightless, lips parted. He looks startled.

There's a gaping hole in Jasper's chest where his heart used to be. An entire chunk of his bones, skin, and flesh—gone. Disintegrated, immolated. The edges are blackened, steaming, and smoke rises from the burnt flesh. Gray shadows creep outward from the ravaged wound.

Caer flings himself onto his knees beside me, a desperate whine in his throat.

"Riordan!" I look up at the White Rabbit, fists clenched so tight my nails draw blood from my palms. "Save him! You can save him like you did me—the vital essences—blood and cum and spit and tears—"

"Beloved." Riordan's voice is deeper than ever, a dark river of misery. "You were human, and still alive. He has been struck down by a god-star. I cannot save him."

Jasper's golden skin is turning gray, death spreading over his body even as I watch. I can't bear it.

"No!" I shriek at Riordan. "You *stop* it. Do something!"

His scarlet eyes shine wet, like pools of blood. "If we were back at the Dread Court, there might be something I could try— but here, I can't..."

West steps past him. "I can preserve him like this, for a while at least." He spreads his hands over Jasper's body, enveloping him in green mist. "The fade won't spread, not until my magic dissipates."

"How long?" Caer chokes out.

"My spell will last for a few weeks, maybe. Enough time for you to get back to the Dread Court. The barrier around the Isle should dissolve now that the god-star is permanently trapped in the scrying stone."

"One has to wonder at the choice of the other god-stars, confining him on this particular Isle, where so many gods'-tears existed," says Dorothy quietly. "It's almost as if they were testing the inhabitants of the Isle, to see if anyone was strong enough to bind him eternally."

"Maybe the other god-stars could punish him, but not bind him," West says. He steps back, looking down at Jasper, whose skin is now pale green, shimmering with magic. "I've done what I can. This should preserve him until you can devise a way to save him, if that's even possible." He shrugs casually, and I feel like slapping him for it, even though he just showed us kindness.

Slowly, heavily, Riordan kneels at my other side. I clutch his arm, a desperate, spastic grip. "I can't be happy until he is all right," I whisper hoarsely.

He nods, his ravaged face more mournful than ever.

Caer looks at both of us with tear-bright eyes. "I want to run," he confesses in a choked voice. "I want to flee far away so I don't have to watch this, or feel it. But I won't. I'll stay, always."

I wrap my arm around his shoulders, and shift my grip on Riordan, circling his waist with my other arm. We bow over Jasper together, the two Unseelie and I, wreathed in mutual pain for the loss of our sweet mate.

Dimly I hear Dorothy saying, "How will we get them to the Dread Court?"

"I have a trove of magical artifacts in my castle," West explains. "Among them is a mirror I once used to speak with a few contacts on the Faerie mainland. There's a particular acquaintance who used to ship me some quality mushrooms from her garden, before the barrier formed around the Isle and we could no longer communicate. I will try to contact Opal. If she can show us her surroundings, Dorothy, you can see the location and transport Alice and the others there."

A golden thread of hope twines through my heart at his words. Fed by that bit of hope, my brain begins whirling through possibilities, picking up and discarding the various bits of knowledge I've gleaned about the Fae and the way they heal. Hunting relentlessly for a chance, for an answer.

At last it comes—the bright flare of an idea—gears clicking together.

"Riordan." I turn to him, urgency in my voice. "I know who can help us."

# 32

# DOROTHY

I stand in the mushroom garden, watching Opal and the others prepare the mostly-dead Scarecrow for transport to the Court of Delight. They plan to ask someone called Finias for help, as well as the new Queen of the Unseelie Court—sometimes they refer to her as Ygraine, and sometimes "the Hatter."

I know they are grateful for the transport to the mainland, but none of them have time for me right now. Nor do I care, honestly. They're decent enough—Riordan is a better brother than I could have wished for, and I'd call the others *friends*—but none of them are as interesting as the one person I left behind.

Not that West will have time for me either. He'll be busy sorting out the mess the god-star left behind. He'll have to speak with all the thralls whose minds were freed when the god-star was trapped. And he'll have to re-establish himself as the ruler of the whole Isle, not just the western quadrant. According to him, the Isle was never one for overseas alliances—operated on a sort of isolationist policy—but with time, under new leadership, some trade and travel will resume.

All of which means that West will be far too busy for the likes of me.

Right before I transported Alice and her boys to the mainland, he gave me an airy wave and said, "Stay as long as you like, Kin-Slayer. No need to hurry back."

But there is a need. A clawing, hollow, hungry need, deep in my gut—the need to argue with him, scream at him, fight him, fuck him. I want him.

My whole being itches to be gone, to be back in Oz. Now that I've been here, to this part of the Seelie Kingdom, I can return anytime, at a moment's notice. Why shouldn't I leave? I can't help with Jasper—I'll only be in the way.

Maybe I should stay here, though. Maybe it is the "right" thing to do, the expected thing, the moral thing: supporting my brother and my friends in this time of crisis. Maybe I should pull on the mask again—shove aside what I want, and fake what's expected of me.

As I ponder it all, I catch Riordan's eye. Frowning slightly, he breaks away from the others and approaches me, scanning my expression.

"You want to leave," he says quietly. "Go."

"I shouldn't."

"You should. You need to discuss your future with your new mate."

I swallow hard, unable to find words. Unable to decide how I should feel about all of it—my link with West, my possible status as his queen...

Riordan cocks his head. "Does it make you unhappy, your connection to him? Do you feel trapped by it? Because you don't have to live with him, or sleep with him again. The two of you can exist apart—"

He must see my eyes widening with dread at the thought, because a teasing smile stretches his mouth. "Ah. So you do love him."

"This isn't what I felt before, years ago, when I thought I loved someone," I confess.

"No two loves are the same. I love Alice differently than I love Caer, and my affection for Jasper is unique as well. And my love for you is far different, yet still strong." He cups my shoulder with his warm, scarred hand. "Sister."

A surge of emotion swells my heart. "You're sure of it? I thought you had to do some test—"

"I did. Back at West's castle, when I was making the potions. I took that drop of your blood, not for the death-simulant, but for the test. We are children of the same Fae mother. You are Dorothy Gale, sister to Riordan Gale of the Unseelie Court."

*Dorothy Gale.*

We stand there for a moment, while I absorb the confirmation of what I already knew, deep in my bones and blood.

Then I hug him, and he hugs me back. Quickly, a little stiffly. It's perfect.

"I'll go then," I tell him. "But you can send a message to Opal if you need me... or..."

"There are ways I can reach you, even as far away as Oz," Riordan assures me. "We will speak again soon."

"I wish you the best," I tell him. "All of you, and Jasper as well."

"And I wish the same for you." He nods and turns away, striding back to the others.

I click my heels together and picture West's castle in my mind. "Take me home," I murmur, and the mushroom garden whirls away.

I stumble as I take the third step and appear in the parlor of West's castle. Fiero jumps up from the rug where he was sleeping, a little dazed, his doggy fur smushed along the side of his snout. Chuckling, I scoop him up and accept several slobbery kisses.

After a moment I put him down and stare around the room at the couches and tapestries, richly-made but a bit neglected. The castle is silent—not a sound of guards or servants, only the clicking of Fiero's nails as he trots across a stone section of the floor between rugs, on his way back to his sleeping spot.

I'm glad we left him here when we went to the Emerald City. The confrontation with the Wizard would have been too dangerous for him. In fact, this whole place has been far too dangerous. It's a wonder he has survived. More wondrous still is how comfortable he seems in this Fae stronghold, far from everything he used to know.

"We were meant to be here, weren't we?" I say absently. "Meant to be in Faerie, at least, if not exactly *here*. Is this home, do you think, Fiero?"

He snorts quietly in answer and settles down for the second half of his nap.

I wander through the halls and climb the steps to the tower where we confronted West. The stand where the scrying stone rested is empty. The big armchair nearby still bears the marks of Caer's claws.

At the back of the large, circular chamber is a curtained alcove containing West's bed—a canopied, pillared monstrosity draped in heavy curtains of green silk. Over-dressed as it is, the bed looks temptingly comfortable. I wish I could take off these damn shoes—it still feels odd to lie in a bed with them on. I suppose I'll get used to it eventually. Maybe West can teach me to glamour them invisible *and* intangible, just for the nights.

If he even wants me around.

Glumly I sit down on the edge of the bed. He's still at the Emerald City, and will be for who knows how long. When he's ready he'll transport himself back here in a blast of green smoke.

Maybe he'll be unhappy to find me here, waiting for him like some forlorn puppy. He probably regrets whatever thoughts he had while we were fucking—I'm sure he wishes he'd never been so stupid as to seal the bond between us. He'd probably rather live alone on this Isle, fucking whomever he pleases and never thinking of me again.

A heaviness settles over my mind, and I slump onto the bed, laying my cheek on one of the satiny pillows. It's been so long since I truly *rested*. And despite my inner turmoil, I feel safe here. Like I could sleep forever, undisturbed, and wake refreshed.

I close my eyes.

A sound and a scent wake me.

The sound first—a crack like a bone snapping. The scent—fresh green grass and summer rain.

The air in the room stirs, and I open my eyes.

West has just appeared in the center of his chambers. He sets the scrying stone with its new star-bright center on the carved stand near the chair. Since it's now the prison of a god-star, he can't use it to scry anymore. But there had to be some sacrifice for what he gained.

West is still green, of course. The god-star's demise didn't dispel all the curses he has wrought throughout Oz. I feel a vague sort of pity for the Isle's inhabitants, many of them harmed by the past years of misrule—but I have only so much space for caring and compassion in my heart, and I use what little there is for my friends. There just isn't room for random strangers.

West's back is to me. I'm not sure he knows I'm here, half-hidden in the shadowed alcove, lying on his bed. I sit up slowly, watching as he whisks his clothing off and summons a faceted crystal cruet to his hand. The amber liquid inside sloshes as he throws himself naked into his chair, takes a long drink, and sighs. I can only see part of him now—his black hair, his shoulder, and the strong jade-green forearm holding the liquor.

"I will not fucking follow her," he mutters, as if he's vowing to himself. "I will not chase after my fucking mate. I will stay here. And drink." He gulps again.

A ridiculous smile spreads across my face.

He *wants* me. *Misses* me, in a dark, possessive sort of way.

I move forward as quietly as I can, but he stiffens, lifting his face, scenting the air. After a moment he settles again.

"I should never have let her in this room," he says conversationally to the scrying stone. "Her damn scent is everywhere."

I don't find it particularly odd that he's talking to the stone. After all, he's been alone for a long time, with no one but his thralls around. I've talked to animals all my life, about the important things that I couldn't discuss with other people. This is hardly different.

Cautiously I slide off the bed and creep across the floor toward him, placing each foot carefully so my silver shoes won't make a sound.

West has set the bottle aside and he's huffing quietly now. His arm is moving rhythmically, and as I get closer, I can see his hand stroking along his bare cock, between his spread thighs. His eyes are tightly closed, teeth gritted and bared, his head tilted back against the chair.

Softly I slip around the small table beside the chair. Then, swiftly, I drop to my knees between his legs, push his hand away, and slip his cock into my mouth.

He startles wildly, staring down at me. "Gods-fuck, Dorothy!"

I ignore the exclamation and continue sucking him.

"You're back," he gasps. "I thought you'd be gone longer...I thought you might stay with the rest of them, on the mainland."

I look up at him, blinking my lashes, and his cock jerks between my lips. I let the tip slip out and say, "I had to come back for Fiero."

"Right, your little dog." He's breathless, his stomach tensing with each hectic breath. "And what you're doing right now is..."

"It's fun." I shrug and slide him all the way into my mouth.

"Dorothy... *shit*," he says brokenly. "Dorothy, stop. We have to talk..."

I make a disapproving sound in my throat, and with a groan of blissful agony he takes my head in both his hands and starts fucking my mouth, hard and desperate. I make helpless gulping sounds as he shoves my head down, down, over and over, until he holds my head between his legs while his hips surge convulsively upward. His cock flexes, and thick cum spills down my throat.

"Fucking swallow it, wife," he says hoarsely, and I do, every bit.

When I pull back, my face is a mess of tears and cum. He summons a cloth from a table to his hand and wipes my cheeks and mouth.

Then I notice it—the difference in the color of his eyes. They're glowing golden.

"Your eyes," I murmur.

"Oh, that..." He clears his throat. "I'm a mated royal now, and the king of Oz. My eyes will occasionally look like this when I'm feeling especially—" he forces the word out as if he's reluctant to admit it— "happy."

"Oh really?" I can't stop a smile from curving my lips.

"Do you want this, Kin-Slayer?" he says quietly. "Do you want *me*?"

I rise and seat myself on his knee. "Before I answer, I want you to know that I'm furious with you."

Humor glints in his gaze. "As evidenced by the way you savored my cock just now."

I smack his cheek. "Don't be an asshole. I'm serious."

"So am I, very serious."

"I want to know what your thoughts were, in the library when we fucked. You know the moment I mean."

"The moment when you looked at me with all the violence of love in your beautiful eyes and my heart nearly broke in fucking two?" he says. "That moment?"

Heat rushes into my face. "Yes."

"I thought that you are the only person I've ever known whom I would allow to carve out my beating heart and flay it before my eyes. With you, life would forever be intriguing, entrancing. I want to witness the heights of your anger and the depths of your depravity. I want to linger with you in your apathy and dive with you into your passion. I want to do all those things with you, for all time. That is what I thought."

I inhale a shaking breath. "And that's why the bond formed between us?"

"Yes." He brushes aside a tendril of my brown hair. "Because you were having similar thoughts, were you not?"

Now that he has confessed, it costs me less to admit my own vulnerability. "I was."

West lifts his hand, and my clothes begin to peel away from my body, separating into curled fragments and falling to the floor around my silver shoes. In seconds I am naked on his knee, all of me—smooth brown breasts, dark peaked nipples, damp pussy, and long legs, ending in silver heels.

"You can live apart from me if you like." His fingertips trail along the flat slope of my stomach. "You can find your own way, and fuck anyone who titillates you. Or you can live here, and give that luscious pussy only to me." His voice deepens, a threat trembling in it. "I am not a kind Fae like Jasper, nor even as honorable as Riordan. I am the king of Oz, a land as dark and wicked as I am. If you decided to leave me, I would try to respect your wishes, though I'm not sure I could. I can't swear that I wouldn't follow you, lock a collar around your lovely throat, and drag you back here. I would *try* to give you your freedom, but I know myself. I know my need for you would overcome me at last, and I would claim you by force."

My human upbringing cries an alarm in my mind—screams that I shouldn't want someone who would say such things to me—that I should run from him, deny him.

But my Unseelie self—the part I know to be dominant—revels in his honesty and his dark lust for me. I *want* someone who desires me so frantically that he would do anything to be with me. I want a mate who would be wretched without me, who craves my company, who worships my body.

I want the utter freedom of belonging to him. Being *his* without question, without end.

But I need to make sure he knows that he will be utterly mine as well. He must understand that my darkness is equal to his, and that it will permit no disloyalty.

Slowly I reach out, curling slim brown fingers around his green cock. "This is mine," I whisper. Then I place my other hand over his heart. "And this is mine. You will not stray from me, or I will kill both of us without hesitation. Do you understand?"

"I believe you, and I understand," he breathes. I can feel his heart racing under my palm, and the knowledge of how I affect him thrills me.

"Prove it then." Rising from his knee, I step onto the armrests of his chair, standing astride him, with my pussy nearly at the level of his face.

He makes a ravenous sound in his throat and tips up his chin, grasping my thighs and pulling me lower until my pussy lips contact his mouth. There's a faint tingle of the alcohol he drank as he begins to eat me out, noisily, sloppily, enjoying me with utter abandon. Tendrils of green smoke curl up my legs and slither against my skin, waking every nerve I possess, sending fresh tingles of arousal through my lower belly.

West breathes over my clit, a scintillating rush of sensation so powerful that I know there's magic in it. My entire pussy feels warm, swollen, exquisitely sensitive, and as he nibbles the little bud again, I whimper, shivering, overwhelmed and desperate for relief.

His hands are spread over my whole ass now, pulling the cheeks apart, and quivers of his magic delve into every crease I own, slip into my second hole, skate up my spine and curl around my trembling breasts. I'm helpless to a fucking predator, a god of sexual torment.

I scream when I come—a pure, shrill shriek of ecstasy. It's an orgasm like breathing the clear, bright air at the top of a high hill—like staring straight into the sun, like welcoming a lightning bolt to the heart. I scream again, while West holds my sex against his face.

Panting, I collapse, and he settles me into his lap, against his chest. His face is nearly as messy as mine was, slicked with my arousal. I pick up the same cloth and wipe his cheekbones, his lips, his chin.

"Well fucking done," I tell him, my voice still shaky and hoarse.

He smirks. "Still angry with me?"

"Yes. You led me through the marking ritual without telling me what it was." He starts to speak, and I hold up my hand. "I *know* you didn't think anything would happen. You still should have told me."

He nods, pursing his lips. "What if I tell you something else instead? My true name?"

My heart jumps. "That might help."

He moves me astride his hips, nudging his cock head inside my slick entrance. As he slips in fully, he says softly, "My name is Darec."

I try out his name over and over as we enjoy each other for hours, until we are both sated with sex and starving for food. Then we dress and go down to the dining hall, where the castle staff serve us a rich meal. Fiero devours his own feast nearby, then settles on the plush rug between our table and the great fireplace.

"You can't free your thralls, can you?" I ask Darec, when the servants have left to fetch another course.

He shakes his head. "Normally I'd be able to alter the level of my influence at will. Since I lost my powers, the spell on them is permanent. Lucky for them, I was never as keen on total control as my other siblings. I only made their dispositions happy, loyal, and hard-working, nothing more. Beyond that, their choices are their own."

"What about the Village of Crows? Do you plan to interfere there and stop their sacrifices?"

He shrugs. "Sacrifice is an Unseelie practice as old as time, and though I may not perform it myself, I see no reason not to allow those villagers to govern themselves as they see fit. As for the crows, they serve a purpose, to protect the Well of Undoing. We can't have its waters being splashed upon us at the slightest provocation, now can we? So I'm of a mind to leave the crows and their worshipers alone. But if they become a more widespread problem, I will deal with them."

Someone like Alice or Jasper might not accept that answer. And perhaps it's wretched of me not to care more about the thralls having total freedom, or the Village of Crows being dealt with—but his answer contents me for the moment. I have other things on my mind.

"I'd like to alter the spell on my shoes—or perhaps layer another spell on top of the existing charm," I tell him. "I want the ability to travel between realms."

"Do you now?" He frowns slightly. "And why is that?"

"So I can bid my parents farewell. And so you and I can go to the human realm whenever we like. It may not be quite as fantastical as Faerie, but I've heard of some wondrous and beautiful places in the mortal world. We could do some traveling."

His face lights up with interest. "And how do you think the humans of your world would react to someone who looks like me? This green skin is a god-star's curse—I can't glamour it."

"Well…" I smirk. "Does it matter? Together, we are more powerful than anyone in that world. In fact… we could conquer it if we wanted to. We can certainly take care of anyone who might dare to oppose us. And I wouldn't feel bad about it…" I hesitate, checking my emotions, my conscience—all perfectly smooth and silent. Satisfied, I smile at him. "No, I wouldn't feel bad, not one bit."

He chuckles darkly. "Kin-Slayer, I do believe you and I have the same idea of fun. I'll help you with your research as much as I can, though you may have to consult with your brother as well. And I think you'll need a little help from this." He reaches for his discarded pants and tugs a small, thick book from the back pocket. "It was a job of work wedging it in there. Perhaps I wear my clothes too tight."

"Not at all." I give him a sultry, teasing smile, but I'm tense, too, eyeing the book. Waiting for his next move.

He sighs and shakes his head, riffling the pages with his thumb. "You don't trust me, do you?"

"You'll have to earn that."

"Consider this my first effort toward that goal." He hands me the book. "Dorothy, I give you the Tama Olc. It belongs to you. And I vow that I will never steal it from you."

The book hums violently as my fingers close around it, and I'm suddenly conscious of Riordan. I believe I could go to him, if I wanted, even without seeing his location first. A blend of the book's power, our familial connection, and the magic of my silver shoes.

But I have more control now, and I'm able to quiet the stirring of the impulse. The book settles under my palm.

West's mouth twitches, and I realize, with sudden clarity, what it cost him to hand over that book. He yielded it to me as Riordan once gave it to Alice—as a mark of love.

But I will be its final owner. It belongs to me, a member of the Gale bloodline—daughter of both human and Fae worlds.

"The things we could do with this, you and I," I murmur, stroking the leather binding.

"I look forward to all of it," he replies.

# 33

## ALICE

"Ready?" Dorothy says, looking around at us.

I survey the hands touching her—my own, Riordan's scarred brown one, Caer's pale slender fingers—and one more hand.

Jasper stands at my side, his tanned arm brushing mine as his palm presses to Dorothy's back. The deep V of his loose white shirt shows a glimpse of the new heart clicking and whirring in his chest—a mechanical heart designed by the Hatter herself and installed successfully with the help of Riordan and Finias. They couldn't force Jasper's flesh to seal around it, or over it—he was scarred by the fire of a god-star, and there's only so much even the most powerful Fae can do to restore him. So the clockwork heart remains visible, nestled between his lungs, surrounded by protective metal plating and the shadow of burn marks.

His chest is no longer smooth and golden, and the crow tattoo across his pectoral has been partly obliterated—but none of us care about that. Riordan, Caer, and I are simply thrilled to have him back with us. Whether his heart is mechanical or not, it remains as big and brimming with love as ever. And all his other parts are intact, thankfully. The first thing Caer said to Jasper when he came back to life was, "Lucky your cock didn't get blasted, or we might have left you for dead." But his fanged grin trembled a little as he said it, and Jasper's new heart whirred faster, right before he threw himself into Caer's arms.

The sex we enjoyed that night was more than pleasure—it was each of us showing our reckless devotion to the others. I can't think of it without blushing hard and feeling a rush of grateful joy.

Weeks later, when Dorothy told me the shoes were ready for a trip back to the mortal realm, I told my three men I would go alone and say goodbye to my family. But Riordan growled, "The fuck you will," and Jasper said, "You need us," and Caer bared his teeth and declared he was going whether I liked it or not.

So we're all holding onto Dorothy now, waiting for her to click her heels and take us back to my former world.

"I'm excited," Jasper says. "Are the rest of you excited?"

"I've been to the mortal realm," Riordan says darkly. "It's nothing to be excited about."

"Just a lot of tasty humans walking around." Caer licks his teeth, then catches my eye. "Not that I'd crave a taste of any mortal but *you*, my sweet mousie."

"Not only because I'd be murderously jealous," I say, "but because eating, kidnapping, or torturing humans is…?"

"Wrong," Caer and Riordan chorus, so dejectedly that I can't help laughing.

"Good boys," I tell them. "I think you deserve a treat after this is done. Don't you think so, Jasper?"

"Yes, and you shall have a treat too, my darling savior." He kisses my cheek.

I can't help blushing. "I've told you not to call me that."

"You protest," he says softly, "but I think you rather like it."

"Oh gods, the four of you," groans Dorothy. "Is everyone *ready*?"

"Yes," we reply.

"See you shortly, wife," West calls from the parlor sofa, where he's munching on a green apple that nearly matches his hand. Dorothy brought us to her castle for the test, mostly because Jasper has been begging to visit Fiero.

"Back soon, bastard." Dorothy replies acidly, but she winks at her mate before tapping the heels of her shoes together and taking a single step.

Instantly the parlor whirls into a tornado of color, wind roaring around us.

Dorothy takes a second step, and another. Abruptly the swirling tempest vanishes, leaving the five of us breathless, standing in the shriveled cornfields I know all too well, under a gloomy gray sky. The bite of winter is in the air now, and the trees are bare and black, like spiderwebs dipped in ink. I suppress a shiver.

"Oh, it's... um... it's nice, your home," Jasper says politely.

"Don't be ridiculous." Caer nudges him. "It's wretched here. That's why she wants to live with us. Well, that, and my talented tongue."

He's not wrong. I love his tongue as much as I love his cock—especially now that his heat is over and the little barbs don't fuse us together during sex. During our time in the Seelie Court, Caer fucked me several times a day until his body finally decided it had pumped enough cum into me, and his lust receded to a more manageable level. As a precaution I took a few of Fin's contraceptive sweets to ensure there won't be any Fae babies until I'm ready for such things.

"I'm going to see my parents," Dorothy says. "It shouldn't take long. Meet back here in an hour?"

I nod and give her hand an encouraging squeeze. "Do you need someone to go with you?"

"No." She shakes her head. "West offered to come, but I prefer to do this alone. I'm going to confront my father about my Fae heritage and find out what I can about my real mother. My parents will be more open to talking if it's just me."

She sets off across the fields, and I turn in the direction of my family's farm. It's within sight already—the shabby house, the big barn, a few other outbuildings. The old barn is noticeably absent from the scene.

As we approach the yard from the road, I notice a familiar horse—the same one that was standing by our gate on that rainy day when Dorothy and I made our unexpected getaway.

"That's Gulch's horse," I mutter.

"Who?" asks Jasper.

"A tavern owner who wanted to marry me. I'm fairly sure he also planned to whore me out to his customers."

Riordan growls deep in his chest—a surprisingly predatory sound for someone with his long, rabbit-like ears. I love the protective impulse the sound betrays.

At that moment, the door of the farmhouse opens and my parents follow Gulch out into the yard. Their discussion halts abruptly when they spot us.

A glorious thrill skates through my stomach as I imagine how we must look to them. Me, with my blond hair flowing free over the blue silk of my dress—a dress both fine and scandalous. I wear a delicate gold collar around my neck, part of a naughty game I've been playing with my partners.

The thin gold chain that usually accompanies the collar is in Riordan's pocket. Jasper took his turn with the collar and leash last week, and he and Caer are very much looking forward to next week, when it's Riordan's turn to play the role of the pet.

Riordan stands at my side, clad in a suit of scarlet and white, his height and bulk a steady comfort to me as I face my parents. Caer is on my other side, teeth bared in a terrifying smile, his tail skimming the back of my leg. He's wearing an outfit Fin made him—all black shimmery gauze and studded leather. Jasper stands beyond Caer, dressed in pale blue pants and an open white shirt, with an overstuffed cloth bag in his hands.

Gulch's sloppy mouth falls open, his eyes bulging in shocked horror. "What the fuck is going on?"

"Alice?" says my mother faintly.

My father can't speak. He's turning purple with rage and fear. Behind him, the children are crowding out of the house, gasping and chattering at the sight of me and my Fae companions.

"I've come back again, but only to say goodbye," I announce. "I'm going to live in Faerie from now on. Pap, I'm leaving you with enough gold to pay your debts and carry the farm through the year. Before I go, I'll also leave a sum of gold in trust with Lord Drosselmeyer, to be used for the education and clothing needs of the children until they come of age. You won't be able to touch it, so don't try. It's for them, not for your drink."

Speechless, my parents stare at me, while the space between me and them seems to widen. The children still hover behind them, unsure whether to cry or rejoice.

Jasper solves the dilemma for them, approaching my siblings with the bag of gifts and sweets we brought. There are clockwork animals of the Hatter's creation and music boxes hand-painted by Clara. And there are sweets concocted by Finias, gently spelled to promote happiness, confidence, and hope.

The children cluster around Jasper, drawn by his innocent blue eyes and beautiful smile. They question him about his mechanical heart and about the gifts he passes around. Meanwhile, Caer, Riordan, and I approach my parents. Caer hisses sharply at Gulch as we pass him, and the tavern owner whimpers like a frightened child.

"What is this?" Mam asks through white lips. "You stupid girl—have you sold your soul and body to demons?"

"Not at all," I say sweetly. "You two were the ones planning to sell me, body and soul. These men are my friends, my lovers. I protect them, and they protect me. They're my new family."

"But—they're monsters," my mother gasps.

"Yes, they are." I smile up at Riordan, then at Caer. "The most lovable monsters in all the realms." I glance back at Jasper, surrounded by children and practically glowing with happiness. "I'm going to talk to my brothers and sisters now, and explain all of this to them."

"You won't," my father chokes out. "I won't allow it."

"Allow?" Riordan says coolly. "I don't believe you have the right to dictate what Alice does. If you'd like to try to stop her, by all means, proceed."

"It's an outrage," snarls Gulch, finding his voice. He steps forward, tugging at the hilt of a dagger in his belt, but Caer lifts one hand, rattling his claws together.

"Give me a reason, bastard," the Cat says silkily.

"Enough," I say. "They get the message. The gold, please, Riordan."

He gives me one of the purses of coin from the satchel slung across his body. We'll deliver the other purse to Lord Drosselmeyer after we're done here.

"Pay Gulch what you owe him," I tell Pap, handing over the purse. "And you—" I turn to Gulch. "Say nothing of this to anyone. As far as any of you know, I was taken by highwaymen again, and this time they're not giving me back. If you breathe a word of this—cause trouble for my family or Lord Drosselmeyer—you'll have to answer to—"

"To your demon consorts," spits out Gulch. "I get it."

Caer laughs. "No, no. You'll have to answer to *her*. She will decide your punishment and command us to carry it out."

"Which we will," Riordan adds smoothly. "With the greatest pleasure."

Gulch pales and nods.

I survey Mam and Pap, taking in their faces for the last time. "Goodbye. Thank you for—for them." I nod to the boys and girls clustered around Jasper. "They are treasures, each one, and I hope someday you will see that."

I don't wait for an answer. Turning my back on them, I approach Jasper and my siblings. "All right then—who wants to hear a story about a girl who jumped down a rabbit hole and ended up in Faerie?"

When we've finished our business and left the mortal realm behind, Dorothy drops us off at the door of our new home. It's a sprawling mansion constructed by Ygraine, formerly known as the Hatter—who, when she's not sitting on her new throne as the Queen of the Unseelie, still enjoys crafting wonderful things.

Ygraine now owns a pair of bracelets from the Isle of Oz—the royal bracelets that enable their owner to build anything they can imagine. Apparently the North Witch left them behind when she was banished, and West discovered them in the Emerald City vaults, after the Wizard's demise. He gave them to Dorothy, to do with as she pleased, and she passed them along to her brother. Rather than keep them himself, Riordan gifted them to Ygraine, as her payment for creating Jasper's new heart.

Delighted with the gift, the Hatter built a house for us, to all our specifications, and in exchange Lir, the King of the Seelie, opened a trade gate in the border wall between the Seelie and Unseelie kingdoms. Maybe one day, when enough trust has been established, the wall can come down entirely.

Until then, my partners and I are the guardians of that gate, and the founders of a new town that's quickly forming around our estate. Riordan never wanted the throne of the Dread Court, but he seems willing enough to take on the joint leadership of the town with me, provided that we still have plenty of time for study and research. Our new mansion contains laboratories, specimen rooms, supply closets, and a library, and he can't wait to fill them with samples, ingredients, and books.

The estate also has gardens where I can finally indulge my love of cultivating and studying plants, and a lovely forest beyond that, in which Caer can roam whenever he has the urge. Last week, we surprised Jasper with a small menagerie containing a few of the Seelie Kingdom's most adorable animals, gifted from the Court of Delight by its queen, Louisa. Jasper was ecstatic and actually sobbed, which shocked both Riordan and Caer so much that they slunk awkwardly off into the garden, while I kissed away the Scarecrow's tears.

Even now, as we stand before our house, Riordan and Caer keep glancing at Jasper apprehensively, as if they're afraid he might cry again. He seemed very reluctant to leave my little siblings behind. They called him "the fancy elf who brings gifts" and appeared more dejected about his departure than mine. I tried not to mind—they're children. I know they'll miss me, just as I'll miss them. I won't be able to visit them often, since Lir and Finias think it best to limit Fae appearances in the human realm, especially around Lord Drosselmeyer's place.

Of course, the Seelie Court can't control what the folk of Oz do, since the Isle is self-governing. Dorothy has hinted that she and West plan to travel in the human world, and though the idea unsettles me, I've decided to be happy for her, and not worry about it.

"Thank you for this," I tell Dorothy, as she prepares to return to the Isle. "Are you sure West doesn't want a vial of water from the Unending Pool, to dispel his cursed wish? Lir has offered to provide one."

She shakes her head. "He wants to keep his transport abilities. And both of us rather like the green skin."

"If he changes his mind, let us know."

"I will." She gives her brother a nod. "Until next time."

"Soon, I hope." Riordan returns the gesture.

With a click of her heels, Dorothy vanishes, and we're alone: the Cat, the White Rabbit, the Scarecrow, and me.

We stand together on the broad, white-stone doorstep of our home, with the flowering vines dripping from the balcony overhead, scenting the blue dusk with delicate sweetness.

I look at each of them—Riordan's crimson eyes, like glowing coals in the gloom—Caer's slit-pupiled cat's-eyes, filled with a sultry violet heat—and Jasper's blue eyes, sparkling with pure, devoted lust.

"It's been a long day," I murmur, a smile curving my mouth. It's a phrase we've begun using with each other during these past weeks of upheaval.

Caer grins. "And how do we deal with long days?"

"With longer nights," Jasper answers.

Riordan says nothing, but he takes the gold leash from his pocket and steps forward, towering over me. The very heat and bulk of him makes me weak and wet immediately.

He bends, his broad lips grazing my ear like heated velvet as he attaches the collar. "Tonight, I will take you. And they will watch."

I nod, my breath catching.

"Hear that, Jasper?" Caer croons. "You and I can have a little fun while we watch them." He drapes his arm across the Scarecrow's shoulders. "Gods, I love how you blush. Makes your cheeks so damn lickable."

Riordan tugs at my leash. "Come, kitten."

I follow him obediently inside, while Caer and Jasper trail after us.

A dazzling array of pink and gold orbs fly upward from Riordan's palm, illuminating the hallway as we pass through the silent house. It's only partly furnished, but I don't mind. It gives us something to work on together. Something to build as we test all the challenges and glories of our new family.

Each of us have our own rooms, all adjoining a great central chamber with a bed large enough to hold half a dozen Fae. Its silken expanse gives us plenty of room to act out our most complex and debauched fantasies together.

Tonight, Riordan draws me close and removes my clothing himself, piece by piece. Last of all, he kneels before me and slides my panties down my legs. He leans in, flicking my clit with the tip of his tongue, and I gasp.

Caer laughs from a few paces away, where he and Jasper are disrobing. "She's always so beautifully sensitive, isn't she?"

"Fuck yes," Riordan replies. "Lie down on the bed for me, kitten. Arch your knees and open your thighs wide. I want to see every bit of your pussy."

Heart pounding, I relax on the bed and part my legs as ordered. Riordan pries back the lips of my sex with his thumbs, exposing my entrance, which I know must be glistening with arousal. Caer and Jasper, now fully naked, peer over his shoulders, licking their lips. The sight of their lithe bodies and erect cocks is almost enough to make me come—I think I could orgasm with a few clever touches.

And Riordan is the expert at delivering such precise stimulation.

"Aren't you going to undress?" Caer asks Riordan. There's a suppressed craving in his voice, a hunger he can't quite hide. Ever since the barriers between the two of them came down, their passion for each other has only increased. More than once,

I've rounded a corner to find Caer on his knees, worshiping Riordan's cock with his tongue or taking its thickness in his ass. Yet their lust for each other never seems to dull their devotion for me. If anything, the fire among the three of us burns hotter than ever. And Jasper is equally entranced, showing his love by cooking for us, performing the necessary cleaning spells on the house, and licking any part of us that he deems in need of attention.

Lucky for me, humans with Fae partners experience a stronger libido, and are able to orgasm more often—otherwise I'd despair of keeping up with them. It's a wonderful part of being in a Fae-human relationship—one I discussed at length with Clara and Louisa when we were visiting the Court of Delight—and one I'm eager to take advantage of this evening.

With a heated glance at Caer, Riordan straightens and takes off his clothes. He does it slowly, one piece at a time, while the rest of us practically salivate for him. His body is the most muscular, rippling with strength beneath the rich brown skin. When he drops the pants, his cock bounces out, huge and thick, glinting with precum at the tip. Jasper lunges forward a little, as if he wants to lick it, but Riordan pushes him back. "I'm taking Alice first. Amuse yourself with Caer until I say otherwise."

With a soft whimper, Jasper flings himself at Caer, and they entwine at once, their cocks pinned between their stomachs as their mouths meet.

Watching my men together is one of my favorite things—but tonight Riordan takes my chin and guides my gaze back to him. "Eyes on me, kitten."

And I comply, because his face is another of my favorite things.

He runs a hand down the thin gold leash, then settles the slim chain right between the lips of my pussy, right over my clit. He works it a little deeper, then pulls it taut, wrenching a gasp from me as the stimulation races through my belly.

"Oh gods, Riordan," I breathe.

His stern expression breaks a little, pleasure curving his lips. He loves eliciting these reactions from me. "Turn over, kitten."

I flip onto my belly, and he threads the rest of the chain length through the groove of my bottom, so it's pulled tight against both my clit and my asshole. The flex of the delicate chain links against those sensitive parts is almost more than I can bear.

Still holding the chain, Riordan smooths his hand over my bottom, his scarred fingers raising delicious chills along my skin. He runs a hand up my spine, then hooks his fingers into the back of the collar around my neck. At the same moment, he pulls the chain suddenly tight.

I squeal as the leash rubs through my pussy and ass. Riordan wiggles it slightly, and with a cry of surprise I come, sharply, wildly, with the tug of the collar against my throat and my arousal soaking my thighs. My clit pulses against the gold chain.

"Good girl." Riordan's voice rolls through my tremoring body, a dark blessing. "Lift your ass for me." The chain relaxes, pooling loose on the bed, and I lift my rear as he requested.

"Look at that little pussy quivering," Riordan murmurs, stroking a finger through my wetness. I jump at the touch, whimpering.

"Gods, I'm going to come," rasps Caer, and I turn my head to the other side just in time to see him stroking both his cock and Jasper's in the tunnel of one hand. He spurts wildly, splattering Jasper's chest and his own, and Jasper comes too, more softly, a creamy fount of cum dripping over Caer's fingers. Jasper's pointed ears turn bright red every time he comes, and I think it's adorable.

Then Riordan enters me, and my mind whites out—a blank, glorious blur at the feel of him, the immense size of him. I moan, my voice joining the faint moans of Caer and Jasper as they kiss, riding out their joint orgasm.

Riordan slams into me, his Fae strength dominating my slim human form. I love it when he tantalizes me delicately, and I love it when he takes me like this—brutal strength, a rough claiming. He thrusts with a violent, frenzied rhythm that means he has abandoned all restraint, he has lost himself completely in me, and me alone.

I come again, shrieking breathlessly at the force of the pleasure rocketing through my belly—but he's still going, still fucking me with all his power. Jasper climbs onto the bed, scraping my hair out of my face and holding it for me while I'm fucked. Caer lies on his belly, watching my expression while he licks Jasper's cum from his fingers.

Riordan comes with a roar, shoving deep inside me. He throbs hard in my pussy, grasping my hip for leverage.

After a few moments, he pats my bottom affectionately, then pulls out. I can feel his release dripping slowly from my sex.

"Clean it up," Riordan orders the other two, and they crawl around behind me on the mattress. Caer rises on his knees, scoops up some of the cum with the head of his cock and slides himself inside me, fucking Riordan's cum slowly back into my body.

"So good," he moans, gliding in and out. "How do you always feel this good?"

"More, Caer, please," I pant, and he increases his speed, driving deeper. My breasts quiver with every thrust, and waves of warmth mount inside me, bringing me closer to the edge.

When Caer shudders and groans, filling me afresh, Jasper takes the Cat's place, kneeling behind me and easing in before Caer's cum has a chance to slide out.

Riordan and Caer lie on either side of me as I kneel there, trembling, with my ass still up. They stroke my back and my hair until Jasper comes with a long, glorious vibration that sends me into another intense orgasm.

After the Scarecrow slips out of me, I turn over and collapse, their essence leaking from between my thighs. Riordan moves in, his chest against my shoulder, and the Cat cuddles up as well, one arm across my breasts, his fingers linked with Riordan's. Jasper lies down behind Caer, and I reach for him, stroking his cheek for a moment before settling my palm against his hip.

"I love you all," I murmur sleepily.

Caer nuzzles his face against my neck and sighs with utter contentment.

"Love isn't a strong enough word for what I feel," Jasper says suddenly. "You rescued me, Alice. You were the first one who thought I was worth saving." He leans over Caer to kiss my mouth. "I adore you."

As he pulls back, he looks at Riordan. "And you—I met you when you were a suit of armor. I remember you speaking to me as you stood guard outside my cell. You were miserable, and yet yours was the first voice that ever held true kindness for me. I think I loved you from that moment. I would have loved you even if your own hands had bound me to the stake."

His voice trembles, sincerity shining in his blue eyes.

Riordan sits up. Reaches over and wraps his fingers around Jasper's chin. "You were a bright light in a world of wretchedness. I wish I'd had the heart to rescue you myself, the first night I met you. Lucky for us, Alice had enough compassion to make up for my cowardice. I will never be able to thank her enough." He draws Jasper's face closer and kisses him.

A tiny flutter passes through my stomach. They've fucked before, but I don't remember ever seeing their lips touch.

"Is that their first kiss?" I whisper to Caer. He nods, urging his body nearer to mine. "I'm so fucking happy, mouse."

"Me too. I'm so full of joy I think I might break into pieces."

"Break if you must, my darling," Caer whispers. "We'll put you back together, every time."

Riordan and Jasper kiss for a little longer, and then Riordan dims the orbs overhead while Jasper pulls the sheets and blankets over all of us.

As we drift into sleep, Riordan releases a long, slow sigh against my cheek—the sigh of someone who has struggled all his life, and has finally found a place for his heart to rest.

That night I dream—a crisp, vivid dream that I know, deep down, is as prophetic as the vision I once saw of the Eater of Hearts coming to my world—a dream Riordan stole from me, a future we changed.

This dream may come true, if we follow our current course. It's a faraway future in which Caer, Riordan, Jasper, and I are sitting at the head of a banquet table, in the dining room of this very house. Dorothy is there, with the West Witch at her side. His hair is longer, and she looks more Fae than ever.

Across from them sit Lir and Louisa, King and Queen of the Seelie Court. Louisa is laughing loudly over some joke West told, while Lir tries to hold back his own laughter and fails.

Beyond those two are Fin and Clara. On Fin's knee is a small pink-haired child with tiny golden antlers and Clara's delicate features.

There are more faces at the table—Ygraine, Queen of the Unseelie, clinking her goblet with that of Opal, a voluptuous blue Fae. There are three tall Fae males, each bearing antlers or horns, clad in heavy robes. With them sits a woman with snow-white skin, long black hair, and dark eyes.

My vision of the rest of the group blurs, and I turn my focus back to those I love best.

Riordan's crimson eyes glow with energy and purpose. There's a notebook at his side, filled with careful lines of script, to which he is adding as he and Fin discuss a new kind of spell.

Jasper, his clockwork heart still ticking, fabricates tiny glittering illusions and sends them across the table to amuse the child on Fin's knee.

Caer's tail curls softly around my leg under the table. His hair, too, is longer—a cascade of black curls around his wicked, pretty face.

The vision fades, and I wake to gentle breathing, the quiet ticking of Jasper's heart, and the sleek intertwined bodies of my three lovers. I settle back into sleep with a smile on my face, soothed by the knowledge that the dream was both a prophecy and a promise—just one shining stop on the long, lovely path I will travel with the Fae who love me.

**Read on to enjoy the Bonus Chapters featuring the guys' points of view from various parts of the story, and an extended scene of Riordan being the pet for the others.**

# TRIGGER WARNINGS

**FOR THE BONUS CHAPTERS**

Brief suicidal thoughts,
gore, violence,
intimate sexual scenes among characters of various genders,
brief reference to sexual and physical abuse,
pet play, light BDSM

# 1

## RIORDAN

I stand outside the prison, a long, low building located directly behind the Temple of Crows. The villagers like to have their outcasts accessible for torture—a frequent pastime in this place.

I do not know how much of their cruelty stems from Unseelie bloodlines, and how much comes from the dominant sway of the East Witch. I doubt they know it themselves. Perhaps, when she enthralled them, she built in permission for such sadistic pastimes. Or perhaps she imprinted them with the desire to torment those whom they will eventually sacrifice—training her subjects to be as ruthless as she is.

The sadism of this place doesn't horrify me—I merely have a strong distaste for it. I believe in causing pain only in the service of a greater purpose. Here, they relish agony for agony's sake. A waste of time and effort.

I was fortunate the East Witch could not enthrall me, thanks to my cursed armor. Certain magics are not compatible with each other—they do not synchronize. Other types of magic leave a signature upon the body, whether Fae or human, complicating the efficacy of future spells. This particular village is a complex tangle of spellwork, arcane influence, and magical coercion. The enthralled Fae are forced to breed as dictated by the East Witch, whose word passes through Glenna, the village leader. Offspring who are somewhat resistant to compulsion or who do not please the East Witch are confined to the prison I'm guarding. They wait their turn to serve as sacrificial offerings to the crows who flap and caw in the cornfields beyond the wall.

It's a wretched place, and it suits me perfectly, for I am wretched.

I thought myself miserable before, when I served my father as a subject for his experiments. I thought myself desperate when I served the Eater of Hearts and searched for a way to end her before she destroyed the kingdom. I thought myself heartbroken when I poured my blood into Alice and silently begged all the god-stars to help me save her.

But that misery, desperation, and heartbreak were nothing compared to what I feel now.

Days and nights run onward in a continuous black river, a viscous tide dragging me through time. I have no source of relief or pleasure—save one. A young Fae male, golden-haired, gentle-voiced. One of the prisoners—the only one whom the East Witch has never been able to compel, not even a little. He is unique among these people, entirely resistant to her magic, and for that the others eye him with jealousy, suspicion, or anger, when they notice him at all.

I try not to walk by his cell too often or watch him too closely. I must not get attached. He is marked for death.

Yet he reminds me of another sweet, curious captive, also marked for death. One who faced the slow advance of fate bravely, with kindness and hope.

He reminds me of Alice.

Now and then the village leader, Glenna, goes to his cell and uses him for her pleasure. He seems glad enough to do it, perhaps because pleasing her keeps him alive longer. The East Witch permits the trysts, or maybe she incites them.

Every time I see Glenna enter the prison, my blood heats, and anger churns in my belly. I know what it is to give my body to another, for reasons beyond my control. I would spare the prisoner that indignity if I could. And yet I cannot help the images that rise in my own mind—visions of the way I would give and receive pleasure with him, if I had the chance. If this cursed armor did not prevent me from touching anyone.

I did not think I would miss *touch* so deeply. I can remember many times when Caer sidled up to me, or brushed his fingers over mine while we played cards, or slunk into my bedroom in the evening when I was reading, making up some ridiculous excuse for being in my room when I knew he wanted physical affection. But I rejected him, every time. And I don't care to explore my reasons for it. I only know that I would give anything, now, to feel his arms around me, his lean body pressed against mine—

My cock twitches at the thought.

Which means nothing. I am unbearably lustful from being trapped in this fucking armor for so long. That is the only reason I'm thinking of my friend in this way.

*But this isn't the first time you've desired him*, whispers a voice in the back of my mind.

I remember sitting astride him, pinning him down, confessing that I could not lose him… I felt it then, the heat pooling in my crotch, the blood rushing to my dick. But we broke apart, and then he left.

It was only the heat of the moment, nothing more.

Growling under my breath, I shift my weight from one metal-clad foot to the other.

The East Witch is in town today. She visits more often of late, to solidify her hold on the people here. I've heard she has a few other villages under her sway as well. Maintaining control of every inhabitant of every village must be a monumental task, requiring constant attention. I've heard of witches before, and I've watched the East Witch's method of operation—it's one of the few interests I have left. The more deeply she suppresses someone's will, the less capable they are of dealing with anything out of the ordinary. She can imprint all the instructions she can think of on their mind, try to account for every possibility, and yet inevitably something will occur that she didn't plan for, and her subject will stall, confused, dazed, unable to proceed with a task or make a decision without her interference.

Because of this, she is constantly having to reinforce her control and tweak its parameters, which means she inevitably leaves more loopholes open. Most of these villagers don't know what to do with those loopholes, but a few have a greater natural resistance or a stronger will. Yet if they attempt to act on their own, outside the prescribed order of things, they are taken by the guards and imprisoned at once.

Today she spent time enthralling a few young children and then went for a walk in the gardens on the west side of the village. I suspect she uses that time to recharge her energy. No one is allowed nearby during her walks.

I've tried to imagine how I might use her to free myself. But I know her to be in league with the Green Wizard, and since I am currently incapable of using magic, it seems foolish to antagonize her. Compulsion isn't the only magic she's capable of.

The afternoon sun beats down, gleaming on my armor, but inside the cursed suit the temperature remains the same—tepid, slightly stuffy, tinged with a metallic odor. I would give anything to feel the fierce sunshine on my skin, or to endure the bite of cold. We Fae are less susceptible to temperature changes than humans, but we do feel them in extremes—and right now I crave those extremes. Anything to make me feel alive again. Anything but this monotony, this dull existence of blue houses, blue trees, and blue-cloaked, glassy-eyed Fae.

"Fuck this place," I grit out.

No one else is around to hear me. Everyone is busy about their own tasks, enthralled to the Witch's will.

For me and the other guards, our duties consist of watching and feeding the prisoners, keeping an eye on the wards that protect the town, overseeing the occasional torture session, and ensuring that no monsters breach the walls. Occasionally we have to fend off the East Witch's brother when he pops in for a visit. He likes to appear suddenly at times and light buildings on fire or set a few prisoners free—less out of pity for them than from a desire to annoy his sister.

I almost wish he would show up this afternoon. But he was here a few days ago, playing his usual tricks, and it's unlikely he would show up again so soon unless greatly provoked.

I tilt my body back a little, so I can view the blue sky through the eyeholes of my helmet. I've adapted to seeing the world in strips—never enjoying a whole, expansive landscape. Always enduring the limitation of my sight as well as my movement. I fucking hate it.

I can't stand it any longer, I can't.

No way out... no fucking way out...

The frantic, furious madness I've been holding at bay swells in my chest until I think my lungs might explode. My heart pounds, booming against my ribs like a battering ram. The suit of armor preserves me in perfect health, with no need of sustenance and no chance of physical damage from the outside—but could I reach such a hideous frenzy that my body destroyed itself from the inside? It's not possible—is it? Could I make myself perish and fade from the sheer violence of my despair?

It's tempting. It's the only way out.

Alice would not want me to think such things. She would want me to endure.

*But I cannot, kitten, I cannot.*

Caer needs me to keep existing, for him, until I figure out how to save us both...

But I have wracked my brain endlessly and come up with nothing—not a shred of a feasible plan. The Cat and I might as well both be dead.

A howl of despair echoes through my mind. I want to roar, to smash things, to crush *bodies*—the rage and panic spiral through my brain, and I open my mouth to bellow my agony aloud.

But a different kind of roar fills the air—the rushing of wind, the rumble of magic. And at the same moment something tugs at my heart. It's as if two forces are pulling at me, in unison—one sharp and imperative, the other powerful, slow, irresistible. Something new is happening, and I laugh aloud, maniacally, not caring who hears, because *something* is better than the hideous nothing I've endured since I made my one moronic wish to the Wizard.

A huge object whirls over the village—a ramshackle building of some kind, carried on a whirlwind. It descends, dropping out of my view with a crash.

That crash came from the gardens—the place where the Witch goes to walk and recharge her magic.

The pull inside me is stronger now, but I dare not leave my post. I have held my tenuous place here by being obedient to the Witch, despite her inability to enchant me. If I abandon my station and go to investigate, she might force me to leave the village. And as wretched as this place is, it gives me a thread of purpose. Something to do. Something beyond wandering the forest, trying to speak with the mad hulking monster that used to be Caer.

Even after I was safe inside the armor, protected from his claws, I made no progress connecting with him. At the mere sight of me he would grow larger, shrieking or snarling before running off among the trees. He doesn't know me anymore. The Fae I used to gamble with is gone. My companion, my partner, my housemate, my—

What he was to me doesn't matter. He is gone.

The sound of running feet catches my attention. Three villagers hurtle past me, heading for the place where the flying house crashed. One of them looks toward me, eyes bright with comprehension, with excitement.

That expression is unusual for one of these Fae. And none of the thralls ever *run*.

My heartbeat shifts into a new rhythm.

A flying house... a shack whisked along by a whirlwind... the image teases something in my memory. I have grown slower of mind as my despair increased, and it takes me a few moments to dredge up the source of that image.

Alice's dreams.

I saw a shack caught in a whirling storm, and a road paved with yellow stones.

Fuck.

I've walked that very road. Why did I not think of the dreams before now? They are not prophecies, exactly, but possibilities, predictions of things that could occur, depending on the dreamer's choices.

The future Alice saw, of the Eater of Hearts conquering her world—that did not happen, because Alice chose to sacrifice herself and end the Queen. But this future—this vision of a building in a whirlwind and a yellow road—that alternate future could still occur.

It might be occurring even now.

Who was inside that house, carried by that whirlwind? Could it be...

Joy blazes up in my heart... but it is doused immediately.

My one consolation in all this has been Alice's safety. Whatever happened to Caer and me, I knew she was safe in her world, living a normal human life. She was happy, far from the dread and damage of this terrible Isle.

But if her dream prophesied her coming *here*—she is not safe. She is vulnerable, likely to become the prey of this village or the monsters beyond its walls.

And that is more unbearable than any wretched thought I've endured today.

---

I remain at my post, torn by the desire to know what is happening and the fear of knowing.

She cannot be here. I will not allow it. I sent her *back*, damn it—she cannot have returned. She has no magic, no power to find her way into this realm. I'm a fool to consider the possibility.

But when a young Fae boy races past me, his eyes alight with newfound freedom, I reach out and grab his arm, pulling him to a halt. My sharp metal fingers slice his flesh, and he frowns, cringing away.

"You'll heal," I say dryly. "Tell me what is happening. Everything you know."

And he tells me a tale of two humans, arriving in a wooden house. The house slammed into the ground, right on top of the East Witch as she walked in the garden—she must have been too stunned to react, too low on energy to whisk herself out of the way. Crushed beneath the building, she faded, and all her thralls were set free.

"And the two humans." I can barely force the words out. "What of them?"

The boy tells me of the West Witch's sudden arrival, and of his conversation with the humans—two females.

"What do they look like?" I rasp.

But the boy frowns. "See for yourself. There's a feast being prepared in the square before the temple. Our two liberators will be sitting with Glenna at the head table." He casts me a final scornful look and races on.

The Witch is dead.

I no longer have to fear that she will banish me for leaving my post. And even if she had survived, news of the arrival of two human women would have been too much for me to bear quietly.

Let the prisoners stay in their cells, or try to escape—it matters not to me. All I want is a glimpse of these new arrivals.

Swiftly I stride away from the jail, skirting the slanted wall of the temple and moving out into the main square of the village. Long tables have already been set up for the feast. The air buzzes with an energy I've never felt in this place before.

Quietly I join the crowd of Fae, sidling through bodies, using my bulk and height to force my way toward the head table. I can't eat anything, of course. Usually I stay away from dining areas at mealtimes—the aroma of the food I cannot eat is torture. But this evening I file along the benches and slide into a spot with the others, listening to the chatter of the liberated villagers. Some of them are raining words on each other like a storm, while others seem barely able to remember how to form coherent thoughts by themselves, without the crutch of the East Witch's compulsion. The magic affects everyone differently, and its absence leaves scars of a different shape on each Fae.

With my place at the head table secured, I can finally scrape together enough courage to turn my helmet and peer through the eye slits toward Glenna and the human guests.

Her fragrance filters through the scent of the food, even before I see her.

Delicate florals, a hint of lemon, and an undercurrent of earth and growing things. There's an addictive twist to her scent, just as there is to the taste of her sex—something entrancing that makes me turn my head farther, angling my helmet to catch a stronger whiff.

A chill races over my skin, and thrills roll through my stomach.

I have been half-dead for so long that the force and suddenness of my emotions catches me off-guard. I feel as if an oillipheist ran headfirst into my chest.

Anger roars in my mind, because she left the safety of her world and came *here*, of all places.

Joy tears through my soul, leaving brilliant gashes glowing in its wake.

Desire throbs in my blood, rabid and undeniable.

To keep myself from bellowing her name, I shift my attention to the other human—a young woman with brown skin and dark hair. When I look at her, I feel a different kind of impulse—an awareness written on my very bones, fused into my blood. This is the sorceress the boy told me about—the one with mismatched eyes who caused the house to fly and to fall on the East Witch. There is something special about her as well. Her presence was one of the two forces tugging at my soul earlier.

I've felt something like this before, long ago, when my brother first came to rescue me from my father and take me back to the Dread Court. His presence spoke to me this way—an echo of our shared ancestry, the call of blood to blood.

I won't deny the brown-skinned girl looks like me. But that isn't proof. I will need hard evidence before I can reach any reliable conclusion about her.

For now, the person who consumes my thoughts and attention is Alice.

She's not eating the food they set in front of her. Wise girl. She can't know all the details of the foul life cycle of this place, but she suspects something amiss, some dark magic—and she is right. I've seen the blood soaking into the soil at the roots of the corn, the entrails glistening beneath the stalks, the globs of wet pink flesh stuck to the swollen husks. I know that the harvested, blood-fed corn is transmuted into all the various dishes here on the feast tables.

Alice turns toward me, and my breath catches.

She's looking right at me. Noticing how I am different from the others. Wondering about me, in that curious mind of hers.

My Alice, my kitten... *mine*...

But I don't go to her, or reveal myself. Disclosing our former connection would raise too many questions among the villagers, and could cause suspicion. I will do nothing that might put Alice in danger. Not again.

I watch her closely throughout the meal as she asks questions of Glenna, gleaning the information she will need to understand this place and survive it. Once more I marvel at her cleverness, her inquiring mind, the diplomatic way in which she interacts with those around her.

As I observe her, I fall in love with her more helplessly than ever.

When the dancing begins, she slips into the enchanted whirl of Fae bodies. Humans are susceptible to our music—it thrills them, lends them grace and energy, and sometimes keeps them dancing until long past their bodies' endurance. Fae dances like this one can be dangerous. I prop myself against a wall, in the shadows, and I wait, planning to interfere if she dances too long and wears herself out.

But she surprises me, as she always has. She catches sight of me at the fringe of the crowd, and I feel that pull between us, like a whispered charm, an invisible cord. An awareness.

She's dancing toward me, her body curving sensuously, her eyes hooded and sultry. She's challenging me, trying to lure me into the dance with her. Naughty, wonderful, wicked girl...

She prowls closer, her gray eyes shining silver in the light of the orbs floating above the square. "Why are you watching me?"

My voice sticks in my throat.

"You don't talk? Or maybe you can't." She examines my armor with narrowed eyes.

My heartbeat is so ferocious I'm sure she must hear it. In this moment I can think of no logical reason why I should not reveal my identity to her. But I can't seem to assemble the right words.

Glenna staggers toward us, her eyes glazed with wine. None of the villagers have been allowed to drink heavily in years, and she's enjoying her freedom to the fullest. "This is Talon." She introduces me to Alice with the false name I've been using. "He'll be your escort to the woods tomorrow."

That's news to me. I suppose I should have expected it—I am usually the one who serves as escort to anyone leaving or entering the village. My cursed, impenetrable armor makes me a useful shield for travelers.

"He doesn't speak much, do you, Talon?" Glenna continues. "He came to us some time ago. The East Witch couldn't enthrall him for some reason, but he vowed to be a good citizen, so she let him stay with us. I've never seen him remove his helmet, or any other part of his armor, for that matter. He doesn't eat, drink, sleep, or piss—not that any of us have seen. Perhaps the armor is actually empty." She reaches out and raps my chestplate with her knuckles. "I'll wager there's something solid in there. Maybe you can convince him to—expose himself."

Alice doesn't react to the innuendo. When Glenna saunters away, Alice lays her hand against my breastplate, over my heart. Her scent rushes into my helmet, filling my nostrils, my lungs.

"You never take off the armor?" she murmurs. "I wonder if you're cursed. Maybe that's why the Witch couldn't enthrall you. Certain types of magic don't mix."

I inhale her scent as if it's a potion that can fortify me for what comes next. "Always so clever, kitten."

Her beautiful eyes widen, and the color drains from her face. In her eyes, I see emotions swirling—a tempest akin to the conflicted storm inside my own chest. She is angry, shocked, sad, anxious—and glad.

When she speaks, her voice is shards of stained glass, beautiful and dangerous. "Say that again."

# 2

## CAER

I stand a few paces from the big bed in Alice's room—a room draped in green, like everything else here in the Emerald City. The heavy aroma of bodies and arousal thickens the air—a vulgar, delicious perfume I haven't enjoyed in much too long.

Back in Mallaithe, I was rarely invited to sex parties. I could never quite determine why. Maybe I was too hungry for touch, too eager to curl up with the others afterward, relishing the warmth of skin on skin. Perhaps it was because those gatherings had a specific purpose, yet I always wanted something more, or different—and the other Unseelie could tell. I never quite fit in.

This orgy with Riordan, Alice, and Jasper is far more satisfying than the few I've attended. I think it's because I care for every one of them, beyond the loveliness of their bodies or the pleasure they can give me. I want them more fiercely and deeply than I've ever wanted anyone.

My asshole is faintly warm, still tender from taking Jasper there. The vibration of his cock sent me flying, as I suspected it would. He's a treasure, and not only because of his dick—though I won't admit it to him.

From the moment I walked out of the forest in my beast form, there has been a mutual enchantment between us. He seemed instantly delighted to see me, and I will never forget the touch of his slender fingers on my muzzle, or his calm voice soothing me with quiet words. He's more tender than I ever was, and somehow his gentleness makes me feel stronger, more powerful, more recklessly wicked. I liked letting him fuck me tonight, and sometime I'd like to fuck him back.

But at the moment, he's licking Alice's clit, while her beautiful body arches off the bed and her blond hair spills in satiny waves. Her breasts and collarbone glimmer with a light sheen of sweat, and she's panting and moaning so prettily I'm hard again.

Jealousy coils in my chest, dark and venomous. Much as I like Jasper, I'm tempted to shove him out of the way, because he's licking *Alice*, and Alice is mine. He already brought her to climax once tonight, and he was lucky I let him do that much. I should drag him out from between her legs and take his place. He wouldn't protest—he'd obey like the good pet he is.

I take one step. Just one.

A band of sinewy muscle wraps around my throat. Riordan's arm compresses my neck as he tugs me backward against his broad chest. "Thinking of interfering, Cat?"

"No," I lie.

He chuckles, and I shiver at the heat of his breath on my cheek. I've lived with Riordan for years, but I've never been this close to him naked.

"Don't try to fool me, Caer," he says, low. "I know you better than they do. I know you hate to share the things you like best."

"I love her," I rasp.

"So do I. And she loves both of us—and maybe him too."

I hiss through my teeth, envy spurting in my chest like hot poison.

"You gave him his first command tonight," Riordan points out. "And he pleased our Alice well. Let him please her again, if she wants it."

"You wish it was you, tasting her," I snarl. "Don't pretend otherwise."

Riordan hesitates for a moment. Then he says, in a deeper, more dangerous tone, "I don't know... I'm not unhappy about my current position."

He presses in closer at my back, his immense cock tucked flat in the groove between my ass cheeks. My own cock bobs at the feel of him there.

Riordan maintains the grip across my throat, but his other hand moves around my hip, across my lower abdomen, to the base of my cock. He wraps scarred fingers around it, and I exhale sharply.

"Shall I teach you a lesson about sharing?" he rumbles against my back. "Shall I show you that Alice isn't the only one who needs you?"

My whole body shudders against his. "Yes."

Riordan keeps one hand wrapped around the base of my cock, but he releases me from the throat hold and slides his big, warm palm to my chest, clasping one of my pectorals. He squeezes lightly and flicks his thumb across my nipple. "If I'd known you would feel this good, I'd have fucked you sooner."

"Ha!" I choke out. "No, you wouldn't. Without Alice, you would never have softened enough. Face it, Riordan—Alice took the shriveled seed of your heart and watered it until it grew. You're like me now—weak and love-sick."

He growls at the taunt. "Not as soft as *him*."

We both watch Jasper as he nuzzles along the inside of Alice's thigh, while she pleads for him to return to her clit.

"Maybe he's not as soft as we think," I muse. "Look how he's tormenting her."

"Fucking hot, isn't?" Riordan's breath is heavier, hotter, a harsh gust against the side of my neck. He inhales hungrily. "You smell good."

"I'm in heat, so my scent is more enticing."

"You think I don't know that?" His fingers tighten around my cock, and it twitches again, helplessly. My whole shaft is burning hard, and I'm leaking more precum than usual. It's fucking *dripping* onto the floor. And still Riordan only stands there, holding my chest and my cock, and *sniffing* me.

I wrench away and shove him back. "Either do it, or leave me alone."

His eyes turn molten, but he just stands there, a tower of muscle and rich brown skin, with that gigantic cock jutting out between his powerful thighs.

I've forgotten my jealousy now. That was his plan, of course, but will he follow through with this game he started?

"Have you ever fucked a male besides Finias?" I ask, with my widest, most mocking grin. "You told me you didn't enjoy it with him. Maybe you're not capable of taking another male like he *needs* to be taken. You're too cold-hearted, too cerebral, aren't you, Rabbit? Not predator enough to manage the job properly. I think I'll go take Jasper's ass, or Alice's mouth." I sneer at him and turn away.

Riordan grabs me. Drags me back in, and clamps his mouth over mine in a brutal kiss. His teeth lacerate my lips, and mine rip into his as well. We suck the blood from each other's torn flesh fiercely. His is the richest, hottest, most delicious blood I've tasted from any Fae.

"Fuck," I gasp. Riordan kisses me hard again, then whips me around. His large palm lands on my spine, bending me over. Then he grabs both my wrists and pins them to the small of my back with one hand.

I barely have time to twitch my tail out of the way before he's slathering my asshole in our blood and his spit—the lubricant of choice for the Unseelie.

I get a second for one deep breath, and then he's wedging the giant head of his cock into my tight hole with one hand, the other still binding my wrists to my back.

Pain rips along my insides, but it's the good kind of pain—the mind-wiping, soul-searing kind that goes hand in hand with excruciating pleasure.

Riordan doesn't give me time to adjust. He barrels into me all the way, stretching me past the breaking point. My body heals around him as he rearranges me into something new—imprints the shape of his cock inside me. I'll be able to take him easily from now on.

Roughly he shoves me, forces me to bend lower—then tugs that huge cock halfway out of me and rams in again. He's thrusting now, thrusting quick—violent, frenzied—oh gods—gods—fuck—fuck—my tail is standing straight up and my whole body is quaking. It feels as if every bone is being jarred loose with the pounding Riordan is giving me. My cock swings helplessly, stiffer than ever, hard and hot and aching. My hands are curled into fists, still manacled in Riordan's grip. I can't touch myself, and it's exquisite torture.

I realize my eyes are closed, and when I open them, I stare straight into Alice's gray ones. Jasper's face is buried in her pussy again, and she's making the sharp little noises she makes right before she comes. Her breasts are so beautiful—plump and creamy, tipped with tight pink nipples. She's watching Riordan fuck me, and the lascivious delight in her gaze makes me grin.

But the grin drops from my face as Riordan shoves himself deeper, thrusts into me more ferociously. I'm a plaything, a cock-sleeve, prey to the most brutal fucking of my life. And I love it.

Oh gods—thrills are soaring in my stomach, blazing across my skin—Riordan pounds me harder and I come, bliss streaking through my cock. The ecstasy is so sharp that I scream. I keep coming, splattering the floor as Riordan hammers the orgasm out of me. Harsh spasms of pleasure jerk more cum from my cock until I have nothing left.

And then he's coming in my ass—a thick, hot, flood that feels as if it's shooting impossibly deep inside me.

Alice came when I did. She's limp and panting on the bed, her gaze still fixed on me and Riordan. Jasper is kissing her pussy, soothing her through the end of the orgasm. His face gleams with her arousal.

Alice's slender fingers twitch against the mattress, and then she reaches for me, a dazed smile on her face. In her eyes I see the reassurance I need—the love she holds for me. The love that drew her back to this realm. The love that prompted her to give her body to me in that field, salving the frenzy of my heat, calming me enough so that I could return with her.

She whispers something as I hang there, impaled on Riordan's cock, my wrists pinioned in his grip. She mouths the words, "I love you."

The warmth that floods over me then is better than the afterglow of sex.

Riordan slides his free hand between my legs, rubbing it over my limp cock. I jump and whimper at the stimulation.

He lets my wrists go and pulls out of me carelessly. My hole squeezes shut after him, leaking some of his cum down my leg as I stand upright again.

I turn, the twitch of my tail betraying the uncertainty I feel. I am nearly too much of a coward to ask him, but with Alice's love strengthening me, I manage it.

"So?" I fight to keep a tremor out of my voice. "How was it? Better than Fin?"

Riordan gives a low growl and pulls me against him, face to face. His heart is pounding—I can feel it through his chest as he tips my face up. Through the gashes in his cheeks, I can see the grit of his teeth. He does that when he's struggling with important words, so I wait.

"You're a thousand times better than Fin," he says hoarsely. "I will never tire of showing you how much I fucking love you, you ridiculous fool."

"Care to bet on that?" I whisper, as he leans in.

"Bet my life," he answers, and kisses me.

# 3

## JASPER

Boots clunk against the stone, heading down the corridor toward my cell. It's the dead of night, but I've been too excited to sleep.

I leap up, propelled by dread and hope. Mostly hope. All the thralls are liberated now, and the East Witch is dead. Maybe that means I'll be set free.

The East Witch compels children around the age of eight or nine, once they begin to understand deeper things and become more of a threat. When she tried to compel me at age nine, and couldn't, she let me live freely a little longer. She said my mind was simple, and perhaps I needed time to "ripen." When she tried again, I was eighteen; and after that attempt failed, I was brought to live here, in the jail. My tattoos were applied soon after, marking me as a sacrifice.

Twelve years I've been a prisoner.

During those twelve years, every time the guards stalked down the hallway, keys jangling, my stomach plummeted with the fear that maybe it was my turn—and at the same time, I couldn't help *hoping* it was my turn, because that would mean fresh air and sky again. Fae are not meant to be kept confined, in the dark, alone in ugly cells.

I crave beauty. I crave the wind through the leaves and the soft brush of grass. I crave the skin of another person—someone besides Glenna. She comes to me often, and I enjoy our times well enough—they are a relief from the monotony of my days. But she does not want to talk to me. When I try to speak with her, she orders me to be silent. If I keep talking, she strikes me. So I have learned to quietly take what pleasure I can with her, and not demand more.

The boots approaching my cell are not hers; they belong to two guards. I tense, waiting for them to pass me by, as usual, anxious to see who they will take this time.

I've spoken with many of the others in the cells along this corridor—those for whom the Witch's control was only partly effective. They were sometimes confused, struggling with the contradiction between her imposed enthrallment and their own willpower, distressed and fearful. I spoke with them, calmed them, sang to them, told them stories. Sometimes they didn't answer—other times they screamed at me to shut up. A few spoke to me civilly enough, and I helped organize several escape attempts—all of them failures. Perhaps I am too much of a fool to succeed at such efforts. But I like to think my stories, songs, and kind words made life a little better for my fellow prisoners, even if they never said so, or thanked me.

I lose them all, one by one. Sometimes they are tortured for the amusement of the Witch and the villagers, then brought back to their cell. Other times they are bound and carried to the fields for sacrifice.

Eventually, everyone in these cells is given to the crows.

I've been here the longest. That's why most of the other prisoners hate me—they think I have an unfair advantage because Glenna likes me, and because the East Witch allowed our trysts. The Witch had the final word on any pairings in the village.

Now that she's gone, maybe Glenna will let me out, let me prove I can be more to her than just a toy for pleasure. I can be helpful. I can be more than this.

Maybe she will love me.

I clutch the bars, waiting as a light-orb dances nearer over the head of the Fae guards approaching my cell. I'm terrified they're going to stop at Mendi's cell—she's one of the newest additions. Her mind has fractured from long years of enthrallment, but she doesn't curse me or scream at me like some of the others do. She has never spoken to me, but when I sing to her, her sobs grow quiet.

The guards walk past her cell, and I breathe a sigh of relief.

And then they stop at mine.

One of them holds a cup. "Will you drink it, or should we pour it down your throat?"

It takes me a moment to realize what is happening.

Grief hollows me out, a chasm widening in my heart.

This is it, then. I know what it means when the guards bring someone a cup of water from the Well of Undoing.

I could fight them, try to spill the water. They'd have to fetch more. But the water is precious, and the guards would be angry, and hurt me more. And spilling the valuable liquid would mean another sacrifice must be made, soon, so that villagers can go to the well and draw more water.

I don't want to hasten anyone else's death, so I will go quietly to mine.

"I will drink it," I tell the guard.

He chuckles and sneers to his companion, "See what I told you? He's too stupid to understand what's happening. It's about time this one was purged."

He hands me the cup, but before I drink, I ask, "Is Glenna continuing the sacrifices then? Even though you're all free?"

"Shut up, fool, and drink," snaps the guard. "Otherwise I might decide to give your cock a try myself before we put you out for the crows."

I drink the water and hand back the empty cup. Already I can feel my strength leaking out of my body, my Fae powers of healing and illusion disappearing, every bit of magic draining away. I sway on my feet, clinging to the bars for support.

The guards open the cell and haul me out. I'm naked except for a pair of ragged pants, the only clothing I've been allowed for a long time. The pants rip open still more as I'm dragged down the corridor, past the cells. There are five other prisoners in the jail, each one awake and watching. I've spoken to each of them—tried my best to lighten their last days. Yet none of them speak to me or smile at me as I'm taken away. They only stare for a moment, and then avert their eyes.

The head jailer nods, smirking, as I'm hustled past him. "It's about time that one did his share. Guess the new mayor's tired of your little cock, eh boy?"

I don't reply, and a few moments later I'm shoved out into the dark street.

The night is cool, and I lift my face to the breeze, inhaling the wondrous freshness.

"The sky," I breathe. "I didn't remember there being so many stars. Have more stars appeared since I was imprisoned?"

"No, idiot. Shut up." One of the guards strikes me across the cheek.

A voice from the shadows. "Leave him alone. Don't you think he will suffer enough in the fields?"

The armored figure of the new guard resolves from the darkness. He's taller than the others, and bulkier. Unlike them, he dresses in full armor from head to toe. I do not know his name, but he patrols the prison hallways sometimes, and I've heard that he, like me, is resistant to the Witch's compulsion.

He stood guard outside my cell once, after my most recent failed attempt at escape. I got all the way to the guards' station at the end of the hall, and perhaps I could have made it farther; but I was caught as I tried to unlock the cells of my fellow prisoners.

After I was beaten and put back in my cell, I remember the armored guard standing there, watching me, then saying, in a low voice, "You should rest. Nothing wearies the mind like ruined hope."

His tone wasn't mocking, hateful, or angry. It was quiet, tired, and kind.

And now he is advocating for me. Ordering the other guards not to strike me.

Gratitude swells in my heart, and I nearly cry out to him. I almost beg him to save me.

*If you help me, if you will claim me and speak to me always in that low, tired voice, I will be yours forever.*

But he is already turning away.

They all turn away. No one has ever cared what becomes of me.

My mother and father mated by the will of the East Witch. Neither of them cared for each other, or for me. On the day I was taken to prison, my mother simply kept working at her loom, ignoring my pleas. As I was marched through town, I saw my father, glassy-eyed, going about some errand. Both of them were slaves to the Witch, too far under her sway to form any attachment to me.

I don't hate them. It wasn't their fault.

The armored guard is walking away, and I'm being hustled toward the village gates. A third guard meets us there, along with a priest from the Temple of Crows. As the priest places a straw hat on my head, I catch a glimpse of markings on the woven crown—ritual spellwork to consecrate my body.

"May the Arcane Murder accept this gift," intones the priest. "May this body and blood renew the magic of the flock, and may the Dark Blessing flow always through our village, sustaining it and bringing us the power we crave."

"Power the East Witch can't fucking steal anymore," adds a voice. It's Glenna, striding up to the group by the gate. She scans me briefly, carelessly, as if I'm a tree that failed to bear fruit, or a signpost that points in the wrong direction. "Everything arranged for this?"

"Yes, Mayor," answers one of the guards.

"Good. The sooner we pay our debt to these humans, the better. Then we can focus on harnessing the Dark Blessing and bringing our village into a new era. I have so many plans! I think I'll invite Tharn and Jeya to my home tonight. It will be a long day, and I'll need to relax at its end. I've been wanting to bed them for years."

I try to catch her eye, but she doesn't look at me again. She nods to the guards. "May the gods smile on you as you place the sacrifice! Go silently, or you may wake the crows."

Then she turns her back on me and walks off again, briskly, full of plans and purpose.

It's too much.

I can feel my soul crumpling inside, thinning to a skeleton leaf. My heart is mourning quietly, a broken, keening sound confined to my chest. I don't let it out, not when the guards creep through the cornstalks with me, not when they brace me against the sacrificial pole, not even when they bind my arms to the crossbeam and coil ropes around my legs. I don't make a sound when several of the crows stir, terrifying the guards—nor do I breathe a sigh of relief when the crows settle into sleep again.

The guards depart, and I hang from the stake, trying to summon the will to enjoy my last moments. I should be able to delight in the pre-dawn crispness of the air, the rustle of the breeze through the stalks, the sparkle of the stars overhead. But as the hours pass and dawn comes, all I can do is mourn, deep inside—mourn for something I cannot name.

I always knew this would be my end, so I rarely let myself imagine anything else. But sometimes I thought about what I would wish for if I ever met the Wizard. No wish I devised ever seemed quite right. I want too many things for the others in my village—joy, compassion, health, freedom, hope—no one wish could ever encompass it all. And every time I tried to formulate what I want for myself, I couldn't quite manage it.

Not that it matters now. Dawn is breaking. I've run out of time, and no wish of mine will ever come true.

My stake is set on a hill, and when I lift my head I can see the gold and green expanse of the cornfields extending endlessly in all directions—except where the belt of the forest forms a taller, darker green. There's a road, too—I can see bits of it coiling through the fields.

Something moves in the cornstalks below the hill, and when I glance quickly in that direction, my straw hat slips off, hanging against my back by its leather string.

The long leaves shift, rasping against each other. The crows are waking. They will be hungry.

But no... the thing coming out of the cornstalks isn't a bird.

It's a young woman—barely more than a girl... and human, by the look of her. Her blonde hair is tucked behind one rounded ear. She wears a blue dress, and her pale face glows with determination.

When she looks up at me, the surprise in her lovely gray eyes shifts into a heated promise. As if she knows me already, *knew* I was here, and *cared* enough to come.

It's impossible, and yet I know immediately that it's true—she is here for me. To save me.

And in that moment, as I look into those bright, confident gray eyes, every wish I could have ever made is fulfilled.

# 4

# ALICE

I fasten the golden collar around Riordan's strong neck, and it magically adjusts to fit him.

I was the only one he would trust to do this. It's his first day of playing "pet"… the rest of us have already had our turn.

He's entirely naked, every powerful inch of him. His brown skin has always been beautiful, but today it's especially lustrous thanks to a liberal application of oil, also by my hands.

As my fingers fall away from the collar, he straightens to his full height. I'm fully clothed, and having him here in front of me, a big, brawny, naked male with eyes of fire and teeth like knives—it kicks my heart into a frenzied rhythm and soaks the lace panties I'm wearing.

He's not erect yet. Even though he consented to this, he's not sure he'll like it. He hates being out of control.

We've given him a safe word if he wants the game to end. But I hope he won't use it.

"Caer, the leash," I say.

The Cat bounds forward, practically salivating with eagerness. He attaches the thin gold chain to Riordan's collar. "May I give him the first order?"

"No." I tug him back. "Riordan wants Jasper to give him orders at first. Isn't that right?"

Riordan nods, refusing to unclench his jaws.

"Fine." The Cat withdraws a little, a sulky expression on his face.

Jasper advances next, his fingers curling around Riordan's leash, knuckles brushing the taller Fae's oiled chest. The Scarecrow looks up at Riordan and swallows nervously.

The corner of Riordan's mouth twitches, and his hardened jawline relaxes a little.

"I think you should, um… kneel," murmurs the Scarecrow.

"Have him go on all fours," hisses Caer.

"Hush." I wrap my fingers across Caer's mouth to silence him. He licks my palm, and when I squeal in surprise, he grins.

"On your hands and knees, pet," Jasper says cautiously.

Riordan lowers himself slowly, with a lethal grace that makes me gasp. Sometimes I forget that he played courtesan to the great Unseelie Queen, the Eater of Hearts—I forget that he has more skill in sexual games than one would think. He's so keen-minded, such an intense scholar of magic and living things—and yet he has more layers beneath that. He is a complex and beautiful being.

"Is this all right?" I say suddenly, anxious that our little game of pretend might bring back ugly memories for him. I don't know everything the Queen had him do.

His scarlet eyes meet mine. "If it's not all right, I will tell you."

Reassured, I pick up the next object we decided on for this session—a string of four small metal orbs with a fluffy white tail at the end. The orbs gleam with the lubricant Caer applied to them a few moments ago.

Riordan plants both palms on the floor. He's on hands and knees now, his perfectly sculpted rear exposed to my view as I circle around behind him. At my nod, Caer steps forward and pulls apart Riordan's ass cheeks so I can see the puckered hole between them.

My first touch—just a fingertip—makes Riordan shiver. I stroke his asshole gently for a moment before bringing the first orb in contact with his opening. This orb is slightly tapered at one end, and it slides into Riordan easily.

He releases a low, shaken sound—and I know him well enough to be sure it's arousal, not pain. Jasper is kneeling at Riordan's front, petting his long, sensitive ears.

"Keep doing that," I tell Jasper. "Keep playing with his ears. He's being such a good boy."

I push in the next orb in the string, then another, and then the last, until only the fluffy white tail is left.

Caer crows with delight. "It's perfect. A rabbit tail for our fine pet. I'll activate it, mousie, since you don't have magic."

He leans in and speaks a word in an old Fae language, and the string of orbs begins to vibrate.

Riordan chokes out a groan. "Oh gods. Fuck... fuck... aahhh..." His beautiful, sinewy body tenses all over... he's practically shaking on hands and knees, and beneath his belly his cock juts out, enormously erect.

"Godsdamn me," breathes Caer, and his voice is stricken, almost tearful. "He's so fucking gorgeous."

I walk to Riordan's head, tipping his face up, loving the feel of his strong jaw in my hand. He's panting, his lolling tongue visible through the gashes in his cheeks. "You can't come until we tell you, pet," I say softly. "Or we'll have to punish you."

"Fuck, Alice," he gasps. "It's too much, please..."

He's trembling, this huge Fae male of mine—precum seeping from the tip of his cock, his strong thighs hard as every muscle in his body fights the oncoming orgasm.

"Give him a break," I tell Caer, and he speaks another word in the old language. The buzzing stops, and Riordan heaves a great sigh of relief.

"Let's go for a walk," Jasper says, rising and tugging the leash. "To the library. You and Caer can teach me that game you like—"

"While our pet tends to us under the table," Caer puts in, practically bouncing with excitement. "Brilliant idea."

His clothes fly off as he races out of the room, headed for the library.

Jasper and I share a look that's half-exasperation, half-fondness for Caer. We lead Riordan down the hall. When we reach the library, Caer has thrown himself into a chair, his tail half-pinned behind him, twitching with anticipation. "Come, pet," he says to Riordan.

Riordan crawls to him, but there's more majesty than submission in his movements. I can't take my eyes off him, and I can't imagine he will last very long in this game if Caer keeps teasing him. He'll get so angry he'll bark the safe word, and then our fun will end.

But before the Cat can give him another order, Riordan takes a long lick up the underside of Caer's cock. Then he takes the whole thing between his serrated jaws.

Caer freezes.

If Riordan bit his dick off, he would heal, but it would be incredibly painful and a horrific breach of the trust among us. It's not as if Riordan hasn't done things like this in the past—but those genital mutilations were limited to his human subjects—criminals stolen from the human world and forced to contribute to the White Rabbit's magical experiments.

This is different. This is Caer, sweet wicked Caer, who hides a soft heart beneath his smirks and claws. I can't bear to see Riordan hurt him.

Riordan moves, keeping his jaws just far enough apart that the tips of his teeth lightly graze Caer's length. Through the wounds in the Rabbit's face, I can see Caer's cock moving inside Riordan's mouth.

Riordan's lips close around Caer's shaft as Jasper and I watch, paralyzed, mesmerized. Caer is whimpering, motionless, not daring to so much as twitch a muscle lest he be torn.

Back and forth Riordan's head moves, his jaws and lips maintaining the exact same position and pressure. Caer's whimpers turn sharp and needy, quicker and shriller—his claws are sunk into the armrests of his chair, shredding the upholstery.

Caer yells out as he comes, terror and ecstasy mingled—but Riordan holds him steady, keeps him from jerking around and slitting himself on the sharp teeth. Through Riordan's cheek-gash I can see Caer's dick throbbing, his cum spurting down Riordan's throat.

When it's over, Riordan withdraws, and Caer collapses into the chair, a look of horrified glee on his face. "Fuck, that was terrifying. I loved it."

"I think our pet deserves a treat, don't you agree?" I look to Caer and Jasper for confirmation, and they both nod.

I set a couple of large pillows by the wall, then slip off my panties. Tossing the underwear aside, I seat myself against the pillows, hiking my skirt up to my waist and spreading my legs wide.

"Here, pet," I command, patting the rug right in front of my open pussy. "Lie on the floor, just here, propped against me. Make sure you spread wide and angle your hips so Caer and Jasper can see your pretty fluffy tail."

Riordan crawls over to me and settles his big frame onto the rug, half-reclining with his back against my chest, with his knees arched and spread, and his pelvis tilted up so Jasper and Caer can see his erect cock, his balls, and his asshole, garnished with the white tail. I unclasp the leash and lay it aside, for the moment.

I love the heavy pressure of Riordan's big back and shoulders leaning against my belly and chest. Wrapping both arms around him, I circle his nipple with a fingertip. "Caer, speak the word."

Caer activates the buzzing orbs inside Riordan, who goes instantly, beautifully rigid from head to toe.

"Fuck," whimpers Jasper, fingers sliding into his pants.

Caer kicks his legs over the armrest of his chair, and though the position is a languid one, his violet eyes gleam eagerly.

I move my palm lower, stroking upward from Riordan's hardened abdomen, along his heaving chest, to his powerful throat, where I cup his jaw again and tip his head back as I bend forward, over him. The tips of his furred ears brush my cheeks, my neck. I kiss him like that, upside down, while he strains and trembles from the delicious buzzing sensation of the orbs inside him.

"I need to taste him," Jasper breaks out desperately.

I nod, and the Scarecrow lunges forward, golden curls tumbling askew as he pops the head of Riordan's cock into his mouth with a hum of frenzied satisfaction. Riordan groans long and loud from the anguish of holding himself back, but he will not beg.

"Wait, Jasper," I say sharply, and he withdraws, his lips wet from Riordan's arousal.

I brush my lips against the delicate pink inside of Riordan's left ear. "Do you trust us?"

He shudders, panting and straining in my arms.

"Do you trust *me*?" I say, more quietly.

"Yes," he grits out, and a thrill of delight passes through my chest.

"Then let your pride go, beloved. Ask for release. Beg us to let you come."

His lower stomach is shining, ridged, tensed with desire, with effort. He groans violently, hips bucking upward, cock yearning helplessly, untouched.

Caer whisks over the arm of his chair and prowls forward on all fours, his tail lashing. He licks his lips. "Beg for it, Riordan."

"And we will gladly grant it," Jasper adds, with a kiss to Riordan's inner thigh.

When Riordan says nothing, Caer's eyes flash, and he speaks another word. The buzzing intensifies inside Riordan's ass, and he yells out, arching up while I grip him tight, holding him against me. The white tail is quivering with the force of the vibration.

"Trust us," I hiss into his ear. "Trust all of us, and yield."

He could easily break out of this—push himself out of my arms, silence the orbs, throw all of us aside and storm from the room. He could use the safe word.

But he doesn't leave, and he doesn't let himself come. He stays in the moment, because he knows, as well as I do, that this is about more than sex. This is our stern, magnificent Riordan finally allowing himself to be utterly vulnerable with us—broken down, submissive, open. Because only once he breaks down every wall can all four of us truly trust each other to the fullest, and make our family into the wonderful unit it can be.

"Riordan." Caer shifts closer, his claws sliding over Riordan's thigh, his violet eyes glowing with a rare, serious tenderness. "My darling, yield."

Riordan's eyes close and his body relaxes against mine.

"Please." His deep voice is hoarse and tight with need. "Please let me come."

"Yes." I lean over and kiss his forehead. "Yes, pet, of course we will. Come for us."

"Come for us, my guardian," whispers Jasper, as his slim fingers glide around Riordan's cock. He strokes firmly, skillfully.

And with a shattered cry, Riordan comes. His release sprinkles his own chest and stomach, my arm and Caer's, and Jasper's hand.

Jasper bends to lick him clean, while Caer slides in and presses his bare body all along Riordan's side.

Riordan lies heavy in my arms, utterly undone. He has relinquished everything—pushed past another barrier.

"I'm so proud of you," I whisper.

He heaves a sigh and reaches up to caress my face. And as my lips meet his, I smile at the thought of every adventure that still awaits us, both in the sanctity of our home and beyond, in the beautiful, dangerous realm of Faerie.

# 5

# DOROTHY

## ONE YEAR AFTER THE DEFEAT OF THE GOD-STAR

"Fuck this kingdom," I say to Darec.

We've been looking forward to visiting this particular country—we heard delightful things about the scenery. We had even heard of a Fae presence there—a rogue clan banished from Faerie long ago. But as it turns out, the kingdom of Revallen is as anti-magic and anti-Fae as possible. It is ruled by a queen both ruthless and careless—ruthless in the persecution of magic-wielders and careless about the welfare of her people. She seems to love piling up money only for the sake of having it, not using it. Which doesn't bother me as much as it should—after all, they're not my people. But I've been deeply annoyed and offended by our reception here.

Darec squeezes my shoulders sympathetically. "We could teach her a lesson."

Usually I would agree wholeheartedly, and we'd devise some wicked plan to carry out together, in vengeance for how poorly we've been received. Some human villages and cities are welcoming to strangers like us, but we've also played quite a few tricks on people in inhospitable places during our journeys. It's been fun, but I'm fucking tired.

"I want to go home," I tell him. "I'm too weary for the teaching of lessons."

Darec's yellow eyes glow brighter, and he gives me one of the sultry smirks I love. "What I have in mind won't require a bit of our energy. I have a golden cap in my vault—very valuable, one of a kind."

"The one that calls the Wild Hunt?"

His eyes widen. "You know of it?"

"Riordan read about it in one of the books you gave me. He told us that when the Wild Hunt is summoned, they will cleanse the summoner's kingdom from unjust rule. Or some such thing."

"That's pretty much the gist of it," Darec replies. "So what do you say? Shall we gift the cap of gold to some poor resident of this land, so they can make good use of it?"

A smile spreads across my face. "I swear that's the best idea you've had yet."

"Really?" He quirks an eyebrow. "Better than the one I had last night?"

"Oh… well…" I feel my cheeks heating. "That was a good one. I'll give you that."

His grin widens. "So we're agreed, then? Shall we let some unsuspecting citizen call the Wild Hunt down upon this kingdom?"

"Yes." I take his hand, a wicked excitement thrilling through my blood. "Yes, we shall. Let's go fetch it. And then, once it's delivered, we can go back to Oz and rest a while."

"Agreed." He squeezes my fingers lightly. "After all, there's no place like home."

If you want to find out what happens when the Wild Hunt is called down upon the kingdom of Revallen, read *A Hunt So Wild and Cruel*... a Fae retelling of "A Christmas Carol." It has midwinter vibes but you can enjoy it anytime of the year.

**She's been a bad girl...**
**They've been summoned for a reckoning.**

When the Fae die, they fade into the ether—but in some cases, instead of going to their eternal rest, they become members of the Wild Hunt, ghost riders who champion a ruthless kind of justice. In *A Hunt So Wild and Cruel*, three majestic ghost riders of the Wild Hunt take physical form to punish Queen Lauriel for her merciless rule. If she can learn to value her people and respect the Fae, she will be spared—but only a true change of heart will save her, and that is not so easy to achieve. As for the three Fae, their failure will mean their banishment from the Wild Hunt and their condemnation to a much worse fate.

**Three ghost riders...**
**One chance to change.**

# MORE BOOKS FROM REBECCA F. KENNEY

### The DARK RULERS adult fantasy romance series

*Bride to the Fiend Prince*
*Captive of the Pirate King*
*Prize of the Warlord*
*The Warlord's Treasure*
*Healer to the Ash King*
*Pawn of the Cruel Princess*
*Jailer to the Death God*
*Slayer of the Pirate Lord*

### The WICKED DARLINGS Fae retellings series

*A Court of Sugar and Spice*
*A Court of Hearts and Hunger*
*A City of Emeralds and Envy*

### The PANDEMIC MONSTERS trilogy

*The Vampires Will Save You*
*The Chimera Will Claim You*
*The Monster Will Rescue You*

### For the Love of the Villain series

*The Sea Witch* (Little Mermaid retelling with male Sea Witch)
*The Maleficent Faerie* (Sleeping Beauty retelling with male Maleficent)

## The SAVAGE SEAS books

*The Teeth in the Tide*
*The Demons in the Deep*

*These Wretched Wings* (A Savage Seas Universe novel)

## The IMMORTAL WARRIORS adult fantasy romance series

*Jack Frost*
*The Gargoyle Prince*
*Wendy, Darling* (Neverland Fae Book 1)
*Captain Pan* (Neverland Fae Book 2)
*Hades: God of the Dead*
*Apollo: God of the Sun*

Related Content: *The Horseman of Sleepy Hollow*

## The INFERNAL CONTESTS adult fantasy romance series

*Interior Design for Demons*
*Infernal Trials for Humans*

## MORE BOOKS

*Lair of Thieves and Foxes* (medieval French romantic fantasy/folklore retelling)

*Her Dreadful Will* (contemporary witchy villain romance)

*Of Beasts and Bruises* (A Beauty & two Beasts retelling)

Printed in Great Britain
by Amazon